Unfailing Love

WHEN HOPE CALLS
···· BOOK THREE ····

Unfailing Love

JANETTE OKE
LAUREL OKE LOGAN

BETHANYHOUSE
a division of Baker Publishing Group
Minneapolis, Minnesota

© 2022 by Janette Oke and Laurel Oke Logan

Published by Bethany House Publishers
11400 Hampshire Avenue South
Minneapolis, Minnesota 55438
www.bethanyhouse.com

Bethany House Publishers is a division of
Baker Publishing Group, Grand Rapids, Michigan

Printed in the United States of America

Library of Congress Cataloging-in-Publication Data

Library of Congress Cataloging-in-Publication Data
Names: Oke, Janette, author. | Logan, Laurel Oke, author.
Title: Unfailing love / Janette Oke, Laurel Oke Logan.
Description: Minneapolis, Minnesota : Bethany House Publishers, a division of
    Baker Publishing Group, [2022] | Series: When hope calls ; 3
Identifiers: LCCN 2021057110 | ISBN 9780764235153 (trade paper) | ISBN
    9780764235160 (cloth) | ISBN 9780764235177 (large print) | ISBN
    9781493437221 (ebook)
Subjects: LCGFT: Christian fiction. | Novels.
Classification: LCC PR9199.3.O38 U54 2022 | DDC 813/.54—dc23/eng/20211203
LC record available at https://lccn.loc.gov/2021057110

Scripture quotations are from the King James Version of the Bible.

Cover design by LOOK Design Studio
Cover photography by Aimee Christenson

Baker Publishing Group publications use paper produced from sustainable forestry practices and post-consumer waste whenever possible.

22 23 24 25 26 27 28   7 6 5 4 3 2 1

With love, appreciation, and respect,
we dedicate this book to real-world foster parents,
the women and men whose personal lives
have been willingly inconvenienced
for the sake of children in difficult transitions.
We know God sees each one of you.
We pray you'll receive courage and endurance,
wisdom and peace,
even in your most difficult days
as you stand in for Jesus in these precious lives.

Contents

CHAPTER 1

Gone

Lemuel staggered forward in the darkness, tucking up his collar as if that could somehow keep the rain from soaking through to his skin. He couldn't figure how the two others ahead of him seemed able to move forward through the stormy night without hesitation.

I can't do it! This is daft. "Freddie," Lemuel called again, whining a little this time. "Come on, Freddie. Wait!"

"We ain't waitin'" came the terse response from farther up the road. "Nobody invited ya. So if yer comin', ya gotta keep up."

For a moment as they rushed past the long drive leading toward the Thompson farm, Lemuel's home for half a year, he paused in place. Trying to think quickly through all the implications of this decision, he found himself panting heavily. He was almost convinced that he should dart toward the safety of his house and sound the alarm instead of following heedlessly. There might still be time to call for help and catch the runaways before they were too far gone.

A prickle of frustration made him cringe. *But I can't tattle. I ain't a little kid. I'm 'most fifteen, fairly grown up. An' I ain't no tattle-tale.* It was one of the hardest of the schoolyard codes for Lemuel to understand and keep. As frustrating as Freddie had been at school after joining them for the last couple months of the year, Lemuel had resolved not to turn him in to the authorities—not even to Miss Lillian and Miss Grace—nor to Mr. Waldin, who watched over him. *So I gotta stay with him. Talk him into goin' home. Make sure he doesn't get into worse trouble. Mr. Thompson—Dad, I mean—he said he doesn't like talebearers. So I'll just follow 'em till I figure how to turn 'em back. Before mornin' maybe it'll all be o'er.*

With a heavy heart Lemuel moved out into the road again. The outline of his home faded into the dark mist of the storm as he blundered forward. "This is stupid," he protested again, aloud this time.

"Quiet," the girl next to Freddie scolded. "Keep your voice down and your boots quiet, or else . . ."

Lemuel fought against the urge to argue. He'd already learned it was pointless where the girl was concerned. He'd have to work on getting Freddie to come to his senses instead. Miss Tilly would be loading the table with supper right now. Lemuel pressed a hand against his empty stomach and muttered under his breath. He quickened his steps in order to keep up.

· · ● · · ·

"Father will arrive tomorrow. And everything will change." Lillian whispered the words aloud as she dressed in preparation for their supper guests, shivering in the second-floor bedroom. An early summer storm was descending from over the mountains.

Lifting her customary gray wool skirt from its hook behind the door, she stepped into it carefully, drew it upward, and fastened it around her waist. Then, pushing her arms into her best printed blouse, which was clearly showing signs of wear, Lillian tucked and smoothed the garments properly, tossing a warm sweater over all.

"Father will bring back the rest of my clothing with him. That'll be a relief." She still wondered why he hadn't agreed just to ship the wardrobe crate back home after it had become clear that Lillian would not follow him to Wales after all. Was it a practical decision as he'd claimed, concern that her wardrobe would be lost in transit? Or merely stubbornness? In truth, Father could be rather set in his decisions. *Never mind, I've been fine without all those clothes.*

With a sigh, she let her eyes move around the room. Father had written that "for the time being" Lillian should remain in the master bedroom. His final telegram had asserted that he would keep his reservation at the hotel in town until the path forward had been considered carefully.

Lillian's mind tumbled. She wished again that she could have spoken to him. It seemed that Father was reluctant to place a telephone call even now that he was back in Canada. *Well, I know him. I'm sure he wants to wait to discuss all the changes in person. He wouldn't want to risk an upsetting conversation when he's still so many miles away. He means it as a kindness. But it's been so, so hard to wait.*

There was a commotion in the foyer below. A last quick twist of her auburn hair, a couple of pins, and Lillian was ready to join the rest for supper. Walter, Lillian's fiancé of just a few months, was expected, as well as her former charges Lemuel and Harrison. She wondered which of them had just arrived.

But as Lillian descended the stairs, she realized the sounds were not a joyful welcoming of guests. Her pace quickened.

"I don't know. That's all they said." The voice was Harrison's, and he was breathing hard.

And then Miss Tilly's words came more calmly. "Where'd ya see 'em, son? How far down the road?"

Lillian rounded the corner to the landing, eyes sweeping the foyer. Grace was already throwing a coat around her shoulders, and Ben and Walter were pushing their feet into boots.

"What's happened?"

"Oh, sis, they've gone. The pair of them. It seems they've run away."

Instantly, Lillian knew without asking which of the children in their care would attempt such a desperate act. It would be Freddie and the new girl. "They went together?"

"Yes, yes," Grace answered. "Stay here. We'll get the car started and search for them." She paused at the door, turning back to instruct, "Pray for us, please. Pray for them! It's so dark out with the storm moving in. It'll take an act of God to find them tonight."

Silence fell as the door closed. For the first time Lillian noticed the other youngsters crowded together in the parlor doorway.

"Come along, Janie, boys." She drew them forward with gentle hands. "I expect Miss Grace and the men will find them. Let's go eat our supper and we'll pray that God will keep them safe."

However, even after supper had been accomplished, there was no word. The wind had become shrill before Lillian tucked the children into bed, staying with them until they'd all fallen asleep, answering questions as honestly and reassuringly as she could. As she pulled the last door shut behind her, she whispered a word of prayer for their tender hearts. Then she returned to the kitchen, where Miss Tilly was seated at the table, hands folded and pressed against her forehead. Her eyes opened when Lillian took the chair beside her.

Lillian found herself articulating aloud the one question that could not be stilled inside of her. "Why, Miss Tilly? Why do these dreadful things keep happening?"

Two workworn hands moved to cover her own, squeezing tightly. "Why'd we have ta go through them things in the past, dear? I guess 'cause now we know what we learnt then. If we hadn'ta learnt it, we wouldn't be set fer this. God leads us forward one step at a time, readyin' an' growin' us for what comes next."

· · • ● · ·

Grace arrived at the kitchen door. Slipping her drenched coat off her shoulders, she let it fall across the washstand.

Lillian rushed to fetch a towel. She glanced at the pendant watch on a chain around her neck. It was past midnight already. "No luck at all?"

"No. And worse yet, we haven't even found any sign of Lemuel."

Lillian shook her head in disbelief. "I thought he just caught the pair of them running away. That's what Harrison said. The boys seemed as shocked as the rest of us. They were just coming for supper when they saw children creeping along in the shadows. Lemuel was trying to talk them out of it. That's why he didn't come inside with Harrison. He was trying to get them to give up on the idea. You don't think . . . ? It couldn't be that he was . . ."

No attempt at an answer followed.

"No, he couldn't have planned to go along with them. It's impossible." Lillian asserted the words she'd wanted to hear from Grace. "It's not like him. I could never believe it." Looking around the room and seeing no eyes meet her own brought an instant lump to Lillian's throat.

As Miss Tilly set a steaming cup of coffee on the table, Grace shook her head and slumped down onto a chair. Her hands enveloped the cup gingerly, drawing in its warmth. She appeared entirely depleted.

Stepping forward, Lillian unfolded the towel. Easing it over Grace's dripping hair, she pressed down here and there in order to absorb as much of the excess rainwater as she could. Grace made no move to assist. Instead, she lifted the hot coffee to her lips.

"You need to rest, Grace."

"Can't. Ben and I came back so we could warm up and change clothes. Then we'll go back out."

"Where's Ben?"

"Barn."

Stepping around the chair so she could see her sister's face, Lillian insisted, "I'll go, Grace. I know the area better than you—better than Ben even—especially as we start searching farther from town. I should go and you should rest."

Grace looked up, her eyes red from the cold and tears. "I couldn't sleep anyway. I have to go."

"Then you understand why I have to come too." Lillian's reply was little more than a whisper, her plea to be included.

"No, no. Please. You should get rest now because one of us should be functional in the morning for the sake of the other children. And don't forget that your father will arrive tomorrow evening—no, in fact, it's already after midnight. Your father arrives at supper tonight."

Lillian draped and tucked the towel as best she could around Grace's damp hair before rushing upstairs to retrieve dry clothing. At least she'd save her sister as many steps as she could. *That's just like Grace, always working the hardest, always doing the most. Well, not this time. I won't let her talk me out of going.*

When Lillian came back, laying a small pile of Grace's clothes on the table, she began immediately to dress herself for the rain, pushing feet into rubber boots, arms into coat sleeves. Her steady flow of words was intended to drown out Grace's further objections. "You'll have to tell me where you've already searched. There's the old cabin where Harrison hid the filly last fall, but I suppose you've already checked there. There's the bend in the river where Freddie spent so much time fishing. There's that trail leading to the old rope ferry, where they could have crossed . . ."

"Oh, sis. We've tried all those. And we've woken up almost

everyone in town. There are probably about a hundred people out searching right now. There's no need for you to—"

"I'm coming." This time Lillian was adamant.

Grace rose from the chair, stepped closer to the hot wood-stove, then peeled away the outermost layers of her wet clothing. Lillian watched the door, wondering how long it would take for Ben to be ready, for him to expect Grace to return to the waiting car.

Soon they stepped from the porch together, arm in arm, stooping down as if by doing so they could dodge the rain. One after the other the sisters lunged onto the front bench seat of their oversized automobile.

A moment later, Ben slid into the driver's place. "Which way now?"

"Wherever Freddie found the foxes," blurted Lillian. "Let's go there."

"We'd have ta walk a ways inta the woods. In the rain. In the dark."

"Whatever it takes."

· · ● · ·

Morning broke and Lillian roused herself from the chaise where she'd fallen asleep sometime after four. Someone had covered her with Mother's afghan. The house was silent. She checked the clock that sat on the mantel. It was now almost six. Summer mornings dawned early, and she supposed that Miss Tilly would have risen already. She hurried to the kitchen but found it empty and quiet.

A flutter of dread ran through her. *Father comes home this evening. And this time he'll bring that woman—Delyth—with him. The one he referred to in his letters. And yet, there's been no confirmation at all about the nature of their relationship. Do they plan to wed? Are they already man and wife?*

Lillian paced as she pondered the dilemma, keeping an ear listening for any other movement in the house. She recited the progression of logic once more. It seemed unlikely that her very traditional father would cross the ocean with any woman if they weren't properly married. He would consider it inappropriate and disreputable. Lillian reasoned that any woman's family would have also insisted on an honorable sequence of events. So, Lillian could only assume they had already made their union permanent. *Is she a spinster? A widow? And what will her expectations be? Where will they live? We can't all crowd in here—and yet, it's Father's house. Does that put our work in jeopardy?*

Stopping at the window, she looked out toward the driveway, wishing someone would arrive with news. *Good gracious, after all the work we've done to present ourselves well to Father—to appear that everything's been under control in his home while he was away—this happens. At the last moment we have children who've run away.*

Sliding down onto a kitchen chair, Lillian draped herself over the table and laid her head on her weary arms. It had been such a long night of praying and searching.

Oh, Veronika, where have you gone? Lillian's thoughts traveled back to the first time she'd heard about the young girl's plight and had first come to carry the ache in her heart for Veronika. She closed her eyes and let the recollection play out in her mind. *Was it only two weeks ago? How did the girl turn the household upside down in such a short time?*

"Children. Attention, please," Grace had said. All faces of those sharing their meal had lifted to Grace, who'd just returned from answering the new telephone in the front hall. The large wooden box hung on the wall near the base of the stairs, still so mysterious and newfangled with its cup-shaped receiver, an earpiece that was attached by just a cloth-covered wire, and a cranking bell for summoning the operator. The children's chatter had quickly subsided as Grace began. "We just received word that we're going to be welcoming two new children."

Lillian had exchanged glances with her sister. She could still feel the concerns that had come to mind on that day—amplified now a hundredfold. Her eyes asked, *Oh dear. What now?* Father was expected on the tenth of July, in less than three weeks. Lillian had been silently concerned about any chance of taking on new children before he returned.

Grace wore a pasted-on smile as she explained, "A girl aged twelve, and a boy aged eight. The girl is—I'm not sure—Virginia? V-something. Veronika. That's it, I think. The boy—I think she said Casper or Cas-something. The line was a bit fuzzy, so I'm not entirely sure. Guess we'll find out soon enough."

There had been excited clapping and exclamations of pleasure from the four children seated around the kitchen table. Even Freddie seemed mildly agreeable to the idea.

Grace had taken her seat again, suggesting they each think of a way to welcome the new pair.

There were many ideas, all spilled out in a jumble of excited voices. Grace clapped her hands to get things back under control. "Remember the family rule. Only one speaks at a time."

They settled.

"We'll go around the table. Let's see. We'll start with Freddie."

Freddie had shrugged his shoulders, a frown wrinkling his forehead. To Lillian, it had looked as though he'd drawn a blank or was totally uncertain how to encourage two new residents.

Even the memory of Freddie's face brought a hitch to Lillian's heart. It was racing again now. *He is gone still—but where?* She could feel her pulse throbbing in her temples too. Still, there was no other movement in the house.

Having spent only a few nights with Ben in the small room in the barn after they arrived, Freddie had soon settled into what had been Lemuel's bedroom before Lemuel had been adopted by the Thompsons. The move came long before winter had rolled away and warmer spring days had descended. Freddie had even attended school for the remainder of the year without too many complaints, much to everyone's surprise. He and Lemuel, who was just a month older, had been in the same class, walked to school together, and had become friends. Still, Lillian had found it difficult not to worry that Freddie was something of a short candle burning down, biding his time before the current comforting glow of cooperation snuffed itself out. And it appeared that she'd been correct.

Rising now, she refilled her tea before returning to her recollections.

"No ideas?" Grace had prompted Freddie for an answer.

Instead of answering her question, Freddie had blurted, "Ya goin' ta put that new boy in with me? It ain't a very big room."

Grace said evenly, "We haven't even discussed that yet. We'll let you know once we've had a chance to talk this through."

Still Freddie seemed to ponder the unusual assignment. Suddenly his eyes had lit up with a surprising suggestion. "We can let 'em see them fox kits I found."

Lillian's eyes lifted now to the kitchen window at the reminder of the kits. They were still in the barn. With Freddie gone, who would care for them? How had he been able to abandon them after focusing so much of his time on their care?

Weeks before, during one of his many trapping explorations, Freddie had discovered a den with five baby foxes. He'd described how the mother was lying motionless nearby. It seemed she'd been attacked by another animal. The boy had carried the babies home tucked inside his coat and, with Miss Tilly's aid, had cared for them faithfully during the weeks that followed. Though he'd allowed the other children to visit them, he still guarded the kits closely whenever they were around.

This had been Freddie's suggestion for the new children. They could share the pleasure of watching the kits grow. It was a significant proposal.

Clapping had followed until Milton cut in with a loud voice. "What if they don't like aminals?"

Grace smiled at his question. But by the incredulous expressions on the other little faces it was clear that no one else shared his concern about the fuzzy little pups being uninteresting.

Freddie frowned. "So long's they don't e'er try ta—"

But Lillian had cut him off before he could finish the words. "I think that's a wonderful idea. We'll watch things closely and have the same rules for the new children as we've already put in place. The kits are still just babies—though they're beginning to look like such sweet miniatures of grown foxes. They still need extra care."

The boy's words echoed once more within Lillian's memory. *"So long's they don't e'er try ta . . ." Did I miss a sign of trouble ahead? Was there growing resentment even two weeks ago—before the new children arrived? But then why did he offer in the first place?*

There'd already been much asking to handle the growing baby foxes, and so the rule was that they were still too fragile—too wild. At present they needed only Freddie to care for them, though eager hands were allowed to gently stroke the soft red-brown fur while he was safely holding one and guarding it. Lillian found it terribly sweet just to watch them scamper from all corners of the barn whenever Freddie arrived to feed them.

That evening when they'd first been told about Veronika and Castor, they'd continued around the table, each child sharing an idea and then discussing it freely with the others. Some would work. Others, maybe not, but at least the children now understood that in just a few days they'd be joined by two more siblings, and each had given thought to how they could do their best to make the new children feel welcomed among them.

· · • · ·

Lillian woke with a jolt. She'd fallen asleep where she'd leaned onto the table. It pained her to confirm that the missing-children dilemma was not just a bad dream. With considerable effort, she rose, stirred up the fire, and slid the coffeepot to where it would heat most quickly. Still the house remained quiet.

At last Miss Tilly shuffled out from her room, already dressed and looking resolute. "Mornin', Lillian. How long ya been sleepin' here? Don't look too comf'table."

Lillian stretched her arms above her head in an attempt to get blood moving through them again. "No, but where I did sleep wasn't much better. I was in the parlor. Did I miss anything?"

"No. Nothin'. But there's a host'a people searchin' still. Arthur an' Harrison took horses west t'ward the mountains with a group'a other men from town."

"Oh, I'm glad there are so many looking."

"And Grace went back out south with Ben—back ta Pincher Creek, where them kids come from."

"What? They left again—without me?"

Miss Tilly froze, her hand still holding the skillet she was setting onto the stove to begin breakfast preparations. "You was asleep. She said she didn't wanna wake ya."

An uncomfortable level of frustration bubbled up in Lillian. She'd been left behind. Again. Even though she did realize it was meant as a kindness, her heart decried that she'd been excluded from sharing the full weight of this event, as if these were not as much her children, her responsibility. Her thoughts slowed as she realized Miss Tilly was still speaking.

". . . around four thirty, Walt and Bucky stopped by an' they set out east along the train tracks."

"Heavens! I shouldn't have lain down at all, I guess." Lillian pushed herself up from the hard wood chair. "I may as well wash up and get dressed. Let me know if anyone comes back."

"Oh, I 'spect you'd hear the commotion."

"I suppose."

"An', Lill, ya might give some thought ta keepin' the others calm. With Grace away, it falls on you."

Lillian agreed. She would certainly listen for the sound of feet in the hallway and be ready to reassure them once again. *Poor little Castor. How will you manage without your big sister? She doted on you like few others I've ever seen.* And then . . . *Oh, Veronika, how on earth could you leave him?*

Cool water splashed onto her face helped revive Lillian, both her weariness and her frustrations. At the basin, she scrubbed with a washcloth, dried herself slowly with the hand towel, and then tackled her tumbling hair. A fresh set of clothing and she began to feel human again. Still no disturbance in the house below. Sighing, she exited to the hallway just in time to find Janie slipping silently toward the stairs. Matty, Milton, and Castor were not far behind.

"Are they back yet, Miss Lillian?"

Lillian accepted the girl's outstretched hand. "I'm afraid not. But loads of people are looking for them. I hope we can find them soon." Her eyes turned toward Castor as she queried gently, "How did you all sleep? Okay?"

He nodded assent with the others, avoiding eye contact with Lillian.

"Do you know something? I was just thinking about how good Freddie is in the woods. He knows all about how to stay safe and how to find his way. I think he's going to be able to keep them all quite well until we catch up to them—don't you think?"

Again, her words were met with silent nods. Passing her free hand over Matty's head, Lillian led Janie away toward the kitchen, wishing she'd had a chance to get to know Castor better. He'd so rarely been away from his sister in the two short weeks since they'd come to Father's house.

And then . . . *No one went north.* The passing thought took root in Lillian's mind, refusing to be ignored. *Unless Veronika is heading south toward her old home, north is not out of the question. Why has no one gone north now that it's light?*

"Miss Tilly, I believe I'll go for a walk. I might stop in at the Thompsons'."

All around Lillian, eyes rose toward her with the same question. Miss Tilly responded, "'Course, dear. June'll be 'specting folk droppin' by. Might know more'n us by now."

"I hope so." But Lillian wavered. "That'll leave you alone serving breakfast."

Janie chirped from across the room, "We can help you, Miss Tilly. Look, we'll set the table all by ourselfs."

Lillian closed her eyes for a moment. *Oh, Veronika, we wanted you here among us. We would have done our best to pour love into your life, if you'd have only let us.* She ran her hand down one of Janie's loose braids before pulling a wrap around her own shoulders. The wet morning was still cool so close to the Rockies, even though it was already July.

And Father will arrive this evening. Please, God, please let us find them before then.

On any other morning the walk would have been enjoyable. But Lillian's muscles were sore now and her head throbbed with each step, filled with worry about the kids who were absent and those she was leaving behind in the kitchen. She wasn't certain what her plan would be. She knew that looking in a northerly direction would require transportation of some kind. *But will June allow me to borrow Lemuel's bicycle? And will I be able to ride it well enough to cover any distance at all?* She'd brought along a short length of rope to secure her skirt, just in case. It seemed a rather frantic idea, but she was determined to do whatever she could to find their missing children.

---- •••◦ CHAPTER 2 ◦•••- ----

Lemuel

Stumbling along behind the two figures in front of him, Lemuel felt his mind clouding. They'd walked all night. He tried to picture what would surely be happening at home now that the sun was beginning to rise. *They'll be lookin'. Mr. Thompson. Miss Grace. Miss Lillian. Maybe the whole town.* He tried to slow his steps, but the new girl called Veronika demanded of him once again, "Hurry up, farm boy, or we'll leave you behind. We need to make tracks."

How on earth did this happen? I never agreed to this! At least, I never meant to. Guilty fear of the consequences for his impulsive choice badgered Lemuel. He'd always tried to do the right thing—be obedient, take care of those younger—and yet, it never seemed to work out the way he hoped. And besides, Freddie was also fourteen—only a month younger than Lemuel. But the girl, she was just a kid. And he had no desire to be in charge of this particularly difficult twelve-year-old.

"We can't keep walkin'," he grumbled aloud. "We've gotta stop."

"Soon's we find a place, we'll rest in the daylight—walk in the dark. No one'll find us that way."

Last evening had started out so well for Lemuel. It was supposed to be just another shared meal at the Walsh house. Miss Lillian and Miss Grace had invited Harrison and Lemuel to join them for supper, which was always something they looked forward to. Even after he'd been adopted by the Thompsons, Lemuel found it difficult not to visit often. He missed the sisters, missed the activity and busyness of their comfortable home. Mr. Thompson's farm was busy too, but it was a different kind of activity. It was work. Hard work. He still loved it best when he could spend time with the horses, but there were other chores as well. The cow needed milking, the stock fed, repairs made. When spring arrived, there'd been a host of additional chores, things he wasn't as excited about joining in on.

And always echoing behind his labor was the memory of similar tasks done for the farmer and his wife, with whom he'd stayed for a few relatively happy years. He still missed the woman. The gentle smile. The wordless encouragement she'd given with just a nod or a gentle hand on his head. But she had died suddenly. Lemuel still wondered uncomfortably often whether there was a new room built onto the house by now, room enough for the widow and her family whom the farmer had brought in to replace his own.

That had been Lemuel's second family, substituting for the parents and brother he'd lost in early childhood. And he was certain the farmer and his wife would always hold a position in his life, a piece of his fractured heart that could never be retracted. He was certain that the sense of loss for that world would never really go away, even if the days he'd spent there hadn't been perfect.

After them had come Miss Grace, Miss Lillian, and the rest. He'd hated to leave them without an older boy to help them out, especially now that George had moved on too. Oh, Lemuel was grateful to be adopted, grateful to live with people as kind and sincere as Mr. and Mrs. Thompson, grateful they'd promised aloud that he would always belong in their family. Always.

But even as their faces came to mind, Lemuel winced. He was supposed to say *Dad* now, and not Mr. Thompson. But that was hard enough to remember when they were at home. At school, where Mr. Thompson was the principal, everything reversed again. At school Lemuel felt it was proper to show more respect among the other kids by continuing to address his new father more formally. No one had actually explained to him what was expected. So it had become easiest just to use the word *sir* instead. That was safe in every situation—just not as workable within his own thoughts.

Then Freddie had settled in at the Walsh house. That caused a whole new issue. Freddie couldn't be trusted. No one was more aware of this fact than Lemuel. They walked to school together and shared the same high school classroom. Lemuel frequently overheard Freddie boast about his plans to his classmates. With growing resentment, he'd tried his best to guard others against Freddie's quick temper. Stepped between, made excuses, soothed over ruffled feelings. Freddie pushed Orville fairly often and teased the high school girls in uncomfortable ways. Freddie took whatever he wanted from the lunch pails of others, even the younger kids. When Lemuel had asked why he behaved that way, Freddie had only grinned. "'Cause I'm bigger. An' you'd better not snitch."

The most galling part of it all was that some people still saw them as the same. Lemuel had heard it said that they were cut from the same cloth. "Home Children" sent from England. Orville understood. Even Lorraine and Elsie seemed to overlook the troublemaker as much as possible. But Elsie Hafner was always just a little too close to informing the principal about Freddie—and in this case, the principal was Lemuel's own father.

What a humiliation that would have been! The worry about such a disgrace had kept Lemuel on his toes. And then, mercifully, it was summer.

Freddie! Glaring now at the pair in front of him, Lemuel reached up to take hold of his flat cap, swinging it down against his thigh repeatedly to shake out as much of the rainwater that stubbornly clung to it as he could. It felt just as soaked when he unhappily placed it back onto his head.

He remembered that when he and Harrison, in their best clothes, had struck out walking together along the short distance between the two houses that felt like homes, he'd been in such good spirits. Harrison, this new brother, still felt somewhat like a random kid whom fate had given him as an adopted sibling. But Harrison had been plenty of trouble too. And Lemuel was growing tired of keeping an eye on him, though he'd never have admitted it aloud.

Now this trek, this reckless act of following after the pair of escapees, felt very much like losing everything again. *No, I'm not runnin' away. I'm just watchin' o'er them. I'm comin' back to Brookfield soon's I can.* But with every mile the pang of regret bore deeper into Lemuel's heart. And his mind was heavy with concern about the effect the dreadful discovery of their absence would have on those he'd left behind.

I can't leave the girl alone with Freddie though. Maybe nobody else knows it, but I do. He could do anything to her. Abandon her in the middle'a nowhere—or even hurt her in anger. An' then there's the money they stole. Freddie, he ain't so good at sharin'. For that matter, neither is she! I don't s'pose neither one of 'em would have the good sense to back down. So I gotta at least try to fix this.

Ahead he noticed a bridge in a clearing beyond the thick evergreens, an old split-log bridge that someone had laid across a creek on this neglected dirt road. "I'm stoppin' at that bridge," he said aloud.

"No, we—"

"I'm stoppin' at the bridge."

"Suit yourself, farm boy. We're goin' on." Veronika shrugged, continuing to stride along.

But Freddie balked. "It's daylight. I'm stoppin' too."

Flipping the long black hair that hung down her back and raising her chin over her shoulder, Veronika turned her face only halfway toward Freddie and said, "We're gonna keep walkin'."

"Fine." Freddie shrugged. "If that's what ya wanna do, keep goin'. But I got the money."

Veronika spun around at last. "We agreed. We'd walk till we got far enough away they can't catch us."

"We said we'd walk till daylight. An' it's day. I'm stoppin' with Lemmy. You can do as ya like."

She stomped a foot. "This was my idea. And I found the money. So I'm in charge."

Freddie stepped closer, looming over her. His words were menacingly quiet. "You ain't in charge'a me. And you ain't me problem, neither. So when I stop, I'm just gonna go right off ta sleep, with you 'round or not."

. . . ● . . .

Lillian walked the bicycle out onto the road. She wasn't certain if she could operate it smoothly and didn't want to be observed in her efforts. Lemuel had taught her to ride it. At first he'd muffled his laughter behind a polite hand. But soon they'd both openly giggled at her wobbly attempts. It didn't help that the large cast-off bicycle had belonged to Jesse and Lou Thompson, the men who'd become Lemuel's older brothers. These were boys whom Lillian had grown up with. Lou was a little older than Lillian, and Jesse was a couple years younger.

The bike was too big for a woman of Lillian's stature. And, to complicate matters, it had a top bar stretching across from under the seat to the handlebars. It had taken time for Lillian to work out how to tie up her layers of skirts and petticoats in just the correct manner in order to be both safe and modest as she practiced.

Oh, Lemuel. Where are you? Why did you go with them?

Glancing up and down the road to be certain no one was near enough to observe her, Lillian braced one foot, gripped the bicycle firmly, and threw the other leg over the seat. Now straddling the bar, foot on one pedal, she pushed off gingerly. Just as the bike began to roll forward, she lifted herself up onto the seat and groped with her toes for the second pedal. *Click, click, click.* She was moving. *Don't stop. You'll fall. Speed up.* With great relief, she'd begun her own odyssey of searching.

It was a marvelous sense of freedom despite the shaking that her body had to endure. She was alone on the gravel road, whisking along, wind at play with the folds of her blouse and the loose strands of her hair. She would begin her search at the corner where she and Lemuel had found a nice patch of wild strawberries. That was where the first crossroads came. From there, she'd need to make a decision.

Since the day they'd first found the berry patch, she and Lemuel had returned together whenever they could, dividing up the tiny fruits and enjoying a good chat in the cool spring sunshine. It had brought to mind her favorite Dickens quote: "It was one of those March days when the sun shines hot and the wind blows cold: when it is summer in the light, and winter in the shade." Though in this part of Canada, such days came more often in May than in March.

Now it was July and the breeze generated by the rollicking bicycle came as a welcome friend. *One mile to go. Watch out for the big rocks. Don't fall. Don't fall.*

If only this were a pleasure trip. Once more, Lillian's thoughts went back to when Veronika's arrival had been imminent, the plan for accommodating her and her younger brother still developing.

After everyone had been tucked in for the night, Lillian and Grace had taken their tea to the stillness of the parlor and settled into their favorite chairs.

Lillian asked about the telephone call and Grace had explained that Mrs. Trenton, the woman who served as the Pincher Creek church's part-time secretary and custodian, had not given much information. She'd said they would send along the Geary children's file when they were picked up tomorrow.

"Tomorrow?" That had caused Lillian to sit bolt upright. The discussion had then changed to particulars. How would they be housed? What was their family situation?

Grace had suggested that, at first, it would depend on how the siblings seemed to be coping. Some children refused to be separated from their siblings. Some were better off staying with other boys and girls. They wouldn't know until the pair arrived. Lillian recalled that Grace suggested they start Castor and Veronika together in Janie's room, moving the just-turned-seven-year-old girl onto a trundle in the room with the little twins, Matty and Milton.

The whistle of a neighbor boy interrupted Lillian's thoughts. She ventured a timid wave and a half smile, managing to keep the bicycle from shuddering violently. Clearly, the kid hadn't heard their news, but there was no time at the moment to stop and explain. Lillian pressed on.

Returning to her recollections, Lillian frowned. She'd asked Grace what she'd learned about the family. Grace had drained the last of her tea and set her cup aside before answering. "Mrs. Trenton really didn't say what happened to the parents—just that they died suddenly—and the children have been left entirely on their own."

"What more do you know?" Lillian had asked.

"She said they are from a farm family near Pincher Creek. Born there. A Canadian father and a Greek-Canadian mother. I remember that because it's an unusual detail." Grace had untucked her feet and searched with one foot for her house shoes. "Perhaps that's something to be thankful for. At least there won't be the added trauma of adjusting to a new *country* that so many of the others were forced to face."

A sizable rock sent the entire bicycle lurching to the left, bringing her perilously close to tumbling. Her thoughts were wrenched back to the present. She was nearing the corner where their strawberry patch was located. Her mind prompted the thought that had plagued her as she'd fallen asleep at the table. *Why on earth would Veronika leave Castor behind? She doted on him like few big sisters did. In fact, she hovered over him as if she owned him, refused to allow others to move in too close to him. So how could she have left without him, with Freddie instead? Whatever could she hope to accomplish without Castor? It makes no sense!*

The bike glided into the grassy ditch. Lillian dragged a foot but, as was typical, had a difficult time slowing enough to disembark with grace. Hopping several times with an uncomfortable sense of losing control, she managed to stop the bicycle and get both feet back firmly on the ground.

With relief, she abandoned the contraption in the damp grass, pulled at the rope that was tying up her skirts in order to release them, and began to search the corner.

There were tiny red berries peeking out among the leaves. Lillian overlooked them. Instead, she focused her attention along the side of the road. *Oh, Lemuel, would you leave behind a clue? If you went with them against your will—and I have to believe that you did—would you please, please go to the trouble of leaving behind a clue?*

Searching in tall grass was never easy. It required a steady succession of parting a patch of loose weeds with her hands, inspecting the exposed ground, then tediously pushing aside a new clump. Lillian's back began to feel the strain of bending over. She was painfully aware that at home Miss Tilly was left responsible for the well-being of four youngsters. By this time they'd be done with breakfast. They might have more questions. It was unfair to put all of that responsibility on the older woman.

At last Lillian stood and looked up toward the sun. *I've been here at least an hour. I've got to get home soon.*

"And I don't even know what I'm looking for," she muttered aloud. "They may have gone an entirely different direction. He most surely wasn't in charge of choosing which way they'd—"

Lillian's foot kicked something and it reflected a flash of light. She reached down into the tall grasses again. *A pocketknife. Lemuel has a nickel-silver knife that Arthur Thompson gave him. But does it look exactly like this? Every boy in town has some kind of knife.*

Brushing away the splatters of mud gently, Lillian dried off the moisture with the hem of her skirt. *If this is Lemuel's, it's a miracle I found it. Oh, Father God, help us to know.*

CHAPTER 3

Ben

The long and lumbering automobile rolled into the town of Pincher Creek. Ben had been there before, just two weeks earlier, when he and Lillian had picked up the new children. Still, he had no hopes that Veronika would have returned to this place. The girl had clearly felt no affinity for this town. And someone had already been notified to watch the homestead where the siblings had lived with their parents—in case that had been the girl's destination.

Freddie was another matter entirely. Ben felt a sting in his spirit as his thoughts went back again to the boy. *Where ya be, lad? An' what on earth ya doin' in the comp'ny a'that child?* There was sorrow and worry that somehow he'd failed to provide Freddie with enough support. But there was anger too. And fear. *God, help us!*

He wondered again if Lemuel had shared these concerns, if that was why he had followed the runaways. Was he trying to protect Veronika from Freddie—or, at least, from Freddie's influence? Ben wondered if the result of his concern for the troubled youth was merely additional heartache for all.

He shifted into a lower gear and heaved on the wheel, making a turn onto the street where the church was located. The maneuver woke Grace, who'd been slouched against the car door asleep for much of their journey.

She startled and sat upright. "Are we there?"

"Yes, miss." He eased the car closer to the wooden sidewalk and puttered to a stop in front of the large brick building. "Take a minute, Grace. Good ya could sleep a little, but give yerself a beat 'fore we go inside."

"Thank you, Ben."

Grace straightened on the bench seat, then tidied her hair as best she could without a mirror. Ben averted his eyes, as if he could somehow give her privacy in such surroundings. "Could be they'll have coffee brewin'."

"Oh, I do hope so!"

She seemed so frail at this moment. Even on the terrible day when Janie's true history had been exposed, Grace had appeared strong to Ben, not quite confident in her own reaction but certainly determined. Now her shoulders stooped in a way he'd never seen before. What was she feeling? Could it be . . . defeat?

"We'll find 'em, Grace. I promise ya." It was a dreadful thing to say. Ben knew it the instant the words had passed his lips. It was a vain pledge that he had no power to keep.

Grace reached for the door handle, offering no reply.

Fighting the urge to strike his fist against the automobile's frame in frustration, Ben exited the vehicle too. *Yer just makin' it worse fer her. Stop talkin'.*

Soon they were seated in the church office. He hoped that Mrs. Trenton would have additional information. They waited as patiently as they could for the middle-aged wife and mother to arrive from her home, grateful that she was able to meet with them on a Saturday. It seemed the woman served at the building only a few hours a week, acting as the reverend's secretary and cleaning the building. Ben knew her type, one of those women who functioned as a pillar for her local church despite the fact that she also had all of the responsibilities of caring for her own home and family.

Ben took in the checkered gray linoleum floor, the rose-colored paint on the walls, the hard wooden chairs. He fully recalled the last time he'd waited in this building. It was the first time he'd met the fiery young Veronika Geary. On that occasion, he'd entered the church with Lillian instead, then waited silently at the door as she'd approached the desk centered in the large office reception area.

By then the sisters had acquired more information about these children and their story from Sid Brown in Lethbridge, who would manage all the legal aspects of their case. Veronika and Castor Geary's parents had died of apparent poisoning. Crushed roots from the water hemlock plant were found in their pantry, ground down to a paste as if someone had been using them in food preparation. The children, however, were healthy. They'd been at school when a neighbor had discovered the bodies. Apparently, it had been a gruesome sight. Sid, however, had been offered no suggestions regarding how this might have occurred. But Lillian and Grace had spoken together in hushed tones about the possibility of suicide or even worse. They'd feared the condition that the children would be in following such a tragic event.

That why the girl's so—so diff'rent? Angry from the first time we saw her? There was no way to know all the causes, but two and a half weeks later Ben was back in Pincher Creek again, still looking for answers.

Regardless of their speculations, it had been agreed by all that Veronika and Castor were in need of compassionate, temporary housing, which the church had claimed to be unable to provide among their congregation. Ben could only imagine how ill-equipped the members had felt in responding to such a difficult case. He wasn't surprised that they'd turned instead to people they considered "specialists" in such things—to Sid Brown's placement agency, which had connected them with the sisters. Grace and Lillian's home was deemed the best solution. Apparently they'd achieved a reputation that had reached here all the way from Brookfield, forty miles away.

On that earlier day, Mrs. Trenton was already seated at the reception desk directly ahead of them, shuffling papers. The woman requested that they take a seat in a waiting room off to the side, then she left the reception area in order to fetch the children from the parsonage. Ben and Lillian sat in the center of a row of chairs, silently waiting. They could see Mrs. Trenton's desk through the open doorway, but only a portion of the larger room.

The memory of the interaction that had followed played out in Ben's mind.

"Veronika, Castor, this way, please." The woman's voice echoed toward them from a nearby hallway. The sound bounced eerily off the hard surfaces of the waiting room. Ben had risen up straighter. With a glance toward Lillian, he noticed that her gloved hands squeezed together more tightly.

A door opened and closed again. Shuffling sounds came from out of sight. Then a girl stepped into Ben's view, approaching the desk where Mrs. Trenton had seated herself. The child was tall for her age and slender. Waves of black hair cascaded down her back. She stood rigidly in an ankle-length cotton dress with shiny brown button-up boots. Her clothing was fashionable, seemingly quite new. Unusual in a farming community—for a farming family. This was not at all how the other children were dressed while in Lillian and Grace's care.

Glancing at Lillian for a clue as to how to respond, Ben had held his tongue. It seemed that Lillian preferred to observe from the small side room rather than make her presence known quite yet. Mrs. Trenton, at her desk, had smiled up kindly toward the unhappy young girl and motioned for her to take a seat on the chair facing her.

Arms crossed closely against her chest, the child had obeyed. Her brother was still out of their range of sight.

With an audible sigh, Ben felt once more what he had on that day. His resolve to remain objective had crumbled. This girl needed kindness. She'd so recently lost her parents. Was it any wonder she was so sullen? Still, he'd questioned, Was it sorrow or simmering anger written on the girl's pinched face?

Mrs. Trenton had tried. "Veronika. It's a very pretty name—for a very pretty young lady."

No change in the dark eyes. If anything, the brows lowered, obvious concern reflected in the somber expression. As the secretary glanced at the papers before her, then back up to the girl, the woman's eyes seemed to soften with pity.

However, it was obvious that her words of kindness hadn't touched the child. Mrs. Trenton seemed to attempt another approach. "Well, Veronika—I have some good news for you." She looked up and smiled again. "It's time for you and Castor to take a delightful little trip. To the town of Brookfield. Your ride has just arrived—"

The girl blurted out, "I don't have to stay here anymore?"

"No, dear. Sometimes our church has cared for needy children in our parsonage until we can place them in area families. There've only been a few others who—"

"They shouldn't have brought us here anyhow. I'm not like those others you helped—those—those wretched little—little street urchins that—"

Mrs. Trenton quickly stopped the sputtering description. "Be that as it may, young lady, as I said, we've made arrangements—"

But the girl cut in again. "Cass too?"

"Yes. Yes, of course. Your brother will go along with you."

"He hates it here," the girl stated firmly. "It's dirty and it's loud. And people keep walking around us, like we're nothing but in the way."

Ben wondered which of the two siblings felt the strong emotions Veronika had expressed.

"We would never separate a brother and sister," Mrs. Trenton assured the child.

Veronika's shoulders seemed to relax somewhat. At least that fact seemed to bring a measure of comfort. "When?" came the next blunt question.

Mrs. Trenton frowned, seemingly unable to hide her strain at responding to the constantly grumbling words, the rebelliously lifted chin. Instead, she laid down her papers and pushed back slightly from the desk, as if she'd concluded it wise to take a few extra minutes to try to put this troubled child at ease. She forced another smile—though again Veronika refused to soften.

"Let me tell you a little about Brookfield, dear. It's a small, very pretty town. I have a brother who farms near there. We live on the prairies here, but Brookfield is in the foothills. It's almost to the mountains. Do you like the mountains, dear? I do. I can see them from my kitchen window, and I always enjoy watching their colors change with the weather and . . ."

No response.

"Well, there's a nice big house—just at the edge of Brookfield—with only a limited number of—of—guests at a time. Two very lovely ladies who are sisters share in welcoming their new—members. Because it's like a big family. I'm told that Miss Lillian and Miss Grace make everyone feel welcomed. Everyone loves Brookfield—"

"I won't. It's too far away. I don't even want to go there. Why do we have to leave our farm?"

"I'm sorry—but, as I've said, we have no resources—"

"Oh, I don't want to stay here," Veronika repeated tartly, leaning forward in her chair to emphasize the fact. "I want to go home."

Mrs. Trenton laid down her pen and took a deep breath. The girl squirmed on the chair, turning her face toward the room's only window. Her arms remained crossed and seemed to wrap around her even more tightly.

Mrs. Trenton took a deep breath and began again, leaning forward, closer to the pain-filled eyes.

The girl had then pivoted away, turning her knees this time and shaking her head. Her back was to Ben. The dark hair that covered it rippled angrily as she displayed her contempt for the explanation. Mrs. Trenton had been shut out completely.

Ben shook his head at the image in his memory. Having lived among the children for over two weeks now, he was more than familiar with the back of Veronika's head, the crossed arms, the simmering anger.

Mrs. Trenton had tried again. "Sometimes things change. But at the Walsh house, they'll understand your hurt. That you feel lonesome and—and sad. So they want to help. To show love. To be a family until—until you can be placed in a new home—with a *new family* that—"

"I don't want another family. Cass doesn't either. We just—"

"I know. You want things to be the way they were. But they won't be, child. I'm sorry, but they can't be. No one can put things back to the way it was before you lost your parents. So we have to do our very best to place you where you'll be cared for. Loved. Protected."

"But we've got uncles! We'll go to them."

Clearly agitated, Mrs. Trenton had spread her palms and placed them on the documents in front of her. "That's why we've kept you here for these three days, dear. The Mounties have done a careful search for your uncles and they were not located.

Something else must be arranged. I'm afraid that you can't stay here any longer."

Veronika did not answer, but her body stiffened. After a moment of silence she shifted back to face the woman. "When?" It was plain that all she wanted at that point was information. Not sympathy. Not understanding. Just the facts.

As Ben recalled the hardness of Veronika's words, his eyes lifted now to where Grace was pacing as they waited. Poor Grace. She'd borne the brunt of most of the arguments with Veronika after the girl arrived in Brookfield. Always patient, always gentle. "Give her time," Grace had insisted again and again. "If we don't push her too hard at first, she may come around. Let's pick our battles. Show mercy. We need to earn her trust—let her know that we won't reject her despite her efforts to push us away."

Ben wondered now, in hindsight, had Grace been wrong? Had they been too lax? Still, Ben knew from experience that plenty of children chose to run away under the constraints of a heavy hand. He opted to trust Grace and not to blame her, even now, for her tender approach.

Mrs. Trenton, a gracious woman too, had been moved beyond such tolerance on that earlier day. "Well . . ." She'd frowned, opening the file again. "That's what I was trying to explain, young lady. Miss Lillian and her driver are here now. You can set off right away."

"Good." Just one abrupt word. But the eyes and body language of the girl belied her simple reply. It was clear that she saw nothing good about her present situation. The word was meant only as a slur against the idea of staying where she was.

Mrs. Trenton had sighed with resignation. It seemed she'd exhausted herself of things she could say or do to bring any comfort to the child before her. "Have you gathered your things?"

"Yes—and Cass's too. But we only have one suitcase each. What about our other things?"

"You won't be able to take anything else with you for now."

"But we have loads of other things. Why can't I take them with us?"

"What do you mean, child?"

"All of my clothes didn't fit in my case. So they wouldn't let me take them all. And we have blankets and books and pictures and—"

"Those will need to be discussed at another time."

Ben remembered how, as if unable to restrain herself, Lillian had risen to her feet at last, passed through the doorway, and approached the desk.

"Hello, Veronika."

The child's eyes fired in her direction with a look of surprise.

"My name is Miss Lillian. We've come to bring you to our home for a little while."

"I don't know you. You could be a kidnapper for all I know."

Ben rubbed a hand across his eyes as he thought back through the short conversation that had followed. It had been painful to hear, only slightly more uncomfortable than the silence that had descended over their vehicle when they'd actually pulled away from the church and set out toward Brookfield.

So is it surprisin' to any that we're back again? That the girl's run off? That all our efforts failed?

At last Mrs. Trenton arrived. Ben jumped to his feet at the sound. She entered the front doors of the church with another person, a man with a pronounced limp.

Grace and Ben moved quickly to meet them.

"Miss Bennett, Mr. Waldin, I'd like to introduce you to Reverend Herbert Mallory."

The man before them was dressed as a farmer. It seemed likely that Mrs. Trenton had summoned him directly from his fields.

Ben extended his hand. "Thank ya fer meetin' us, sir."

"'Fraid I don't have much time," the reverend answered. "But we'll drive out with ya to the Geary place. Let you have a look around."

"Thank ya," Ben repeated.

Grace fell in step behind him. "I assume you've heard about what happened last night?"

"Yes, yes. Very sad. But not too surprising according to Mrs. Trenton."

As they exited the church, Ben stopped in shock when he saw a large tractor parked in front of the building—evidence that his suspicions had been proven correct regarding the man's dual occupations.

"My farm's just over that ridge." The words were spoken as if no further explanation were needed. And then, "Is that your auto there? Guess I'll just jump in with you, then." Reverend Mallory's suggestion came matter-of-factly. Ben hid a smile.

CHAPTER 4

Long Saturday

In her haste to return on the bicycle to the Thompsons' farm, Lillian tumbled down onto the road. The spill caused a scrape on her hand and a few unbidden tears of frustration. She was trembling now, and far less coordinated in her efforts to move quickly. Soon she arrived at the long lane leading to Lemuel's new home. She coasted to a clumsy stop in front of the house, more than willing to cast aside the difficult conveyance.

Without pausing to rinse her hand at the pump in the yard, Lillian hurried inside to show the pocketknife to June Thompson. The small woman recognized it at once: two blades, a pearl inset on the handle, and a scratch on the smaller blade where Lemuel had damaged it while learning to sharpen it properly. Without a doubt it was his knife.

"Praise the Lord! You found something!"

Lillian's questions poured out. "Can you think when he might have left it there? Did he have it recently? We've been there together before, but I think he would have told me if he'd lost the knife back then. What do you think? I'm not certain, but could he have left it last night for us to find?"

June pushed a wave of yellow curls behind her ear. "He must have. . . . He didn't mention losing it, and he used it most days." And then, "Oh, your hand, Lillian."

"I'm all right. I took a spill."

"Let me just—"

"No, please. I need to get home."

"Of course. But don't neglect it, dear. You can't risk an infection." June's slender arms reached up to hug Lillian quickly before allowing her to hasten away. For a moment Lillian softened. No words of comfort nor expressions of worry were necessary, both of them fully aware of the precious lives at stake. And Lillian was determined not to start crying again.

She struck out for home at a brisk pace. June Thompson was already on the telephone, making the discovery known to as many townsfolk as owned telephones. *North. They would all need to concentrate their efforts on searching to the north.*

The children were playing in the side yard of the Walsh house. As soon as they noticed Lillian emerge through the bushes that lined the road, they hurried toward her.

"Did ya find 'em?" Milton called out first.

"Not yet." Lillian's skirts swished from side to side with the force of her hurrying steps.

Matty added, "Where'd ya go?"

"I went to the Thompsons'. Where's Miss Tilly?"

"Kitchen."

Lillian slipped between the twins, but as her eyes moved toward the back porch, she noticed Castor, half-hidden behind a bush. The expression on his face brought her to a halt. She held out her hand. It was still trembling a little. But the boy remained where he was. "We're looking for her, sweetheart. Lots of people are out looking for Veronika and the boys."

No movement. His eyes filled with unasked questions.

Janie came closer, acting the part of a little mother. "It's all

43

right, Cass. You can trust Miss Lillian—and Miss Grace too. Everybody's looking. Are you scared?"

He pushed out a lip, shaking his head.

"Are you lonely?"

Another shake of his head.

"Come on and play. We'll let you be 'it.'" Castor followed Janie away from the porch and into the sunshine of the yard.

With a heavy sigh, Lillian hurried up the steps. "Miss Tilly!"

The kitchen was empty. "Miss Tilly!" she called again, louder this time.

Heavy footsteps descended the stairs. "I'm here. I'm comin'."

"They went north."

Miss Tilly appeared on the landing.

Lillian gestured toward the window. "I found Lemuel's pocket-knife in the grass along the road."

"What? Where?"

"At the crossing. The first intersection."

"Up by Raskopf's, then. Ya call the p'lice station?"

"No, but I'm sure June has. I stopped to tell her."

"Good."

Lillian moved to the basin, then lifted the pitcher of clean water to pour over the raw patch on her hand. "Where are Grace and Ben? Are they back yet?"

"Still at Pincher Creek."

"Have you heard from them?"

"'Fraid not yet."

"Oh dear, that's entirely the wrong direction."

· · · ● · · ·

It was damp under the low log bridge. There were bugs and the smell of decaying weeds from the creek beneath it, little more than a runoff for rainwater. Lemuel hated sleeping outdoors. It brought back too many unpleasant feelings that he kept carefully veiled in his memory. Looking down the length of his body toward his feet, he realized he'd been unconsciously rubbing at his arm exactly in the place where it had been broken by a kick from the old black gelding the previous summer.

The eerie realization was enough to send him from their hiding place despite the daylight. He crawled out slowly, carefully, from under the row of split logs, leaving Freddie and Veronika asleep. *If I could find a house, maybe I could get a message to—*

"Hey, where you going, farm boy?" It was the girl's voice.

"Can't sleep," he answered.

Veronika emerged with no effort to keep her movements quiet. "Are you making a plan to turn us in?"

"I just can't sleep on the ground. I hate it too much."

"Well, maybe we can find an old barn next time."

Frustration was bubbling up. "You don't really think you're gonna get away, do ya?"

"'Course I will. I'm smart and I'm strong enough to walk forever. There's no reason I can't get all the way to my uncles in Sundre, with or without you."

"What? Did you say *Sundry*? Is that a town? I don't even know where that is, so it can't be close by. How on earth do ya expect to find 'em? How do ya even know if yer uncles're still there?"

Veronika tossed her head. "They will be. I can feel it."

"When's the last time ya heard from 'em?"

"When Cass was born. My *mána* sent them a letter and got one in return. I found it when I packed my suitcase and kept it. That's where I got the name of the place where they live. I brought it with me, in my bag. It says, 'Lukas and Stephanos Karagiannis, Sundre post office.' That's my uncles—Mána's brothers. So I'm going to find them there."

"But isn't your little brother eight now? It's been *eight years* since your mum heard from 'em? What if they've gone—"

"Then I'll find out where they went next."

45

Lemuel grimaced. It was a waste of words to argue with the twelve-year-old. "Veronika, I don't have any idea where Sundre is. We'll have to stop and ask someone eventually."

"That's fine. I know that it's north. Mána said they were straight up the Cowboy Trail. That's the name of a road."

"But it's not the road we're on! This is just a dirt—"

"Ba! Don't be so ignorant. We can't use it till we're farther away from town. It'd be too easy for them to find us. But the road is just a little bit that way." She pointed vaguely northeast. "Tonight we'll be far enough from town that we can cross over to it and then we'll just travel straight north. Maybe we can even hitch a ride. But you'd better not turn us in, farm boy. I'm warning you."

Lemuel scowled toward the trees and dusted off the sleeves of his coat before feeling controlled enough to answer. The girl's dark head came up only to his chin. He was well aware that she was no match for the strength he'd earned through his labors on the Thompson farm. Now, Freddie on the other hand . . .

"Veronika, you have to know that I'm not afraid of ya. Ya can't possibly think you can hurt me. I'm only worried 'bout what'll happen to ya if I don't stay with you."

"Farm boy—"

Enough! She'd pushed him too far. "My name is Lemuel. Ya'd better start to use it or—"

"Fine then, Leh-mule. I'll call you that instead. Leh-mule!"

Spinning on his heel, Lemuel walked away. He was worried what he might say or do out of anger if he didn't keep her at a distance for a while. Never had another child aggravated him as much as Veronika.

· · · ● · · ·

"Do you know anything of the Geary family? Did they attend your church?" Ben listened as Grace made the most of their traveling time, quizzing Reverend Mallory and Mrs. Trenton for any additional information they might know regarding Veronika and her family.

"No, I'm afraid not." The pastor cleared his throat as he tried to sort out an answer to Grace's question. "I paid them a visit when they first came. Oh, that was years back now. Martin Geary said he didn't put much faith in religion, except where it taught good citizenship. He said he figured too oft it just caused wars instead." The man's words drifted forward from his seat behind Ben, as if the memories were buried rather deeply. "Martin stopped in for coffee sometimes though. Well-read. Always enjoyed a good chat on politics and such."

Mrs. Trenton chimed in. "Oh my, but they had a fight to keep that little girl alive, didn't they?"

"That's right. I'd forgotten about that. Veronika caught the polio. How old was she, Eunice, two? Three?"

"She was about three. It went to her spine, I think. She got some paralysis from it and had a hard time walking for months. I think they feared she might never fully mend. But by the time she started school, it seems she'd recovered."

Reverend Mallory shook his head and sighed. "Nothing puts a scare in a parent like a sick child."

Mrs. Trenton placed a hand on the seat in front of her, leaning forward to catch Grace's eye for emphasis. "The girl recovered, but I don't think Mrs. Geary ever truly did. I don't like to tell tales, but in this case it might just be pertinent information. Eleni Geary smothered those kids. There's just no other word for it. School was about the only thing the children did without her—and my daughter used to say they never bothered with friends there either. Veronika just led Castor in and out, played alone with him at recess. Poor little boy." A pause. "Both of them, I mean. And then to lose their parents. That was their whole world."

Grace quieted. It seemed their answers had given Grace a great deal to process.

From the way the Geary children had been dressed, Ben expected to find a substantial, prosperous farm. He was quite surprised at the modest homestead they were approaching when Reverend Mallory directed him to turn into a muddy lane. The wooden house and its farm buildings were small compared to other farms around them. There was no automobile in the yard, merely a covered buggy waiting forlornly in the open end of the barn. Two horses sauntered up to the fence, as if hoping for some attention from whoever was arriving.

"I expected we might see the police," the reverend said, seeming to speak his thoughts aloud. "Guess they're done investigatin'."

A strange feeling suddenly came over Ben as he brought the automobile to a stop. He found it difficult to move—to *want* to move. The thought that this was where two people had died only three weeks ago was suddenly overwhelming. This was where Veronika and Castor had lived. He shuddered to think what they might find that would explain the turbulent girl.

Slowly he exited the vehicle and moved toward the house as if walking in some kind of unearthly dream. Ben felt that his footfalls on the wood porch floor sounded too hollow, echoed too much. He found it difficult to trust even the door handle as he reached for it.

However, the house was perfectly tidy inside, comfortably furnished, though an odd odor lingered in the air, even though the windows were open to catch the breeze. Allowing his eyes to scan the front room, he felt it was difficult to believe what had occurred there. He crossed the area slowly, trying to understand, then walked forward far enough to see inside the first bedroom.

A patchwork quilt had been torn from the bed. It hung now, suspended from the footboard by one taut corner. The bedsheets had been removed, were not in sight, leaving the mattress stripped bare. Cast-off rags were scattered here and there on the floor. A basin lay overturned against a wall. The rag rug was stained with ugly splotches.

Recoiling from the sight, Ben lifted his gaze from the floor. Two bowls sat on the dresser. A blue-glass medicine bottle lay on its side. He turned away, pulling the door closed behind him in order to spare Grace from any view of the room, the scene of a disaster that was by now three weeks old.

Grace had turned toward the kitchen area instead. She was glancing at remnants of a meal still half-prepared on the work area. Shriveled peels and moldy chunks of vegetables lay across a cutting board.

The reverend's voice came unexpectedly, causing Grace to lurch back in surprise. "I heard the Mounties took their stew pot. To see if they could find any trace of poison in it. But that's little more than local gossip, I suppose."

Grace inhaled loudly. Her eyes turned to Ben, a look of horror in them.

Instinctively, he took her arm to help her steady, remembering the bedroom scene. "We don't have ta stay here. Or ya can wait outside whilst I search."

"No, no. I want to see if there's anything we can learn about the children."

Reverend Mallory seemed unsubdued by the situation. His voice was uncomfortably loud. "Like I said, I didn't know 'em well. Martin Geary, he was a pretty quiet man. He once said that he'd fallen on some hard times back East and was makin' a fresh start in the West—like so many around here did. We're a community built up of folks starting over and brand-new immigrants. That's about the only kind of folk who'd brave the hardships of frontier life."

"What do you know of Mrs. Geary?"

"Eleni? Well, she was another thing entirely. She had a reputation in town of being kind of bossy. Had an accent too. I think she was Italian, or Greek. Not Martin, just the wife. But she sure doted on those kids."

Ben's eyes fell on a shelf of books beside a well-stuffed chair. "What's gonna happen to their farm? Their belongin's?"

"Auction. There'll be an auction on Saturday next."

Ben drew a book from the shelf. It was an illustrated encyclopedia of animals. Next to it was a book of fables for children. "So soon?"

"I was told the place is leased. The owner has to get it ready for other renters. He's hoping to get new folks in before the crop's ready to bring in."

"But the kids?" Grace's words were rich with concern. "Won't they be allowed to come take whatever they want to keep first? That is, if we can find her soon . . ." Grace's voice trailed off.

"That I don't know, miss. Except, as I say, the auction is Saturday, week from today."

Grace closed her eyes. It looked to Ben as if she were overwhelmed by the thoughts she was trying to process. "What about the proceeds of the auction? Will that go directly to the children?"

"I'm sorry, Miss Bennett." The pastor made a sucking sound through his teeth. "I don't mean to sound callous, but I'm not a lawyer. So I'm afraid I just can't say—and I wouldn't want to give ya false information."

"Where are their bedrooms, sir?"

Looking at the watch from his pocket, Reverend Mallory answered, "Seems the kids shared a room. It's directly ahead of you. But if you want my opinion, you'd better take what you think they'll want now. No sense in thinkin' you'll come back this way, and I don't know who may come by next, or what they'll carry off."

With a pleading look, Grace asked permission of Ben.

It was impossible for Ben to deny her such a request. "Whate'er ya like. But, please, miss, don't open that first bedroom door. Ya don't wanna see in there."

A nod. Grace began to load clean flour sacks that she'd discovered stacked neatly beside the kitchen washbasin. Ben carried them out to the car two at a time, choosing his path carefully in the grassy patches where the mud was less of an obstacle. There was plenty of room in the back of the automobile, even when Grace began using blankets to wrap up clothing and possessions in large bundles. Their only limit was the impatient reverend, who continued to check his watch and shake his head at regular intervals.

"That it, then?" he asked at last.

Again Grace lifted her eyes toward Ben. "The parents' bedroom? What if there are photographs?"

"I'll go."

Pressing back his shoulders, Ben entered cautiously. He would search the scene of calamity for the sake of the children, and because it was Grace who'd asked him.

CHAPTER 5

Commiserating

"Yer gonna have ta calm down, Lillian. Yer scarin' them kids."
Miss Tilly was beating eggs for the meringue topping on her strawberry pie for supper with Father. She paused only an instant to speak the words quietly, her eyes fixed on Lillian.

"Am I? Scaring them?"

"Yeah, I think ya are."

"Oh dear."

There'd been so much to worry about, Lillian had momentarily forgotten to try to appear confident for the sake of the children. Her heart had fluttered uncomfortably for much of Saturday afternoon and by now her stomach was churning. Her long-awaited reunion with Father was fast approaching. "I'll try."

"With as many folks as are lookin' north just now, I wouldn't doubt but them kids'll be home 'fore ya know it."

Lillian groaned. "I do hope you're right."

In spite of the strain of it all, supper was being prepared. The table had been set. There was no way to know if Grace and Ben would arrive home before Father and Delyth appeared, but there was no way to postpone the meal. Lillian was suddenly aware that the children should have been her most important focus at the moment.

"Would you mind, Miss Tilly, if I went upstairs to speak with them? I feel I should try to spend some time listening better if I'm to know just how they're all feeling."

"'Course, dear. I'm fine here fer now."

Lillian rinsed her hands carefully, dabbing at the scraped area on her palm. The children were playing in the attic, a favorite hideaway where toys could be strewn about without reproof. She opened the attic door quietly and moved up the dark, U-shaped stairwell. There were no lights in the large open space, and the children were not allowed to bring candles or lamps with them, so the two small windows at either gabled end were the only sources of light.

"Janie? Boys?"

"We're here, Miss Lillian," Milton answered. "We're pr'tendin' ta be hunters."

Lillian climbed higher until her head rose above the attic floor. As expected, the evidence of their play was scattered across the floorboards, now at her eye level. "I see." Climbing the remainder of the steps and lowering herself to a seated position at the top, Lillian waited while her eyes adjusted a little.

"Ya wanna play, miss?"

"I believe I'll watch for a bit."

Janie came closer and sat down on the edge of the step beside Lillian. "Did they find the kids yet?"

"No, dear. We haven't. But we believe we're getting closer."

"Oh. All right." As guilelessly as she'd approached with her question, the seven-year-old girl scurried away, carrying along a stuffed gingham bear with button eyes that she'd helped to sew. "I'm gonna hide now, Matty. And I bet you can't find me."

For now, it was enough for Lillian just to observe. They didn't seem distraught. They seemed to be managing well enough. Her eyes rested on Castor. But even the young boy appeared to be taking the disaster in stride. He seemed fully engaged in the play.

It brought to mind previous conversations with Grace. There were often no exterior signs of the turmoil that children were facing. And sometimes, Grace had warned, even the children themselves were incognizant of the effects of their personal traumas. However, this could often surface later in life, particularly in the teenage years. Grace explained how the mind and heart sometimes adjusted, tucking away the pain for a while. Perhaps that was a mercy. Perhaps that was what was sheltering Cass just now. Though he'd been a little withdrawn from the adults, the boy appeared to engage fully with his new playmates.

In her mind, Lillian returned to the first day she'd met Castor. His brown eyes were large and apprehensive, his dark brows pressed low over them. All through the time they spent in the church building, Veronika had kept him tucked close behind her body as if shielding him from the new situation. But Lillian was certain that Cass had risked an interested peek as they'd emerged from the building. Despite the circumstances, he'd seemed intrigued by the large and somewhat awkward automobile that was to carry them away. It gave Lillian hope that maybe it was simply Veronika's efforts that held the boy in check.

Still, the siblings had been almost silent on that first ride to Brookfield. Lillian had soon given up on trying to coax conversation from them and folded her hands together in her lap, watching the rolling landscape whisk past, the mountains looming larger with each fold of prairie. She wondered what Grace would have said, how Grace would have managed to interact with them.

It had come as a relief when their automobile finally pulled into the yard at home. Lillian had seen the flash of a small face in the kitchen window and, even from the yard, she could hear the sound of scampering footsteps and excited voices from within.

Castor had emerged from the back seat to look around. It was Lillian's first opportunity to observe him when he was free from his sister's grasp. He had a lovely mop of curly copper hair that appeared it could do with a cut. A dusting of freckles was sprinkled across his nose and plump cheeks. His clothes were too tidy and pristine for such a young boy. But, now that he'd been set free for a moment, it was his shy grin that had quickly won over Lillian's heart. At last acting on his own, Castor took a cautious step forward when three other children and two women tramped down the porch steps and surrounded him. Freddie, who'd been chopping wood not far away, hadn't bothered to approach.

Castor extended his hand to the nearest stranger with well-rehearsed manners. "Hello, miss. I'm Cass Geary."

Miss Tilly accepted the handshake with a chuckle. "My pleasure. You can call me Miss Tilly if ya like."

Grace welcomed him next with a warm smile, one hand on his shoulder affectionately. "I'm Miss Grace. Welcome to our home, Cass."

"Thank you, miss." And then quietly he'd added, "You've sure got a load of kids here."

A strange thought had come to Lillian's mind as she watched those initial introductions. *He has no accent.* She hadn't realized until that moment that all of their charges had come with a foreign accent, some far more pronounced than others. Strangely, it seemed out of place to have a child join their group who spoke with the sounds of Lillian's native land.

Still Veronika had not moved from the car. Ben was in quiet conversation with her from the front seat. Lillian could see the girl shaking her head, and Ben, though carefully controlled, seemed to be a bit lost as he continued to speak with her. Lillian thought she overheard the words "not goin' ta rush ya."

Grace moved to the still-open car door. Taking a step closer,

Lillian heard Grace speaking. "You must be next to starving. We've saved some supper for you. We tried to wait, but we didn't really know when you might arrive and everyone was getting hungry—and cranky—so we went ahead." She made an attempt at laughing softly.

Oh, Grace, you tried so hard. We all did. And look how it turned out. Well, I guess she meant what she said, even then.

At last Veronika had announced from inside the vehicle, "I need a privy. But I'm not staying here." She looked around, concern suddenly clouding her eyes as she searched for her brother. "And Cass too. We're not staying." Clearly against her preferences, it seemed that Veronika's physical need would force her to move from the vehicle.

Grace stepped aside and let the girl pass, pointing to the path past the kitchen porch that led to the small outbuilding behind. They all watched as the girl ran down the well-worn trail. Freddie made a gesture of greeting as she passed near him, which went entirely ignored. Grace had turned to Ben.

"How much luggage do they have?"

"A couple cases."

"Just set them here and—I'm sorry, Ben, but you might need to leave. Take the car to the Thompsons' and park it there for the night. Let's not give her the option of barricading herself in the back seat."

Ben had blinked in surprise but then nodded. It seemed that his departure might be the only way to be certain the car wouldn't be used as leverage.

They'd hurriedly unloaded the luggage, and Ben followed Grace's orders. He was already disappearing from view when the girl returned. Lillian feared a wild tantrum—but there was none. The girl glowered in turn at both Grace and Lillian but said nothing further.

If only that had been the end of it. Lillian smoothed the folds of her skirt, ducking her eyes in the dim light of the attic so that her thoughts wouldn't be evident to the youngsters around her. *If only winning that battle had set us up for better days. But that was not to be.*

Veronika's face had turned bright red with anger as she swung around and picked up her case. "I am starving." And she'd marched off toward the house. Suddenly she whirled back, her eyes wide with terror. "Where's Cass? Did that man take him?"

Lillian began a frantic scan of the yard. Had the young boy climbed back into the car unseen? Surely not! Yet where had he disappeared to?

"Pst . . ." Grace had pointed a finger nearby, toward the corner of the house. Castor was squatting down in the bushes beside the steps and rubbing his hand tenderly over the silky side of Miss Puss, who was enjoying the affection. Lillian exhaled her relief.

Veronika had strutted up to him and clamped a hand down on the boy's shoulder. With a wistful glance behind him at the kitty, Cass had followed along without a word of objection. He never seemed to protest Veronika's demands.

The recollection struck Lillian suddenly, bringing her attention back to the present. Castor was notably different now that Veronika was absent. Here he was, playing in the attic, laughing and scampering with his peers. She tried to remember the sound of his laughter while Veronika was present, uncertain that she'd ever heard it then.

That first evening really hadn't improved as it had moved along. Allowed to travel around the new home only a short distance by his sister, Castor made tentative efforts with the other children who were close to his age. In the cool of the early summer evening following supper, they managed to conduct him on a stop-and-start tour through the yard, from the tall swing to the roughly constructed tree fort that Ben and Freddie had made, then from the spindly young chickens in the hastily assembled coop to the old haystack behind the barn that had been turned into a slide. So long as Veronika could observe him, Cass was allowed to explore.

Lillian had maintained her own view nearby on the back porch, listening to snatches of their conversation that carried across the yard. She'd chuckled to herself. Every now and then, the children had to stop and ask one another to repeat words because of the difference in their varied accents. *They'll get it figured out soon enough. It took me a little while too.*

Once they'd returned indoors, Lillian had become aware that managing Veronika would be a whole new experience. That memory caused her eyes to close, even now. Nothing pleased Veronika. She'd flatly refused the idea of sharing a bedroom with Janie, stating emphatically to Grace that she would not "sleep with a foreigner for the risk of head lice."

So Grace had whispered aside to Lillian that they yield for the time being. Just as they'd supposed, Veronika and Castor would stay in Janie's room, while Janie's bedding would remain on the trundle that had been moved under Matty and Milton's bed. It meant that their temporary solution for Castor, a smaller mattress stuffed with fresh straw, might become permanent. Castor seemed perfectly pleased at the notion of sleeping on a bed of straw on the floor.

The sisters had set their minds to ignoring the girl's frequent tirades. But Veronika was muttering under her breath the next morning all the while that Lillian laid out their cases on Janie's bed and began unpacking them into the topmost drawer that had been cleared for them, hanging her pretty dresses on hooks behind the door where her own childhood dresses had once hung.

"I shouldn't need to share a home with gutter-prowlers at all—because I'm actually a Canadian. I was born here. They should

58

put all those ragpickers from across the ocean in one place by themselves, because I don't belong with any of them."

Lillian had winced at the scathing words, unable to refrain from comment as Grace had suggested. "We don't prefer to use words like that in this house. I think you'll come to understand that—"

"Well, my mána talked about those lazy immigrants. Their kind should have never come to this country at all, taking up places for good Canadians."

Rashly Lillian countered, "Wasn't your mother from Greece?" If only she could have taken the question back. It was instantly pure fuel for further defamation.

"Yes. But she's no soap-dodger like those others. She came from a *good* family. Important people. When she married him, my papa always called her his own Greek goddess."

"Hmm. That's nice, dear." Internally, Lillian had wrestled with her own feelings. It was one problem that the child was so abrasive and used such foul terms to refer to immigrants. But there was also the sorrow over the fact that the girl's precious parents had been lost. *I can't judge her just now,* Lillian cautioned herself. *Surely some of this behavior is due to grief.* It was, however, growing easier to see why the folks from the Pincher Creek church had not found a place for Veronika among their own families.

Finally shaking off her brooding thoughts, Lillian rose from her seat at the top of the attic stairs, ready at last to join the children in their play. At first she was given the role of one of the hunters. Soon Milton chose to pass along to her the small carved elk that had been their prey instead. Lillian was tasked with hiding it stealthily somewhere in the dimly lit room while the others covered their eyes and counted. Then the hunters were turned loose to track it down.

After a short time Lillian felt it was too urgent that she return to the kitchen and their preparations for important guests. Father would likely be in town by now, checking in at the hotel. *Oh, and I wanted his return to be a happy time! It's been so long since I've seen him, and so much has happened. When Grace and I took on these children, we certainly never imagined it would end up like this.* Immediately, Lillian prayed against the thought. *No, this isn't the end of anything. We'll find Veronika. I'm sure we will—and Freddie and Lemuel too.* The thought of Lemuel brought a fresh wave of concern. What was he doing with—?

"Miss Lillian." Matty interrupted her worried thoughts. "Can Cass sleep with us t'night? He don't wanna sleep alone again."

Castor edged closer, standing just behind the twins the way he had hidden behind his sister when Lillian had first met him. Now it was Matty who spoke up on his behalf. It seemed they'd been discussing the boy's problem. Castor's dark eyes were round with concern that he might be left on his own.

Lillian had no strength nor desire to deny the request. "Of course, dear. I'm sure Cass would like to have some company. We should have thought of it last night too."

A smile broke out immediately, the brown eyes showing relief. "I can pull my little bed in their room. It'll be like a sleepover."

"That sounds nice."

And then, "Miss Lillian?"

"Yes, Cass?"

"Do ya think my sister's all right? Ya think she'll come back soon?"

Lillian melted down to the boy's level, looking into the troubled eyes. "I think so, sweetheart. I think that there are so many people out looking right now that they'll find them quite soon."

"I don't want her to be gone forever."

Lillian closed her eyes for a second before daring a question of her own. She reached to grasp Castor's hand gently and was pleased when he received the affection. "We don't know where she went, son. Where do *you* think she was going?"

His answer was oddly confident. "Oh, I know. She's goin' to Sunday."

"What?"

"To Sunday. We got two uncles. I told Miss Tilly at breakfast, soon's I got up. They live in a place called Sunday. Mána said so."

The hope that was momentarily rising immediately subsided. She'd heard Veronika speak about the uncles before. The Mounties had done a search for them even before Sid had been called to arrange a placement. Castor's childish revelation had obviously not been deemed useful.

"Who's Mána?" Milton interrupted.

The boy's lip suddenly began to quiver. His eyes filled with tears. "That's my mother. We call her Mána 'cause we're Greek."

Broken by his sorrow, Lillian pulled the boy down onto her lap. He didn't resist but burrowed his face into her shoulder as she stroked the back of his head, fingers gliding through his copper curls. "I'm so sorry, Cass. I'm so sorry all this has happened."

Janie's hand reached out to pat Castor's back. "I told him all about my mum and dad, Miss Lillian. An' he told me 'bout his."

"He did?"

"Uh-huh. When we were swingin'. His mama is so beautiful, right, Cass?"

The little head nodded. Lillian pulled a cotton handkerchief from her waistband and held it where Castor could receive it.

"He said that she's got black hair too. Just like Veronika. An' his papa is so smart. He used to read books to them every night after supper—even when he was so tired out from workin' on their farm. That's why Veronika's so smart too, Cass said."

"That's true, darling. She's a very clever girl."

Matty knelt down on the floor beside them empathetically. "Our mummy had white hair."

Lillian reached out a hand to touch Matty's arm but waited breathlessly, too afraid to trust her voice, when Milton added, "That weren't our mummy, Matty. That were our old granny."

"Oh, then what did our mummy look like?"

"I don't 'member. But I wish I did."

Tears were rolling down Lillian's cheeks now. All of it hurt too much. She felt as if her heart were being strangled by so many grieving children surrounding her. It was all too much.

Then came the weight of another child pressing his way onto her lap. Lillian made room for Matty, pulled him closer, welcoming him.

She wanted to speak but knew full well that she should probably keep the particular words she was thinking to herself. But Lillian's heart was crying out silently, *My mama had brown hair, just like Miss Grace. A woman in town commented on that when she met Grace. I was so happy that someone had remembered Mama. But Mother's was a color closer to blond. Dark blond.* A sob escaped despite her efforts to stifle it. A fresh flow of sorrow fell unhindered down her cheeks. Yet her arms were occupied with holding so many little bodies close that there was no free hand left to wipe away her own tears.

"It's okay to cry, Miss Lillian." Janie's hand had moved to Lillian's arm. "Sometimes when we're supposed to be sleeping—me and Matty and Milt—we just cry for a while. It feels better crying if you're not alone."

Lillian reached to pull Janie close too. Milton, the only one left out, spread his arms around them all, leaning his small body over them.

"Stop it. You're squeezin' me," Castor objected.

Milton giggled. "It's a lemon squeeze! I'm gonna give ya a lemon squeeze."

And then they were all giggling. Lillian released them back to their play. Her own heart recovered far less quickly from its moment of grief. She left the attic but retreated to the bedroom instead. Father and Mother's bedroom. It was several minutes before she was able to return to the kitchen. Only one thought was enough to call her back.

Father will arrive in an hour. How on earth will I ever be ready?

CHAPTER 6

Supper with Father

The sun had made its broad arc across the sky and grown hot during the day that Lemuel spent at the side of the dirt road. All evidence of the night's rain had evaporated under its bright rays. Now the giant sphere was lowering again toward the western horizon. Still Veronika refused to allow their journey to proceed. Freddie had long since disappeared into the woods to set a trap for their evening meal. This left Lemuel alone with the girl. He tried to feign that he was sleeping, but he doubted she believed it. At last he raised his head, running a hand through his hair, only to discover a bit of twig that had lodged there. He freed it and dropped it on the ground, next removing one of his shoes in order to ferret out a bit of rock that had found its way inside. *What're we doin' here?*

Though Lemuel had exhausted every argument he could think of to convince Veronika to head back, he made one last attempt. "If we go back now, I think they might not be too mad. We've only been gone a day. But if we keep on, they'll get the Mounties lookin' for sure. An' then we'll be in for it."

"Not me." She shrugged, making no effort to turn her face toward him as she answered.

"What d'ya mean? You're the one who's most to blame."

"But I'm not going to tell them that, am I, Leh-mule? I'm going to say that you tricked me into coming because you want to keep all that money for yourself."

A tingle of fear. Lemuel answered with what he hoped sounded like confidence. "They won't believe ya. An' they know me better'n you."

"Miss Grace and Miss Lillian might know you. Your new family too, maybe. But those Mounties won't. And Freddie told me all about that trouble you got into with them not so long ago— when your brother stole a horse."

"He stole her to rescue her—an' he stole her from our dad. That's all over with."

"For you, maybe. But Mounties don't forget about that stuff. They probably have a big file of papers in their office with your name on it. So when you get in trouble again, they'll read what you did before and they'll send you to jail. After all, this time it'll be for kidnapping a poor little girl."

"I never tried . . . Ya didn't come . . . That's a lie!"

"Won't matter. People believe girls from good families more than they believe gutter trash like you."

Lemuel felt as if his brain were about to explode inside his head. "Ya wouldn't dare."

She faced him then, a smug smile on her face. "Oh, don't you think?" Then she fluttered her dark lashes in mock coyness.

'Course she'll lie to everyone. She'll say all that an' more.

He made up his mind. He'd do whatever he needed to see that they were caught. The very next house that they passed, he'd break away from them and knock on the stranger's door. He'd ask for a ride back to Brookfield, and he'd pour out the whole miserable story. Surely he'd be believed. And even if he wasn't entirely convinced that he could still avoid trouble, he was sure it could only get worse from this point on.

While the girl's back was turned, Lemuel pulled the loose wool sock from his foot and stuffed it into his pocket. That would be the second clue he'd leave behind when they set out by darkness. First the pocketknife and now a sock. From then on, everywhere they went, he was determined to make a trail that could be followed. The pledge was followed by a heavy sigh. Realistically, he had precious little to drop along the way. It would have to be bent twigs and drawings in soft mud from now on. *And who'd notice such little things way out here?*

· · ● ● · · ·

When Ben and Grace arrived back at the Walsh house from their trip to the Geary farm, the smell of Miss Tilly's supper greeted them as soon as they opened the back door. Ben's stomach pinched from hunger. It was only then he realized they hadn't remembered to eat lunch.

"I'll unload the children's things inta the barn, Grace."

"Thank you, Ben. That's probably best. We'll need the car for church in the morning."

Reaching for a bowl of meat scraps that had been set aside, he stepped out again, pulling the door closed behind him. What he wanted most was to spend some time with Janie, listen to her chatter, and enjoy some less complicated moments. He went instead to the task of securing the Geary children's possessions, hoping that the rest of the current crisis could be sorted out soon.

As he entered the barn, fuzzy balls of red fur scampered toward him from every direction, clearly expecting to greet Freddie, their pseudo-mother. For an instant they hesitated, eyeing Ben cautiously. As much as he appreciated the small critters who'd lived for weeks under the same roof as him, their presence was now merely another reminder that the boy was gone. He began to toss the scraps a piece at a time to the floor. Yips followed as the foxes gulped down the sustenance he'd brought to them. They disappeared instantly to private corners when he turned to unloading the car.

Ben was only half-finished before Janie made an appearance. "We were playing in the attic, Mr. Waldin, me and the boys. We were hunting a deer. That one you made us."

"Ya were? Hope ya didn't get hurt er lost in them deep, dark wilds up there."

The girl shook her head solemnly.

"An' now ya've come ta help me, eh?"

She laughed. "You're teasing me. I can't lift all those heavy things. What's all this stuff, Mr. Waldin?"

It seemed prudent not to share too much more information with the child. "Just some things we're goin' ta store fer a bit. Not fer keeps, so ya don't need ta concern yerself."

Perching on the running board of the automobile, Janie chatted amiably. "Cass gets ta sleep in our room tonight. An' Miss Lillian says her daddy will be here any time now." As if sharing a confidence, Janie added, "I think Miss Lillian's a little worried. Milton said it's a'cause we're living in her daddy's house. Is that right, Mr. Waldin? Is this Miss Lillian's daddy's house?"

"It is. But ya don't need ta worry, bunny. He knows all 'bout us stayin' here."

"That's good. But how come Miss Lillian seems worried about supper?"

Ben squatted down so he could meet the girl's curious eyes. "Well, there's a great deal'a fuss jus' now. She's worried 'bout Veronika, an' Lemuel, an' Freddie too. We're *all* worried 'bout where they've gone."

"Oh, me too. We prayed with Miss Tilly for them at breakfast—and at lunch too."

Ben smiled. He hoped God would hear and answer the children's prayers.

"Why did Freddie go away?" She frowned up at him. "I thought he liked it here with us." As Janie often did when they were sharing a quiet conversation, she pulled out the long gold chain with a pendant cross that hung around Ben's neck. He always wore it, though few others were aware. His sister, Jane, had given it to him long ago, and Janie liked to play with it, seemed to enjoy the feel of its weight and the sound that it made as she scooped it up into a golden puddle in her pudgy hand.

It took Ben a few moments of watching her fiddle with the chain before he was ready to answer. "Freddie's got some hurts what need healin'. His hurts happened long b'fore he come to live with us. So I were ne'er quite sure he'd stay fer long. But I was hopin' . . ."

"Was it 'cause of that money too?"

"What money? What do you mean?"

Solemnly Janie explained, "That money that you kept in the coffee can behind the wall in your little room."

Ben's eyes clamped shut. *No! He wouldn't!*

There was no reason for secrecy now. If Janie knew, then all of the children did. Ben hurried to his private room in the corner of the barn, placed one boot on the cold top of the little woodstove, and hoisted himself up to where the boards were loose. He pulled the right one out of its place and reached a hand into the space behind it. Sure enough, the can was gone. All the money he'd been saving up in order to procure a place for himself, for Janie and for Freddie.

"Who tol' ya, Janie? How'd ya hear . . ." But it didn't really matter. Freddie had taken Ben's hard-earned savings. *This weren't*

68

a rash act done in anger. They planned it. An' they got funds fer their journey too. Blimey!

· · ● · · ·

Walter's vehicle rumbled up the driveway. Lillian knew the sound of it by now, only this time he wouldn't be alone. He'd offered to fetch Father and the mysterious Delyth from the hotel, bringing them to supper. *At last! Oh, he's home at last!* With an encouraging nod from Miss Tilly, Lillian set down the wooden spoon she was using to stir butter into the mashed potatoes before scurrying toward the front door. Though she'd fretted all day about how she'd explain the current situation, she was no less exuberant to greet her father after he'd been gone so long.

Father stepped out of the back seat of Walter's car just as Lillian opened the front door. There he was, dressed in his traveling suit, with a printed silk waistcoat beneath it and a wide black tie. Instantly, Lillian was a little girl again, greeting him at the door just as she'd always done when he'd come home from one of his business trips. Nostalgia swelled a lump in her throat. She caught his eye. His face lit up, and she hurtled down the steps toward him, allowing herself to be swept up into his arms.

"Well, well, Lillian," he said over the top of her head, "you're a sight for sore eyes, you are."

"Oh, Father. It feels like you've been gone forever."

Clearing his throat, he agreed. "We've a great deal to catch up on. But first, there's someone I'd like to introduce you to."

Lillian loosened her hold, took a step away. *I don't think I'm ready for this.*

"Lillian, I'd like to introduce you to Delyth, the woman I wrote to you about."

A woman standing behind him stepped forward, slipping her arm through Father's. Lillian's mouth went dry. She was young, much younger than he, slender and in the prime of life. *How can this be? Father is fifty-two! She looks closer in age to me. Have we all been entirely wrong in our assumptions? Is she just a friend he met, a distant relative who . . .*

Grace's words from close at hand broke into Lillian's toppling thoughts. "It's so nice to meet you both at last. I'm Grace. Grace Bennett. Lillian's sister."

"Grace?" Father's smile widened. "I've read so much about you in Lillian's letters that I feel I know you well, dear." With two broad hands he engulfed Grace's more slender fingers. "To make your acquaintance at last is pure delight."

"We've been anxious to welcome you home again, sir."

Shoulders back, Father turned toward Delyth. "And may I present my new bride, Mrs. Elliott Walsh—"

Lillian gasped audibly, interrupting Father's words.

A shadow crossed his face. "I mean, Mrs. Delyth Walsh. My new wife, my . . ."

The unfamiliar woman brushed aside his fumbling words. "O-oh, it's so nice to meet you, Gr-race." Her face lit with a confident smile. Her words arched and curled as she spoke them with a thick Welsh accent, rolling the *R* in Grace's name. "Elliott and I are so excited to meet you, we are. But you can call me Dell, if you like. I answer to either."

The woman was speaking now with Grace. Lillian continued to gape in shock. Delyth was nothing like the sensible, middle-aged woman Lillian had imagined from Father's letters. She did not fit the concept of a new wife that Lillian had finally come around to envisioning as possible. Instead, this woman's skin was taut and light-complected. She had fair hair tucked up under a fashionable hat. She was tall and poised and outgoing. She was holding Father's arm. In fact, she was angled toward him, standing far too close.

The words of the conversation that continued without Lillian's participation filtered into her consciousness only a few comprehensible phrases at a time: ". . . neither of us looking to mar-ry . . . We discovered we were soul mates—enjoying the same aspects of life. . . . So we opted for a simple wedding at my family home. . . . Elliott, poor soul, is such a br-rilliant man, just needing someone to look after him."

What about me? Lillian's fingernails pressed painfully into her palms.

"Well, won't you come in?" Grace invited. "I know we'll want to hear all about it."

"Thank you."

The group began to move toward the house. Father and Mother's house. Lillian was frozen in place. It was Walter's hand under her arm that roused her from confusion. Bewildered, she looked up into Walter's pained eyes.

He whispered, "Okay, so she's not quite what we expected. But let's not judge her yet."

"Huh?" Lillian's feet still refused to obey her efforts to follow.

"Try not to panic, Lillian."

Panic? I'm just trying to breathe.

· · ● · · ·

Supper proceeded despite Lillian's stupor. Places were assigned and taken. Children were relegated to the kitchen, as all dining room seats were required for the adults. Lillian's attention remained on Father, who was given his traditional place at the head of the table, centered in front of the large bay window. Lillian was still waiting for him to explain more about Delyth. Yet the explanation did not come.

Miss Tilly had assigned Lillian a place to Father's left. Delyth was seated at his right. This meant that Lillian was now directly across from the stranger. So she kept her gaze averted.

"I've wondered about yer voyage." Miss Tilly drew their new guests into beginning the conversation. "How'd that go?"

71

Father traded knowing looks with Delyth. "It was rough for a little while. But we soon got used to it."

"Yes, but for the most part, it was delightful." Delyth laughed, letting loose a garble of incomprehensible words, and Father answered her in kind. Then he cleared his throat and looked around the table. "Forgive us, please. We'd agreed to speak only English instead of Welsh. But it's a difficult transition for us to make—and a difficult habit to break."

Habit? Lillian's fork stabbed at her potatoes. *Other than a Welsh word here and there, English is all you spoke before you left.*

"How was the last part of your trip?" Walter advanced the conversation. "It must feel like it takes forever to ride across Canada by train. You'd have seen most of the country by now, Dell. What did you think?"

"I loved it! And we spoke to some cowboys on the tr-rain. Such a romantic notion to me. R-riding across the flatlands, chasing cattle, and cooking over a campfir-re. But that's what you do for a living as well, Walter. Elliott told me about you. How exciting! I'm pleased to meet you in per-rson, I am. We've got horses where I'm from too. Some like yours here, but most are just humble beasties that pull the coal carts out of the mines." She looked around the table as if seeking confirmation. "A fair bit smaller than your-rs. Just ponies, they. Do you enjoy it, Walter?"

"I do. In fact, I miss workin' the cattle if I'm gone too long. It's a feelin' of freedom and simplicity you don't find in many other situations—at least when things are goin' well." He chuckled. "But I don't do much cookin' over campfires. I don't do much cookin' at all, really. I prefer just to be fed by more skilled cooks than me." He raised his fork. "Miss Tilly, as always, you've outdone yourself."

The woman waved off his compliment and the affirming sounds that came from around the table. "What kinda upbringin' did ya have, Dell? Ya from the city er a farm?"

"Me? Oh, neither. My family owns property. I have a gr-rand-mam who married a Scotsman of means. So I've a bit of a silver spoon, so to speak. Not a gr-reat fortune, by any account. But there were veins of coal discovered on his lands. And that's how I came to see the ponies pulling their little car-rts."

"We got coal here too," said Miss Tilly. "Under the prairie and in the mountains, both. My husband and some'a my sons worked as miners."

"It's a hard life, that. Your men *ear-rned* their daily bread, I'd say." Miss Tilly nodded slowly, her face solemn.

Grace asked, with humor in her words, "You were well off but you didn't have a pony of your own to ride? As a child I always imagined that was what being wealthy meant. A pony of one's own."

"Oh no, my mam was far-r too worried to let my sisters and me loose on such a beast. My brother, though, he followed my dad wherever he went, lear-rning the work of overseeing. They tended to drive in an automobile—but sometimes they'd r-ride my father's thor-roughbreds." The conversation lagged, so Delyth continued. "We had dogs though. Most were just hounds for hunting. But we also had two beautiful collies, and a little cair-rn ter-ricr for the house. As a girl I loved spending my time tr-raining and fuss-ing over them." Another pause, and Delyth laughed. "Listen to me, talking like a pepper mill. I'm afraid I'm pr-rone to excessive words, I am."

Lillian was suddenly grateful that so little of the conversation was being required of her. It was work enough at the moment just to listen and try to absorb. She kept her eyes on her food, with short glances around the table to gauge reactions.

Walter was seated beside her. He caught her eye with a look that seemed to wonder how she was faring. Lillian's eyebrows rose high as she returned a weak smile. She felt his shoulder lean gently against hers.

Grace was asking, "What about the rest of your mother's family? Did you live near them?"

"Oh, Elliott can tell you all about that! Can't you, *cariad*?" She laughed and gave him an amused expression. "I have a large family, I have. Some of them lived near our home. But we visited often with all the r-rest of them. That's how Elliott and I met—at the family par-rty welcoming him back to Wales. He and my father had been friends as lads. And we're r-related if you go back thr-ree generations. How does that go? You're my mother's father's father's son's daughter's son?"

Finally, Father answered a question. "I don't think they have an actual name for our familial relationship. But I'm grateful that we're family and most pleased to have met you." His voice was tender.

Lillian set down her fork. The food was no longer a sufficient distraction. She'd lost her appetite.

A look of compassion suddenly clouded Delyth's eyes. "Ah, but tell us more about the missing childr-ren. Walter told us just a little as he drove us from our hotel. Is there anything new to r-report?"

Grim looks were exchanged. Lillian held her tongue. So Walter spoke. "We realized they must've headed north. Lillian found a knife along the road that belonged to one of the boys. We think he must've left it behind as a sign for us to follow."

"Left it?" Father's head tipped to one side in uncertainty. "That seems a strange action for a boy who's running away."

Miss Tilly, who'd just returned from the kitchen with a refilled bowl of creamed peas, was quick to counter. "Ah, we don't think Lemmy was runnin' away. We think he was goin' to keep them others safe—'specially the girl."

For some time Father quizzed them all on their interpretation of the recent events. Ben and Grace shared what they'd found at the Geary house, using guarded language just in case Castor was listening to them from the kitchen, though the steady noise of words and laughter from the other table made it unlikely. Lillian's depleted heart found it difficult to comprehend the new information. *My father is married again. To a woman not much older than I.*

CHAPTER 7

Sunday

When darkness had finally descended over the quiet house, Lillian retreated to the master bedroom and cried in solitude on Mother's side of the bed. Mercifully, sleep claimed her quickly after its lack during the previous night. And suddenly it was morning again.

She rose, fetched a cold washcloth, and returned to bed. Lillian's head was aching and the children would wake soon. Placing the damp cloth over her puffy eyes, she tried not to think at all, but her mind swirled in fitful bursts.

How can Father show up with a new wife—a young woman—and not feel the need to discuss it with me at all? How can he not understand the way it would make me feel? I should talk to him about this—but there's really not much I'd like to do less than that today.

She wasn't certain what to think about Delyth. On one hand, the woman seemed to have an outgoing and positive personality. In fact, she was rather charming with her melodic speech. On the other hand, what on earth was she doing marrying a man so much her senior? What had she gained by not choosing a husband closer to her own age? It made her suspect. Though, even having learned so little about the woman, Lillian doubted now that it had anything to do with Father's money. It seemed Delyth would have been better off financially if she'd stayed in Wales—despite marrying a successful Canadian inventor.

Now it was Sunday—the second sunrise since the nightmare of missing children had begun—and there'd been precious little progress. Soon the house would be humming with children needing to be fed and dressed despite the heavy weight of worry. Against every inclination of her body, Lillian rose and dressed for the day.

Where had the runaways spent their second night? How were they feeding themselves? Were they safe? Ben had called Lillian and Grace aside to admit his stash of hard-earned money had been stolen. That had been a dark harbinger of a much more serious set of circumstances. These children had committed a crime. They had taken advantage of a safe home and trustworthy guardians. With each hour that passed it seemed less likely there'd be a quick resolution. The circle of distance they could have traveled was ever widening, particularly if they'd hitched a ride.

Oh, Father God, she prayed, *please protect them. Give Lemuel wisdom in whatever he's facing. Give him words to say that might sway the other two. Keep Freddie from making further catastrophic decisions. And please, please put a hedge of Your protection around that young girl. Keep her safe. I don't think she knows the severity of the choices she's making—how this could change everything about her life. She's only twelve. Just twelve.* Lillian tried to remember what it had been like to be twelve.

However, instead of those memories, the pressures of the current moment brought to mind the time of worry about the stolen filly. *God, You worked on Harrison's behalf—You protected and saved Lemuel in that trouble. I know that You're good. I know that—that You have power to act far beyond what I'm capable of doing, with all of my fears and confusion. I'm going to try to trust in Your power. I've learned I can trust You already through caring for these children. I'm going to try not to panic. But, honestly, this is just so frightening.*

Lillian adjusted the lace collar on the dress she'd chosen for church, looking in the mirror that hung over Mother's dressing table in order to do so. *It feels almost impossible not to fret about it all. I love these children so much. Even Veronika, though she's only been with us for a couple weeks.* Tears were pooling in Lillian's eyes at the thought. *I worry especially for Veronika because I know how much she's hurting right now at the loss of her parents. Oh, I wish she could have trusted us—listened to us. I wish we'd have been able to get through to her.*

Lillian stared at her own miserable reflection. *It's just so hard to show love to difficult people sometimes, God.* But as soon as the thought had formed in her mind, she paused in shock that she'd tried to explain such a thing to her heavenly Father. With a humble heart she whispered aloud, "Well, You know."

· · · ● · · ·

The second night of walking had been even more tiring than the first. Since their little party met no one along the road to whom Lemuel could expose their presence, his mind had hummed with ideas on how to drop clues. As much as he hated to do so, he'd torn three strips of cloth from his own shirttail as he walked along, mentally apologizing to his new mother for such a wasteful action. Three pieces of his best Sunday shirt were all he dared take lest Freddie notice and become suspicious.

Then, feigning the need for a privy break, Lemuel had stepped away by himself for just long enough. He'd snagged the first strip on a barbed-wire fence that turned up the lane of one of the farms they passed. Sadly the house was surely too far away for him to be heard if he were to dare to yell. Freddie and Veronika would be long gone before anyone could dress and investigate—and the money would be lost.

It was a perplexing dilemma that Lemuel was trying to manage, a little like fishing. Mr. Thompson had taught him that if you pull too hard on the line it could break, but give too much play and the hook wouldn't become properly secured. Lemuel had the oddest sense that he'd need to reel the runaways in just a little at a time, but not so much that his tenuous hold on them would snap.

The second and third pieces of shirt were left along the way where he hoped they were close enough to the road to be conspicuous, hooked on a thornbush and strung from a low-hanging tree. Lemuel prayed they'd be seen easily by passersby. But he was well aware that they were woefully small in such a vast wilderness.

At last Sunday morning had dawned and they'd retreated to the shelter of an abandoned shed in a patch of woods beside the road. Lemuel had fallen quickly into a fitful sleep. When he gave up sleeping just an hour later, he heard voices outside the door—the same two voices he'd already come to loathe.

"But I don't like fish. You said you'd kill us some meat."

Freddie growled a response. "If ya don't like it, get yer own."

Everything inside Lemuel wished he could crawl out through the shed's back window and just keep walking, putting distance between himself and the pair of runaways. But then the foolish girl would be left unprotected. And the thought of Mr. Waldin losing all of his money brought a determined shake of his head. Besides, the smell of fish roasting over a fire was too tempting to ignore.

As Lemuel emerged from the shed, rubbing his eyes against the bright sun, he saw the girl sitting cross-legged, picking at the exposed white flesh that was still skewered through by a rough stick. It made Lemuel's mouth water instantly, though he would likely have been grateful for anything that could have eased the hunger pangs in his belly.

They'd encountered little in the way of civilization on this road. Few farms. No nearby houses. Just a fence here and there jutting out from between stands of thick pines. He wondered how far they'd come, how many hills they'd passed. Not as many as twenty miles from home, he reckoned. *How far through the trees would I hafta go to get help? Pro'bly not that far at all. I bet people aren't too far out of sight if I only knew which way to run.* It was a sickening thought. Traveling at night greatly limited his options.

"Freddie, I was just thinkin'—"

"Well, don't. That ain't yer job."

Lemuel fell into silence once more.

If I can just get ahold of Mr. Waldin's money, maybe I can take off and get help for the girl. Lemuel hadn't seen the funds exposed at any point, but he'd been studying Freddie. There weren't many places where a boy could hide the bundle of bills. He had no backpack, only pockets and socks. It was likely too much bulk to hide inside a boot. Of course, it could be dispersed throughout Freddie's clothing.

Maybe I can jump him and pin him, take it by force. But past experience advised him that the idea was foolhardy. He'd known boys like Freddie. They didn't fight fair. And Lemuel was well aware that, though a little smaller and wirier, the other boy was armed with a knife. The thought caused prickles to stand up on his arm. *I shoulda found somethin' else to leave by the road. I shoulda kept me knife.* But it made little difference. Lemuel knew he'd never have raised such a thing against another. After all that he'd been through in his short life, no matter how bad his situation had become, he'd never been that kind of desperate.

Still, there was little extra risk in exerting his opinion through conversation. He kept his voice low and calm. "Why'd ya do it, Freddie? Why'd ya leave? I thought you liked Mr. Waldin."

Sharp eyes cut at him from across the wavering smoke of the small fire. "I ne'er tol' him I'd stay. Always said I might—*fer a while*. He's got Janie if he wants a kid. He don't need me too."

"But why? What was wrong with the Walsh house that ya couldn't endure it? They treated ya right, I know they did."

Tossing another handful of sticks onto the flames, Freddie sat silently for some time. Just as Lemuel had come to believe his question would be disregarded, the other boy answered with startling transparency. "I ain't no farm boy, like you. I don't b'long here. Them school kids—they're dull and slow. Figure I'll do what Mr. Waldin done. I'll go ta sea."

Lemuel froze in place. *Does he have any notion how far he is from water? He can't be plannin' to go back across Canada again, can he? He'll never make it on his own. And what about her? What's Freddie said he'll do for her? What deal did they make 'bout the money?*

A deep breath. These words were risky. "So ya just stole from him? How's that right?" Lemuel kept a keen eye on the boy seated on the other side of the fire. If Freddie made a move, there was a thick piece of stick near at hand that Lemuel could use to defend himself.

It was the girl who answered for Freddie. "I told him to take it. We need it now, and that man doesn't. He gets paid and so he can earn more. They call it 'survival of the fittest.' That's what my papa read to me from his books. And anyway, when we get to Sundre, my uncles can help Freddie get back to the coast. They'll put him on a train. They'll write a letter that says he can travel on his own. That's what I promised him."

Lemuel rolled his eyes. They'd both completely lost their minds.

· · ● · ·

Ben walked up to the house quietly, then stood in the doorway, listening for evidence that all the inhabitants had departed.

Through all of the Sunday morning hubbub he'd waited in his little room in the barn, puttering around with an old lock he'd been trying to repair. He'd attended church with the family on the first Sunday after his arrival but had opted out with a variety of excuses for his absence after that. It wasn't that he hadn't enjoyed the sermon. The pastor, known simply as Bucky, was down-to-earth and ordinary. However, those qualities were not at all what Ben had been raised to expect in a man who ministered before the church.

There were no robes and no candles. There was very little in the way of an altar at the front of the humble room, just a podium from which the pastor taught and another man led the singing. Even that had no accompanying organ music. Merely a piano. Ben wasn't certain if the casual atmosphere counted as church at all, doubtful it would appease the God he'd been avoiding for most of his life.

Having paused at the back door long enough to convince himself he was alone in the big house, Ben strode into the kitchen. A quick tap of his fingertips against the side of the coffeepot told him Miss Tilly had left some there. He smiled to himself again at his suspicion she'd done so on purpose. There was even evidence that she'd prepared extra breakfast with his needs in mind, leaving the tin serving plates sitting to the side of the stovetop to keep things warm. His absence at breakfast on Sundays had certainly not gone unnoticed, and yet the woman had seen to it that his needs were met.

To his relief, Ben had grown to have great respect for the busy matriarch of their home. True, she wasn't really part of Lillian's family, but to Ben she felt like the heart of it all, the one upon whom everyone else depended. A sort of mother to all—kind, unless you trespassed on her sensibilities. Then she'd let loose words of reproof to child or adult alike.

Seated now with a plate bearing the leftover bacon, eggs, and potato hash, Ben let his mind wander back to the months he'd spent in the Walsh household. For the most part, he'd managed to stay out of Miss Tilly's way, helping as best he could to keep the home functioning smoothly. He'd been careful not to cross swords with her by judiciously respecting her rules.

Freddie was another story. As much as Ben had urged him to fall in line, the boy had continued to push against the restrictions he claimed to feel. If Freddie was told to fill the woodbin, he'd bring in only half. If he was asked to clean the ash from the stove, he'd allow some to spill across the floor. Annoyances mostly, which required constant rebukes. But Ben suspected they were done on purpose—or certainly by wanton carelessness, at the very least. The lad could have done better if he'd had a mind.

Yet, it was rare for Freddie to make the same blunders where Ben was concerned. For the most part, they worked together without incident. So, even though Ben wished it weren't so, it was Miss Tilly who had taken the brunt of Freddie's negligence. As much as Ben had tried to be a buffer between them, the older woman had done most of the reproving of Freddie.

Until Veronika had arrived. That girl was like gas on a fire. Where Freddie had undermined, Veronika had gone for the direct attack.

She didn't like the way Miss Tilly spoke. She dared voice aloud that the woman sounded like an ignorant fool. Lillian had gaped in horror and hurried forward to deal with the child directly, but Miss Tilly had quickly dealt with the comment herself, appearing unfazed. "If ya choose ta use yer words ta try an' harm others, there'll be a cost ta ya. Fer that, missie, you'll be washin' up supper dishes with me."

At breakfast, Veronika criticized the way Miss Tilly cooked the sausage patties. She was immediately invited to help with breakfast preparations for the next day. And true to her word,

Miss Tilly had woken Veronika earlier than normal so that the twelve-year-old was ready to stand next to the hot stove in order to ladle pancakes into the skillet one after the other, enough to serve the entire household. It seemed that those events had served to turn Veronika's attention away from the kitchen for the most part. Next, she'd faced off with Ben instead.

Ben chuckled to himself, lifting a stocking foot to rest on the nearby chair. Miss Tilly's skin may well have been tougher than his own. *Not all that surprisin'.* Ben hadn't been able to brush aside the words quite as skillfully when the child had chosen a family meal setting to ask, "Why do you eat with us in the dining room, Ben? When you're just the hired help?"

He'd frozen, unable to think of a reply. The uncomfortable silence was broken when Grace had stated calmly, "Veronika, I'd like you to apologize to Mr. Waldin. That was not a kind question to ask. We consider him to be part of our family here."

"I won't," she'd insisted.

"Then you may be dismissed. Go up to your room."

Veronika had risen with a smug expression on her face until Grace had added, "No, dear, please leave your plate."

"All right, I'll leave. But I'm going upstairs to pack. Cass and I will be gone in the morning." This had become a frequent threat. Nothing and no one pleased Veronika. Only Freddie seemed to enjoy her presence immensely.

Maybe we shoulda seen this comin'. Maybe we missed all the signs. Ben speared a chunk of potato. *Is there somethin' we shoulda done different?*

It had been later that same night after the children had been put to bed when Lillian and Grace had called Ben and Miss Tilly to a meeting in the kitchen. Ben had taken the seat nearest the door. The women gathered around one end of the table, speaking in hushed tones. Ben noted the tightness on Grace's face. As much as she was trying not to be affected by the new girl, he could tell that Veronika was wearing away at Grace's confidence too.

"What will we ever do with her?" Lillian had moaned quietly.

Grace kicked off her house shoes beneath the table and leaned down to rub her tired feet. "Pray! Plead! I've never had my patience so—so tested in my life. And we thought this situation was going to be easier because the children weren't foreign-born."

"I didn't know it was possible for a child to be so demanding and difficult. She's like a—a little monster." Lillian whispered the last word almost inaudibly.

Grace straightened in her chair. "We just have to keep reminding ourselves that she's a hurting, wounded child. She's likely so confused and broken that she's lashing out at anything and anyone. I expect it's just a cover—a way to cope so that she can feel she's in control of a situation that's completely out of her control. Imagine—losing everything!"

"Well," Miss Tilly muttered, "she ain't got no trouble being *tough* enough. She's as stubborn a youngster as I've e'er seen. No tears. No weakness. Seems ta me she's just beggin' ta be sent away. That's why I keep her close ta me as much as I can. We get ta sendin' her to her room, we might ne'er see her again."

Ben had never considered such things. He'd been surprised at how insightful these women were in regard to the children. His family home had been painfully simple—obey or suffer the consequences.

The thought brought Ben's hand to rest on the table, tracing the bowl of his coffee spoon. In the silence of the empty house, he closed his eyes to hide his thoughts more deeply still. *But if I hadn'ta pushed back at Dada, what then? Would I 'ave been rewarded fer it?* It seemed doubtful. Ben's father was not the encouraging kind—still, there was no way to know for certain what might have been if Ben hadn't chosen to run away too. He'd been fourteen. The very same age that Freddie was now. He shook his head and reached for his coffee mug.

On the night of their impromptu meeting, Lillian's response had been more emotional than Grace's. "How are we ever going to be able to help her? Heal her? We thought we had some challenges with the others, but—but this Veronika—I've no idea how to reach her. I have to be honest and admit I've had the thought that it would be so tempting to just send her back to the church. To say we can't keep her here either."

Grace had stood to her feet slowly then, pushing her empty teacup into the middle of the table and reaching down to reclaim her shoes. "We have to try. She's got no other place to go. And I keep remembering one thing Mrs. Copsey used to say: '*You can't punish the hurt out of a child.*' If they're acting out because they can't cope with what they've suffered—even when it looks exactly like rebellion—the children themselves don't even really understand their own behavior. They're acting out of their hurt. And that has to be handled entirely differently. It takes time, but they have to learn to trust first." Ben had studied Grace's expression carefully as she'd shaken her head and sighed. "I just wish I could ask Mrs. Copsey for advice on this one. Veronika is something else. I hope that someday we'll understand the human mind better—so we'll be able to help people through their childhood traumas in ways that don't merely deal with their actions, punishing their hurts and driving them down deeper inside."

As Ben finished his solitary breakfast, he thought back to those words that Grace had used regarding Veronika. In fact, he'd pondered them often ever since. "*You can't punish the hurt out of a child.*" How did that speak to the woundedness in Freddie? It was bewildering to be responsible for children. Who could ever be certain about the right thing to do? At least until much later, when the results would be all but set in their character.

Pensively, Ben stood to fill his coffee cup again. At any rate, it wouldn't hurt for him to spend some time in the afternoon driving the backroads toward the north. He was quite certain he wouldn't be missed on a sleepy Sunday.

· · ● · ·

Midmorning, following a much-welcomed breakfast, Freddie had spied an open meadow behind some tall evergreens where it appeared a farmer had been harvesting a crop of hay. He'd motioned for Lemuel and Veronika to follow him. Near the edge of the field he'd found a rickety wagon half-filled with dry, cut grasses. The pitchfork that had been used to toss the hay from the ground to its wooden bed stood against the side of the wagon. Lemuel knew how much work such a load implied.

Without pausing for discussion Freddie climbed up over the side and dropped into one of the soft hay valleys. "This is the best bed ever."

"But they'll come back. They'll find us," Veronika objected.

"No, they won't. It's Sunday. They'll be in church."

"But after that—"

"It's s'pose ta be a whole day a'rest, kid. A whole day. We got as long's we want."

Veronika had turned to Lemuel for confirmation. He nodded without comment, hoping she wouldn't feel the need for more discussion. The wagon was a risk, but a risk that Lemuel was rather pleased to take. If they were discovered here, out in the open, all the better. And if they weren't, at least he'd get some much-needed sleep. With the soft bedding, the warm sun shining down on them, he'd hardly tipped his flat cap down over his face for shade before he'd surrendered to slumber.

All too soon he felt a shaking of his foot. In a half-dream state he pictured the farmer that they'd assumed owned the rig reaching over the side, agitating him awake. It seemed an unfathomably long time of coming to his senses before Lemuel's eyes opened into the bright sunlight. Instead of a man's face, large brown eyes stared back into his. Soft dark lips that hid a row of thick, straight teeth were clamped on his pant leg. It was a horse that had been shaking him.

CHAPTER 8

Upping the Ante

Veronika woke and moved in the hay beside Lemuel. Seeing the long furry face pressing over the side of the wagon, she shrieked. The horse's head jolted upright and the large beast spun several steps away.

"Shh," Lemuel hissed. And then, already on his knees and holding out a comforting hand, he called softly, "It's all right. We won't hurt ya. Ya just wanted some hay. Come back. Don't go."

The horse was a chestnut mare with a white star on her forehead and white boots. To Lemuel's surprise, she had a leather halter around her head that was attached to a lead rope trailing along the ground.

Lemuel climbed over the side of the wagon slowly, eyeing her skillfully. Her body was healthy and muscular. Her mane and tail were trimmed straight. Yet she was caked with muddy patches over her back and legs, and all of her dark body needed a good brushing.

Patiently, one careful movement at a time, Lemuel edged closer. He held out his palm, low and flat. Her nose reached out to sniff it. Her lips flapped against his callused skin, tickling it with long black whiskers.

Lemuel reached his second hand to grasp the lead rope. Instantly, he controlled her. She belonged to him. He felt a rush of satisfaction for securing her safely.

"Ya caught a horse!" Freddie's shout sent the mare heaving her weight backward.

Lemuel held tightly, kept his balance as she dragged him two big steps over the grass. But she calmed quickly and allowed him to approach again. He muttered just loud enough for Freddie to hear, "Can ya keep your voice down? Please."

Soon the mare was tied to the wagon and mildly munching on the sweet hay she'd been so interested in. Freddie was lying on his back again, staring up into the clear sky.

"We can go faster on a horse. Even if we take turns ridin'."

Oh no! That can't happen! Lemuel tried not to let too much of his worry show in his answer. "We can't keep her. She b'longs to somebody 'round here. We have to take her back. Stealin' a horse gets ya sent to jail."

"Are you kidding?" Veronika was quick to agree with Freddie. "We didn't steal her. We found her. No crime in *finding* a horse. This is perfect. We can go faster now. Can't we all three ride on her? She's pretty big."

In his mind Lemuel knew the suggestion was possible but not wise. Two riders were plenty. However, he also knew that even if he and Freddie each took turns walking—leading the mare with the other two aboard—their speed was likely to double. He had no intention of sharing the information. *Freddie doesn't know much about horses. What can I say that'll make him doubt the idea?*

But Lemuel's thoughts were interrupted by the other boy. "I know yer goin' ta tell us we can't. But we *are* goin' ta keep it, Lemmy. And we are goin' ta *ride* it." Freddie laughed aloud. "What is it folk say? Ya shouldn't look a gift horse in the mouth?"

The smile on Veronika's face faded. "What does that saying mean? Why would you look in its mouth?"

There was no attempt at profundity in Freddie's reply. He said dourly, "It means . . . we're keepin' it."

. . . ● . . .

Lillian had managed to dodge Father and Delyth's presence in their home through the Sunday meal and all the way through putting the children down for naps. She was fully aware that he couldn't be put off forever. And, even though it seemed impossible to turn her attention away from the missing children, Lillian had been assured over and over that the search continued, that it was even more effective now that they were able to focus to the north.

Descending the stairs, she walked directly into the parlor. Father was seated in his favorite wingback chair again, one leg crossed over the other, a book in his hands. Regardless, Lillian closed her eyes in horror. It was the new woman, and not Mother, who was resting on the chaise. The plum-colored velvet chaise had been brought from Calgary just for Mother—so that she might convalesce on the main level of the house during the day instead of alone in her bed. The chaise held such potent memories of Mother for Lillian that it evoked even the smell of her rosewater perfume. Many people had been seated there since, but only this woman had offended Lillian with the act. Although she knew the reaction wasn't fair, still her heart cried out indignantly.

Lillian forced herself not to falter in her plan. "Father, I was wondering if you'd like to take a walk. I thought it would be nice for *the two of us* to stretch our legs a little." *There. I've invited him and defined my terms. What will he say? Will he press to bring Delyth along?*

"I was thinking the same thing, dear. We can go out back through the woods where you used to like to walk with me."

A sigh of relief. "That would be so nice."

Their conversation began with catching up on all the residents of the family house and moved on to a summary of the events that he'd missed while in Wales. These things were precisely what Lillian had longed to share with him for many months. Their letters had served as a lifeline but were not the same as conversing. Lillian wanted to read his face, hoping she hadn't disappointed him with any of her decisions.

To her great relief, Father was very gentle and supportive. He asked questions for additional information but did not criticize or chastise her choices. In fact, so much so that Lillian began to feel an unanticipated and uncomfortable rising sense that Father was all but releasing his claim on the family home—that he was busy with other plans of his own.

They're going back to Wales. He's planning to leave me. Can it be? The foreboding idea made it increasingly difficult for Lillian to share her thoughts. The pauses in their conversation stretched longer.

At last she felt she couldn't restrain herself. "I was so surprised by Delyth, Father. You must have noticed."

"Surprised, dear? Why were you surprised?"

Lillian stopped short on the familiar path lined with towering lodgepole pines. The trees suddenly felt like onlookers, listening in on their private conversation. Her voice lowered. "Because you didn't tell me about her."

Father seemed amazed. "I did. I wrote to you several times."

Wringing her hands in an effort not to feel like a whining child, Lillian began again more slowly. "I know you did, Father. But I wish you could understand. Up until only a couple months ago, I had supposed Delyth was a *man*—a distant cousin whose acquaintance you'd made. That was how little I gleaned about her from your letters."

It was Father's turn to be taken aback. "But there was an entire letter devoted to explaining our relationship. I was as honest as a man could be."

"What letter?"

Silence. "You didn't receive a letter—special delivery?"

"No."

"How is that possible? It was the only one I sent that way. I thought it would . . . It was supposed to be more . . . I can't believe it didn't arrive—at all?"

Lillian turned her back and began walking up the narrow path again. She could hear his footsteps following after. He was clearing his throat periodically the way he did as he gathered his thoughts. Emerging out of the trees and onto the back field, Lillian waited for him to come alongside her, to speak first.

"I believe I understand now, my dear. It's a terrible misfortune. I wrote an extensive letter explaining my relationship with Delyth—how we met and how my affinity for her had grown." One of Father's large hands came up to grasp rather roughly at his forehead, sliding down his face until he was gripping his own chin. His cheeks had flushed red. "I think I understand now, Lillian. I had no idea you knew so little. I'm afraid I must ask for your forgiveness, then. Lacking that letter, I can see why you'd be overwhelmed."

Words failed her. There seemed no proper response. Instead, Lillian leaned forward until her cheek was resting against his chest. Strong arms drew her close.

"Oh, my dear daughter, my letter would have explained that Delyth has been, for me, a grace from our Lord I did not seek nor expect. We met when I first arrived in Wales, at the family gathering that welcomed me back. Her father had been my childhood friend, so I was promptly invited to stay in their home rather than in the rented cottage I'd arranged. It was an easy friendship that formed between us."

Stepping an arm's length away, Lillian watched Father's face silently as he explained further, struggling to keep her mind clear enough to comprehend his words.

"She's never been married—but, as the spinster daughter of a wealthy family, she enjoyed more freedom than most women her age. She's educated and talented, well-read and a poet in her own right. She also enjoys the outdoors. So we hiked together—the three of us. I appreciated the fervor of her conversation—even during the times when she argued politics and business with me."

Is that a blush rising in the apples of Father's cheeks? Lillian swallowed down a response.

"I suppose you could say that Delyth pursued me. I, having not considered such a relationship, remained rather oblivious to her interest, so that she was forced to be rather forthright. One night she told me that she'd never intended to remain unwed, but that she'd simply not found a man for whom she felt a strong enough affinity to surrender her freedom. Imagine my surprise that she might consider me as such! And, I assure you, I was equally flabbergasted that her family, upon hearing of our mutual interest, was in favor of such a union." Father cupped a hand under Lillian's chin. "My only regret is that you weren't there with me to share in this happiness, to get to know Delyth over time as I did."

Lillian took a second step away. "You married her without me."

"Sweet child, there was no other way. Her family would never have allowed me to take her away if we hadn't married first." His heavy eyebrows lowered. "And I doubt I'd have considered such a thing besides. No, dear, there was no way around that point being settled first."

Lillian could only whimper aloud her most frightening question. "Are you going back with her—to Wales?"

Father's arms drew her close again. "No, no, of course not. I have no desire to leave you, Lillian. We plan to stay. You're my family, the only one of my little family that I have left. I want to be here with you, dear. And so does Delyth."

Even though Father was crushing her tightly against his rounded stomach, Lillian finally felt that she could truly breathe again.

· · · ● · · ·

Ben was fully aware that his gas was running low in the car. He'd checked the level with an improvised dipstick before he'd left the farm in the afternoon and figured he had about two hours of fuel for searching. Sam Caulfield, one of the men in town with whom Ben chatted often, claimed that the newest automobiles included a special gauge the driver could read in order to know how much gas the tank held. The thought made Ben chuckle. *This old gal is lucky ta have a brake pedal!*

Ben's estimated time limit would expire soon, and it was several miles back to town. He had fuel for only one more branch out from the larger road. He'd driven these dirt lanes very slowly, stopping often at crossroads to check the ditches for clues. If there had been anything else Lemuel had managed to leave behind, Ben didn't want to miss it.

The current thinking by the officers involved with this case was that the children went only a little ways north in order to avoid approaching town. They were convinced that, once they'd passed about a mile north of where Lillian had found the pocketknife, they'd turned east in order to get to the main routes and more traffic. The Mounties' gravest concern seemed to be that the trio had found someone to give them a ride and then moved quickly out of reach. They'd sent a special bulletin to other Mounted Police stations across southern Alberta to watch for children traveling alone who met their descriptions.

Ben was duly worried about that particular outcome too, but he had a nagging suspicion that Freddie would be uncomfortable with such a plan. The boy liked to be in the wilds. He preferred solitude to strangers. And, though there were few good roads that traveled north and south in this hilly part of the country, Ben was determined to search as many of the inconsequential routes as possible. And he was particularly pleased that one advantage to living with deeply religious folk was that Sunday was a day off—even for him, so that he answered to no one.

At the moment, the Walsh home was a little too chaotic for his preferences. Not just because of Freddie's escapade, but because of Lillian's father's return. The young woman's shock was evident, and yet her father seemed almost unaware. Ben tried to imagine how he would have felt if he'd come home from sea only to find his dada remarried. The thought made him slightly ill, no doubt because his mother was still living. He wasn't certain, though, that it would sit well anyway.

Maybe tomorrow, if the kids were still gone, Grace and Lillian would allow him to take a longer trip—perhaps overnight. Then he could truly have a good look around these roads.

Turning up what appeared to be little more than a dirt track through a narrow path of grass, Ben slowed for a moment. He doubted that this could truly be considered a road—supposed that it led only to a farmhouse or, more likely, an abandoned cabin. But he'd determined to try every option, so he crept slowly along, watching for places where the recent rain may have left the trail impassable.

The trees gradually crowded closer. The thought suddenly occurred to Ben that he might not find a spot wide enough to turn the cumbersome automobile around, that he might have to drive out again in reverse. Then the road curved and he puttered to a stop. It was a bridge. A poor excuse for a bridge—simply a row of split logs laid across a small creek. It was probably intended to be used by riders on horses, or a wagon. Ben had no desire to test it with his heavy automobile.

However, just at that place, the corridor of trees widened and the ground became more even. He had a glimmer of hope that he'd be able to maneuver the vehicle in a way that would get it turned around. If only it could be done without ending up stuck in a hidden muddy patch.

Leaving the car parked, he walked out to inspect the area around the bridge and stopped short. Something gray lay in the ditch. He moved closer. It was a sock. A knitted wool sock. The same kind worn by almost every local farm boy. He passed it by, studying the ditch on either side of the car. There seemed to be enough room to turn around. The ground appeared solid enough.

So Ben slid back into the driver's seat and began carefully backing up and pulling forward in succession, each time angling just a little more until he'd turned in a half circle and was ready to drive away.

But that sock. What if it was something deliberately left behind? It was likely that no one would be able to identify it, even if it were Lemuel's. But, on the other hand, after traveling all this way, it seemed senseless to ignore the one thing he'd seen that might have been an indication of the children's presence. So Ben left the car once more, pulled the lump of fabric from the damp ground where it had become embedded, and tossed it onto the floor on the passenger side. It was time to return to the farm. He'd pushed the gas as far as he was willing for this excursion.

. . . • • . . .

"Are ya goin' ta hold it whilst I climb on, or am I goin' ta hold it fer the girl?"

Lemuel glared back at Freddie. "We don't even know if she's broke for ridin'. This horse might be—"

"Yer makin' that up. Who's got a horse ya can't ride?" Freddie's eyebrows lowered threateningly. "Get on, Veronika."

"No." Lemuel pushed his body between them, taking the lead rope from Freddie's hands. "Don't put her on first. I'll hold the rope. You can try next. But don't ne'er say it was me who stole her. This is yer doin'. Not mine."

They'd spent most of Sunday sleeping in the hay, the horse contentedly grazing while tied to a wooden wagon wheel. The lack of food for the children themselves was becoming a serious issue. Their one blessing was that cold, clear water had been easy to find in the creek that followed along beside the road they were on. Miss Lillian claimed that many of these streams came directly from mountain glaciers. Whenever Lemuel rubbed a handful of the clear water across his face, he found it easy to believe. It was like washing with ice. At least the frequent drinks had helped to slake their hunger a little. But after they'd slept, as the sun was lowering to the west and Lemuel was rubbing the horse down with handfuls of hay in an attempt to remove the worst of the caked-on mud, Freddie had returned to announce that his snare trap was empty. They would go without another evening meal. It was a disheartening discovery. Such that, at this point, all three were in rather foul moods.

"I'm sorry, girl," Lemuel whispered into the horse's ear, one hand on the lead rope and one hand raking comforting fingers against the muscles of her broad neck. "Steady."

They need not have been concerned. Freddie scrambled from the wagon onto the mare's back without incident. She stood patiently in place.

"How d'ya hang on ta this thing?"

An unbidden smile. Lemuel tried to keep his amusement from showing itself in his voice. "Ain't ya rode a horse b'fore?"

"No. I'm from a town."

Lemuel moved closer to where Freddie's leg dangled, looking up at the concerned teen. "Right here. This bump here, right b'fore her neck, is called the withers. And this tuft of hair don't hurt the horse when ya hold it. So you can grab hold here."

"I'm goin' ta fall."

I hope you do. Lemuel patted the mare's solid shoulder. "Squeeze yer legs. That helps."

Veronika was far less awkward than Freddie. She climbed on behind the older boy without complaint. It seemed she may have been more experienced.

Lemuel turned to leave the pasture. He knew all too clearly the seriousness of the offense of stealing a horse. He'd been accused of it and jailed for it last fall. Setting out, only one thought helped. *I can't leave her to this pair. So I'm goin' to see she gets back to her owner. It'll just be a day or two, then I'll bring her right back here where we found 'er.* He was already gambling with the hope that his actions could be seen as protective rather than criminal. Would it be worse to be accused of horse theft than of kidnapping a child? He'd been clear to the others that he wanted nothing to do with their decision, but he also knew for certain that Veronika would twist the truth—would accuse him of every kind of trespass—if he forced her into a corner.

At such times, his mind filled with the face of the farmer's wife who'd taught him to read. The farmer had commanded that he not bring shame on her with his actions. How much did he dare to compromise on that promise before he would need to allow the rebellious pair to strike off on their own? What if he'd already passed the point of no return? *Why does life gotta be so hard to figure out?*

CHAPTER 9

Monday

After a Sunday during which Lillian felt as if they were all pretending that normalcy hadn't completely vanished, she was ready to see something accomplished on Monday morning regarding the runaways. The children had been gone now for three long nights, and it seemed that no progress had been made by all of the search parties. She and Grace began with a group meeting before breakfast for the adults in their household plus Walter.

Lillian was first to make a suggestion. "I want to go into town and get a map of the area around here that shows who owns each property. That way we can divide it up. We'll keep track and know that we've covered every road. We can also stop at every home to ask if anyone has seen the kids—or evidence of them."

"The McRaes got a map like that pinned up at the post office," Miss Tilly said over her shoulder as she added another shovelful of coal to the stove. "Bound ta be another copy somewhere. Ya need more coffee, Walt? Yer cup's empty."

"No thanks, ma'am."

Grace was less encouraging about Lillian's idea. "The men

from town have already divided up sections. I know that over Saturday and Sunday they've knocked on most of the doors in our area—particularly to the north. I think by now they've covered every farm within ten miles in that direction." She seemed to hesitate before adding, "I don't think most of the men are going out again today. They're likely returning to their regular work. And . . . it's possible, unfortunately, that the children didn't actually go north."

Lillian recoiled. "You don't think Lemuel left the pocketknife on purpose?"

"Oh, sis, I don't want to sound like I doubt that. But I think we have to keep an open mind to all possibilities."

"But they could be *anywhere*, then."

"Yes." Grace's face was pinched with concern. "I'm afraid they could be. And if they went west into the mountains, I can only imagine how hard it is for them to find food and shelter. You didn't notice any missing food they might have taken, did you, Miss Tilly?"

"Not a crumb, and I woulda knowed it."

"I'm afraid they weren't well prepared for this." Then Grace added glumly, "Except for Ben's money."

Faces grew even more solemn. Heads began shaking at the disheartening thought.

But Lillian was still struggling with Grace's suggestion. *I'm sure he left it. He left his knife specifically where he thought I'd look—the place where the two of us went together. I've got to trust that he did it on purpose. It's all I have to go on.*

In the brooding silence that followed, Ben suggested quietly, "Think we got a photograph'a the girl 'mong her things. Don't ya 'member it, Grace? I can check the barn fer that. Ya got any photos'a the lads?"

Why haven't we been taking pictures? Lillian groaned to herself. *We should have photographs of all of the children by now! There's a little Brownie camera sitting right upstairs. What a foolish thing to have overlooked.*

Then Walter's words brought Lillian out of her silent self-reproof. "I'll check with the Thompsons. It's likely they have one of Lemmy." Turning to face Lillian, he asked, "Will you come with me?"

Lillian nodded, still frowning. And then argued, "But I think you're exactly right, Grace. They didn't take food—as if they were heading toward the wilderness. They took money—so they must have been going somewhere they could *purchase* supplies. And that means toward the towns—not west." It was a small but encouraging thought.

Ben seemed to stir himself. "Then we go ta the closest towns next, show 'em whate'er photos we got. Ask at any place a body can buy food fer twenty miles ta the north."

"The Mounties have already sent bulletins to all the towns," Walter said.

"No." Lillian pressed her opinion further. "They've sent them to the towns with police stations. There are little towns around that don't even have post offices. That's where we should start. Anywhere there's a little grocery. The little hamlets are far more likely to be a stopping point for the children than larger settlements."

Heads nodded in agreement. And as Lillian put herself in Freddie and Veronika's shoes, she felt certain it was true. A town or city would mean more chances for Lemuel to turn them in. Freddie would realize that. He was nothing if not shrewd. But if they stayed away from concentrated populations, they could buy food from a corner store in the middle of nowhere and still manage to slip past the few people living there.

However, if Freddie went into one of those little hamlets, he'd need a story—a believable reason why children would be traveling alone in a remote location. People in rural communities would certainly recognize a stranger and feel free to ask questions. The explanation would likely be memorable. It might make them easier to find. She determined in her own mind to remember to request that outcome as they prayed together daily for the lost children—that someone would notice them and that God would lead them to that person.

Following the meeting, Lillian climbed into Walter's automobile, scooting over close beside him on the long bench seat. They headed for the Thompsons' farm. Lillian felt depleted from their discussion, not very talkative. She was still annoyed with herself for not having thought of taking pictures long before this.

"Are you okay?" Walter asked, then quickly amended his question. "I mean, I know you're not okay. But do you wanna talk about it?"

Lillian didn't feel much like talking. "I'm all right. I'm just struggling this morning." She turned toward him, studied the side of his handsome face as he drove. "I haven't paid much attention to you, Walter. I'm sorry about that."

"Don't apologize. I understand. You were so excited about your dad comin' home, and then all this just erupted underneath you."

Lillian let her head fall against Walter's shoulder. "That's exactly how it feels. Like a volcano just burst up from nowhere. Yes, that's exactly how it feels."

"I'm glad you were able to talk to him yesterday. It seemed like you were in better spirits afterward. I take it you worked some things out."

Lillian sat upright, half-turned toward him. She realized that she hadn't shared their conversation with Walter. "I did. We did. And, oh, you'll never guess. Father sent a letter—special delivery. It told all about Delyth and him. But I never received the letter."

"What?"

"Yes. So when he arrived, he thought I already knew. He was just giving me time and space to adjust to having her around.

He never guessed I didn't know anything specific about her. He felt very bad about that."

"The letter was lost?"

"Well, he got to thinking about it later and remembered he'd given it to a secretary to mail. The man apparently didn't send it—or, at least, must have done something wrong. So, that explained my father's lack of—of clarification when he arrived."

"Ah, I see."

She settled back against the seat. They were already turning into the Thompsons' lane.

"Do you feel any better about it now, Lill?"

"A little. I mean, she's nice. She's pleasant, but . . ."

"But?"

"Well, it's not as if I'm ever going to call her *Mother* or anything." Even expressing the idea aloud felt offensive to Lillian.

The car slowed to a stop in front of Lemuel's house. Walter's words were gentle. "What'll you call her?"

Lillian rolled her eyes. "I'm going to start out by calling her Dell just like she asked us to. And—and then, I just won't bother to stop."

Walter squeezed her hand and laughed a little. "Maybe he won't notice."

Lillian groaned. "Father notices everything." And in her mind Lillian added, *But I refuse to accept a third mother—especially one not much older than I am!*

"Well, you'll know soon enough. Aren't you having tea with them later this morning?"

"Don't remind me."

• • • ● • • •

Before he was ready to set out searching for the day, Ben drove into town to gas up the automobile and to get the daily mail. He asked Sophie McRae at the post office if copies of the posted map were available and was told to go to the town office, a single room on the second floor of the local bank building. Ben had climbed these stairs regularly since he'd arrived in town. On the same landing across from the town office was the entrance to the small public library.

Finding the town office locked, Ben stopped in at the library desk instead. He kept his voice low. "'Scuse me, Mrs. Orlinger. I'm lookin' fer a map'a the area, like I saw hung up at the post. D'ya know if they have extra in the office there?"

"We had them here, actually," she whispered back, eyeing another woman at a table toward the back of the room. "But we're all out now. They used them up when they were lookin' for the kids."

"I see. Well, are they gonna make more?"

"I'm not sure how soon they can be printed. I'm sorry, Ben. I'll send one over as soon as they come in."

"Thank ya. 'Preciate it, ma'am."

He stepped away and she called him back, her voice rising with concern. "No word yet?"

"No, nothin'. Still lookin'."

"Well, I'm praying for you all. We're *all* praying for you."

"We 'preciate that too, Mrs. Orlinger. Every prayer helps, I'm sure." Ben hoped that it would make a difference, that the Good Lord would show mercy for the sake of the lost children. He'd accept help from any direction at all and was painfully aware that only God knew their location at the moment.

Failing in the secondary purpose for his visit to town, he decided there was nothing else to do but return home. He'd promised Janie that she could ride with him in the freshly gassed-up car for a little while. He couldn't imagine why such a thing would interest her but assumed she merely wanted his attention all to herself for a few hours.

The money Freddie had stolen was a huge blow to Ben. He'd

hoped it meant independence for him—a chance to make a search for his family, to set up a home of his own somewhere in order to care for Janie himself. Sadly, these seemed to be competing goals. How could he settle down before he'd found his parents and sister? *Where* would he settle if he ever accomplished that task? But he was determined that whatever decision he made, it would be the one that was best for Janie more than any other consideration.

In fact, a couple weeks earlier he'd stopped in at the office of Mr. Wattley, the local lawyer, to inquire about officially adopting Janie, in addition to his current standing as her legal guardian. It wasn't an expensive proposition but would require a day in court when the circuit judge was in town. There was just one concern that might become a problem. The solicitor had explained that some judges were not amenable to allowing single men to adopt. If Ben were to marry first, it would make the process much simpler.

Casting that idea aside quickly, Ben was still uncertain how the child would respond to officially having him for a father. It would mean leaving her new "family" at the Walsh house in order to live with him. Perhaps it would help if the other children were placed in families first. Matty and Milton were expected to be settled with the Caulfields soon—as soon as their paperwork could be completed. Catherine was increasingly anxious to have them with her.

That left only Castor. Ben doubted that the new boy would be in a family any time soon—even if Veronika returned immediately. The girl was problematic. Her troubles would delay what would otherwise have been a fairly easy placement. He shuddered to think how long their situation might drag out. He wondered if any family would be willing to bring a child like Veronika into their midst. And, without a place for her, Castor was also in limbo. Additionally, there was the daily understanding that new children could arrive at any time.

When Ben returned to the farm, he parked by the back porch, intending to leave again shortly. He gathered the mail from beside him on the front seat, wondering what he'd missed while in town. Would there be additional reason for activity—additional news?

It was still early, and the house seemed quiet. Miss Tilly was mixing the large tub of bread dough for the week. She looked up and nodded toward him in greeting. Ben could hear Grace in the parlor, reading to the children. Lillian was either absent or upstairs. He set the mail on the table.

"No maps left?"

"No, all of 'em gone."

"Guess I'm not surprised." With skillful hands, Miss Tilly tossed a dusting of flour across one corner of the kitchen table and tipped the dough out onto her work surface, ready to begin kneading. She explained, "Well, Lillian's gone ta town fer a visit with her dad an'—an'—her dad's wife." A stifled chuckle caused the woman's round shoulders to bounce a little. "I'm not sure what ta call 'er."

Ben met her eye, noting the twinkle there.

She added, "Life's perty funny, if ya can keep yer humor 'bout it."

He wasn't certain Lillian was ready to be amused just yet. "Don't seem quite right ta me. He's well beyond her age, if a day."

The hands were working the dough again. "Reckon ya can't know how it feels lest ya've lost a spouse yerself. If I'd found another husband, maybe I'd have been happier too. An' if he'd been younger 'an me, well . . . don't see no good reason to complain 'bout that." Her shoulders bounced again with mirth.

Ben froze. He hadn't expected such words from her. "Oh? Ain't ya happy here, Miss Tilly?"

The woman's face fell, suddenly pensive. "I am. Fer certain, I am. But there's a whole smorgasbord a'ways ta find joy. An' I won't deny that sometimes I feel I'm missing a flavor er two

107

here an' there." And then she amended her declaration further. "Mostly, though, I'm glad I knowed what few folk do—what it is ta be loved well. How 'bout you, Ben? Ya feel a little less 'an all yer wants are met?"

He wasn't certain he'd ever known what it was to have his wants fulfilled. How could he answer such a question? "I'm fine. Fine as is likely, I guess."

"Hmm." She went back to working the dough.

· · · ● · · ·

As Lillian walked up the driveway after Monday morning tea with Father and Delyth, she noticed the large family automobile parked beside the back porch. It seemed that Ben had been out to town. She supposed he'd left the vehicle so close to the house because he planned to be off again soon on another search.

Her visit with Father had gone quite well. They'd sat for tea at the hotel restaurant and chatted together. Lillian had learned much about Father's trip and listened to long descriptions of his favorite sights. The countryside he'd seen in Great Britain sounded almost mystical, made vivid by Father's detailed narrative. In addition, Delyth's comments were rich with sentiment for her homeland. But Father held a particular interest in castles. As he described them, Lillian found it difficult not to picture them as looming stone monuments commemorating the strong power that one group of people exerted over another. She listened attentively while trying to conceal her own distaste, her concern for the common folk who had been crushed under such oppression. It wasn't a conversation she'd have preferred to have just now. Still, after so many months spent waiting impatiently to have Father home again, she could hardly challenge what he wanted to talk about.

By the time Lillian arrived home to the mudroom, unpinned her hat, and placed it on a shelf above the tumbling row of shoes, she'd traveled through a wide range of emotions. She wanted to give proper attention to this very important man—to get to know his choice of a new wife. And yet, the pair of them felt rather foreign to her now—and at no time more than when they shared private words in Welsh with each other. At those times, Lillian felt completely forsaken and uncultured.

Her mind, however, was still mulling over Father's startling disclosure this morning and its implications. He and Delyth were planning to purchase a home. He'd described their goal as a modest house in town, adding that it should be small because they also planned to travel together frequently.

That notion hadn't surprised Lillian. Her memories of Father were mostly of his comings and goings due to his occupation as a railroad man and inventor. The fact that he now planned to continue traveling for pleasure fit well with Lillian's idea of him. In fact, she'd often listened to stories of how he and Mother had roamed together in the years before Lillian had been adopted by them. The couple had traveled mostly by train—to both ocean coasts—and had even ventured into the United States. But once Lillian had arrived, Mother had stayed home in order to give Lillian the best upbringing she could manage.

Even while Father had been explaining their plans, Lillian's mind moved to the obvious question. *What about the large house? My childhood home? Will it be sold?* At last, Father had taken her hand and cleared his throat. "Lillian, dear, Dell and I have spoken about it at length, and we'd like to give the home you grew up in—the home your first parents built—to you and Grace." Even now the words replayed themselves in Lillian's mind over and over. "*To you and Grace.*" Father had added, "God has blessed us well, and we feel this is an appropriate way to demonstrate our gratitude to Him."

Lillian had never imagined such a thing. The future of the children living with them was instantly more secure. They could be provided a home for as long as was needed. There was no reason to fret any longer about rushing them into new families.

It was a lovely revelation to Lillian's heart. She was excited to share the news with Grace and Miss Tilly when they were alone later. But then Lillian's thoughts went to Walter. *Dear Walter. What happens when we're married? Will he be content to simply move in here with us?* Try as she might, she couldn't quite imagine Walter's presence in the current situation. He seemed out of place—though not because of the children. They all doted on him. But this man didn't really *belong* so close to town. And how could he also raise cattle? Lillian reached for her everyday apron and tied it behind her back. She was well aware that Father's acreage was not nearly large enough for such an enterprise.

As much as Lillian had been thrilled to have Walter back in Brookfield after his short attempt at working for the oil industry in order to build up a pool of funds to fulfill his true aspirations, his return had pained her too. Now that he was back on Tommy Gardner's ranch, sleeping once more in the bunkhouse with the other men, Walter's pay had been greatly reduced. How would he ever get the land he wanted?

CHAPTER 10

Backroads

Hopping down the back porch steps with her feet together, Janie seemed pleased to join Ben during Monday afternoon's time of searching. She chatted away, explaining some of her recent exploits. The car was ready, and Ben had been given a hand-drawn map to find two little hamlets hidden among the nearby valleys. Maybe it was just Janie's presence, but Ben had a heightened sense of expectation. Perhaps this would be a blessed excursion.

Ben held the driver's door open, and Janie crawled across the front seat.

"Eww. What's that?"

"What?"

"It looks like a dirty, dead thing."

Ben slid into the vehicle, his eyes following her pointing finger. "Just a sock I found b'side the road."

"What are you keeping it for?"

"I ain't. I thought . . . Here, I'll take it away."

Pinching the cleanest corner of the fabric between two reluctant fingers, Ben flipped the sock out of the car and toward a bush. He'd explain it to the women inside the house later—maybe give it a quick rinse before showing it to them.

They set out together. It was a lovely warm day with a cool breeze. Miss Tilly had packed a picnic. Ben planned to stop somewhere scenic so they could make a good memory to counteract all the hustle and worry. He feared that the younger children were being adversely affected by the current crisis. If there was any way he could help Janie to feel more secure, he wanted to take the time.

Turned backward and up on her knees on the broad front seat, Janie watched out the back window and commented on the amount of dust that was trailing in the air after the car. Then she stretched out beside him for a time, tucking her arms under her head. Ben wondered if she was going to nap. But instead, she rose up again and began bouncing on the passenger end of the bench seat, making the springs inside it creak in ways that delighted her. All the while she was chatting in a stream-of-consciousness fashion. And, as was typical, the little girl blurted exactly the topics he'd hoped to avoid. "Mr. Waldin, are Lemmy and Freddie and V'ronika in trouble? They've been gone so long—since Friday, and it's Monday."

"Well, it was wrong'a them ta run away. But we wanna find 'em so we can bring 'em home again 'cause we love 'em—not ta punish 'em."

"But this isn't V'ronika's home. She doesn't like it here. She keeps telling us that."

"I know, bunny. But she's young an' she needs somebody ta take care'a her, even if she ain't happy 'bout it. She still misses her mum an' dad an' the home she shared with 'em. Ya understand about that, don't ya?"

"Uh-huh." Janie was looking out the open window now, allowing her hand to play in the air that streamed around their vehicle.

"Mr. Waldin, am I in your family, or am I in Miss Grace and Miss Lillian's?"

"Ya belong with me now, 'member? We found that paper what says yer mine."

"But are you always going to live in the barn? That doesn't seem very nice."

He studied her in short glances as they bounced along in the heavy automobile. *What's she thinkin'? Does she wanna stay with the sisters instead? Is that what she's leadin' up to?* "No, Janie. I plan ta find a place'a me own."

"And will I live with you then?"

Should he offer a choice? Or should he simply declare it? "I hoped ya'd wanna. I plan ta adopt ya so yer *always* in me family."

Her face turned toward him. Her eyes were shining. "I do. I want to stay with you, wherever you go. You're my favorite, Mr. Waldin. I'm glad I'm in your family."

Ben's heart had begun to pulse with emotion and relief. He labored now to keep his answer steady. "I'm glad too. I love ya, child."

"Me too." And she turned back to the window.

Ben blinked hard to maintain his composure.

But Janie wasn't finished. "Mr. Waldin, what am I going to call you? When you 'dopt me? Will I still call you Mr. Waldin?"

The truth was that Ben had wondered about that too. He turned the question back to Janie. "What would you like to call me?"

"Well, I already had a daddy. So I don't think I'd like to call you that."

Ben sighed. He'd expected as much.

"But I never had a papa before. Maybe you could be my papa." Her voice changed tones as she explained matter-of-factly, "That's like a daddy, but just a diff'rent word."

"I'd like that," he managed to answer. "I'd like to be your papa."

For Janie the matter seemed to be settled. Her next question was about lunch. But Ben returned her focus in order to clarify one last point. "Would ya like ta begin callin' me that now? Instead'a Mr. Waldin? That's so long."

She shrugged. "I can wait till after I'm 'dopted."

· · • ● • · ·

After another sunset on Monday night, Lemuel and the other two set out once more. The horse seemed confused to be expected to travel again in darkness but fell good-naturedly into step behind Freddie. When the moon had arced halfway across the night sky, Lemuel noticed increasing evidence that a town was near. He'd observed that their road had become gradually more pronounced, wider with fewer patches of weeds between the rutted dirt tracks. And along the side of the road there were more shadowed lanes and trails leading away from it. The mare that Lemuel had dubbed Star had been steady and seemed content to allow them to lead her along. Now her ears pricked forward from time to time as she seemed aware of activity somewhere in the night around them. Freddie was visibly more agitated. At last, from his turn riding high up on the mare's back, he whistled to Lemuel.

Then he hissed, "We gotta stop. We're too close ta a town. Someone'll see us."

"All right."

Veronika slid off first, holding tightly to the crook of Freddie's elbow to slow her descent. "How close do you think we are?"

"Not sure. But close enough."

Her face brightened a little. "Good. We can buy some food. Give me some money, Freddie, and I'll go—"

Freddie dropped down beside them. "No. I'll go an' check it out. You stay here with the horse. I might be a while."

Lemuel shrugged. He'd surrendered to the fact that there was no sense in arguing. But being so near to a town would surely

114

provide opportunity to expose the runaways. So he led the horse off the road and through the trees to where he could hear another creek burbling along in this valley. Holding the lead loosely while Star took a long sip, Lemuel eyed a patch of soft dirt on the other side of the stream. Maybe this could be used to leave a message behind. Then he passed the rope to Veronika so that he could lean down and drink as well, raising the water in his cupped hand.

"How far do you think we got last night?"

"Can't say."

North was an easy direction to manage. The mountains ran beside them to the west. As long as they continued to keep them so, staying in the rolling foothills, they could be relatively certain they were on course toward their destination. But Freddie had begun to worry aloud that they'd never reach the proper road Veronika claimed would be easier—the Cowboy Trail. He frequently grumbled about it.

Lemuel dropped down in a patch of soft grasses and slipped his shoes from his aching feet. He planned to soak them in the icy water for as long as he could endure it.

Veronika's voice broke out, too loud and too close. "Hey, where's your other sock?"

He merely muttered, "Lost it," and lowered himself nearer to the rocky creek bed.

"Lost it? Lost it where?"

Lemuel shrugged.

"You know what, farm boy? I hope you're not getting any ideas about getting us caught. Don't forget that I'll just tell them you made me come along. Who are they going to believe? You, a street rat from across the sea who already got in trouble with the police, or me, a girl from a good Canadian family?"

Lemuel forced himself to squelch his response. In truth, he'd considered leaving the other sock when they'd begun walking for the second night. But it had seemed so very unlikely to Lemuel that such a common item would draw attention that he'd chosen not to bother. Besides, whenever he stopped throughout the night to take his shoes off, he'd switched his one sock to the opposite foot. That way he was able to keep the spots that were rubbing raw inside his shoe to a minimum. It seemed prudent to hold on to at least one sock for that purpose. But his good shoes were showing wear from so much walking. He cringed.

Veronika had begun to natter at him like a magpie with accusations and warnings.

Fine then, I'm gonna go to sleep till she stops talking. Flopping down onto the soft grass near the creek, Lemuel closed his eyes. Sleep was his only comfort in this bizarre new world. *Just, please don't dream*, he instructed himself. *I hate it when I dream.*

· · · ● · · ·

By Tuesday morning, Lillian had managed to gather a picture of Lemuel and one of Veronika. However, there weren't any of Freddie. As she and Walter set out for their turn at searching, she had the photographs beside her on the seat, tucked into an envelope.

They'd been assigned two churches and a grocery store. Because of the remote and widespread locations, those goals were all that had been deemed practical for today's journey. Lillian had still stubbornly refused to head in any direction other than north.

Walter seemed unusually quiet. After several attempts at beginning a conversation with him, Lillian asked softly, "Is there something wrong?"

He stirred himself, shifting in his seat. "I'm sorry. I didn't mean to seem sullen. I've just got a lot on my mind, I guess."

She leaned up against his shoulder, slipping her hand under and around his arm. "Want to talk about it?"

"Sure. Well, it's not really just one thing. It's—well, the kids, of course."

"Of course."

He gave her a questioning look. "Honestly, Lillian, I'm not sure this is the time to bring up anythin' else. In light of the kids."

A long pause. "I think, Walter, that there's *always* going to be something happening with the kids. I suppose if we're ever going to talk about other things, we'll need to just go ahead and talk regardless."

"I suppose you're right." Walter exhaled, closed his eyes for a moment. "I was hoping we could discuss *our* plans."

Lillian smiled down at her lap. Something inside her had instantly begun to tremble at the idea of having such a conversation. "I'd like that." She could feel Walter's shoulder relax a little. *It would be wonderful to choose a date for the wedding. It would make the promise of it feel more real.*

"Well, I've been reading about property that's become available because of the Dominion Lands Act. They've opened up a new area not too far from Brookfield, and I found out that I could get a quarter section now, and a second quarter section once I've built a house on the first one—and, of course, cultivated forty acres of it."

"Oh, I see." She tried to redirect her own thoughts. "Well, that's a lot of land. It must be very expensive."

"No, Lill, that's just it. The government is selling off the land in order to get the area settled. The only cost is a ten-dollar fee for each quarter, and then fulfilling the requirements by developing it within three years. I've checked into it before, but there was never land near enough."

"You don't have to buy it?"

"Nope. It's a great way for a man like me to get started. We could own a half section in just a few years and use it for runnin' cattle." His voice was rising in excitement as he shared his thoughts. "Tommy said he'd help me out with a few head for startin' up and that I could use his bulls when I'm ready. We've already put together a rough plan."

Lillian held her breath. Her voice squeaked a little as she asked, "Where would that land be?"

"I'm not sure right now. I sent a letter askin' them to mail me the application and a map of available lands. I know there's kind of a rush whenever new areas open up. So I'm tryin' to work quickly. That's one reason why I hate to keep puttin' off talkin' to you about it." He hesitated. "You haven't looked up at me for a while, Lillian. What are you thinkin'?"

"I'm—well, I'm excited about that."

"Are you?"

"Yes, of course. I want to see you get the land you've always wanted, Walter." She dared a glance up toward him, hoping to exhibit more confidence than she felt. "And I know how hard you worked while you were on that oil rig. And then you came back to Tommy's instead of working for as long as you'd planned. I know that was hard for you. I can see that—that my undertaking with Grace has slowed down your own goals. I don't want to do that to you."

"But I wanted to be with you more than anything else, Lillian. I just couldn't stay away for so long. Still, without enough money to invest, I can't get enough land around here to make a reasonable attempt at ranching."

"Yes. I see." Mentally wrestling with whether or not to remind Walter about her inheritance money from Uncle Saul that was still sitting in the bank, mostly unused, Lillian answered quietly, "I want to support you in the best way I can." After all, there hadn't yet been time to discuss those surprising funds with Father.

His arm slipped out of her grasp and reached around her shoulders, drawing her closer. Lillian allowed herself to melt against Walter's side. She hoped her stilted breathing didn't betray the tension she was feeling. *He won't want to live in Father's house. He'll have to build a home on his land instead, and I'll need to live there too. And who knows where the land will be?*

"Are you all right, Lillian? You're very quiet."

She lifted her face up toward him with effort. "I'm just thinking about it all. It's exciting. You would get your land so much sooner that way. That's wonderful."

"*Our* land," he corrected.

"Yes, our land."

Her mind was still buzzing with the implications of the new land. The land would likely be remote. She'd heard stories of early settlers who'd taken the government up on just such an offer, and most described a laborious and isolated life. Lillian had never really been a farm person. Sure, she'd helped her mother to raise chickens and tend a vegetable garden in the years while Mother was still healthy—and that had seemed work enough. The rest of what they needed had been purchased with Father's income. Lillian wondered how much she'd have to learn in order to be the wife that Walter would need for homesteading together.

Her lower lip began to tremble, and she bit it instead. *I have trouble and worry enough for this one day in just searching for the kids. I'm not going to carry that extra burden now too. Father God, please help me not to worry about this until I know more. But that is going to be hard.*

"Is that the town?" Walter's voice brought Lillian out of her prayer.

She looked at the road ahead. "Well, it's a few buildings around an intersection anyway."

"It's Harstad, I think. Population—well, about seven. But they do have a grocery store of sorts."

Curious eyes watched them from nearby windows as Walter pulled up in front of the only public building. A small sign posted by the door was the sole indication that there was a store inside. Walter knocked and then tried the handle. It opened, and they tentatively pushed inside.

"Hello?" Walter called.

"Welcome, friends. How can I help ya?"

The front room was rather dim compared to the bright sunshine. The space was crammed full of all types of goods in rather haphazard fashion.

"We're not shoppin' today. We're actually lookin' for some children. We have pictures here." Walter reached for the envelope that Lillian had carried into the store.

"Well, I ain't seen nobody I didn't know, but I'll look at yer photographs so I can watch fer 'em, if ya like."

"Thanks. I appreciate that. We think that the three of them are traveling together. This is the oldest boy—his name is Lemuel Thompson. He's almost fifteen. And this is the girl—she's twelve. Her name is Veronika Geary. She has long black hair."

The store owner was examining the pictures carefully. Without looking back he called over his shoulder, "Fern, can ya come out here fer a minute?"

A woman emerged from the back. "What is it?" She sounded put out that she'd been disturbed.

"Look at them pi'tures. See if ya seen these kids."

Fern pulled a folded pair of glasses from her apron pocket and settled them on her nose. "Kids? Wanda Palmer said something ta me 'bout that. Said some kids've gone missin'."

Lillian stepped forward. "There are three of them. But it's unlikely they'd be seen together. Two of them have run away and the third is probably just trying to keep the others safe."

The glasses tipped down off Fern's nose. "Why's that?"

"Well, we're not certain just why he went along. But this boy, Lemuel, he's not the type to run away."

"That so?"

Her husband handed the photographs back to Walter. "We ain't seen 'em, but we'll keep an eye out. Might want ta put in a call to the police."

"Oh, believe me, we have," Walter assured him. "They've put

out a bulletin to all their stations. But the kids have been gone since Friday night, so we're out lookin' for them too."

The woman bristled. "Since Friday? 'Round here? They walkin'?"

"We're not exactly sure which direction they went from Brookfield, which is south of here. But, yes, ma'am. We suspect they're walkin'."

"Hmm."

The store owner scratched his head for a moment and frowned. "Son, that's not so good. We got a mountain lion pesterin' farmers in this area. Been seen several times—twice not too far from town—out 'long the backroads. Likes ta stay near the creeks, I hear. We're all on the lookout fer it now."

"No, that's not good." Walter's face had washed white. "Would you—do you mind? Can I leave our names and how to get in touch with us?"

Lillian had preprinted small cards with their contact information. The store owner took one willingly.

As they were turning to leave, Walter added, "I hate to ask, but could you please call to let us know any news about that cougar—one way or another?"

"O'course, son. They got a telephone a couple'a towns over. I'll be sure ta let ya know should somebody shoot it."

They walked to the automobile in silence. Walter opened the door and Lillian slid across the seat. At last she ventured, "Well, at least it's not a bear or a wolf or something."

Looking down at the steering wheel, Walter spoke quietly. "I wish you were right. A mountain lion's about the deadliest thing in our woods here." He shifted into reverse and Lillian closed her eyes. For the first time, she hoped that she was wrong—that the children had gone south, or east or west. Any direction but here.

CHAPTER 11

Floundering

Freddie had fashioned a slingshot out of a Y-shaped tree branch and a flexible rubber tube that he'd purchased when he'd made their first stop for groceries on Tuesday morning. Of all the things he could have splurged on in his excursion back into civilization, Lemuel was disappointed that making a slingshot seemed to be the boy's top priority. But Freddie continued to boast about hunting in the woods and eating off the land, puffing out his chest as he explained how well he could provide for them now. However, Lemuel had been perpetually hungry over the weekend, and so far he preferred the two loaves of bread, the block of cheese, and the homemade beef jerky to Freddie's speculative endeavors. They shared some of the food while seated beside the bubbling creek before settling in to sleep for the day. They'd opted to reserve the apples with the other leftovers for when they woke up in the late evening.

All this had been acquired because Freddie was good at lying. He had woven a story of camping with his father and two older brothers a little farther into the mountains. He'd described how they'd all gotten sick on jars of the home-canned provisions that they'd brought along, and how the others had sent him walking out to purchase more supplies. He further explained that was why he was choosing foods that need not be prepared or cooked. When enthusiastically relating the tale of his exploits to Lemuel and Veronika upon his return, he'd described how he'd made the incident amusing to the store owner, using vivid details to portray the discomfort of one brother in particular. And when asked why he hadn't gotten sick too, Freddie had retorted, "Well, I don't *like* pork. And we think 'twas Mama's canned meat from the pig we butchered last year what done 'em in."

Lemuel was still amazed at the quick thinking involved. How much of the narrative had Freddie planned—and how much had he made up on the spot? There was certainly nothing wrong with the function of the boy's brain. Lemuel wondered why Freddie had done so poorly while in school. Clearly, it wasn't a matter of ability.

Veronika, conversely, had listened with rapt attention, as if learning at the feet of a master. Lemuel shuddered to think what kind of education she was receiving as he moved Star to a patch of fresh grass. It was late afternoon with nothing to accomplish but trying to fall back asleep in readiness for another night of walking.

Then Lemuel remembered the patch of wet ground beside the creek. *If I'm ta write somethin' in the mud, it'll have ta be after dark or the others might see.* After their simple meal, they rested again and even Lemuel drifted off to sleep.

But his heart raced as he woke a couple hours later and stole silently away. Freddie and Veronika appeared to be sleeping. This might be just the moment he needed.

With slow and cautious movements, he slipped down the embankment toward the river. A stick served well as a pencil. Using large letters he carved *Call the Mounties. Lemuel Thompson,*

Alfred Jones, and Veronika Geary were here. Tuesday, July 13. His heart raced even more as he crept back to where he'd been lying and eased himself down again. No movement from around him. It seemed he'd accomplished his desperate mission.

I could be home right now. With Mum and Mr. Thompson. Wonder what they did today without me. Wonder if Harrison got to drive the team with the hay wagon behind it. Lemuel shifted, his mind buzzing, adrenaline still pulsing through him. Sleep would be impossible.

It was still hard to think of Mr. Thompson as "Dad." And yet, it hadn't taken him long to realize why. Though he had few true memories of his original mum, he felt an aura of kindness and love whenever he thought of her. And even the farmer's wife had been gentle and nurturing. This new mum, June, though nothing like the other two, was just as easy to appreciate—joyful and amusing, full of life and the unexpected. But she shared one quality with both of the others. When she looked at him she truly saw him, seemed to understand him.

And then there was also the food. Each mother was associated with food in his mind. So as Lemuel stretched out in the failing light of the day, he closed his eyes and conjured up pictures of this new mum setting food on the table. There'd be back bacon and sunny-side-up eggs for breakfast. When poked with his fork, the eggs would ooze their golden liquid across his plate and Lemuel could drag the thin pieces of fried meat through it. At lunch, after their soup or reheated leftovers, there was almost always her soft white bread spread with raspberry jam to serve as dessert. Lemuel enjoyed that bread and jam more than anything else in their lunch meal. But dinners were best of all. Slices of pot roast, steaming potatoes, creamed peas. Or thick stews served with fresh cornbread.

Mothers were easy to surrender to. *Is that why I felt so at home with Miss Lillian and Miss Grace too? Women are comforting—they focus on loving instead of on training. No, that's not really true. All of 'em pushed me to learn and to work. But I felt like I was doin' it to make 'em proud or something. It seems diff'rent with a father.*

The fathers in his life, even Mr. Thompson, whom Lemuel admired so much, felt more distant. Strangely, the memories of their interactions seemed to come from a distance—over his head or across the room. His mental images of Mr. Thompson were of forking hay side by side in the barn, or leaning over a harness or an engine needing repair. It was as if the work, and not the relationship, were the reason for any time spent together—even when they were fishing or hunting. With a mother, the relationship seemed to be more the true motivation.

There was one last distinction that he'd slowly come to realize. Life had taught Lemuel two miserable rules. Fathers would eventually leave him, but mothers were taken away. And so he had become entirely cautious now about holding on to either too tightly. And in light of what was happening to him now, he supposed that the Thompsons would disappear from his life again shortly too. Perhaps this time, it would be truly of his own doing. He had inadvertently sacrificed his new family for the sake of two kids he cared rather little about. At least when he'd intervened for Harrison's sake, it had been for a boy he'd known well—a boy who had become his brother—rather than two relative strangers.

All I wanted to do this time was stop somethin' had from happenin'. And here I am—a cast-out again. An' I don't even have me knife. Wish I'd kep' me knife.

· · ● · · ·

Driving out from the foothills and onto the prairie, Ben felt as if he were exiting a strange labyrinth. He'd spent so much time during the last three days in the automobile, weaving in and out of every branch of the valley roads, that an excursion farther out onto the grasslands where he could see in all directions was just what he needed to clear his head. It was Wednesday morning, and Ben was headed roughly in the direction of the Szweda farm. So it would be well worth stopping there.

Due to the arrival of the Geary children, it had been four weeks since Ben had dropped by to check on Vaughan and Michael, the two boys who'd been placed with the Szwedas after Milton and Matty had been given up by the older couple. On this visit the boys seemed to be doing much better. A bedroom had been provided for them in the attic space of the house. It could be reached from the large enclosed porch by a ladder through a hole cut in the ceiling. Ben tried to stifle his true feelings as he climbed up behind them on the ladder for a look around their area. He doubted that it was much better shelter than the barn had been. *Well, I hope the lads feel it's more of a civilized place ta be, at least.* Their mattress still rested on the floor, but there was a small table beside it with an oil lamp. Ben was also pleased to note a small stack of books there.

"Ya gettin' much better with yer readin'?"

Vaughan nodded vigorously. "I like it. Them 'ventures make me feel like I'm traveling, Mr. Waldin. Just like ya said."

"Me too. I like the one ya left of Sir G'wain. I like how the story come from England too."

Ben rubbed his hand over Mickey's short, dark hair. "You can be proud'a comin' from there, lad. An' when yer bigger, I'll lend ya me Shakespeare—if I still got it, that is."

On the drive across the prairie, Ben had considered telling Mickey and Vaughan about the children who'd run away. But he'd quickly decided it was best not to pass along such disheartening information—or to put ideas into their heads.

However, as he was standing beside his vehicle preparing to leave, Mrs. Szweda marched across the yard, a newspaper flapping from her hand. "You there! You jus' wait."

The boys exchanged glances and looked up toward Ben. He merely shrugged.

She continued to rant. "I seen this. It's yer notice in the paper. Says ya lost some kids."

Ben felt his eyes squeeze shut and tried not to let his dismay show on his face. He put a hand out to rest on Vaughan's shoulder as if he possessed more calm than he truly felt. "That's true. I ain't gonna deny it. They run away."

The expression on Vaughan's face, the wide questioning eyes, tore at Ben's heart. "Who? Freddie?"

Ben nodded. "Him and a girl ya don't know."

Before he could also explain about Lemuel, Mrs. Szweda stood before him, shaking the paper toward his face. "Ya talk like yer so much better'n us. But ya ain't. Ya come out here, pesterin' us 'bout our boys—an' ya can't keep'a watch on yer own. Don't figure ya got much ta say now, do ya?"

Ben accepted the newspaper from her hand. He rolled it up unconsciously as he formed a slow reply. "That weren't our doin', ma'am. We give 'em all that I 'spect from you."

"Nah! Ya ain't any better'n us," she growled.

Ben turned to the boys instead. "I want ya to know, lads, that we're lookin' fer 'em. I been out searchin' every day since Friday—an' we called the Mounties—and most'a the townfolk been out a time or two. We're gonna find 'em. An' then I'll come right back out here an' tell ya."

Two heads nodded in unison, but the expression on the boys' faces was one of deep concern. Ben wondered if they'd ever contemplated the idea themselves. He hoped it wasn't true. "I'll come back an' see ya soon," he promised. "An' I'd like ta hear how far ya got in yer Sir Gawain."

"Yes, sir."

As he drove away, the newspaper that Ben had tossed across the car mocked him from the passenger seat. *Maybe we're not any better'n the likes of 'em after all.* Then his own conscience argued back. *Of course we are! But the children aren't prisoners. They got minds'a their own too.*

· · • ● • · ·

In the midst of their Wednesday night journey, Star had begun to limp. Lemuel suspected that there was a stone or something trapped in her hoof, but he wanted to be thorough in following the practices that his new father had taught him. First he lifted the foot carefully, using the point of a stick to scrape away the little pockets of mud that were trapped among the softer parts under her hoof. Again by habit he'd felt his pocket for the knife he'd kept there before remembering that he'd left it beside the road in hopes of being discovered. Clearly that sacrifice hadn't accomplished anything, and he wished he hadn't bothered. By the light of the moon, Lemuel found no obvious object lodged in the mare's hoof. Still, there was no way for him to have a good look until it was day.

Next, he felt the mare's leg, beginning by grasping her pastern gently, moving upward a little at a time, sensing for swelling or radiating heat, which could mean that there was an injury. Still, there was no indication that Star had been hurt. All the while the placid horse stood peacefully, nickering from time to time as she munched on the long grasses at the side of the road.

"She's gotta see a farrier," Lemuel insisted. "If we keep walkin' her, she might go lame."

"Oh, we ain't gonna do that. If she gets lame, we'll just leave her behind. Leastways, we'll get what we can outta her first."

"No." For the first time Lemuel had absolutely no intention of conceding to Freddie.

The boy's voice lowered in a threatening fashion that had become tiresomely familiar. "You ain't in any kinda—"

"No," Lemuel repeated and headed off the road, into the trees.

He knew a creek was close by. He decided to lead Star to where she could stand in the stream and drink, taking advantage of the soothing cold of the water washing around her leg.

For some time, Lemuel waited alone in the stream. His own stripped feet had gone numb. He began to wonder if maybe Freddie and Veronika had proceeded on without him. *Fine. I'll just turn meself in an' get help fer Star. I don't care anymore.*

He felt keen disappointment when he saw the others emerge from the woods and step out onto the creek bank. "We talked it over. I'll take her ta a farm and make up a story. Have the farmer look her o'er." Freddie was becoming bolder about his ability to deceive the locals.

Lemuel argued back. "But it might not be somethin' a farmer can fix. I couldn't see nothin'. But this is the fourth night we been walkin' her. She's gotta have a break."

"She can sleep all day, jus' like the rest'a us."

"No," Lemuel insisted. "You don't know nothin' 'bout horses. I'll check her again in the mornin'. But me an' Star are done fer the night."

"I got a better idea." Freddie had raised his slingshot and was aiming it at the horse. "How 'bout I shoot her right here? That's what they do ta horses who get lame, right? If she can't help us, then why keep 'er?"

Lemuel lunged in front of the mare's head. "Are ya daft? Have ya lost yer mind? Put that down."

Even Veronika balked at the threat. "You can't hurt her, Freddie. She's just a horse. You can't hurt her."

"Can do as I please. Watch me."

"No!" Lemuel intervened again, raising his hand as a feeble shield. "Look, she'll be all right. She just needs to be off her feet fer a while. Give her the rest'a the night an' tomorrow. Bet she's better before we leave by dark."

"Ya got till then. But no longer."

The pair retreated into the trees. Lemuel could hear them bickering through the darkness. He hurried to put on his shoes. It was time to leave. He would lead Star to the nearest farm and ask for help. None of it mattered anymore. Freddie had become a complete menace.

Glancing in all directions, Lemuel opted for an opening on the far bank. He would circle around through the woods until he could emerge again farther up the road. But there was no path here and he was painfully aware of the lack of stealth he was achieving. Star's broad body snapped twigs as she obediently pressed herself farther into the woods. Her heavy feet crunched over unseen things on the forest floor. Still the sound of Lemuel's heart pounding in his own ears seemed to drown out even the mare's movements.

Then there came a noise that pierced the gloom and made his hair stand on end. It was a scream. His first thought was of Freddie. *He's done it now. He's hurt the girl!*

Turning back, Lemuel hurried through the woods in the direction he thought their camp had been. As he approached he could hear the sound of sobbing.

"Stop it. Yer not hurt. Get up."

"I can't. I can't. It's my leg. You hit me with your stupid slingshot."

"I weren't shootin' anywhere near yer leg."

"Did too. You hit me! Right here."

Lemuel's worst fears were coming true. Freddie had harmed Veronika with his unchecked aggression. Guilt for having left her flooded Lemuel's mind. What would Mr. Thompson think? Miss Lillian? Miss Grace? He should have been watching out for her.

Veronika was slumped on the ground. Freddie was walking away from her in disgust. "I didn't hit her," he insisted even before Lemuel had a chance to pose the question. "Weren't anywhere near her, I tell ya."

"Then it must have bounced or something. He did it! It was Freddie. It hit me in the knee. I think he knocked my patella off."

Lemuel let go of Star's lead, rushing to the girl's side, dropping onto the ground in front of her. "What happened? What did he hit?"

Her hands were clutched behind her leg, drawing one knee up close to her chin. Her skirts were now bunched and disheveled. "It hit me in the knee, I said. I think it knocked my patella clean out of place."

What's that—a patella? Is that a girl thing? Lemuel cringed and offered, laboring over his words, "Do ya want me to look at it?"

Veronika's eyes grew wide in horror at the suggestion. "You can't, you dumb farm boy. You can't look at my bloomers!"

Instinctively, Lemuel tucked his hands behind his back, giving her even more space. "Then what do ya want me to do?"

"Just leave me alone!"

For several long moments Veronika remained immovable, crying loudly and refusing to answer questions. At last Lemuel tied Star to a tree and settled himself against a fallen log. There seemed to be no way to help her. So once the girl had quieted at last, he fell asleep, utterly exhausted.

As the sun rose on Thursday morning, there was no improvement in the girl's disposition. Now two members of their party were hobbling as they tried to walk. *What's a patella anyway?*

Lemuel found himself wondering if he had that particular body part too. *She said Freddie hit her in the knee. She's been holdin' her knee.* Yet the mystery of the female child was too much for Lemuel to comprehend. He decided to merely defer to her description, no matter how Veronika explained it.

Lemuel led Star back to the stream and searched under her hoof once more, finding no obvious cause for her limp. Last night he'd set his mind on turning her over to a local farmer, hoping that perhaps he could claim to have found her wandering along the road in this area rather than wherever they had truly been. He hoped that she'd be returned to her original owner, even though he was aware it would be a surprising outcome at this point. They'd traveled miles since finding her in that hayfield.

The girl's injury raised new and even more difficult problems. As much as he wanted to, now Lemuel was reluctant to strike out on his own. Freddie, having hurt her once, was all the more likely to hurt her again. It didn't help that Veronika's suffering was loud, demonstrative, and annoying. The complaints she made caused Lemuel's teeth to grind. He could only imagine how it was affecting Freddie.

But how could Lemuel abandon her now? He was the girl's only source of protection in this wild and dangerous place. It seemed his only option was to remain with Veronika for the time being.

As expected, Freddie disagreed with Lemuel's suggestion of surrendering Star. "Ain't gonna happen. But we'll give her one more night a'rest. It'll serve the girl too. That way, I can do some huntin'. We can make a fire—maybe a bit'a shelter."

Veronika voiced her own frustrations from where she sat cross-legged on the ground. "We should have found the right road by now. I don't know how far we've come, but something is wrong. Don't you think?"

"Mountains on the left," Freddie muttered back, pointing westward with the pocketknife he held in his hand. "You two said we're good so long's we keep the mountains on the left."

It seemed pointless to argue. Instead, Lemuel tried to figure a way he might make a crutch for the girl.

· · ● · · ·

Freddie insisted that he be the one to lead Star down the winding lane and up to the farmer who was working in his field half a mile from where they'd been camping since the middle of Wednesday night. It was now Friday morning, almost a full week

132

from when they'd slipped away. Freddie would ask this farmer to assess the mare because that particular farm was isolated and there appeared to be no one else at home. So the teenager reasoned that, if necessary, he could run at the first sign of trouble and be long gone before the man could alert the neighbors. By now, Freddie had scoped out most of the surrounding countryside and felt himself quite an expert. He'd also caught several fish and shot his first rabbit.

Lemuel's heart thumped in his chest. He coached the boy over and over again about what questions to ask. Freddie's casual manner gave Lemuel no confidence that the horse would receive good care—would be examined properly. Clearly Freddie merely wanted a way to dismiss Lemuel's fears so they could begin moving again.

For what seemed an eternity, Lemuel paced behind a row of thick bushes that shielded their hiding spot from the small road. Veronika had hobbled up the little path behind Lemuel, grasping for handholds on trees and hopping with exaggerated movements and moans in the process. She rested behind him now, head tipped back so that the bright sun glowed on her face and neck. The woods were always damp and a little bit chilly.

At last Freddie returned, accompanied by the familiar rhythm of the horse's irregular footfalls. Freddie's smug face was all that Lemuel needed as an answer.

"What'd he say?"

"Ya gotta gimme time ta get off the road b'fore we talk."

Veronika muttered, "You can talk and walk. Just tell us."

Freddie lingered a moment more, as if lording the power of his information over them. At last, "He said she's got a bit'a arthritis, he thinks. Says her leg joints're thicker'n most. Says I might'a bought a bad horse. I didn't tell him how far we been ridin' 'er." The boy laughed at the farmer's gullibility.

"We're givin' her up, then?" Lemuel's heart was hopeful.

Freddie smirked again. "Ya know what? I think we'll vote on it."

Veronika nodded along with Freddie at the suggestion, flipping her long hair in Lemuel's direction and lifting her chin. Lemuel's shoulders drooped. It would be two against one, and Freddie knew it. But when Freddie posed the question officially, his own hand rose in favor of stopping where they were. "We got trees here—an' game ta hunt. The man said there's a town just north'a him. We can buy more supplies. I say we find a good spot and set up a camp fer a while."

Veronika's face turned bright red, but she seemed to choke down her argument. No doubt her concession was partly because she much preferred riding at night to walking—especially in her current state. It seemed to Lemuel that the mare was more of an asset than the girl wanted to admit. So they angled off down the path that they'd broken through the bushes, Veronika hopping and waving her arms, stumbling along.

Lemuel remained in place, the mare's lead clutched in his hand. He could simply walk away. Freddie was no longer standing guard. And the farmer would still be near at hand. There was nothing keeping him from heading home—except for the injured girl. With a glance over his shoulder in each direction, Lemuel followed the others back into the secrecy of the woods.

· · · ● · · ·

Lillian had put a mark on the calendar each evening before retiring for bed. The children had been gone a full week. The pang of fear that she felt whenever she thought of them had become a wound in her spirit. It took effort to suppress.

But life around her moved doggedly on. Somehow during that first long week, Father and Delyth had found a little house they thought might work for their new home—one of only two unoccupied houses in town. They brought Lillian along to look at it on Saturday morning, just one week since they'd arrived in Brookfield.

It had been owned by an older couple, one of the first to settle the area. The husband had passed away almost a decade before, but Lillian had known the old widow who'd attended Mother and Father's church across town. Walking through the home was like attending a wake. The idea that this might belong to Father felt impossible.

Delyth, however, was brimming with ideas. "Oh, fir-rst we'll paint the house yellow. That'll cheer it r-right up. And then we'll paper the foyer. I found the most lovely flor-ral pattern in a catalog at the dry goods store."

The main floor was nicely laid out with a parlor, dining room, kitchen, and workroom. Delyth intended to completely overhaul the kitchen, putting in modern conveniences such as indoor water and a built-in icebox with a small door opening to the outside where ice blocks could be loaded into the proper compartment without carrying them through the house. She even intended to install a chute for coal delivery from the outdoors. On the second floor were two small bedrooms tucked up under the sloping roof.

At first, Lillian had expected Father to request some of the furnishings from their current house. After all, everything in it belonged to him. She'd even begun a mental list of what she and Grace might need to replace. But when she finally braved the question, he'd taken her hand and answered affectionately, "No sense unsettling any of you there. We don't need much, and we've the resources to buy what we need."

Though Father did not say so directly, Lillian surmised that Delyth wanted her own home, not the remnants of another woman's life. The furnishings, other than Father's desk and personal effects, were to remain at their original house. This was a great comfort to Lillian. It had been two years now since Mother's passing, and the echoes of her presence remained dreadfully important to Lillian. She was relieved at the thought of retaining all her cherished keepsakes.

Still, she worried about the land Walter was considering. *He'll find property to start his ranch, and then he'll be required to build a house and live there. That means that I will have to live there too, of course. So Mother's belongings will pass to Grace along with my family home.* If only Lillian might be allowed to take some of the most precious items when she married. What would she choose? The piano? Probably not suitable for a humble cabin. The dining room suite? Unlikely. The dressing table and mirror? For the hundredth time Lillian wished there could be another solution, one where she'd be allowed to stay in her own home, yet still marry Walter.

And Ben? How long will he be willing to stay before leaving to find his own family as planned? What on earth will we do without him?

Throughout the week, Ben had been gone more than most of the others, searching the backroads of the foothills north of Brookfield. His face had begun to show the strain, eyes hollow from not sleeping enough, wrinkles etched across his forehead. Only Janie seemed able to pull him out of his melancholy.

· · · ● · · ·

Lemuel's party had relocated to a rough little overhang of rock that Freddie had discovered farther up along their stream. They'd been in the same area since Wednesday night, and Star was only just beginning to improve. If they were ever to ride the mare again, how long would it be until they were in the same predicament just a little farther down the road?

The jagged recess in the hillside had failed to offer quite the protection that a proper cave would have given. Its open sides caught any slight breeze, but at least it was shelter enough to keep them dry as they slept, certainly helpful since it had rained quite hard last night. The sound had made Lemuel's heart ache just a little bit more, wondering if anyone had seen the message he'd left in the mud at the creek's edge. Surely by now the storm had erased it.

Veronika, despite her injury, had set to work immediately, weaving a wall of branches on either side of the shelter, though it seemed to Lemuel that her work made no difference at all, that any breeze had no difficulty in flowing straight through her barrier. However, he said nothing and obediently supplied her with branches from the surrounding trees. It gave the girl something to focus her attention on while she rested. Freddie, on the other hand, was gone much of the day, setting traps and trying to improve the distance over which he could fire his slingshot accurately.

Lemuel kept a fire going, which had immediately become the hub of all activity. Fish from the stream were easy enough to acquire and delightful to eat when cooked over even their meager flames—though not necessarily as tasty for breakfast, lunch, and supper. Three piles of moss and dried leaves had risen in the narrow space between the fire and the back of the rocky overhang as each one of them tried to fashion a comfortable spot for sleeping. For Lemuel, the best part of it all was that night had once again become a time of rest rather than of stumbling along in the darkness, trying to head north.

Had it not been for the pleasure that Freddie took in his hunting, Lemuel was certain they would have been on the move again already. Veronika was not as distractible.

Sitting on her makeshift bed she muttered, "I'm telling you, farm boy, if the two of you aren't ready to leave by tomorrow, I'm going to take that horse and keep on going without you." The girl took two more thick sticks from the supply Lemuel had gathered and poked them into the fire, frowning as she seemed to contemplate her few options. "I suppose you'd go home again, if I did. You're just staying to care for that horse—not me." For a moment, a rare glimmer of weakness showed in her eyes.

Lemuel stared back at her. "Well, there's the matter of Ben's money. But if you an' me agree to turn Freddie in, then . . ."

"Don't be ridiculous. I'm not giving up. We've got to be getting closer. It can't be too many more days."

Standing to his feet, Lemuel answered, "I don't know much 'bout where we are, Veronika, but look—we ain't crossed any of the big roads that head west into the mountains. An' I know we shoulda if we're gainin' ground. So we can't have come very far."

Her voice became stony. "He'll hurt me again if you leave us. You know that, don't you? Freddie'll kill me with that slingshot next time—or kill that horse. You'd better not leave us, farm boy. It'll be your fault if he does it."

Backing away in shock at this new tactic, Lemuel stepped out of sight before crouching behind a tree. She'd never said such a thing before. But the girl was tricky. Did she mean it—or was it just a way to manipulate him? Lemuel's mind began retesting what would happen if he simply abandoned the pair. He'd mentally calculated the risks so often that now he dreamed about it all whenever he put his head down.

For one thing, he didn't know how badly Freddie would treat Veronika in his absence—or if her knee would ever heal at all. Lemuel had offered her a ride into town on Star's back in order to see a doctor, but Freddie had refused. Even Veronika seemed disinclined to seek out medical care.

If I leave 'em, won't Freddie just take off? He's got the money. How much can her uncles really matter to him? So, there seemed to be only one rational alternative. He could make a run for it to the farmer's place, or the small town, hoping to bring back help before the other two realized he was gone. He'd leave in the night when they were both asleep—taking Star with him if he could—risking that they wouldn't flee before he returned.

"Nine days we've been gone," he muttered to himself. "That's long enough."

But when Freddie returned, he seemed to sense the change of mood. "Tell ya what we're doin' from now on, Lemuel. I ain't gonna sleep here with ya no more. I'm gonna be out there in the woods somewhere, watchin'. Might be by the road. Might be near that horse. So, if yer thinkin'a takin' off, Lemmy, ya might wanna think twice. Ya might get away all right, but then again, ya might get hit with a rock 'fore ya get very far." Freddie laughed.

· · ● · ·

On the second Monday morning after the children's disappearance, a telegram arrived from the church in Pincher Creek in regard to the proceeds of the Geary property sale—money that would now be held in trust for Veronika and Cass. What struck Lillian first was that it was more than the amount that Veronika had stolen from Ben. *Such a shame! If she'd waited rather than taking matters into her own hands, she'd have had more money by now.* But Lillian corrected herself immediately. The funds would never have been given to the girl directly. They would, of course, be held until the siblings were older.

Shortly after lunch, Grace spoke with Cass about the money's arrival. He was interested in the idea of it, but more concerned to learn that some of their belongings had been sold. So Lillian followed behind as Grace made a special trip with him into the barn in order for the eight-year-old to see for himself the items that she and Ben had rescued. That seemed to alleviate most of Castor's concerns.

Nonetheless, it had broken Lillian's heart to have listened to the little boy's prayers each night. "Please keep my sissy safe, God, so she's got food to eat and a place to sleep."

And each night, Grace would add after him, "And please bring them all back to us soon. Amen."

At first, the repetition seemed incidental to Lillian. But even before the first week had passed she'd begun to suspect more significance than what was evident at first. Then she'd listened more closely and noted that Castor never prayed that Veronika would return. Cass prayed only that she'd be kept safe and fed.

Little by little Lillian began to notice subtle changes in the boy too. Cass was blossoming. He laughed more. He spoke more often. He interacted with the new adults around him in delightful ways. And, particularly where Grace was concerned, Cass began to initiate affection. He'd reach for her hand or slide up onto Grace's lap. As much as it was a familiar process to Lillian with new children by now, something about this particular child seemed unique. Was the boy attaching himself especially to Grace? Or was it the other way around?

Lillian walked daily to the Thompsons' farm to trade updates with June. Arthur Thompson had all but given up on farming. Instead, his automobile was in constant motion, searching for his lost son. This left tiny June Thompson, along with Harrison and her adult son Jesse, shouldering the burdens of the summer season on their farm, the care of their livestock, as well as all of the housework. Lillian knew that it was a great deal of work for the trio, but June made no comment or complaint. Still, it was clear by the peas that hung heavy on their vines in the vegetable garden that no one had been tending it. The hayfield that Lillian passed while walking on the main road had been mowed almost two weeks ago but had not yet been baled. Lillian wondered if there might be long-term effects for Arthur Thompson's family should it take much longer to find Lemuel. Making a mental note, she planned to return again as soon as it was light the next morning in order to harvest as many peas as she could for June. The kids might be willing to help shell them if they could just be coaxed to sit still for long enough.

· · ● · · ·

Just after breakfast on Tuesday morning, Lemuel stretched himself in full view of Veronika and murmured aloud, "I think I need a walk. We've been sittin' still too long." Freddie had disappeared into the woods after breakfast and there'd likely be no better time to make his move.

"Are you coming back?" Veronika asked quietly from her place by the fire. "You're not leaving me to Freddie, are you, Lemuel?"

Lemuel hated the feeling of telling a lie—even to the girl. "Oh, I'm comin' back. Don't worry." That was honestly his plan at least. To get help and then return.

He struck out toward the stream first, certain even in his own mind that the charade was pointless, that he'd never outwit the girl. But she was next to immobile, and if he was careful to move quietly, he could circle back toward the road. Still, there was Freddie to worry about. Unconsciously ducking his head for fear of projectiles, Lemuel renewed his determination to press on.

With hopeful steps he approached the road, eager to get the worst behind him. But there stood Freddie, grinning like the cat that just swallowed the canary. "Well, I thought ya'd never get here. Been waitin'. What took ya so long?"

A deep breath. Lemuel struggled to put together a terse reply, then realized that nothing he said would matter. Freddie was always watching him now, enjoying their game of cat and mouse far more than he did his hunting.

So Lemuel spun on his heel and headed back toward camp, feeling heartsick and frustrated at the impossible predicament his good intentions had gotten him into.

· · ● · · ·

When Lillian visited June Thompson, she was overjoyed to hear that Lou, their oldest son, who'd moved to the United States for employment, was considering a return home. Though the pixie-like woman was smiling broadly as she spoke the words, there were unchecked tears streaming down her pink cheeks. Lillian wasn't certain exactly which emotion accompanying the announcement had caused the flowing emotion—her joy or her loss. Regardless, Lillian reached arms out so they could share a long embrace. It was a rare glimpse of the heavy strain that June had been carrying.

As usual, Lillian and Grace's hired man, Otto, arrived to work around the house on Tuesday afternoon. Even after Ben had come to stay, the decision had been made to continue employing Otto to care for the yard. He was an older man, single, and without many resources. When Miss Tilly took it upon herself to suggest that he might be paid with baked goods rather than cash, Otto had accepted readily, exclaiming, "Yah, yer bread vill be good, Mrs. Tillendynd. Better than gold, it is." And now that Ben was so frequently absent, there was a growing list of work that needed to be accomplished in addition to the care of the yard.

Before leaving for the day, Otto stopped at the front porch, where Lillian was shelling peas for June. "Miss Valsh, I finished the mowin' and the veedin'. The hedges I vill clip next time, yah?"

"Yes," she agreed. "That seems reasonable. Was it terribly difficult to get that gutter piece secured again?"

"I tink I got it. If it come loose again, I'm goin' to need to replace the vood board behind it before I nail it down again."

"I see. Well, thank you."

"Oh, an' Miss Valsh?"

"Yes?"

"I found an old sock under yer bush there. I didn't know if it vas one of the kids'. So I left it on yer back step."

"A sock? I don't remember anyone saying anything."

"Jus' ordinary vool."

142

Lillian frowned. "I'm not sure who left it there, but I don't think there's any need to keep it. Would you mind just throwing it on the burn pile with the weeds you pulled?"

"Sure. That I can do."

Lillian thanked him and went back to her work with an appreciative smile. It wasn't the first time she'd been grateful for Otto.

CHAPTER 12

Surprises

The newspaper that Katrin Szweda had given Ben on the previous Wednesday had been relegated to the floor in the back seat before he'd even arrived back in Brookfield. It lay there still, entirely forgotten. It was Matty who rediscovered it while searching for a spot to conceal himself. The youngsters were playing hide-and-seek while they waited to be called for lunch. "Mr. Waldin? What's this?"

Ben was lying on the ground nearby, draining motor oil from the engine. He pushed up from the barn floor. "What, lad?"

"This bunch'a paper. Can I have it?"

"Oh, huh. I fergot 'bout that. Not yet, lad. Might have a look at it meself first."

"All right." The boy hunched down again as if suddenly remembering that he was supposed to be quiet. He crept away toward the back of the barn, causing the little foxes to scatter to their respective hiding places in one quick flash of their red tails. They'd become less and less comfortable around the children. Ben supposed it was probably for the best. Eventually they'd need to be entirely wary of human contact if they were to survive in the wild, though the thought that the sweet little critters might vacate the barn before Freddie returned made him a little sick at heart.

Rather than returning to his position on the ground, Ben slid onto the second bench seat in the car and stretched his legs out beside himself in a reclining posture. He was due for a break, and it seemed prudent for him to have a look at the newspaper before it was discarded. He'd been aware that Lillian's father had set up notices in many of the area papers but hadn't seen one in print. The small gazette was only six pages long, making it easy to find the classified ads section.

Missing children: two teenage boys and a twelve-year-old girl with long black hair have run away from Brookfield, Alberta. Their names are Lemuel Thompson, Alfred Jones, and Veronika Geary. A reward of one hundred dollars is offered for any information leading to their return. Please contact your local Royal North-West Mounted Police immediately.

Ben hadn't known about the reward. He was pleased to see there was an incentive provided for getting involved, though he hoped that the size of the offering wouldn't bring profit-minded scoundrels crawling out of the woodwork.

Then his eyes fell on another, much shorter ad. *Skilled English tinsmith looking for work. Leave message at post office, Denholm, Alberta.*

Ben sat up so quickly he tore the page by accident. This town was close to where Vaughan and Mickey were living. It was only a few miles away from where he'd visited just last week. Could it be that his family had settled so close to him? Yet how many English tinsmiths could there be in this area?

Slamming the car door and clutching the paper in his hand, Ben hurried to the house. Miss Tilly was just about to make the request for help with setting the table. Ben hollered rather discourteously, "Look't this! Look here," while holding the paper out to her. "This one. This ad."

She read aloud, "Skilled English tinsmith . . . Could that be yer dad, Ben?"

"It could be. I think it could. An' I was there not long ago visitin' the lads."

Miss Tilly let out a whoop. "Lillian! Grace! Come see!"

Soon they were all gathered around the humble pages as Ben held them out. "It's as like as not ta be him. Don't know many other tinsmiths here 'bouts. He could still be lookin' fer work. Been only about six months since their voyage to Canada, an' travelin' woulda took some time." Ben's face fell. "Though, I hope this ad ain't placed on account'a their bein' in a lowly state."

"Well, you've got to go see them," Grace was the first to insist.

"No, I b'lieve I'll use the telephone first, if I may. I'll ring the post an' get a name 'fore I drive that far again."

Lillian said, "Well then, call now. Just make your telephone call right now."

A deep breath. Ben was almost afraid to take the dramatic step. "All right. I'll do it at once. An' you can let me know the charges so I can pay ya later."

"Oh, don't be silly!"

Ben lifted the receiver and cranked the small handle to summon the operator and place a call. He heard a voice answer, "Where would you like to call, please?"

"The post office, in Denholm, Alberta."

"One moment, please." Several clicks followed. Ben's eyes moved to each woman's face. They stood in a close group surrounding him, holding their collective breath on his behalf.

"Hello, Denholm post office," a man's voice answered.

"Hello. I'd like ta ask 'bout the advertisement fer a tinsmith."

"Yes?"

"Who is it? I mean, can I ask the name'a the person what took out the ad?"

"Yes, sir. Man's name is Waldin. William Waldin."

Ben's fingers contracted suddenly at the confirmation, causing him to nearly lose his hold on the telephone receiver. For a second he struggled to get a proper grip on the earpiece. "Can I leave him a message? Please."

"'Course. Ya got a job fer him?"

"No, sir, he's my dada—my father. I want ya ta tell him I'm comin', soon's I can."

"His son? No kiddin'? Yeah, I'll give ol' Will the message. He'll be right glad to hear from ya, I'm sure. Yer mum too, no doubt." And then, "What's yer name, sir? An' when ya comin'?"

"I'm Ben. Ebenezer Waldin." He shook his head to try to clear his thoughts. "Tell him I'm comin' this evenin'. I'll leave right away an' get there in just a couple hours, I s'pose."

"Good, good. I'll send my son Davie ta tell 'em now. They're stayin' in the hotel. Stop at the desk. It ain't hard ta find once yer here."

"Thank ya, sir. Good-bye."

The room seemed to swim around Ben. His hearing became foggy. He was aware that the sisters were shouting with joy, but the sound seemed to come from somewhere beyond. *Jane. I'm goin' ta see me sister, Jane, soon.* And then he made another realization. *An' I'm takin' Janie along. I'll introduce her ta me sister. Janie, meetin' me own Jane!*

Abruptly leaving the group of women behind without further comment, Ben headed straight out to the barn to find his little girl.

· · • ● • · ·

Janie had fallen asleep on the front seat beside Ben, which gave him some much-needed time to gather his thoughts. After long months without any contact with his family, it was all happening so fast. He wondered what their situation would be. He wondered if his parents would be nursing a grudge that they'd felt forced to leave England without him. He wondered about Jane and hoped that she'd been well since their departure.

The little town of Denholm was like any other. A short main street along the through road with only a few additional buildings scattered beyond it. It clearly served as a center for the area farmers. There was a railroad behind the short row of buildings. Alongside it not far down the tracks stood a large grain elevator, the hallmark of a prairie town. Ben wondered what had led his family to such a rural location.

As he pulled up in front of the two-story hotel, Janie stirred. She rose and rubbed her eyes. "Are we there?"

"Yes, bunny. We're here."

He turned off the engine and opened the car door. But before he'd planted both feet on the ground, the hotel door flew open and a young woman rushed toward him, blond hair streaming out behind her. It was Jane. Ben's eyes filled with tears. She flung her arms around his neck, and they laughed together as he lifted her off the ground and spun her around the way he'd done when she was young.

At last she gasped, "Bless us! You're here! I can't believe you're here."

The car door's hinges squeaked. Their eyes turned in unison to see Janie making a slow exit behind him. His sister's face spun up to his, her eyes filled with questions.

"Jane, I'd like ya ta meet me sweet little Janie. We're family—me an' her."

His sister's blue eyes grew wide with wonder.

"I'll 'splain later."

Jane adjusted her garments and smoothed her hair, as if to return to proper decorum. "Hello, child. Ya say your name is Janie?"

"Yes, ma'am." Little Janie had suddenly become shy, eyes to the ground, a small hand grasping at Ben's fingers for comfort.

148

"She'll warm ta ya," he said, "sooner 'an ya think." Then he added, "Where's Dada and Mam?"

Jane turned toward the hotel, her face a little pinched. "Inside, but, Ben . . . Mam's not doin' very well. You should know that before ya see her."

He felt his emotions lurch again, as if he were a ship just hoisting the sail only to be struck by an unexpected gust. "What is't? She sick?"

"No, but . . . well, come inside. They'll want to see ya right away."

Ben followed his sister into the hotel lobby, Janie trailing along behind him. Inside he found his father and mother waiting, seated on two matching wingback chairs. Dada rose as they entered, but Mam remained seated. Tense ridges in Ben's forehead deepened with worry.

"Mam." His voice rasped with emotion. "I'm so glad ta fin'ly find ya."

"Ebenezer. It's truly you. Thank the Lord in heaven!"

He sank to his knees beside her chair. "Mam, what's wrong!"

"Not a thing." She smiled back at him, her warm hand coming to rest on his cheek. "There's nary a thing wrong as I'm lookin' at yer face. At long last, me Ebenezer returns to me."

The echo of a door closing down the hallway startled Ben. He turned his head toward it and found that Dada had walked away without comment. After so many months and so many miles, they'd not exchanged one word of greeting. Ben laid his head on his mother's lap and allowed rare tears to fall as she stroked his dark curls gently, the way she'd often done when he was small.

* * * * * * *

Lillian locked the front door and blew out the oil lamp in the parlor, moving to the dining room and tucking the chairs neatly under Mother's table in the shadowy dusk. Ben would not be returning until the morrow. She wondered what he'd found in Denholm, hoping that his reunion had gone well but concerned also that he might be drawn away from Brookfield now. She'd hate to lose him, even though she wanted him to be with his own family again. Her thoughts tumbled back and forth, stirring her turbulent emotions.

Through the large windows, the twilight sky was just fading into darkness and the first stars had begun to appear over the town. On impulse, Lillian stood in the center of the bay window and looked out over the field toward Brookfield. She'd come to dread going upstairs to bed, passing two empty bedrooms that belonged to Freddie and Veronika.

Lillian's mind ventured back to near the end of the first week with the Geary children. The siblings had been given a few days to adjust to their surroundings, to observe the way the household functioned, and to come to know its residents. However, Lillian had observed a strange relationship between the pair of children. Veronika seemed reluctant to allow her brother to move too far out of sight, hovering over him instead. And, whenever Veronika spoke to him in whispered instruction, it sounded to Lillian like she called the boy "Torrie."

At first, Lillian had presumed she'd misheard, but repeated occurrences affirmed the nickname. She had mentioned her confusion to Grace, whose eyes opened wide with realization as she said, "Well, that does kind of make sense. His name is Castor. She's just using the second half of it for a pet name. I've seen it before. It's like a shared bond between siblings. I don't think it's anything to worry about."

"Oh, I see. Sure, I suppose it's just their way of feeling closer."

So on another occasion when Lillian had overheard the pair playing in the attic as she passed the open door, she'd lingered for a moment to listen.

"I'm going to save you, Torrie. Here I come, flying out of the clouds, swooping down." Scampering footsteps followed.

Castor's laughing voice answered back, "Hurry, here comes the Minotaur. Ah, he's goin' to get me, Polly. Help!"

Lillian froze. *Did he just call her Polly? What are they playing at?*

"He's swinging his axe, Torrie. Duck! Now run to me. Hurry, he's getting up again."

Thump, thump, thump.

"I got you. You're safe now."

"You saved me, Polly." Castor's words were breathless with the efforts of his play. "Are we gonna be stars now?"

"Yes, yes. Now we're stars in the sky. And whenever you look up at night, you'll see us. Right there beside Mána and Papa, all together again."

At the time Lillian had continued past, her heart aching for them. She thought, *I need to remember this moment, that even when I don't see her hurting, she's just a precious child. She's trying to come to terms with her terrible loss.* And then immediately, *I'm so glad they have each other.*

Framed by the large bay window, Lillian wondered for the hundredth time how Veronika could possibly have run away without Castor. Clearly the smaller brother meant the world to her. It seemed impossible that this devoted sister had intended to desert him. *What was it Cass said about their uncles? That they live in Sunday? I wish I could figure out what he meant by that.*

Lillian had seen the pair together often after that day, playing and talking in their private world. Sometimes she heard the pet names repeated softly. On one occasion while Lillian was weeding in the garden, she overheard Janie call out to "Torrie" from across the yard. Veronika had swooped down with severity. "You can't call him that. Only I get to call him that."

Rising to intervene, Lillian had watched closely for Janie's reaction. The girl shifted gears without a glimmer of hurt on her face. "Okay. Cass, c'mon." Even the children had found ways to adapt to the Gearys' idiosyncrasies.

But then Lillian recalled how the stakes had been raised one particular morning about a week after their arrival. Each day following breakfast, while reminding the other children of their chores for the day, Grace had mentioned to Veronika and Castor that they were not expected to help out just yet, that they could be free from obligations until the following Monday while they got used to sharing the household.

Then a new week had begun. As each child waited to receive an assigned morning task, Grace invited the new children closer so she could explain their system and involve them in the procedures. Castor listened carefully.

"So what would you like to choose as your chore for the week? Here's the list of options you have. Then we'll trade again next Monday so that each person gets a new task."

Castor seemed to be contemplating his choice when Veronika spoke up. "You don't need to pick, Torrie," she muttered, giving him a nudge and using the pet name. "That's just for the foreigners." And she turned to leave the room. One hand pulled Castor by the arm so that he would follow her lead.

"No. Wait." Grace stood. "First of all, we do not have any foreigners in this home. All these children have been given their Canadian citizenship. And secondly, if you live here, you are part of this family. You have privileges—and you have responsibilities. You may choose what you'd like to do for the week—or it will be assigned to you."

Lillian was surprised at the firmness in Grace's voice. *Is Grace ready now to stand her ground in dealing with Veronika?* The girl's face had registered disbelief also. She'd blinked and retreated back a step. Then her chin lifted. She still had not released Castor's arm.

"We don't have to," she'd said, and there was iron in her words.

"We're not foreigners. Mána said that cleaning somebody else's house is work for dirty immigrants and poor folk. The kind of people who made me sick when I was little."

The room fell silent and still. Grace managed to ask, "What did you say?"

"I got really sick—when I was little. Mána said it was the foreigners who made it happen. Mána said they're dirty and that they carry diseases. And I'm never going to be like them." Veronika turned to go, drawing her brother behind her.

While she stood at the bay window deep in thought, Lillian's mind had begun to combine the discarded memory with more recent disclosures. *Is this the source of Veronika's terrible prejudice? Her mother openly blamed immigrants for causing the polio she had as a child?*

"Wait." Grace had moved until she was blocking the path to the stairs. Somehow Castor had managed to free his arm and was rounding the table in the opposite direction.

Grace took a deep breath. When she spoke, her voice was controlled. "That's fine, Veronika. If that is your choice, then you may leave the kitchen. But you should know first that the rule here is that if you will not work, you will not eat. Since you're a child, we'll provide only for your needs. You may eat as many vegetables as you like from the garden. The green beans, carrots, spring onions, and lettuce are all ready right now. There are still apples and blocks of cheese in the cellar. But you may not sit at the table with the rest of us. Understood?"

Veronika's eyes widened, then her jaw tightened. She whirled and fled up the stairs to her bedroom.

Castor, on the other hand, had soon acquiesced. Before long he was merrily sweeping the floor of the back porch and tossing the dustpan of tracked-in dirt back outdoors where it belonged. Later he helped Matty carry the piles of freshly washed and folded clothing up to the second-floor bedrooms. The occasion marked the first time Castor had stepped out from under his sister's authority. And Veronika had clearly not been pleased. Instead, she appeared to have increased her own determination.

Even when Grace had attempted to speak with her later on several occasions about the declaration she'd made, all efforts were futile. This would not be a quick victory. This was likely to be a war that the young girl would wage with those around her for years to come.

When the table had been set for lunch that day, the only plate missing was in the spot that had been claimed by Veronika. For two days she'd refused to eat any meals, though Miss Tilly had reported evidence of discarded carrot tops, and of pea plants that had been rather roughly handled while they'd been harvested. At last Veronika had surrendered, but by then Lillian and Grace were beyond anxious for the child's well-being. They'd come to doubt that their own judgment and experience would be equal to the task of subduing this willful child.

If we'd known then what we know now, would we have handled all of that differently? Did we just end up pushing her away instead of helping her to see herself as part of the family?

Lillian looked out now into another night sky descending over the mountains and pulled her arms tighter against her stomach, thinking about the store owner's warning of a nearby mountain lion. "Oh, Father God, keep them safe. Please bring them home to us. You must have a plan for all of this. I don't know what You're doing, but I'm still choosing to trust You."

CHAPTER 13

Junctures

Ben quietly pulled the hotel room door closed. Though it was far later than the rules back at home decreed, little Janie had fallen asleep at last. Jane had gently tucked her into her own large bed, singing the nighttime lullaby Ben remembered from their grandmother.

Now he and his sister were free at last for some private discussion, moving stealthily down the short hallway and back to the lobby area, which had been deserted long ago. Ben motioned for Jane to take one of the wingback chairs and settled himself in the other. From his position, Ben could keep an eye on the hallway with Janie's door.

"Where ta begin?" Jane's smile was rich with feeling. "I've missed ya. Do ya know how much I've missed ya?"

It was an impossible question for Ben to answer, but he was certain their exchanged gaze was a sufficient explanation. Then Ben burst out with, "Oh, yer letter. I found it at the port."

"Ya did? I hoped ya would." Her eyes sparkled. "I knew ya'd be straight for the bookshops. Oh, but Mam did fuss that it took me

155

so long ta deliver 'em, though I wouldn't let her put me off from it. I knew ya'd come. I had to believe it."

"But ya left nothin' in Winnipeg? Er did I miss it?"

"No, no. There wasn't time. We switched trains and headed out again. Dada had the scent of a job by then. . . ." Her voice trailed away.

"But that didn't work out?"

"No. Nothin' did. We went from one place to another. No jobs. Not for an old tinsmith, and a foreigner."

"I'm sorry, Jane. That must have been hard."

She brushed at the folds of her skirt, as if needing an excuse to divert her eyes elsewhere. "We managed. I got a job."

"Ya did? You?"

Her face lifted. Jane scolded back, "Well, don't say it like ya think it couldn't be done. I'm not so useless as all that." But the dimple on his younger sister's cheek betrayed her humor despite her tone.

For a long time Ben sat with rapt attention as Jane related the chronicle of events that had brought them through the recent months. It was difficult to hear. Dada had worked at odd jobs in an effort to establish a reputation wherever they moved. Each rumor of a better opportunity elsewhere set them packing up again. Ben's heart ached with his longing to have been with them, to have lightened their load and cared for his family.

At last Jane's voice took on a hushed tone as she described her first offer of a job. "There was a woman. I met her at church. She said they needed seamstresses in Calg'ry. Mam thought she'd do the work too—right alongside me. So we up and headed to the city. But, what with the cost of a place ta live and food for three, all our pay was gone each week. And Dada had no success at findin' a job. And then . . ."

Is she blushin'? Er are her cheeks turnin' bright red in shame? Jane's eyes had been averted again. Ben held his breath and waited for her to finish her story.

"And then . . . I met Lloyd Pender."

"Who?"

Jane's fingers were twisting themselves together in her lap now. She was raising up the little knot she'd made out of them to conceal her face. But where Ben could still see her rosy cheeks, they were punctuated by her deep dimples. Jane was smiling. "Lloyd Pender. He lives here in Denholm."

"A man who lives here?"

Her words began to flow. "I met him in Calg'ry. He was just in for a day or two, and I was introduced to him at church by that same woman who found me a job. But then Lloyd kept comin' back, and soon I knew it was mostly ta see me. We got ta talkin' and I learned more an' more about him. He was certain that I could be hired on as a cleanin' woman at this hotel, and that Dada could get started with his tinsmithing here in this town. There's a blacksmith already who works with various metals and sells his products to a shop in the city. Calg'ry had become too much for Mam, so we came ta try our luck here instead."

"Who is he? How old is he? Does he own the hotel?"

Jane rolled her eyes. "So ya still hear only what ya want, eh? Well, fine then. I'll answer yer questions. He's twenty-eight an' his wife died a couple'a years ago. They didn't have kids yet. Now he's workin' a farm south of town with some of his family. But he's got a nice little house by a pretty little stream, and a steady income—much as a farmer can e'er have. And he's kind, ever so kind. He picks me flowers and leaves 'em at the desk for me."

"Is he plannin' ta marry ya?"

Jane giggled. "What do *you* think?"

"I think he'd better be makin' his plans known fer sure. Don't wanna see ya get strung along—"

"Oh, Ben. Stop it. You can meet him in the mornin'. He plans ta come ta meet ya. Then you'll know."

It was growing late, and the stillness of the building around them provided Ben the courage to ask what he knew must come next. "An' Mam? What is it that's ailin' her?"

Jane's face fell. "We don't even know. She's seen a doctor in Calg'ry and another one here. Maybe it's homesickness. Maybe it's just age. But she's run herself down and can't seem ta get started again."

"They don't know?"

"They don't. An' Dada, well . . ."

"What?"

Jane leaned forward, reached for Ben's hand before answering. Even in the pale lamplight he could see her eyes were rimmed with the glint of tears. "He loves ya, Ben. I see it written on his face whene'er your name is mentioned. But he's too proud ta show it. Too proud ta forgive ya for what he thinks ya've done."

Ben's eyes closed in anguish. "Me runnin' away?"

"No, not that. Not really. Heed me now, please. By my way'a thinkin' he wishes he could'a allowed for that. What he truly blames ya for is his own needing of ya—that he couldn't make enough wage to care fer us without a son workin' at his side. Do ya see it? If he forgives ya for not bein' with us, then he has to admit that he's ta blame that we couldn't make ends meet."

A heavy sigh. "I shoulda stayed."

"No." Jane squeezed his fingers tighter for emphasis. "You had ta leave. An' the money you brought from time ta time aided us more than your labor at home woulda. Dada has to work it out in his own heart. But Mam doesn't blame ya. Neither do I."

Ben and his sister continued conversing and reminiscing until both grew tired. As Ben settled into the back seat of the automobile to sleep for the night, his mind played the words of their conversation over and over. Guilt for his absence plagued him still—but not just because of Dada. Ben had been at sea for almost all of Jane's first marriage. He'd been sailing to Spain on the day of her wedding. He was returning from Morocco when the terrible accident that had shattered Jane's world occurred. In fact, Ben had only met her husband once, and that was after he was bedridden. Try as hard as he might, Ben could not even remember the man's name. The realization made him ashamed of his own failures where Jane was concerned.

But now there was a new man—a man who seemed to have nothing but good intentions for Jane and their family. So why was Ben bristling? He rolled over, facing the back of the bench seat, his feet now tucked awkwardly against the door in order to fit in this new position. He knew precisely why he'd recoiled. He had finally arrived to take care of his family, and he was too late to help. *Why does love always feel so tangled up in guilt? Near inseparable, it seems.*

·· ● ··

Late on Wednesday evening, Freddie announced that they were moving on once again. "Yer horse's been restin' fer a week now. We ain't givin' her no more time, an' that's that."

"We could have gone days ago," Veronika argued. "We've been here since Saturday. You were the one who decided we'd stay. It was your hunting and playacting that slowed us down this time."

Freddie's eyes danced in amusement. "I thought it was you what was hurt. That's what made us stay put. Yer knee that ya claim I hit."

Veronika pushed herself up and limped theatrically toward him. Lemuel rose to his feet too, in fear there might be another altercation between them.

"See, I can walk just fine. And, like I kept telling you, I could have been riding all along!"

"Yeah, that's fine, all right. Ya walk worse'n that ol' horse."

The girl's scowl remained, but for some reason it seemed that Freddie now had the power to command their movements. And it was a strange feeling to decide to move again. There was really nothing that needed doing. Nothing to pack up or put away. No door to lock. Slipping on his sock and shoes, untying Star—those actions were all that were necessary to be ready to go. As they walked away from the doused fire that Lemuel had nurtured for days and the soft pile of bedding he'd grown accustomed to, Lemuel felt a twinge of regret. He muttered, "Ya shoulda warned us, Freddie. I'da tried ta sleep fer some'a the day if I'd known."

When they reached the road, Freddie tugged on Star's rope to bring her to a stop and motioned with a thumb to Veronika. "S'pose ya expect ta ride now. Me an' Lem'll take turns leadin'."

· · ● · ·

Ben had called from Denholm first thing on Thursday morning with news that he and Janie would be back late in the day. His voice sounded different somehow, richer and more confident. The change made Lillian smile. It was just as well. Their day would be busy enough.

Walter had been in contact with the little town's grocer once more. He'd organized a group of men from Brookfield and the outer farming community to track and hunt the mountain lion that stalked their woods, and they planned to leave at noon. Arthur Thompson had even contacted Raymond Calling Owl in order to get a message to Running Fox, the boy's tribal chief. Since the presence of such a dangerous predatory animal was of concern to his people as well, a Tsuut'ina guide was provided, much to everyone's relief.

Lillian watched from the kitchen window as the men from town gathered in the yard before setting out together in the strange array of vehicles they'd assembled. Constable Hayes stood talking with them, his bright red tunic setting him apart from all the others. A lump tightened in Lillian's throat as she thought about the courage these men demonstrated by their actions, their willingness to put themselves in harm's way in order to safeguard a small town and three lost children who may or may not even be in the area.

"Miss Lillian, are they gonna kill it?" Milton's voice came from the stairwell beside her, causing Lillian to jump.

"Oh, well . . . Yes, Milton. We hope they can find it."

"So it don't eat V'ronika an' Freddie?"

Lillian took hold of his shoulders and drew him close for a hug. She was thinking, *We try so hard not to let the children overhear what's happening—with all our stealthy late-night talks—and yet, they always seem to know.* Four little pairs of ears made secrecy a formidable challenge. Aloud she answered, "We don't know where they are, honey. We don't know if our children are anywhere close to this animal. But we don't want to take any chances, and we don't want the cougar hunting close to anybody's town, anyway."

"Are we gonna eat it if they shoot it—like Freddie did with those birds?"

"No, dear. We don't eat mountain lions."

"Think they'll find the kids too?"

Lillian closed her eyes. "I hope so, Milton. That would be an especially wonderful outcome."

Miss Tilly called Milton away, setting some used brown wrapping paper and a pair of scissors on the kitchen table. "Why don'tcha cut yerself out a farm—or a zoo, if ya like?" she suggested. "Call them other kids. They can help too."

Milton was off up the stairs to round up the other boys. Miss Tilly approached Lillian. "Maybe ya want ta head ta the yard 'fore they leave. I think Walt's been eyein' the front door. Seems he's hopin' ya'd come out."

It was all the impetus Lillian needed. Walter was standing next to his car, speaking with Pastor Bucky and Ernest McRae, the town's postmaster. As she drew near, Walter excused himself and approached her instead. Her eyes begged the question she didn't dare to speak out loud.

"We'll stay in groups," Walter assured her. "Three or four men together. It's unlikely we'd be attacked that way. Cats tend to pick off isolated prey."

Like a child alone in the woods. Rather than expressing her thought aloud, Lillian leaned closer so that Walter could slip an arm around her shoulders and draw her to his side. He pressed his cheek against her hair and whispered, "These men know what they're doin', Lill."

"I know. It's just . . . well, a person hears stories. Ugly hunting stories. And it's hard not to worry."

"We'll keep as safe as we can."

"I know you will. I just . . ."

The men were beginning to load into the cars. Walter was moving away. Lillian fought back tears, following behind him and laying a hand on his car as if she could keep him from leaving. But with a last wave, even Walter pulled away.

When Lillian had mentioned to Ben on the telephone earlier the plan for a hunt, he'd apologized for not participating. But Lillian was certain that he would not have been asked to join their party anyway. He was not experienced enough with tracking or hunting.

She'd assured Ben, "There are already more men helping than I would have imagined."

"I shoulda just gone along, leastways."

As thrilled as Lillian was that Ben had found his family, her heart pained her too. Poor Ben. He was being tugged in all directions now. Here in Brookfield and his home with Janie. Out in the wilds toward Freddie. And to his family in Denholm. Lillian, of all people, knew well how it felt to have to decide which family members to pursue.

162

Even after a long night of walking, Lemuel struggled to close his eyes. The sun had risen high overhead on Thursday before he was able to force himself to move away from the small fire he'd managed, its flames working hypnotically on his fatigued mind. Their new hiding spot was beside a spur of railroad tracks that headed west toward the mountains or east toward the prairie. A small shed had been built within a stone's throw of the rails, and it was equipped with a single bed. Naturally, this had been offered to the girl. Freddie and Lemuel had dropped to the ground behind the building instead. But even Veronika lingered with them, hesitating to retire inside.

Lemuel was thinking wearily, *If I could just follow them tracks, I'd come ta a town. It'd be a sure thing. Or maybe I could hop a passin' train and just ride away.*

"How far ya think we come?" Freddie's question interrupted. "We must be almost to the Cowboy Trail. Aren't we?"

"Who knows?" Lemuel muttered, then spit into the dust beside him. He'd convinced himself that there was one last tactic to apply. As he'd trudged along during the night he'd made up his mind.

Loud enough for Freddie to hear, Lemuel asked Veronika, "When we get to Sundre, ya gonna get yer uncles to get me a train ticket too—like yer gonna get fer Freddie?"

She laughed. "You want to be a sailor now?"

"No, no. I just wanna ride it back to Brookfield."

This time it was Freddie who laughed. "Ya dumb mutt. Why ya wanna do that?"

Lemuel let the question go unanswered. This pair would never understand the ache in his heart to be home again. But if he couldn't get away from them, then he was determined to see this thing through instead. So he'd made a first effort to remind them of their shared goal. He hoped they could cooperate together long enough to arrive at their destination soon. His presence should help to mitigate disputes, and he'd have at least delivered the girl to safety. It seemed that nothing would recover the money for Ben, unless the uncles would be able to talk some sense into the pair. At any rate, tomorrow, after another long night of walking, would be Friday again—the end of their second week. He had a plan. *Just get 'em there. An' then go home.*

CHAPTER 14

Hunted

Needing to keep her mind off the hunt for the mountain lion, Lillian mustered her crew of four children and set off for town. All around them were people on the move, walking in and out of shops, chatting with one another on the sidewalks. It felt refreshing to be among them, sharing the pleasant day—just what Lillian had needed. The boys ran ahead so they could have extra time choosing their books at the library. Janie, recently returned from her trip with Ben, stayed at Lillian's side, calling out to friends as they passed by.

While they crossed in front of the dry goods store, Janie asked, "Miss Lillian, can we buy Miss Tilly a new hankie?"

"What do you mean? Does she need one?" Lillian paused beside the large store window.

"She has ordin'ry ones. But on Sunday the other ladies have fancy ones. An' Miss Tilly doesn't. I thought maybe we could buy her a nice one too."

Brushing a gentle finger under Janie's chin, Lillian took a deep breath. "Sweetheart, there is nothing I'd like to do more with you right now than to buy a gift for Miss Tilly. Let's do it."

Inside, the shop was busier than usual. Lillian led Janie to the small display of handkerchiefs and allowed the girl to touch each one—unfolding, inspecting, and refolding them by turn. At last she chose one with a sky blue ribbon weaving in and out of white lace around the edges, a spray of darker blue flowers embroidered in delicate stitches in one corner. "It's perfect," Janie declared. "Miss Tilly likes blue the best."

Lillian asked Daisy McCodrum, the young woman who worked behind the counter, "Is it possible to have this gift-wrapped—in a box if you have it?"

"Yes, I'm glad ta wrap it for ya, Miss Walsh. If you'll just gimme a minute, I'll get the paper and scissors from the back."

Now the unsupervised boys were a growing concern to Lillian. She didn't want to leave them unattended in the library for too long. "Yes, I think we have time for that. Thank you, Daisy."

The clerk hurried away. Lillian stepped back and explained quietly to Janie, "Miss McCodrum is Vernon and Ervin's eldest sister. Which of those boys is in your class at school, dear?"

"Ervin. Vernon is younger than me. They have a sister Esma too who's . . ."

"Why, Lillian. Hello."

Looking up, she was surprised to find Father's wife standing before her. "Oh, hello. How are you, Delyth?"

"I'm well, dear-r. Just out enjoying the day and making plans for the new house."

"That's nice." And then, "Do you remember Janie?"

Delyth crouched in her stylish narrow skirt so she could greet Janie properly. "I do remember you, dar-rling. I'd know your pr-retty blue eyes anywhere."

Janie smiled a thank-you. "We're buying Miss Tilly a new hankie. But it's a surprise. Please don't tell anyone."

"Oh, I wouldn't spoil your surpr-rise, lass."

An awkward pause. Delyth rose to her full height, then patted Janie on the head. Lillian scrambled in her mind for some way to keep the conversation going. "What are you shopping for today?"

"Cur-rtain fabric. I've in mind to begin sewing. We'll move into the house soon, and I want to be prepar-red."

"Oh, that's nice. You're welcome to stop by and use our sewing machine anytime you'd like. It was . . ." Lillian halted herself mid-sentence. She'd been going to say that it had been Mother's, but she doubted the words would sound like beneficial information to Delyth.

Janie spoke up loudly, covering over Lillian's near blunder. "We're going to the library. The boys have gone ahead of us."

"Oh, that's lovely. Are you going to pick out a new book to r-read?"

"Yes. We each get to choose one."

"What do you like best, lass?"

"Aminal—I mean, a-ni-mal stories."

"Ah, me too."

Daisy McCodrum returned. She placed the handkerchief in its box and began to wrap it carefully in a sheet of printed paper. A piece of ribbon lay on the counter beside her. "Do ya want this on yer account, Miss Walsh?"

"Yes, thank you, Daisy."

Another awkward pause. Lillian could think of nothing else to add. She smiled at Delyth, and the woman forced a smile in return. It was the young clerk who broke the silence. "My mum's got yer yard goods cut, Mrs. Walsh. She put 'em in a box at the counter with that diaper flannel ya picked out. It's ready for ya whenever yer done shoppin'."

Delyth's face pinched a little. Lillian managed to keep her gasp inaudible. She retrieved her small package from the counter and excused herself as graciously as she was able, muttering something about the boys waiting in the library. Janie trailed along behind.

. . . ● . . .

Ben sat looking out on the field behind the barn, resting on the threshold of the oversized door that faced it. Normally this rear door was kept closed, but he'd opened it wide enough for the little foxes to get to the back field as often as they chose. Since this door was set well above the ground, the proper height to access the barn from the bed of a wagon, the little kits were required to jump up almost three feet in order to enter. But this was no longer a difficult task for them. Their legs had grown into tight little springs, launching them easily up from the dirt and through the open doorway. For a long time, Ben sat and watched them play. They kept a wary eye on his movements but seemed willing to allow his proximity.

He'd promised himself that he wouldn't name the kits. That pledge was rather easy to keep while Freddie was the one caring for them. But now that they were Ben's responsibility, his will was faltering. He found himself whispering things like, "Keep it up, Sideburns. Little Bitey Boy is goin' ta get ya." Then immediately he wished he'd made no such distinctions.

He wondered if the mountain lion had been tracked and shot yet. It was Friday morning, and there'd been no word by telephone. Walter had mentioned that their intention was to spend a second day hunting, if need be.

The whole idea of it made Ben rather sick to his stomach. He'd seen a photograph of a mountain lion and despised the idea of killing one, and yet, it could not be allowed to harm the children. *Life's got a way'a givin' us no good choices. Just loathsome ones.*

Chewing on the corner of a fingernail, Ben spat the broken piece into the dust. The sudden sound made the little foxes react in unison, dropping their bellies to the ground, freezing in place but ready to flee. Their synchronized movements were elegant and precise. Ben smiled and held himself in check again so that they were soon back at their play.

His thoughts returned to his previous musings, hoping the other men would not bring the big cat's body back with them as some sort of trophy. He'd like nothing less than to be required to look at it. And he would never allow Janie to be subjected to such a sight.

His family came to mind next. They were settled now in Denholm, Dada having confirmed arrangements with the local smithy to share his workshop. And Ben had been introduced to Lloyd Pender—had even paid a visit to the man's farm. Not only did Lloyd offer a comfortable home for Jane, but many members of the Pender family lived in the area as well—providing a network of resources and support. There was no doubt that Ben's sister would be well cared for from now on. In fact, she and Lloyd's family were already as thick as thieves. *Who wouldn't love her though? Me priceless Jane.*

Though they were only two hours away, Ben worried that he might not be able to accomplish anything at all for their benefit. In addition to a rather comfortably constructed home, Lloyd's property had a small log cabin that was still intact, which Ben's parents had been offered as a home once the younger couple had married and settled in together. Mam would soon have all the rest that she needed—even her meals would be provided by Jane's hand. And Dada had already begun making preparations to construct the workbenches and acquire the tools that he needed to begin his craft once more.

The frustrating reminder brought Ben to his feet. Dada had spoken only two sentences to him during the visit. After hovering in the background all day, refusing to participate in the flow of conversation, Dada had finally stepped forward as they'd begun their farewells. By this time, little Janie had already been loaded in the automobile in order to set out for home and the light was fading away. At first, Ben hoped he intended to offer some type of congenial good-bye. But just as Ben was opening the driver's door, Dada had muttered, "G'on 'bout yer business, then. S'pose we'll see ya again in a year er two."

Ben wiped a hand across his eyes. *Maybe Jane is wholly wrong in her perspective. Maybe he ain't so complex. I failed him as a son, an' he wants me ta always know it.* Aloud he stated with resolve, "Gonna see 'em soon again, anyhow—an' regular from then on—weekly, if I can manage it. Leastwise, fer Mam and Jane. Might even ask Doc Shepherd 'bout her ailments."

The kits scattered at Ben's words. However, he was already moving anyway. It was time to burn the trash. He figured that he might as well do some work as he pondered his options. Gathering up what he'd set aside during the week in the corner of the barn, he headed out to the pile. Already heaped on top of the thick layer of ashes in the pit were layers of dried weeds from tending the garden. Ben could tell that Otto had added to it from his yardwork on Tuesday. *It'll be a smoky fire t'day.*

But there was something gray half-hidden among the refuse. For a moment it looked like a dead animal. *The sock. It's that ol' sock I found an' ne'er asked the sisters ta look at.*

He drew it out and beat it against a tree branch until all the clumps of dried mud had fallen off it. It was just a very ordinary piece of clothing. However, now he could tell that the heel had been mended. Ben hadn't noticed that before. *There any chance a mama would know her own work?*

Abandoning his chore, Ben covered the distance to the Thompsons' farm with long, purposeful strides. He knocked on the door and it was opened quickly. June's kind face peeked out from the shady entryway.

"Mrs. Thompson, sorry ta disturb ya."

"Not at all. It's good to see you, Ben." She motioned him inside.

However, Ben shook his head to decline the invitation. "I'm not fit fer sittin'. Been sortin' refuse. But I been meanin' ta ask ya 'bout this old sock I found whilst I was drivin' backroads." Now that he was face-to-face with Lemuel's mother, he hardly dared accuse her of being responsible for the dirty piece of discarded wool. He wished for a moment he'd attempted to wash it first.

June reached out her hand without hesitation, examining the item and its stitching, even turning it inside out.

"It's his," she whispered. "I'm sure of it." There was silence as she swallowed back emotion, raising the dirty stocking to cradle it against her chest. "Where did you find it, Ben?"

"On a backroad, ma'am. I can take Arthur there when he gets back from the hunt." He hesitated. Her countenance was crumpling. The poor little woman needed someone to comfort her, hug her. Ben understood how much the children's absence cost a grieving heart each day. However, words would have to be enough. His voice softened. "It's somethin', missus. It gives us a d'rection. Shows Lillian was right 'bout north. It's a good thing. It'll help. I'm sure."

June Thompson pushed a hand up into the pile of yellow curls that crowned her head. She closed her eyes for a second and breathed deeply, managing to regain her composure. "I'm so thankful for you, Ben. I know how hard you've searched. Arthur will be glad to have this encouragement too. He's been beside himself with . . . Thank you, Ben. This is a blessing. A wonderful blessing." Her lip had begun to tremble despite her efforts at control.

Ben tipped his hat and nodded farewell. The door closed rather quickly. Almost instantly Ben could hear weeping. He froze in place. *Should I knock? Should I try ta speak ta her through the door?*

A voice called from across the yard. Spinning to face the sound, Ben saw Jesse Thompson waving at him from behind a fence. He hurried across the grass toward the young man.

"Yer mum needs ya. She's cryin'."

Jesse's face fell. He was climbing over the fence before he'd even begun to reply, "What happened?"

"I found somethin'. A sock. It was Lemmy's."

There was a thump as Jesse's boots dropped to the ground again. His face had grown puzzled. "But that's good. That'll help, eh?"

"Yeah, it's good. But, but . . . she needs ya." Ben gestured toward the house. "She needs comfort."

The young man sprinted toward the door. Ben headed for home. In the sunshine he processed the revelation. *The sock belongs ta Lemmy. June was sure. I gotta get back ta me map and figure where that old bridge be.* And then a new thought. *They stayed on the small roads. They didn't hitch a ride—at least not at first.* Ben released a sigh. That was a good thing. However, his next thought brought a shiver of fear. *Then they could be right where that big cat is by now. God, help 'em!*

. . . ● . . .

Lemuel woke to the sound of Veronika's voice. She was arguing with Freddie again. The sun had just begun to drop from its zenith in the sky. Yet a cool breeze filtered through the trees beside them. There was no point in rising and he was still tired. Lemuel closed his eyes again, wishing he were back at home, even if it would be a day of hard labor. His mind flashed to Mr. Thompson and Harrison. They were probably cutting the hayfield, the large metal mower rattling along behind stout Mirabella. Or, they might be using the rake instead to gather the scattered hay into rows. It would all be much more work for only two people. Perhaps Jesse would join them to help. How Lemuel longed to be with them—coveting even their day of labor.

But angry voices broke through his respite, ending his imaginings. "I'm not eating that, Freddie. It's disgusting."

"Then we'll eat whate'er *you* got. Aw, what? You ain't got nothin'? Guess beggars can't be choosers, then, eh?"

"But it's dead!"

A scoffing laugh. "Oh? So ya wanted ta eat it alive, did ya?"

This was becoming the strangest argument that Lemuel had yet endured. "What's goin' on?" he called out at last, refusing to rise from his position on the ground.

Their footsteps approached him and without warning a clump of mottled flesh landed in the grass beside him. Lemuel leapt to his feet. "What're ya . . . What is't?"

"It's a lamb leg, that's what."

Disgusted, Lemuel spat out his next question, "Freddie, how on earth d'ya kill a lamb? Don't ya know we could—"

"He didn't," Veronika interrupted. "He found it! In the woods. And he still plans to make us eat it."

Lemuel's mouth gaped open. Words would not form.

"Look't," the other boy muttered, gesturing with his hands in frustration. "It's clean. I cut away all the chewed parts. Took only what was fresh and good—just like I'd shot it meself. Only better— 'cause it ain't no ratty little squirrel this time—it's a whole leg'a lamb. Thought ya'd both be proud'a me—thankin' me, at least."

Grimacing, Lemuel managed to say, "All right. Go ahead and cook it, then." He was already turning away, searching for a new place to rest, advising over his shoulder as rationally as he was able, "Veronika, no one's gonna make ya eat it. But it might look better to ya once it's cooked."

Settling farther from the activity around the fire, Lemuel lowered his cap back over his face and tried to ignore their continued banter. Then suddenly a new thought brought him back to his feet. "Freddie? Freddie, where'd ya find it? Near here? What killed it, d'ya think?"

Freddie merely shrugged. "Must'a had big claws an' a big mouth. Think it was a bear?"

"I dunno, but we'd best build a bigger fire. I don't wanna meet up with whate'er took down that lamb."

· · · ● · · ·

The hunting party had not returned by supper on Friday. They'd likely spent another long day in the woods. Lillian hadn't shared the news about Delyth's pregnancy with Miss Tilly or Grace. She'd felt too ashamed. She was simply grateful that Janie had not understood enough to blurt it out at an inopportune moment.

But sitting in the parlor after the supper dishes had been washed and put away, while Lillian was struggling to read for a few moments, she found herself doodling numbers on a piece of paper instead. Father was fifty-two. Delyth was thirty-seven. Lillian was twenty-six. Only eleven years younger than this *stepmother*, far closer in age to Delyth than to her baby. The half sibling would be twenty-six years younger than Lillian. She sat forlornly, chewing on her pencil and mulling over the importance of such a difference in ages, figuring other numbers as well.

When this new little sibling was ten, Lillian would be thirty-six. By then she supposed she and Walter would have their own children as well. Would they call Father's new baby "aunt" or "uncle" as they grew up side by side? What would people think? Would they laugh behind Father and Delyth's backs? Would all of these children get teased in school?

However, there was no way to surmise where exactly Walter might find land. It seemed unlikely that Lillian would be raising her children in Brookfield. The lands that the government released were likely to be in remote places, thereby fulfilling the intention of drawing settlers into new areas. There might not even be a school yet where they would live. The new thought squelched the fears Lillian had about her children sharing a school with Delyth's baby. It suddenly seemed better to stay in

Brookfield, where her family could be given the benefits of friendships and a proper education.

And besides, what would Mother have thought about Walter's desire to move her daughter to unsettled areas of the province? Mother had spent such effort to see that Lillian received every manner of training available even in their small town. But for Lillian and Walter's offspring, there would not be a grand piano for lessons in Walter's humble home, nor painting classes, nor French tutoring, nor children's clubs.

Lillian set the pencil down. Her heart cried out, *Father, I know I'm running ahead of You again. I know I'm worrying about my future, and I'm sorry. Why is it so hard to remember to trust You? Please help me to wait and not worry. Help me to believe that You are going to bless me and not harm me as I follow Your plans for my life.*

The prayer helped a little to fend off Lillian's turbulent feelings. But as she rose to gather the children inside from their evening play, the numbers she'd written on the paper circled in her mind like mosquitos, buzzing around and pestering her despite her efforts to be free from them.

CHAPTER 15

Stopped

Welcome back, lads! Did ya have success?" Despite Ben's apprehension that he might see more of the results from the hunt than he wanted, he'd hurried to the yard in the failing light to greet the returning vehicles. He needed no response. Their faces answered his question before he'd finished speaking.

The men were moving slowly, exiting the vehicles without fanfare. They were clearly spent from their two-day venture and unenthusiastic about sharing their accounts. Standing in the yard only long enough to express polite farewells, the group disbanded and headed to their own homes and families, their vehicles chugging and rattling away one at a time. Only Walter remained beside his car.

"I b'lieve Miss Lillian's in the parlor readin'."

Walter lingered. "Actually, I'd like to speak with you for a moment, if it's a good time."

"O'course."

Walter rubbed a hand across his eyes. "We saw no evidence of them. Anywhere. I'm afraid the men are losin' heart to continue searchin' for them, and I don't know what that'll mean to—"

Ben stepped nearer. "But I found somethin', Walt—a sock. Mrs. Thompson said it's Lemmy's. She's sure."

"What?" The word was pronounced with little enthusiasm.

"I found a gray sock on a backroad—on one'a the first days I looked. He must'a left it fer us—like he did his knife. I figured out the place on me map. I can take ya. An' it weren't on a big road. Hardly a trail. I think we been stickin' too close ta towns. Them kids kep' deep in the hills."

"Well, if that's true, they can't have gotten very far. It would take much longer to travel that way." Walter's eyes had brightened. "When? When did you find it?"

"'Fraid it's been nigh unto two weeks since."

A frown. "Well, it's a sign anyway. We haven't had any sign of them for so long. So that's good."

"But, Walt . . ."

"Yeah?"

"Wouldn't that . . . Wouldn't it put 'em 'round where that big cat be? Or d'ya think they didn't get so far north as that?"

Walter's eyes closed as if trying to pull up a map in his head. "The cougar was seen farther east, that's where the town of Harstad is, the place where Lillian and I stopped. But it could be . . . I just don't know. I guess an animal like that would likely stay west of the town, between there and the Rockies. That's where we were lookin'. We went maybe ten miles west of town. And we saw lots of tracks, but none of them fresh. Could be it went right back where it came from. That's what we were hopin'."

"That'd be good—'less headin' west took it closer to the kids."

"But all of us lookin'—we didn't find any evidence of the kids there at all."

"Ya might not'a been far 'nough out."

They stood in silence, eyes cast down to the ground. At last Walter spoke again. "I'll talk to Arthur. He'll want to go back out." Sighing and shaking his head, Walter added, "He's pushin' himself too hard. I don't know how he can keep goin'. But he's not likely to give up any time soon—'specially with a new clue."

"But, Walt, Arthur ain't done hayin' yet. Saw that when I was passin'. I don't know much 'bout how it's done here but I seen the cut grass still layin' in the field."

Walter thrust his hands into his pockets. "Jesse got it cut a while back. And he was goin' to try to rake it this week but their rake busted. Last I heard he's tryin' to fix it still."

"A rake? We got plenty'a rakes here."

"No, I mean a machine rake, drawn behind horses."

Ben pondered the dilemma, then offered, "I can come with ya—when ya go out next."

The suggestion brought Walter's face up again. He seemed to be choosing his words cautiously. "Can you handle a gun?"

"Nope. But I ain't near as tired as the rest'a ya. That's gotta count fer somethin'."

"True," Walter admitted. "That's bound to make a difference."

· · · ● · · ·

Lillian's relief that Walter and the other men had returned was short-lived. Arthur wanted to head back out immediately, insisting that if they left tonight they'd arrive in the proper area and be ready to begin again by sunrise. He agreed to settle, instead, for sleeping at home for one night first, starting fresh the next morning. They gathered together around Mother's table, making plans long after darkness had fallen. Lillian and Grace, Walter and Ben, and the Thompsons.

Even Miss Tilly joined them, offering what she knew of the places they intended to search. "There's roads what aren't on yer map—but they ain't good ones. See here, where this road branches off? There's a way ta keep goin' this a'way." Her finger traced a new line onto Ben's worn map. "An' another here where this one dips near the river 'bout in there. But yer gonna have ta ford the river if ya use that one. Ain't been too much rain, so should be all right. Takin' Walt's car makes more sense 'an takin' ours."

"We could take horses," Jesse Thompson suggested.

Heads around the table nodded. Walter leaned forward onto his elbows. "We'd cover less ground, till we got past the roads. I don't know. What do you think, Arthur?"

"It'd slow us down—loading them up and getting them out there."

"True."

Lillian allowed her eyes to settle on Arthur Thompson. It had been increasingly apparent to her that the situation was exacting a heavy toll on him. Dark skin wreathed his eyes. Even his face seemed stretched thin beneath his neat peppered beard, like it was turning to fragile paper. She'd never really thought of Arthur as *old* before. Somehow, it seemed that worry was advancing the clock for him. *Perhaps he's just been losing weight from the strain— and he'll look the same again once this is all over.* Lillian hoped that would be true, that Arthur—and everything—would go back to the way things had been before the children had run away.

Deep in the night, drawing up the covers on Mother's side of the bed, Lillian prayed about the troublesome thought. Even as she whispered the words into the darkness of her room, she felt a check in her spirit. Things were never going to be the same again. They could not be. And worse yet, there was no way of knowing how things would change after it all played out. She prayed instead for the children: for Lemuel, and Freddie, and Veronika. For Castor and Janie. For Milton and Matty. *Oh, Father God, protect them. Keep them in Your plan for their lives. Draw them to You through everything that happens to them. All of those hard things that they've known in their short lives—it isn't fair, Lord. But I know You didn't promise to make things fair. You promised to redeem it all instead.*

Even after her time in prayer, Lillian's thoughts refused to quiet. They drifted to her own life, her own strange ambages that had led to losses. She dared add to her prayer. *I wouldn't have chosen the things in my life that You assigned to me either. Losing my first parents when I was too young to even remember them—and watching my second mother die slowly. So as much as You've helped me to put my life into perspective—to begin to heal—I can't claim to understand the . . . the why of it all. For me, or for all of them.*

· · • · · ·

There was little in the way of a moon on this cloudy night. So the shadows along the road blended with the darkness, making it difficult to walk carefully enough. A chill breeze blew down out of the nearby mountains. Lemuel found himself stumbling along, leading the horse while Freddie and Veronika took their ride. Rather than remaining near the edge of the road, Lemuel walked down the center, taking advantage of as much moonlight at his feet as he was able.

He was thinking about how tired he was, then corrected himself. He wasn't short on sleep. He shouldn't feel tired. He'd slept fitfully through another long day. So it wasn't truly physical fatigue. He determined that it must be in his mind. His body was just following suit. Maybe this was what people meant when they claimed to be "sick and tired." Perhaps it was his mind exerting control over his body in a way that made him feel physically exhausted. His whole being—body, heart, and mind—was rebelling against the situation. Still, the logic of his physical efforts seemed far easier to process than the emotions he was feeling just now.

What's causin' me gloomies, then? Am I sad? No, not really. More like numb. I jus' can't feel nothin'. That's what's wrong. Something inside me is shut off again, like it used to be whenever I was lost.

It was a strange choice of words. *Lost.* He'd honestly never labeled himself that way before. *But I was lost when I was little and lived on the streets in London. And I was lost when I was older and the farmer left me alone back in Lethbridge. So am I lost again? Not really. I got a home an' a family now. So why does it feel the same?*

He thought about Mr. Thompson and Mum. He'd been promised he would always be part of their family. Did that mean the Thompsons loved him more than anyone else did? Than even Miss Grace and Miss Lillian? No, he didn't really believe that was true. He'd come to believe that the sisters loved him in a way that stayed the same—even from a distance. Then what did it mean to be *family*?

As he trudged along, clarity began to unfold the layers of his thoughts. He found that at last he could admit the truth—at least to himself. He did feel closer to the sisters than to anyone else. By contrast, he did still feel a little like a stranger in his new home. Not because he wasn't treated well. In fact, it was partly because he was treated so well that it didn't feel quite real. It felt like the kind of politeness that you'd show to a guest, not someone in the family. Jesse, for one, behaved like no older brother Lemuel had ever observed—kind, polite, a little distant. So maybe Lemuel was still just an outsider, after all. Maybe that's how he'd always feel.

His mind certainly believed Mr. Thompson and Mum were telling him the truth. Yet somehow it all felt too *arranged* that he would stay with them until he graduated from high school. Then he hoped to go to college to become a doctor. If only the strange feeling that countered what he believed about the Thompsons would go away, the sense that their kind promises lay just on the surface of his skin, like they couldn't soak down all the way into the heart of him.

Was he even right to have any expectations about his future? After all, he'd never stayed put in a family before. Maybe he was just cursed to keep getting lost from people who loved him. It wasn't *their* fault. It must be something about *himself*.

181

Finally, judging by how far through its arc the hide-and-seek moon had descended on its cloudy path, Lemuel estimated that he'd done about two hours of walking. So he slowed to a stop. Dawn seemed delayed by the overcast sky.

"Ya switchin'?"

"Yup."

There was no movement from above him. "Ain't time yet."

"'Tis." Lemuel dropped to a seat on the grass by the road, leaning back on his arms. The ground was damp and cold. Star took a step closer to him, reaching out her soft nose to sniff at his hair. Her broad lips were grazing down toward Lemuel's ear before he gently pushed her away.

Veronika dismounted first, clutching Freddie's arm in order to slow her descent. She said nothing.

Freddie's feet landed on the ground next. "I'm hungry."

Lemuel waited silently, watching.

It was the girl who responded. "We're going to stop as soon as the sky brightens. You can wait."

"If I'm gonna walk, then I'm gonna eat first." Freddie's voice was quiet and threatening. "Ya don't wanna give me time, then you can walk fer a change."

"You know I can't," Veronika muttered back.

"Yer as able as ya wanna be. Jus' lazy, I figure."

It was the girl's turn to manipulate. "But I'm the one carrying the food, eh? If you want something to eat, you're going to have to ask me nicely."

On hearing her reply, Lemuel began to rise. He couldn't understand why the child would choose to deliberately provoke Freddie. She knew the speed and the depths of his anger. Why . . .

But rather than approach her, Freddie was walking away along the road. The darkness was claiming him. This hadn't happened before.

"Freddie?" Lemuel called after him. "Where ya goin', lad?"

No response.

Lemuel turned toward Veronika instead, trying to sound like the voice of reason. "He's right. If he wants ta eat, he gets to. He's the one what's done all the huntin'. It won't take him long."

Strange laughter burst out of the darkness where Freddie had disappeared. The sound of it made Lemuel's skin tingle with fear and spun him around. The disheartening chortle was followed by Freddie's lowest voice challenging savagely, "Agree with him, er else."

Veronika pushed herself between Lemuel and Star, hobbling toward Freddie. Though Lemuel threw a hand out to catch her arm, she continued out of his reach until the shadows had swallowed her too. Her speed had surprised Lemuel. He could hear her arguing, "You don't get to decide everything. If the farm boy can walk without eating first, so can you."

Something alarming was happening. It was heralded by the icy sound of Freddie's laughter instead of his more familiar rage. It was amplified by the girl's goading words. Lemuel rushed forward, trying to force himself between them, but Veronika was moving too quickly.

"Don't you dare!" she shouted into the shadows.

At last, Lemuel was near enough to Freddie to see the threat. The boy had chosen a stone from the road. It was loaded now in his slingshot and aimed toward the advancing girl. Lemuel made a leap to intervene. He felt a flash of searing agony and then nothing.

CHAPTER 16

Shock

Ben, Walter, and Arthur paused in each valley west of Harstad to search for a while. At noon they discovered some shoe marks in a patch of soft dirt beside the road. One set only.

"Think it's one of them?" Arthur asked.

"Might be. Two of them might have been walkin' on the hard ground of the road." Then Walter noticed, "Wait, there's been a horse here too. And it's followin' in line with these prints. See? Here—and here."

Arthur crouched down for a closer look. His fingers traced the shape of the indent. "The boot print must just be some local farmer, then. But let's keep an eye on these, just the same. We might see where the man went. There aren't too many people out in this area, and we can ask him if he's seen anything." He walked forward, following as many footprints as he could find. "It seems like the horse is limping a little. He probably won't be walking it far in a state like that."

Ben's eyes rose to the woods as he asked, "Then this man an' his horse might be near?"

"Maybe. Or maybe not. It's impossible to say for sure. But at least the tracks are fresh. So we'll keep an eye on them as long as we can."

"What d'ya mean? How fresh? T'day?"

Arthur rose and crumbled a clod of dirt that he'd picked up from the roadside, comparing it to the soil around the print. "Yesterday—maybe. Probably not more than that though. I wish we'd brought along a Tsuut'ina guide. I'm not nearly as good as . . ." His voice trailed off as he spotted another line of hoofprints farther up the road. At last he repeated, "Yesterday or last night. That's my best guess."

From time to time, particularly in the valleys where the moisture along the roadside made the ground softer, the tracks reappeared. Ben found it difficult to keep his hopes in check. He tried to remind himself that, even if they didn't find the children, if it were only a farmer from the area, perhaps he would have noticed the presence of strangers.

At last they found a lane to a homestead, far back from the road. Walter eased their vehicle up the rutted drive. A stocky black dog barked ferociously, its hackles raised along its neck and back, warning them to leave. The dog had circled the vehicle twice before an old man exited a nearby shed and approached them, commanding the dog to "Go lay down." It retreated reluctantly as far as the bushes and dropped to its belly, panting and licking its white teeth.

Walter rolled the window down in order to speak with the man, as if he were reluctant to put his foot out of the vehicle. "Good afternoon, sir. We're lookin' for three children who've run away. We wondered if you've seen any sign of them in your area."

The man ambled closer, crossed his arms over his red flannel shirt, and tipped back a little on his heels. "I ain't seen nothin'. But I ain't been out fer a couple weeks, neither." He paused to spit on the ground. "Old Claude here, he took ta barkin' in the middle'a last night. Might'a been yer kids on the road there.

185

Then again, might'a been a fox near the hens. Can't say either way. Sorry."

"Thank you, sir. We appreciate you lettin' us ask." Then Walter added, "Say, does this road keep goin' straight on from here, or does it turn east? It's not shown on our map."

The man's eyes squinted in amusement. "Not surprised it ain't. Not much more'n a trail. But it goes pret' near straight fer two miles till it comes to the crick. Only that bridge there, it ain't built fer autos like yers. Yer gonna have ta go 'round the other way. Back 'bout a mile an' up from there."

"Oh, there's not a crossing on this road?"

"Not there. Valley's too narrow."

"I see. Well, you've been very helpful. Thanks. Maybe we'll go as far as we can and then turn back around so we can search the other side too." Walter's hand dropped to the stick shift, preparing to withdraw.

But the man took a step forward. "Ya say it's kids yer lookin' fer? Runaways?"

"Yes, sir."

He shook his head as he added, "Ya might wanna take care. Been a cougar nosin' 'round these parts." His hand came up to tug on an ear, making the gray hairs that grew from it stand out farther. "How far ya goin', son?"

Walter hesitated. Arthur answered instead, calling out from his side of the car, "Until we find them. As long as it takes."

The man whistled to his dog. It rose instantly and trotted to its master's side, the tufts of fur down its neck upright again, though its eyes were lifted upward and fixed on the man. He said, "Don't know if ya want our help. But me an' Claude'll come with ya if ya wanna check down ta the bridge. If that cat's out there, he'll know it. Yer kids too. He's a good tracker."

Without hesitation, Ben pushed the back door open for the man. They would take all the help they were offered.

The dog launched himself up onto the seat next to Ben even before he could move aside. His long red tongue hanging out, Claude the dog panted and drooled, shoving his large shaggy head into Ben's lap. Having little experience with dogs, Ben recoiled and raised his arms as a shield in order to keep the dog from encroaching too close to his face. He was glad that at least there was no longer any trace of aggression in the dog's eyes.

For a moment the man disappeared back into his shed. At last he came out into view, this time carrying a rifle. As he joined them in the car he stated, "Name's Beake. Lonnie Beake."

Arthur was quick to thank him. "We're so glad for your help, Mr. Beake. A dog's the best kind of scout of all. I know you must have other things to do today, but we're so grateful for your time."

"Jus' the right thing ta do."

Ben turned his shoulder away from the flapping tongue beside him, shifting closer to his window to make more room on the bench seat for the newcomers. The man chuckled, throwing his arm around the thick black body and drawing it close against him. "Claude ain't never been in a motorcar b'fore. I think he likes it."

* * *

Lillian was the one nearest the telephone when it rang shortly after lunch. She shooed the children away from the area so that she could hear and cautiously lifted the earpiece. *It can't be Walter yet. The men are certainly not where they could place a call.* Speaking into the receiver, she gave a tentative "Hello?"

"I have a Mr. Sidney Brown of Lethbridge for Miss Grace Bennett."

"Yes, operator. Yes. We accept."

Several clicks and then a crackling sound. Lillian asked, "Sid? Are you there?"

"Hello? Yes, it's Sid. Is this Grace?"

"No, sorry. It's Lillian. But Grace is here. Would you prefer to speak with her?"

"Hello, Lillian. No, that's fine. I can speak with you. It feels strange though. This is the first time I've placed a telephone call to you there instead of going through my secretary. How do you like having one at your house?"

Lillian smiled. She wasn't certain how to answer. In truth, it was a strange and rather shocking feeling for life to be interrupted at any moment by the shrill ring of the telephone's little bell. She was glad for the advantages it brought but had not yet grown accustomed to the technology's presence in her life. "Well, it's certainly more convenient than driving, but I'd rather be in person for a good visit," she answered honestly.

"I suppose so." Sid laughed. "Well, I wanted to check in with you. I've been keeping up with the details about your search for the missing children. But I also wanted to see how you and Grace are doing with it all. You must be about played out by now."

Lillian stifled a groan. "Yes. Yes, we are."

"And I don't suppose you've heard from Arthur's group today? I doubt they're able to get in touch with you."

"No, we probably won't hear from them at all before they return. We don't expect them until late this evening."

"Sure, sure."

Lillian surveyed the children around her, then waved a hand to summon Milton's attention. She placed one hand over the receiver and whispered, "Would you please fetch Miss Grace? Tell her that Mr. Brown is on the telephone."

The boy nodded and hurried up the stairs.

"Well, I have news for you. Though I'm not sure you'll feel ready to receive it."

"Oh?"

"There are two things actually. The first is that the Caulfields have been approved to adopt Matthew and Milton, at last."

Lillian exhaled her relief. "Oh, that's wonderful. Catherine will be so glad to finally have them with her. It's taken such a long time—months."

"Yes, and that's because they're one of the first families to adopt while we've been working out a new system with the Viney Boggs Mercy Society. I'm sorry it's been such a trial for them."

"Well, the boys have been thriving here, but I know the Caulfields have been anxious to see this resolved." The familiar tangle of excitement and sadness followed immediately. Lillian would miss the twins. They'd added so much levity to the household. She knew too that Janie and Castor would not be pleased to see their dear little playmates depart. However, for the good of the small boys, it would be best for them to be settled in a permanent home and away from the trials and unpredictability of living here.

"But there's something else." Sid's voice heralded news that was less desirable.

"Something else?"

"Yes, there are three children needing immediate care. We were hoping to place them with you."

Lillian's mouth widened and froze in surprise. "With us? Now?" *How can he even ask when we're still looking for Veronika and the boys? How can we even be considered suitable?*

Grace arrived. Lillian greeted her with a bewildered expression and made room by the receiver, holding the earpiece between them. She said aloud, "Grace is here, Sid. Can you repeat that for her, please?"

Exchanging a series of increasingly concerned glances, they listened as Sid explained the situation. Three sisters had been cared for by an aging grandmother in a community near Lethbridge. But it had been disclosed to authorities that the children's father had returned to the area and for some reason this had prompted the neighbors to intervene. The children would not be considered adoptable. However, they needed care for an indeterminate length of time.

Lillian could read in the frowning expression on Grace's face that this was a new situation even for her. She asked, "Sid, will anyone know where the girls have been placed? Will they be told anything about us?"

It wasn't the first question that Lillian had expected from Grace. *Is there a need for secrecy? Whatever for?*

But Sid's answer illuminated the implications. "They will not. The Mounties are dealing with the custody issues at their end of this case through our agency here in Lethbridge, and the officers involved would be the only ones with whom you'd interact. No one else would know where the children have been taken—not even the grandmother, and certainly not the father."

After several more questions, Sid seemed to press a little harder. "I know the timing is terrible for you. But I'm afraid we need to have an answer right away. The girls are being held right now at the local police station and being watched over by officers. For obvious reasons, we don't want that to go on for long. We'd like to see them in proper care by tomorrow if we can."

Everything inside of Lillian begged to decline. She wanted to insist that someone else be found this time. But Grace's eyes were softening. Grace was ready to accept them. With a heavy heart, Lillian moved a step away, her soul far from willing to even consider such a thing. *Not now, with children still missing. How can we be asked to flip-flop again? We'll have to pack up Matty and Milton for their new home, but at the same time clean the rooms and reorganize, so that tomorrow we'll have new children among us again? Children with troubles that we haven't faced before. It's impossible to consider such a thing.*

As Lillian set the earpiece back in its cradle, Grace grasped her arm. "I know you're not ready for this, sis. I'm not either. Not at all. But if God is asking us to step into this new role, I want to be quick to accept it."

Lillian attempted a nod. Then her face crumpled in defeat and tears began to flow. Grace's arms reached out, drawing her close. "I'm not ready," Lillian whimpered. "I can't just turn my feelings off and on like that. Can you? Not now! And besides, it's going to take time for my heart to let go of Matty and Milton. We both know how long that's going to hurt."

"Yes, of course. I understand, sis. I really do."

"Not to mention that we're in the middle of a huge crisis! How can he even ask?" With effort, Lillian stopped her own flow of words, suppressing the accusation that would have followed. *And how could you say yes to him, Grace?*

Grace's words were more controlled. "I do know what you mean. I feel all of that too. But we don't get to decide when children need us. We agreed to be available to God whenever He calls, and I want to be faithful in that. I know you do too, sis. Even when it doesn't feel like the right time."

"Oh, Grace, if there was ever a time that didn't feel right . . ." Lillian let the remainder of the sentence go unspoken. Instead, she muttered, "I'm sorry. But I'm just not ready this time." Grace's head against Lillian's shoulder moved in a nod. Lillian felt the pressure begin to lessen, grateful that even Grace had a limit to what she was willing to tackle.

Then Grace added softly, "All right. Take the time that you need. I'll manage the best I can."

Lillian pushed away. "What?" They studied each other for a moment.

With resolve, Grace repeated the same message. "I'll do what I can to shield you from this."

Now Lillian's head was spinning, trying to understand what Grace was saying. "But—but *you're* still going to accept new children. Even knowing that I'm not prepared? As if you'll do this without me?"

A shadow had fallen over her sister's face. "Yes, if I need to, I will. I don't think there's any choice, really."

Sorting through her thoughts, Lillian found no response that she felt should be uttered aloud. Instead, she dropped her arms to her sides, her gaze to the floor. "I'm going to finish the ironing."

Leaving Grace standing in the foyer, Lillian spun away and retreated. She wiped at the tears that had fallen on her cheeks, only to find that they were quickly replaced with fresh ones. She was grateful that at least the ironing was set up out of the way in the workroom, where she could find some momentary solitude.

·· · ● · ··

The presence of a dog in their search party changed everything. Nose to the ground, Claude covered an area far beyond the men's ability. At each stop he swept the ground beside the road and traveled in and out among the trees. One whistle from Lonnie Beake brought him back again, red tongue flapping, with what appeared to be almost a smile lighting his face.

Soon they were approaching the small bridge. Ben was certain he knew what the other men were thinking. Could this man and his dog be hired for the day? Would there be any incentive strong enough to retain their services?

The automobile rolled to its final stop on this stretch of road. Lonnie's door opened again before the vehicle had slowed to a complete stop. The dog launched out, hitting the ground hard and heading straight down the embankment toward the creek where it passed under the small bridge, nose to the ground. The men followed more slowly, gathering at the side of a narrow ravine, pausing before crossing the wooden span on foot.

Then the barking began in earnest. Claude was heading up

the other side of the creek bank, lunging farther down the road directly ahead of them. This was new. The men traded glances.

"Could be the kids." Ben took a step forward onto the bridge, his eyes searching ahead.

"Could be the cat." Lonnie whistled and waited. The dog did not return.

A wave of fear passed over Ben. He heard a double *snap-snap* just behind him as Lonnie Beake cocked his rifle. Arthur and Walter rushed back to the automobile, retrieving their guns from the back compartment. Ben stood motionless with empty hands.

Lonnie's chin gestured toward him. "Ya ain't got no gun?"

Slowly shaking his head, Ben glanced back to where Arthur and Walter were still loading theirs. Should he advance with the others? Or should he retreat into the car? Freddie might be near. Ben's eyes skimmed the ground around him. He lifted an arm-length piece of thick branch. It was bent awkwardly in the middle. Perhaps it was laughable to the others, but it would have to be enough. Ben had no intention of retreating to safety just now.

With tense steps, the men moved forward. Lonnie whistled again. Claude's barking had changed. Rather than expressing the excitement of discovery, the noise had become a staccato of throaty yips. Their pace quickened. They crossed the little bridge. Ben followed close behind, his stick raised to one side.

Ahead, the dog rushed out from the trees, stopped in its tracks, and yelped at Lonnie before lunging into the bushes once more. Arthur's pace quickened first, his steps hurrying forward. He yelled, "Lemuel! Freddie! Lemuel!"

Walter took up the shouting. "Boys! Are you there? Veronika?"

At first the sound of their yelling seemed strange to Ben, but it dawned on him slowly that if it was the cat, it might not be drawn nearer by the noise but instead be frightened away. He joined in the chorus.

They came to the place in the bushes from which Claude was repeatedly erupting and returning. Ben entered the shadows last. They were on a steep hill that dropped into a wooded valley. Branches scratched at his face, his hands. Then Ben heard a guttural cry.

"Oh, Lemuel!"

Chapter 17

Discovery

The boy was lying in a small recess of the hillside among the trees. His body had been almost fully covered over with leaves such that they would surely never have found him had it not been for the dog. Lemuel's face was bathed in blood.

Ben's first thought was of the cougar. Had the boy been attacked? Where were the others? What had happened to them? Were they . . . ?

Arthur was digging the motionless body out from among the leaves, tossing aside the coat that had been wrapped around Lemuel in order to inspect for injuries. He was repeating Lemuel's name over and over again. Each time it was spoken, the word became more of a lament.

He's dead. The cat killed him. We're too late.

But suddenly the men were scurrying.

"We've gotta get him out."

"We can't carry him. We don't know how else he's injured. We gotta try not to hurt him worse."

"Make a travois. Find some branches."

Ben stood bewildered as they quickly assembled an improvised stretcher. Two long branches were laid side by side, with enough space between them to tie their jackets as a cradle for Lemuel's body. The thickest end of each tree branch pointed up the hill toward the road. On the downward end, there remained two fans of smaller branches and pine needles.

It occurred to Ben that they'd need a path out through the thick underbrush. His would-be weapon became a tool as he swung it repeatedly in order to break branches and move them aside, clearing their way up the hill. At last, the men followed slowly behind. With Arthur and Walter each holding the thickest part of their assigned branch, they dragged the contrivance forward a little at a time, trailing the lower end of the travois where it fanned out, moving as gently as possible. Lonnie followed behind on alternating sides, keeping it from snagging as it progressed. The process seemed to take impossibly long.

Once they were out in the sunlight, they laid the contraption on the ground. Arthur was instantly on his knees, leaning across the body to wipe the matted blood from Lemuel's face.

"He's got a wound above the eye. Very near his eye! It's quite deep. But it doesn't seem to be a bite or a tear." He brushed the hair back tenderly. "I can't tell how it happened. Maybe he ran into a sharp tree branch or something."

Ben's eyes lifted. He spun slowly in place and searched around him. *Where's Freddie? Did he just leave Lemmy here? Where's the girl?*

The upper end of the travois was being lifted again. More quickly now, the whole assembly was dragged along the road back toward their waiting vehicle. Lonnie whistled for his dog.

Aren't they going to look around? What about the other kids? As much as Ben understood that Lemuel urgently needed care, his feet refused to follow.

Claude woofed from the tree line beside him, commanding

Ben's attention. The brown eyes were locked on Ben's, as if willing him to understand. Claude bounced on his front legs twice, then raised his nose to point up into the trees above them.

It's the cat. Oh no! Ben stumbled back several steps. The men were far from him now. Lonnie was carrying all of their guns. Ben was completely unarmed and out of range of their help.

A snapping sound came from above him. Claude woofed again. Ben's eyes searched the greenery. And then Ben saw a dangling boot. He hurried closer. He spied a second boot, an arm. Freddie's face peered down at him from over his head.

"Freddie!"

A terse answer came through gritted teeth. "Shh. Leave me be. I ain't goin' back."

"What? Lad, what d'ya mean? We found ya."

There was the shrill sound of a whistle from up the road. Claude darted away.

Freddie muttered again, "I ain't goin' back. Ya can't make me."

Ben reached his arms up toward the boy, holding them suspended empty in midair. His mind was too cluttered with questions to summon words. His mouth hung open uselessly.

"Ya know I mean it," Freddie insisted. "Ne'er said I'd stay with ya anyhow. An' now I'm goin' on alone."

Ben fought the urge to shout back in desperation, kept his voice as steady as possible. "The girl? Where's the girl? Freddie, come down. Talk ta me, please."

No movement above. "I dunno. She left us this mornin'. Said she was goin' on alone."

"Oh no. Oh, lad." Ben's chest tightened further at the thought of the twelve-year-old girl entirely by herself among the hazards of this wilderness.

Freddie's voice changed. His words became a negotiation. "Look't, sir. Ya leave me be an' I might find her. I can catch up ta her. Ya leave me be, I'll go on."

"But I can't. I have to . . ."

At last the boy began to descend, swinging his body weight from one branch to the next with agile arms. His feet struck the ground next to Ben. "Ya make me go back, ya lose her fer good." Seeing Ben's hesitation, Freddie added, "I'll leave again anyhow, Mr. Waldin. Ya know it."

Walter's summons came from up the road. "Ben! We're ready. Ben!"

Ben closed his eyes. "I can't leave ya here, lad. Not here. There's a cat—a mountain lion . . ."

"All the more reason ta send me fer the girl." He grasped Ben's sleeve. "Jus' one thing, Mr. Waldin," Freddie muttered. "It was me what took yer money. I wanna give it back t'ya."

"What?" Ben shook his head in an attempt to understand. "But I know ya did, lad."

Freddie's expression was one that Ben had never seen. Tears were pooling in his eyes. His voice cracked with emotion. "I'm sorry, sir. It ain't right, what I done. I'm sorry. So sorry." He wiped his nose on his sleeve and continued hoarsely, "I took advantage'a ya—an' . . . an' of Lemmy too. When ya both've been better ta me than anyone else. So here's yer money." A lumpy sock was pressed into Ben's hand.

"Ben! Ben!"

"I have ta go, lad. Lemmy needs care."

"I know it. 'Cause it's me fault, sir. I hit him, with me slingshot, in his eye. It were me. An accident, I promise! But I can't come back, ya see. They'll put me in jail . . . er somethin'."

"Oh, Freddie." Ben extended his arms again, but the boy eluded him, slipping away from his reach. "No, no, Freddie, please." Ben felt his body straining to move in two directions. There was not enough time to convince the boy. "Take the money, lad. At least take the money. Keep yerself safe. Find the girl if ya can. But take the money. You'll need it." He tossed the sock forward and turned his back. Stumbling up the road again, Ben clutched at his chest. *Oh, Lord, why?*

· · • · ·

The four young children had gathered around the kitchen table for supper, chattering away to Lillian and Grace regarding their latest expedition into the field beyond the barn. They hadn't informed them yet about the call from Sid. It would likely be their last meal together, the last before they'd be joined by new residents and bid farewell to Matty and Milton. Lillian was doing her best to keep her emotions in check.

Miss Tilly was just settling a bowl of steaming roasted vegetables in the center of the table when the sound of someone bursting through the front door interrupted them even before their meal could be blessed. "Miss Grace! Miss Lillian!" It was Harrison.

Instantly there was pandemonium, a rush of bodies toward the foyer.

Harrison cried out, "It's 'im! It's Lemmy. They found 'im."

"Oh, praise God fer that."

"No, no! Lemmy's bleedin'—dyin' maybe. Ya gotta come."

"Dr. Shepherd?" Lillian asked.

"Walt went fer 'im, an' come back already too."

Lillian locked eyes with Miss Tilly, who waved her onward. Scrambling out the door still in their house shoes, the sisters followed Harrison across the yard. Once on the road, the boy shot out ahead. They hurried as quickly as their skirts would allow, arriving at the Thompson farm out of breath and trembling.

There were two cars in the yard. Ben was seated on the grass next to the path leading to the house, his head in his hands. Grace rushed inside while Lillian paused beside Ben, hoping to gather a little more information before entering. She laid a hand on his shoulder. "How is he?"

Ben shook his head, refusing to raise it. "Hit in the eye with a rock, hurt bad."

The few words drew more questions. "But how? Who?"

Slowly Ben pushed himself up to his feet. His head hung low. "It were Freddie what done it. Not that he meant ta. Were an accident."

Instantly Lillian searched the yard. "The others? They're here too?"

"No, miss. We left him there."

Ben's answers were frustratingly brief. Lillian grasped at his wrist, giving his arm a shake. "You left them behind? The others?"

His face came up at last. Ben's gray eyes had become a storm of sorrow. "I'd no choice, miss. Freddie, he wouldn't come. Said he was goin' after the girl. She were already gone. An' by then the men were loadin' Lemmy in the car. I had ta leave him. Don'tcha see? I had ta." His voice crackled with regret.

Lillian threw her arms around his waist. "Oh, Ben. I'm so sorry I sounded critical. I know you did your best. Your very best. Always."

He pushed her gently away, turning his head to the side to hide his tears. "No, miss, I didn't. I don't know what I shoulda done, but this ain't right. Him out there still. The girl as good as lost. An' the other boy . . ." Ben's eyes rose to the house. Lillian saw his body shiver at the thought.

Her mouth had become so dry the words were difficult to form. "Lemuel? How bad is he?"

"The doc's with him. It bled a mess. Might lose his eye. An' he might even . . ."

Lillian recoiled. "Oh dear."

"You should go inside, miss."

It was Lillian's turn to shiver in horror. "Yes, I should." Instead, she turned again toward Ben with a sudden need to express one more thought. "It's not your fault. Do you hear me? You did everything you could to save that boy. For as long as I've known you, you've done nothing but work to help him. He refused to let you. That's all."

"I left him, miss. I left him."

Lillian touched his arm helplessly for a moment. Then turned toward the house, unable to even imagine what she might face inside.

· · ● · ·

A strange humming sound came first. Lemuel wondered where the noise was coming from. It seemed to vibrate through his entire body. He tried to open his eyes. A flame of pain blazed up inside his head. It confused him that he hadn't felt the anguish of it at first. He hoped that if he kept his eyes closed, his head perfectly still, the throbbing might slowly fade once more. What had caused the terrible pain? It seemed imperative that, though his body was refusing to cooperate, he should search out the cause.

However, there seemed to be no light at all where he was lying. His foggy brain told him that it must be night. He'd been asleep. But where? Was he back in the cave? In the grass along the road? What was under his back that seemed much softer than either of those places, more comfortable than he remembered?

His arm lifted in the darkness. He was pleased that it seemed to obey his brain's instruction to move. But then something seemed to have caught hold of his hand. From far away, someone seemed to be speaking to him. Still, the hum inside his head made the words unintelligible.

So he tried to move the other hand instead. Finding it free, he brought it up to his forehead. However, rather than hair, his fingers discovered cloth. Was he trapped under the blankets? No. His arms were free. This cloth seemed tightly bound against his forehead, even over his eyes. *Why?*

Aware next that his mouth felt crusty inside, Lemuel licked at his lips and discovered them cracked and sore. Almost immediately, there followed the sensation of water passing slowly over them and into his mouth, a welcome relief. He'd needed a drink so desperately. Was it Freddie who'd given him water? The girl? How long had he been sleeping? Were they properly caring for Star? He should rise so that he could check on her.

The humming grew louder, the unintelligible words faded further away. Then sleep reclaimed him.

· · · ● · · · ·

Lillian sat on one of the Thompsons' kitchen chairs that had been placed at Lemuel's bedside. She tried not to give in to the desire to surrender to tears. This situation was far too much like sitting next to Mother in her final days. The memory of such raw emotion that had been kept at bay for so long rose now into the forefront of Lillian's mind. She discovered that those feelings of loss and grief had not truly been conquered, but were only lying dormant in the recesses of her heart. The awareness of their return, multiplied by her fears for Lemuel, was overwhelming. And, though in some sense she wanted to flee, Lillian found her desire to remain where she was tugging at her even more strongly. Her wounded heart refused to retreat.

This room, however, was rather crowded with people coming and going. Dr. Shepherd and his nurse, Faith, came frequently. Grace rushed back and forth between the houses, taking care of what needed to be done at home. Jesse Thompson, Ben, and Walter visited every few hours. June, however, was at the center of it all, in constant motion, tucking and fussing, commenting and praying aloud. Lillian sat quietly on the far side of the bed, hoping that her presence was not a nuisance to anyone.

Because this was June and Arthur's own bedroom, Lillian felt like an intruder in the intimate space of her neighbors. The master bedroom just off the kitchen had been easier to access when the injured boy had been carried into the Thompsons' home, rather than the one upstairs that Lemuel shared with Harrison. This room had delicate yellow and blue flowers sprinkled across the white wallpaper. It had lacy white curtains over the windows and a tufted rag rug on the floor. There was a tidy little dressing table that held June's hairbrush and hairpins and hand mirror, as well as a table for the basin and pitcher they used when they washed up for bed. Lillian dropped her attention back to the boy before her, trying not to let her eyes travel around the small bedroom any longer, trying to preserve her neighbors' privacy as much as possible.

Lemuel lay in this place of honor where he could be cared for best. By contrast, tall Arthur Thompson had retired to the stuffed chair in the corner of the room, where he had fallen into a sporadic sleep. His long legs folded at odd angles and stretched out by turn, and his head hung back in a strange way.

Memories rose into the forefront of Lillian's mind. She remembered how often she'd forsaken the bedroom chair during her own long hours of watching in Mother and Father's room, simply lying down on the bed beside Mother's frail form instead. *Oh, how I miss you. I wish you were here again today to brush my hair back and tell me it's all in God's hands.* Lillian's fingers twisted her handkerchief tighter in an attempt to keep her tears from falling. *Oh, Mother, I love this boy. How could I ever bear losing him too?*

CHAPTER 18

Resettling

"G race?" Ben had noticed the young woman from across the yard as she lifted a wet sheet from her basket in order to pin it up on the clothesline. He approached tentatively. He'd been worried that she was overtaxed with all that had fallen into her lap while Lillian spent her time at the Thompsons'. Everyone was worried about Lemuel. Truth was, Ben needed company just then too. His own turbulent fears were more than he could bear in solitude. If only he could help out, it might allow him to control the strain for a time. He'd heard, too, that new children were expected soon. "Can I help ya?" He rubbed his hands down the seams of his pant legs, then checked his palms to be certain his hands were clean.

A feeble smile. "Oh, I can manage. I just need to get these things hung so that they'll dry before dark."

"O'course ya can do it, but I'm glad ta help ya."

"Well, I don't doubt that you have other things to do." Grace pushed a lock of stray hair away from her eyes with the back of her hand. "When I told Sid he could send the girls here, I had no idea that Lemuel would be . . ."

Poor Grace. "I got nothin' what I need ta do fer now. I got time an' I'd rather not spend it alone an' thinkin' too much. Here, let me lift fer ya, an' you can pin. So's I don't soil them clean sheets."

Together they moved down the long double line, leaving behind two rows of white bed linens flapping in the breeze. Ben struggled to find something to say to alleviate the heavy silence without bringing up any of the current difficulties. Grace certainly didn't need more emphasis on those. At last he said, "Ya know, this puts me in mind'a sails blowin' in the wind, in the rigging high o'er a schooner."

She seemed pleasantly surprised. "Oh, yes. I can see that now that you mention it—how this would make you think of the days when you were a sailor."

A shy smile. He was grateful to hear her voice sound somewhat normal again, not quite so strained and tired. "Well, I didn't truly sail, miss. In point'a fact, I'm a seaman. Sailor ain't quite the right word. An' me ships were steamers—the large, lumberin' workhorses'a the sea." He raised the basket higher so that the corners of the sheet were less likely to tumble to the ground as she pinned.

Grace was smiling, as if his words were carrying her away for a moment. So Ben pressed further. "But I been sailin' too. An' there ain't nothin' so grand as feelin' the strong wind pressin' inta the sails, drivin' the ship 'cross the water. Nor as pretty as the white cloth billowin' out against a blue sky. So quiet, it is. Just the wind an' waves all 'round."

Grace's eyes lifted toward him. One of her eyebrows rose in concern. "Do you miss it terribly, Ben?" She'd paused, clothespin in hand, watching him for a response.

There was nothing to be gained by denying the truth. "Yes, miss, I'm 'fraid I do. Most oft at night. Whene'er I see the moon risin' in a clear sky." He hoped he hadn't shared too much detail.

He'd hate to shatter the fleeting pleasure of the moment, so he added hastily, "But I like it here too."

Grace chuckled to herself, her hands busy again. "Of course you'd say that. You're not one to complain. Are you, Ben?" Shaking the wrinkles out of the last item in the basket, Grace anchored its first corner carefully. "We haven't had much opportunity to speak lately. Everything has been quite chaotic. I'm sorry about that. I haven't been a very good friend to you."

Ya think'a me as yer friend? Clearing his throat, Ben answered carefully, "I got no reason ta complain. I been well treated here— better'n I deserve, I s'pose."

"Now, Ben. You know that's not true. I haven't even asked about your family since the first night you got back. Have you had any more word from your sister, Jane?"

"Got a call this mornin'. She was checkin' on the boy. An' shocked ta hear what happened." Grace's face was falling. Ben struggled to change the subject again. "She's plannin' a fall weddin'."

A sigh. "Oh, that's nice. You must be excited for her."

Am I? Excited? "I'm *glad* fer her, miss. I hope she'll find happiness an' start her own fam'ly. She d'serves that."

The task was complete. Grace reached for the basket. "Thank you."

"Oh, you can leave it with me. I'll watch 'em an' bring 'em in when they're dry. I can do that much."

"Thank you. I won't argue. Not today, anyway."

"When're the new kids comin'?"

"After supper. It certainly helps that they're all girls this time. That makes it easier to set up the bedrooms. With Matty and Milton off to their new family, we'll put these sisters in their room. Janie will be back in her old room, and Cass—oh, I'm sorry, Ben. But we've decided to put Castor in Freddie's old room."

"'Course ya did, miss. He ain't plannin' ta . . ." Ben fumbled to sift through thoughts that were impossible to express. At last, "I s'pose it'd be easier without us in yer way at all."

A look of shock passed over Grace's face. "Don't you believe it," she insisted. "You're not in the way at all—and neither is Janie. We're so glad to have you both here. Please, please, don't ever think of yourself as being in the way. I'd rather you both think of yourselves as family—as *belonging* here. That's how I think of you."

"Thank ya, miss." Ben's eyes fell to the basket he was carrying in his hands. Her strong response was entirely unexpected.

With a pat of his arm, Grace retreated into the house, loose strands of brown hair blowing around her face as she strode away. *She's a beauty,* Ben thought. *She's a true beauty, inside an' out.*

· · · ● · · ·

Late in the afternoon, Lemuel spoke. He merely whispered for a drink and the room sprang to life. Lillian rose to her feet, gasping. She watched as June poured a little water at a time over Lemuel's lips, her hand cupped gently under his chin. Arthur roused and leapt from his chair, then leaned across the bed and took Lemuel's hand. "Son? Lemuel?"

"Where am I?"

"You're home, darling," June reassured him. "You're back at home—in our bedroom, mine and Dad's, so we can take care of you."

The boy swallowed slowly, licked at his lips. "Where's Freddie?"

Arthur brushed back a tuft of dark hair where it stood upright at an odd angle because of the bandages still wrapped around Lemuel's wounded eye. "I'm afraid we don't know. The others weren't with you when we found you."

"They left me?"

Silence descended as concerned looks were exchanged around the room. At last Arthur replied, "I'm afraid they did, son."

Lemuel licked his lips again and muttered, "Figures." The resigned fashion in which he spoke the word tore at Lillian's heart.

Dr. Shepherd took over and began a series of medical questions. Lillian silently excused herself from the room. It seemed too personal a moment to be a bystander. Lemuel was as safe as he could be, with family surrounding him who cared deeply for him. Still, her tears fell freely as she began the walk home again.

Though she was glad to carry along the good news that Lemuel was now able to speak, Lillian dreaded the work that lay ahead of her, and the emotional investment she knew it would require. There would be three new children to welcome and to begin to understand. It would require her full attention and commitment, and yet Lillian would rather have stayed with Lemuel—even though he belonged with Arthur and June now. Her heart simply refused to let go of him.

It was a strange feeling, a vexing problem that was difficult to articulate. She found herself wishing that he would have come home to Father's house instead of theirs so that she and Grace and Miss Tilly could care for him. Blinking hard at the shocking thought, she wondered if claiming Lemuel was perhaps the first time she'd ever truly coveted. However, she had no idea how to repent of such a feeling. The contemplation of it all left Lillian feeling even more ill-equipped. How could she, at this moment, turn her interest to strangers?

* * ● ● * * *

Just after supper there came a knock at the door. Grace opened it to find the bright red coat of a Mounted Police officer. He removed his hat respectfully. "Good evening. My name is Sergeant Jernigan. Are you Miss Grace Bennett?"

208

Grace nodded and shook the man's hand. While they exchanged pleasantries, Lillian remained where she was at the base of the stairs, hands holding tightly to the banister, her whole body reluctant to step nearer.

"Well, miss, I'm here to accompany these lovely young ladies to your home. May I make the introductions?"

"Of course." Grace smiled. "Won't you all come in, please?"

Hat in hand, the sergeant led three timid girls into the entryway. Two sets of eyes remained on the floor, but the middle-sized sister seemed to defy the situation, her gaze traveling boldly around her as she investigated the foyer of this unfamiliar home. Lillian smiled weakly as their eyes met. The girl nodded in response and resumed her inspection.

Officer Jernigan continued, as if they were all simply meeting at a church event in town, "This is Mamie Voss. She's the eldest. And next comes Irma."

Irma Voss spoke aloud. "Hello." Something in the way she was refusing to be subdued by the difficult situation charmed Lillian a little. Then, almost by deliberate choice, she steeled herself against attaching too much. *We don't even know how long they'll be with us. I'll be kind, of course. But there's no sense in getting too close to them.* Ashamed, Lillian quickly rebuked the private thoughts, grateful that no one else could overhear them.

"And the youngest sister here is Ora."

"We're glad you've come to stay with us for a bit," Grace murmured gently. "We hope you'll feel at home soon."

"Thank you, ma'am," Irma said.

"I'll retrieve the bags," said the officer, excusing himself to the porch. Grace left the door standing open behind him. From her place beside the stairs, Lillian could watch Officer Jernigan opening the trunk of his police car, removing several bags.

The sisters remained in place, like three statues lined up in a row.

Grace filled the empty silence. "We have your room prepared for you, girls. I'll take you up in a minute so that you can settle in. This is my sister, Miss Lillian. And you may call me Miss Grace. We're not so formal here."

Irma's eyes moved to Miss Tilly, who had just joined them in the entryway, then turned back to Grace with a questioning look.

"And this is our dear housekeeper, Mrs. Miriam Tillendynd. But we all just call her Miss Tilly."

"Are ya hungry, gals? I got some chicken an' biscuits still in the warmer."

Two of the sisters stood silently in place. Irma spoke up. "Yes'm. We ain't had our supper yet."

"Well, follow me. We'll dish ya up some plates."

The girls trudged forward down the short hall and into the kitchen, passing where Lillian stood. She smiled again, but Irma's attention was on Miss Tilly now, and the other sisters still refused to acknowledge their surroundings. Lillian's heart stirred a little more. She wondered about their story, and what they'd been through. She hoped they'd soon be able to speak about it all, to accept the safety of their new surroundings.

With a sigh, Lillian received two cases from Officer Jernigan and followed Grace up the stairs. *Are we merely replacing Veronika? Is that how quickly it can happen? If she were to come back home tonight and find her bedroom already given back to Janie, what on earth would she say? And Freddie, should he ever return seeking his bedroom too.* Lillian shook her head to clear it of the sorrowful thoughts.

. . . • • . . .

Gradually, Lemuel began to improve. At first, Dr. Shepherd insisted that the bandages should remain in place, that the injured brain needed to be allowed a chance to recover before taxing it with the work necessary for sight. With the gauze dressing wrapped snugly around his head and eyes and it feeling very much like an executioner's blindfold, this was the strangest world Lemuel had known yet, unreal and isolated. He groped in the darkness just to fluff his own pillow or to find the chamber pot next to the bed. It was a humiliating ordeal.

After a second night's sleep in his parents' bedroom, silently enduring much discussion occurring all around him, his family decided that a place would be arranged for Lemuel in the parlor instead. A cascading array of bumps and thumps down the stairs indicated that the feather tick from the guest room was being carried down as he'd been told. They'd decided that a board could be laid across wooden crates to fashion a makeshift bed for him in the center of the parlor. With the thick brocade curtain that hung in the doorway to the parlor drawn shut, it would make a semi-private area for him. Unfortunately, this room was the only access to the stairs leading to the second floor. So he knew that Jesse and Harrison would pass through it periodically.

Next, Mr. Thompson took Lemuel's arm and lifted him to his feet, insisting that they pause for a moment to be certain he could maintain his balance. The chagrined boy felt like a cripple, wishing that they would leave him alone to fend for himself instead. He already suffered with remorse enough at the trouble he'd caused when he'd decided to pursue the pair of runaways. Returning home as an invalid buried him deeper in his feelings of guilt and shame. Surely now the Thompsons would realize how sorry they were for having adopted him. He began to wonder if Miss Grace and Miss Lillian would take him back if he were turned out again. However, even that seemed unlikely. It felt as if trouble were somehow orbiting him, no matter how hard he tried to do the right thing.

Sitting on the edge of this new bed, Lemuel listened for the sound of the curtain being drawn closed, the footsteps departing, before allowing himself permission to explore a little. He was only slightly familiar with the room. The parlor was not a place where he'd spent a great deal of time. This was a room largely kept for the purpose of entertaining guests.

First, he tried to remember where the breakable things were kept. There was a clock on the little shelf above the coal bin. He could hear it ticking dutifully. That should be easy to avoid. He recalled a china doll that stood on the table between the brocade chairs. An oil lamp sat directly behind it. And there was a row of family pictures on the mantel. They included a photograph of Lemuel receiving the science award at the end of the school year and one of Harrison in the yard, holding up a particularly large fish that he'd caught. The thought of his own image there came as a peculiar comfort. He couldn't recall having his photograph displayed in any other home he'd known.

Slowly, carefully, Lemuel felt for furniture around his new bed, trying to get a good sense of the layout of the room in relation to where he was now. He quickly realized that the area rug would prove especially helpful. So long as he could feel it under his feet, rather than the cold wood floor beneath and beyond it, he could keep from bumping his shins into furniture. It was enough information to remember for the time being. Even with so little activity, he felt oddly tired already and returned to the bed, his hands traveling over it slowly to locate his pillow and the edge of his blankets. This was a feather mattress—one of only two in the house. He and Harrison shared a straw-stuffed tick in their bedroom upstairs. Even Jesse had a straw mattress in his room. The straw beds were not nearly as decadent as sleeping on feathers. Lemuel laid himself down across it and sank in deep, felt it conform to his body, and was quickly drifting off to sleep once more.

Suddenly, he sat bolt upright. "Mum!" he called out to the vacantness around him. And a second time, louder, "Mum!"

Swift footsteps approached and the curtain swished open. "What is it, son?" This was Mr. Thompson's voice.

"I just remembered somethin'. I shoulda said so before. But I know where they're goin'."

"What? The other kids?"

"Yes, sir. They're goin' to a town called Sundre. That's where Veronika thinks she has a couple uncles. I'm sorry, sir. I shoulda thought to say so before."

Mr. Thompson cleared his throat. "That's good to know, Lemuel—where they're headed." A weary sigh escaped him. "I don't suppose those kids realize how far away Sundre is. And, unfortunately, the police already knew about that lead and have checked it out thoroughly. The uncles had lived there once, but no longer. And none of the folk in town kept in touch with them. But, still, it's very helpful to know where the kids are headed. I'll make a call to Officer Hayes right away. I'm certain that's information he'll appreciate knowing."

No uncles waitin' at the end of the road. Well, that figures too. "Yes, sir," Lemuel murmured aloud.

"Do you need anything else? Can I get you some water?"

"No, thanks. I'm all right. I'm just gonna sleep fer a bit. I'm kinda tired out now."

"That's wise. Sleep as much as you can. And please don't worry about anything, son. We'll take care of it all now. You just need to rest so that you can get better."

"Yes, sir."

"Oh, and, Lemuel, I thought you'd like to have this back." Footsteps crossed the room toward him. "It's your pocketknife. If you put out your hand, I'll give it back to you."

Lemuel raised a quick palm and felt the familiar tool pressed onto it. It was a strangely satisfying feeling to have possession of it again.

"Good night, son." The footsteps retreated across the room.

"Good night, sir."

A pause. The curtain had not been lowered again. Lemuel

remained upright, braced by his weary arms that pushed up behind him from the mattress. He was listening closely until, at last, he heard Mr. Thompson clear his throat. "Can I ask you something, Lemuel? Now that you're feeling a little bit better, I just wanted to know. Why was it that you went along with them? I mean, I think it was . . . But I just wanted to ask you directly."

Lemuel took a deep breath, dreading the confession he must make. "I didn't plan to go, sir. I'm sorry now I did. Me an' Harrison just found 'em near the bushes on the road, and I thought that maybe Freddie . . . well, he ain't such a great guy to trust. An' that girl, she's so young an' all. It didn't seem right to let 'em both go off alone. I thought I could talk 'em into goin' back—or that somebody'd find us real quick. I'm sorry I did it. Honest, I am. I just couldn't think of nothin' else to do."

The sound of movement in the room drew closer. Lemuel eased himself a little farther away, concerned that he might be in trouble for his actions. Instead, he was surprised to feel a gentle hand on his shoulder. The sensation made him shudder a little. The strained voice that followed only deepened his concern.

"Lemuel, I have to tell you that I think you're a very exceptional young man. I'm so proud of you for taking responsibility for others in an impossible situation."

These were not the words of reproof that Lemuel had expected. Hadn't he caused a considerable nuisance for the Thompsons? How could this new father be commending him?

"Your mother and I thought we would bring you into our home and begin to teach you about love." His voice broke, followed by several deep breaths. "But *you're* teaching *us*, son. You're teaching us what it is to sacrifice for the people around you. I'm proud of the young man that you are. I'm so proud to be your father."

Lemuel faltered. He wasn't certain how to respond to such unexpected emotion. "Thank you, sir," he answered warily. After all, he'd only done what he felt was unavoidable. He didn't even like Freddie or Veronika very much, and even less now that he'd been forced to spend so much time with them. Surely Mr. Thompson had misunderstood something about the situation. Would he feel differently, then, when he came to comprehend it better?

CHAPTER 19

New Ground

After the children had been put to bed on Tuesday evening, Lillian waited for Walter's expected visit. There was so much to tell him, and yet she knew that she'd prefer just to sit quietly instead, to feel a sense of peacefulness in withdrawing from the constant tumult. The knock came on the door and Lillian grabbed up her jacket. "I'm just going out for a bit. I won't be long." And before Miss Tilly could object, Lillian had joined Walter on the porch and pulled the door closed behind her.

His eyes widened in surprise.

"Could we just go for a walk tonight? Or maybe a drive? Do you mind?"

"Of course. Whatever you'd like."

Lillian rushed forward down the steps and into the car without even pausing as usual for Walter to open the door. She slid across the seat and waited for him to follow.

Walter took his place at the steering wheel, making no move to start the engine. "You seem . . . anxious. Is there somethin' wrong?"

Lillian's eyes rose to the front door. If Miss Tilly determined that their time alone would be inappropriate for some reason, she was certain to chase Lillian down. "Can we go? Please?"

"All right. I guess that's fine. We'll go into town and get dessert or somethin'."

"Sure. That's fine. Or just sit somewhere—or even drive for a while."

Walter consented without further explanation. The car rumbled into motion, faltering for only a moment as they reached the road. Then Walter turned away from town and out toward the country. Lillian sighed in relief. He'd seemed to understand her need to withdraw from the world for a little while. She snuggled her shoulder a little closer to his side, and he smiled down at her.

For a while they chatted about trivial things like the little foxes that had grown so big, the quality of this year's wheat rising up in the fields, and how Tommy's spring calves were turning out. Anything at all that didn't relate in any way to the recent tribulations or to the newest residents of their home. The land rolled past and Lillian felt herself begin to relax. It was a blissful sensation.

The sun started its retreat behind the tall evergreens around them. Lillian was well aware that it was growing late. Too late for a single man and woman to be unchaperoned on the country roads. Yet she found herself willfully disinterested in acknowledging the fact, so pleased instead to enjoy the time away with a man as entirely trustworthy as Walter.

She wondered, though, at the reason for *his* impulsiveness. It was unlike Walter to be so frivolous with his time, so whimsical in his decisions. Lillian sat forward and reached out to roll down the passenger side window, filling the car with a wild breeze that made the loose strands of her hair dance all around her face. She closed her eyes, sighing with contentment. Walter's arm around her tightened a little.

At last she felt the car slowing unexpectedly, turning down a little rutted trail just wide enough for the automobile to bounce along successfully, the tall grass swishing along under the vehicle. Lillian's eyebrows rose quickly to express her query.

"Oh, I just thought I'd show you somethin' while we're out. I've been kinda excited to bring it up, and this seemed like the perfect chance." He was wearing a broad smile, his eyes dancing.

"Show me something? Where are we?"

The car rolled over the grassy crest of a hill, and a valley view opened in front of them. The bulging hills on either side held splotches of color, emerald-toned patches of trees, yellow summer grass, and rocky gray protrusions—as if the nearby mountains were leaking out from their hiding place beneath the hills, contending with the nearby prairie for ownership of this intermediary landscape. In the bottom of the valley was a meandering creek, so clear that Lillian could see the stony bed plainly.

"What do you think, Lill?" Walter's voice had changed, had tightened with emotion.

"It's beautiful. What is this?"

He cleared his throat. "It could be . . . home. Our home."

Lillian felt a paralyzing surge of electric emotion, her mind jumbling with warring reactions. *Oh, it's so beautiful. But it's so far away. How long did we drive? More than an hour. For our home—mine and Walter's. But what about the house I have now?* Speechless, she struggled to take it all in. Then she heard him exiting the car. He held out his hand to encourage her to follow. Obediently, Lillian scooted out from under the steering wheel and took her place beside Walter. They stood together in the tall grass.

"I can just picture it," he gushed. "We could build a house over there, right on that little ridge. That way we'd get a good view of the valley but not suffer the full force of the winds that blow down off the mountains—especially in the winter. We'd run cattle down below, where they'd have the stream. And then

I'd raise hay and plant crops in that area over there." A pause. "You're not saying anything, Lillian. Are you all right?"

Lillian raised her eyes quickly. *Oh, don't be offended, Walter. How do I answer you? This is so sudden.* "I'm taking it in." She attempted a warm smile. "I'm listening to you. It is beautiful, just so beautiful."

"It really is. A rare gem. I'm praying so hard that it works out." He laughed aloud. "Do you know what? *This* is what I see in my mind now every time I close my eyes. Honest, pretty much every time I blink, I'm back here."

Oh, Walter, your heart is set on this, isn't it? How do I follow you here? My own heart feels like it's being pulled in so many directions at once.

• • • ◉ • • •

It was more difficult now for Lillian to find an excuse to visit Lemuel, to endure the conviction that she was out of place in the Thompsons' home. There was an overriding sense that they had a great amount of work to do in rebuilding their life, and Lillian felt like an unnecessary weight for them to bear in the process. Still, she longed to spend time with Lemuel each day.

On Wednesday morning it occurred to her that perhaps he'd enjoy sharing a book while he convalesced, the way they used to in the fall evenings with the original five children they'd taken in. Hazel and George were in Hope Valley with the Akerlunds. Bryony had remained in Brookfield with the Moorelands, and Harrison and Lemuel were with the Thompsons.

Favorite book in hand, Lillian closed the door behind her on her own house as she struck out the short distance down the road. Adjusting to the new girls seemed different than it had with the others. Each attempt to speak with Mamie resulted in near silence. The teenage girl's answers were as brief as possible before she'd turn away. *How will we ever help you if we can't even speak with you?*

Little Ora was even more shy. She would physically obscure her eyes behind her raised hands or, more often still, behind one of her sisters' shoulders. This behavior might be understandable in a child who was four or five, but Ora was ten.

At first, Grace had worked doggedly to be allowed into their tight little circle. But even Grace had been sidelined by the Voss sisters. It seemed that Miss Tilly was to become their chosen protector instead. Their first days were spent either in the kitchen helping or beside Miss Tilly in the garden. In fact, with only the older woman present, Lillian had overheard the girls actually interacting with one another and asking questions of the woman herself.

Privately, Grace had instructed with resolve, "Whatever works, Lillian. If they feel safer with her than us, we'll keep our distance. And Miss Tilly deserves the extra help besides. The girls are very good workers—the garden and the house have never been better kept."

As she strode along in the morning sunshine, it suddenly occurred to Lillian that perhaps Miss Tilly reminded them of their grandmother. She was certainly the closest thing to that type of relationship that the Walsh house could offer. "Bless you, girls," Lillian whispered aloud. "I hope you can be back with her soon—at the very least for a visit." And then a second thought flashed like a jolt in her mind. *What if they could speak to her on the telephone? I wonder if that could be arranged. Or they could write to her.*

Sadly, the postmark on a letter was liable to betray their location, but special delivery would not. Lillian made up her mind to speak with Grace about her ideas once she returned home.

· · · ● · · ·

It was time for the doctor to remove the bandages from Lemuel's eyes. It had been all that he could endure to keep from tearing them away on his own using his precious pocketknife, which was now safely back in his pocket. But he had dutifully resisted the urges.

During the four days that he'd worn them, he'd become comfortable making his way around his parlor bedroom, into the kitchen, and outdoors to the privy. He'd gone with Harrison a couple of times to the stables, where he spent time with the horses. The smells and sounds of that place were his greatest comfort.

He still wrestled with the memories of Freddie and Veronika, wishing they'd be found safe and wishing them retribution by turn. *How could she just leave me there? They must'a thought I was dyin'. An' I probably was.* And he worried about what had become of Star.

Dr. Shepherd had cautioned Lemuel often about the seriousness of his injuries while Lemuel had been impatiently waiting. The doctor had laughed once, patted him on the shoulder reassuringly, and stated, "After all, young man, it was a rock to the noggin that took down that giant Goliath."

Lemuel just wanted the bandages to come off so that he could resume life the way it had been before he'd gone after the wayward pair of kids.

Now he sat on one of the kitchen chairs, drawn up next to the large kitchen window so that the doctor could have as much light as possible to examine him by.

"I'm here, Lemuel. On your left," his mum encouraged from close to his side. "Dr. Shepherd is in front of you and his nurse is to your right. They're getting their equipment ready to cut the bandages away. Dad is standing by the stove. Jesse and Harrison are over near the sink. We're all here for you." Mum had been his best caregiver, chattering aloud about who came and went from the room he was in, explaining all that was going on around him as naturally as if it were something she'd always done. His darkness had been softened by his mother's efforts. Lemuel reached out for her hand despite the sense that the action might make him appear weak. At this moment, it seemed worth the risk, even necessary.

There was a tugging and the sound of scissors. Then the layers were carefully unwrapped. Lemuel resisted the urge to lift his hand to feel his head, squeezing tighter to his mum's hand instead. The last bandage was gingerly peeled away, accompanied by several pinching sensations as it released from the raw skin beneath it. At last he was free of all the layers.

Slowly he opened his eyes. Light from the window pierced them, and he clamped them shut again. More slowly still he began to allow bits of daylight in, a little at a time. The room came into view, fuzzy and spectral. He recognized the vague shape of a white-aproned man in front of him.

"How well can you see, son? Can you make out my face?"

There was a pink blur hovering above the white before him. One slow blink at a time and the blur developed eyes and a mouth. Lemuel began to relax a little. "I see yer shirt. I see yer face a little."

"That's very good. Can you tell me how many fingers I'm holding up?"

His eyes tracked the movement in front of him. Lemuel was certain he could make out a pair of digits held up above the fist. "Two?"

"That's right. How about now?"

"Four."

"Yes, that's good, Lemuel. That's very good."

The room behind the doctor was beginning to emerge. The black of the stove gradually came into focus until there were distinct sides and a top—even the teakettle sitting near the back.

Then the soft green of the walls grew patches of hanging pictures and the corner of the hutch. Finally, the shape of Mr. Thompson became distinct from the rest of it all.

"I can see you, Dad." With Lemuel's deep relief, the word slipped out before he was able to consider its implications.

Mr. Thompson's shape grew larger. His voice was tight with emotion. "I'm so glad, son. So very glad."

Lemuel felt a hand on his right shoulder and turned toward it. But something was wrong. He turned his head again, back and forth. "Doc Shepherd?"

"Yes?"

"I can see what I'm lookin' straight at, but it gets blurry to the side."

The man before him leaned closer, concern drawing his eyebrows together. "Which side, Lemuel?"

"The right side." That was the eye that had been injured.

Moving a little at a time, Dr. Shepherd tested the extent of Lemuel's sight. He quickly determined that the injured eye had not healed completely, that the peripheral vision had been diminished. Lemuel could see well through the uninjured left eye. He could see normally through the range of vision on the right until he was just past the center of his view. At that point, the shapes grew fuzzier and fuzzier until they faded to black.

Mr. Thompson's deep voice from the shadow of Lemuel's right asked, "Will it continue to heal?"

"We can't be sure. I wish I could give you a better answer than that. But I've seen some amazing things. The capacity for the body to repair itself, for the brain to adapt over time, can be nothing short of miraculous. And it's a good sign that you have as much sight as you have so quickly after taking off the bandages. I would expect at least some improvement to follow, even today. I'm just not certain how much."

Lemuel peered up toward the doctor again, and his mind

began to calculate what it would be like to have only the sight that he could manage now. How much would that hinder his future? Would he be able to ride horseback without running into obstacles hidden from view? Would he be able to farm alongside the others without risking further injury? And what about his dream of becoming a doctor someday? Would that dream be extinguished too?

He lowered his head and bit hard on his tongue to keep the tears from forming. *I knew it wouldn't work out for me. I knew it.*

· ·• ·•◦•· •· ·

News that Lemuel's bandages had been removed and that the results had caused a mix of joy and concern reached the Walsh home quickly. Harrison delivered the information, once more out of breath from his haste. Ben had just returned in the automobile from a long drive to visit his family. From the open barn door, he'd watched the familiar eleven-year-old boy leap up the stairs of the front porch and in through the door, not bothering to knock. Without hesitation, Ben had hurried to the house himself, concerned about any news that needed to be delivered so rapidly. His thoughts turned immediately to Freddie. Was there an update?

Ben entered the back door just as Harrison's boisterous announcement filled the home from the front. "Lemmy can see! 'Cept 'e can't see so good in 'is right eye. Doc says it might get better. But 'e ain't sure yet."

The reactions that Ben could hear as he slipped off his work boots in the mudroom were varied. Female voices exclaimed one after another, "Thank God!" "Oh dear." "How poor is his vision?"

"That's all I know," the boy insisted. "'Cept that it's so good ta see Lemmy walkin' again, not feelin' 'is way like a blind man."

Ben hurried up the hallway just as Harrison excused himself rather abruptly and headed back out the door, leaving a brooding silence behind. Unwilling to disturb the tumbling thoughts with which the women were grappling, Ben held his tongue. This was both pleasing and serious news.

At last Miss Tilly ventured, "Well, he's alive. He's healthy. He's home again with those who love him. So much ta be grateful fer in that."

"That's true," Lillian answered slowly. "We've much to be thankful for."

Grace squeezed her hands together, interlacing her fingers and raising them up to press against her forehead. Ben could see the turmoil that was taking place in her mind. It showed in the little groan that escaped her lips, the tension of her raised shoulders, and the pinched expression on her face. Then Grace released her clenched hands and covered her face with them instead before lowering them at last to announce, "It's not enough. I'm sorry, it's not enough. It's not that I'm not grateful—I'm so, so glad for all of it. But I'm not satisfied with this outcome. I'm going to keep praying that he'll be fully healed. I just feel that God has more in store for him. Maybe it's just because I love Lemuel so much—but then again, God loves him more, much more, than I. So this time, I'm just not going to stop praying yet. I'm going to believe that there's more to come."

Silence followed. It was broken by Miss Tilly, who dusted her hands on her apron and nodded. "If ya feel the Spirit leadin' ya to pray more, then ya best do just that. Don'tcha give in b'fore God gives ya the nudge. We'll all join ya, dearie. Won't we?"

Lillian nodded her assent quickly. Janie, who'd been peeping out from the parlor in the row of interested children, crossed the room to stand beside Ben, lifting her large blue eyes up to his. "We'll pray too, won't we, Mr. Waldin?"

Ben squirmed for a good answer. Yet there was no way out. So he nodded in agreement, promising that he too would offer up prayers for the sake of the young man. Turning and walking away as the little group dispersed, Ben wondered how he would accomplish such a task and what possible good his participation could do.

During the long afternoon as he completed his work on a larger coop for the chickens, he wondered why Grace had spoken that way about praying. Was this a tantrum she had determined to throw against the most powerful Being in the universe? Such a thing was entirely out of character for the dear woman he'd come to know, and would hardly have been approved by the likes of Miss Tilly. So what gave Grace the audacity to refuse to accept the apparent results of all of their previous prayers? Did she feel she knew more than the Almighty about what was right for this boy? Or was there something more that she was leaning into, some understanding that she had of how God acted that Ben had never observed someone call upon previously? It was ponderously difficult for his mind to understand.

CHAPTER 20

Forward

Lillian, I'd like us to have supper with your dad and Delyth. Do you think you could get away tomorrow night, if it works for them?"

Lillian had been attempting to avoid Father ever since learning about Delyth's pregnancy. She cringed at Walter's suggestion. "I'm not sure. The new girls are still just settling in. I'm not certain it's the right time to—"

"I already asked Grace. She said it'd be okay."

Walter was pressing this request. That was unusual for him. Lillian wondered what he planned to accomplish with the meal. "Oh, well, you see . . . Grace would never tell you no outright, Walter. But she might still need my help with the meal and things. We've been anxious to begin doing devotions with the children again in the evenings. We let that practice slip when we were all so focused on finding the lost kids. And I promised to accompany them all on the piano." Even in Lillian's own ears, it sounded like a rather hollow excuse. Miss Tilly handled the bulk of the care for the Voss sisters—overall they were far more help than they were work, and the children could easily sing a cappella during their evening devotions for a night. Lillian and Grace had already discovered that the three new girls had lovely voices, though it had been difficult at first to coax them to join in.

"I'm sure she wouldn't mind for one night." Then Walter asked softly, "Is there some reason you're avoidin' your dad, Lill?"

Lillian turned her face away from Walter while she struggled for an answer. The children were playing in the yard on this Thursday evening. She could watch them easily from where she and Walter were seated on the front porch steps. Irma was pushing Janie on the swing. Her own little sister, Ora, was mothering the rag doll that Miss Tilly had stitched up for her. Mamie sat on the grass beside Ora, plucking up a few blades at a time, staring off toward the road beyond the bushes.

It was so difficult to put her emotions into words. Even for as often as Lillian had tried to sort through them in her own mind, the thoughts seemed disjointed and elusive. Instead of answering his question, she whispered, "I ache for them, Walter. These girls seem to be struggling much more than the others did. Even Veronika, though she acted out, didn't feel so . . . so far away."

"The new girls? They're very quiet. I noticed that."

"It's more than just quiet, Walter. They don't trust us. They're like little birds that have fallen from the safety of their nest. They still need to be nurtured by somebody. But how on earth does a person show them love when they're not even able to trust yet? I can carry on a conversation with Irma, but we're all well aware of the fact that it doesn't mean she's not hurting too. Her eyes are just—I can't really describe it—just fractured. Something deep inside her is broken. I haven't gotten more than a couple words from Mamie—and *nothing* at all from Ora." Lillian paused contemplatively. "Maybe it's because the others have lost their parents to death. It's a cruel fact, but one that carries the weight of permanence. These girls want nothing more than to go back home to a grandmother who loves them and raised them. So how can they suffer through their time here with us instead?"

"I understand, I really do. And you know I support everything you do here for these kids. You know that, right?" Walter's words were slowly whispered and tender.

Lillian's mind flooded with all the time and effort he'd sacrificed while looking for Veronika and Freddie and Lemuel. She turned her face up toward him, searching his brown eyes for recognition of how highly she regarded him. "Of course I do, Walter. We all appreciate it so much. And no one more than I. Not just what you've done to help, but being someone I can talk with about it all. I can't imagine going through all this without you."

His head dipped lower, the lines of his smile spreading on his face. "Well, I'm glad that's how you feel."

"You know I do."

His eyes twinkled back. "Then how about you come away with me for just one night? I'd have thought you'd be glad to have supper with your dad. I know how much you've missed him. Is it because of Delyth? You still feel strange around her?"

Still? It's only been three weeks, Walter. So, yes, I still feel uncomfortable around this stranger who's married to my father—especially now. It occurred to Lillian that it might be best to share with Walter what she'd overheard. It would likely make her reluctance more reasonable. "I have to tell you something. It feels a little like gossip—and I don't want it to be like that."

"I've never known you to be a gossip."

"Well, I certainly try to avoid it. And I haven't said anything to *anybody* else. But the truth is, I saw Delyth in town last week, and she was shopping for . . . for fabric for a baby layette."

Walter showed no sign of understanding.

"Delyth . . . is expecting . . . a baby."

At last Walter drew in a long breath that demonstrated his comprehension.

They sat for a moment in silence. Lillian fought the urge to flee in shame, even from Walter.

"Well . . . I think we should be glad for them. Don't you think?"

How on earth can I explain this to him? This time her own words came slowly as she labored over them. "Walter, my father is in his fifties. It's embarrassing enough that people in town know he came home with such a young bride."

"Oh, Lill, it's not like she's seventeen or anything. She's in her thirties. She's older than you and me."

Lillian pursed her lips. She managed to keep her voice low and controlled. "Yes, as you say, she's closer in age to his *daughter* than to his first wife."

"Hmm. I didn't look at it like that."

"I'm certain people are talking."

"Oh, people always talk." Walter ducked his head again, trying to make eye contact, as if prompting Lillian to smile. "We can't be bothered by what *people* think. You'd have never brought all these kids here if that was how you made decisions."

Lillian shrugged off his comment. "Well, how would you feel if your father was going to have a new baby? Can you imagine how you'd feel about that? Not another niece or nephew in your family—but a little brother or sister."

This seemed to strike a chord. "All right, I see that. I suppose I'd feel kind of sheepish about announcin' that to the world too. Is that what you're reluctant to talk about with him?"

"I have no idea how I'll manage. I can't even bring myself to tell Grace."

They sat in brooding silence. Lillian watched Ora take a turn on the swing while Mamie pushed her. Janie had run off to play with Cass in the tree fort.

At last Lillian ventured quietly, trying to keep her voice from breaking, "I'm a little bird that fell out of my nest too, Walter."

"Oh, sweetheart, what do you mean?" His face moved closer as he leaned forward.

"I'm so much like them. My happy little childhood was shattered by losing my first parents." Lillian tucked her feet closer beneath her, dropping her head down toward her knees and folding her arms around them. She'd rarely spoken so openly to Walter about such feelings. "I look at them, and I *feel* all those things again. If I look too closely into their eyes, it's as if I see my own reflection there. I can't describe it. In fact, I don't really want to try any harder."

She felt a gentle hand on her back, sliding slowly up to caress the arch of her neck. "That's what makes you so good at what you do here—you and Grace. You both know what it's like."

Lillian scrunched her eyes tight to keep the tears at bay. "But did you know the truth is that it hurts me to love them? It means being willing to see that reminder of my own broken childhood in front of me day in and day out. It would be so much easier just to walk away from all this. I'm struggling to force myself to try to build relationships with the new girls. I feel I'm more like an impersonal machine right now—just going through the motions of caring for them."

The pause that followed swelled with significance. Lillian's deepest feelings had been spoken aloud. She wondered exactly what he'd perceive that she intended by articulating them. Would he assume she was glad to be given a way out by marrying him? Because that wasn't what she'd meant at all. She found herself wishing that she'd never spoken the thoughts aloud.

Walter's fingers brushed against her cheek. "That's who you are, Lillian. It's how you love. With all your heart and soul. Just like you loved your mum. It's why you simply had to find your sister once you heard that she might still be alive. You amaze me. More and more all the time."

Lillian released the hold she had on her knees and raised her head, sinking back against Walter. "Thank you," she whispered. "Thank you for listening and really hearing me."

. . . ● . . .

Having spent two long weeks of searching through the foothills, Ben was at a loss now with nothing to do but remain at home. There was plenty of work around the Walsh house, but his heart was no longer in it. He found himself staring into space instead, wondering where the boy was now, if he'd been able to find Veronika, if they were safe.

If worry for the missing children wasn't distracting his mind, then he was plagued by the sense of guilt he felt for knowing where his family was living now but still remaining apart from them. However, what were his options? There was no room for little Janie and him at Lloyd Pender's tidy prairie farm—neither in the fine home that Lloyd would share with Jane nor the little cabin where his parents would soon live. And Ben had none of the skills necessary to work alongside Dada as he set up his tinsmithing business. It felt like a farce to even become involved—inserting himself into the good fortunes of the moment when he'd abandoned them all during their difficult times.

Bringing the axe down hard into the meaty white center of a log destined for the stack of firewood that fed the ever-hungry woodstove, Ben's mind went back to Freddie. He missed the boy terribly, missed his company and his ideas. Traps and hunting and shelters in the woods—all this seemed to be constantly swirling in the boy's mind. "I hope yer doin' well with it now, lad. I hope yer thrivin' there."

The money—well, that could be replaced. With enough time Ben could earn it back again. And then? Would he ever truly settle in a place of his own nearby with little Janie? Should he attempt a move to Denholm instead? Or was it enough to visit his family weekly and focus on the important relationships that he'd achieved here in this place? Heaven forbid that the boy would return and discover that Ben was gone!

The axe froze in midair above Ben's head. Then he lowered its head to the ground as a new thought connected all of the others: the worries about the missing teenager, the pain of feeling responsible for his family yet unable to care for them properly. Was this how Dada had felt?

Ben loosened his grip on the axe handle, and it slid lifelessly to the ground among the wood chips he'd created. He slumped onto the upright log that he'd been using as a chopping block. How many years had passed between when he'd run away at fourteen and now? For all that time was *this* the burden that Dada had been carrying in his heart? Was this the pain that he'd been silently tending? "No wonder," he uttered aloud. "No wonder he can't bear ta look't me."

Drawing his crumpled handkerchief from his pocket, Ben wiped at the sweat on his face, trying to figure out a way to set everything right again.

· · ● · · ·

Lillian requested that she and Walter walk into town to meet Father and Delyth for the meal that had been arranged. There was no reason to drive such a short distance when the summer evening was blessed with a cool breeze from off the mountains. She smiled up at him as he took her hand and they struck out together. However, she found conversation difficult. Walter seemed to comprehend her reticence fairly easily, not seeking an explanation but merely giving gentle support. It was such a delight to have him nearby again, to be able to communicate with each other with just an exchanged glance or a gentle touch. *What a gift he's been in my life! What would I do without Walter?*

Father had made a reservation at the hotel in town. During their main course, conversation among their little group remained comfortable. First Lillian gave an update on Lemuel's condition, which was met with genuine concern. Next, Delyth gushed about progress on their little house and Father explained how they would soon be traveling west by train to see the Rockies and the Canadian coast.

"That'll be an amazin' trip." Walter sat forward in his seat, anxious for more information. "I know they're buildin' up those rails as fast as they can—but never fast enough. I met a few men who'd worked on them when I was at the oil rig. Do you know if they've finished the spiral tunnels for Kicking Horse Pass yet?"

Father said confidently, "Yes, they have. And that's just the place where we'll travel through. It's a marvel of modern technology! Mankind has begun to subdue even the mountains, which almost sounds like a holy pursuit."

But Lillian allowed her mind to drift away, grateful that Walter was holding Father's attention so that she could have a moment to her private thoughts. She watched how Delyth's eyes remained on Father's face, only periodically turning toward Walter as she added a comment of her own now and then. *Is it somehow possible that Delyth feels about Father the way I feel about Walter?*

Still, Lillian was certain that the conversation would soon turn to their impending baby announcement. She wondered if Father would seem embarrassed at such a confession. Yet, he hadn't been reluctant to introduce this young woman as his wife. So Lillian doubted that the expected child would give him pause. She took her time over her meal, cutting her roast beef into far smaller bites than necessary, playing with the fresh greens as a way of avoiding eye contact, only half listening.

At last, Father cleared his throat. "I'm told, Lillian, that while you were shopping in town you overheard information that we'd been keeping to ourselves for some time."

Her eyes lifted obediently, but she tried to keep her thoughts from being too easy to read. "Yes, I believe I did."

"Well then, I'm glad to take this occasion to talk about it openly. Delyth is expecting a child in December."

Walter gave his hearty congratulations, which helped to conceal Lillian's more tepid response. However, Father was undaunted.

"What do you think, dear? That you'll finally have a little brother or sister?"

Lillian cringed. She wanted to blurt back, "*I already* have *a little sister. Her name is Grace.*" Instead, she held her tongue and dropped her face again to her plate for a moment.

Delyth spoke next, laying a hand on Father's arm. "Of course, Elliott hasn't forgotten about Gr-race. He simply means that 'twould be the gift of a sibling from himself, you see?"

"Yes, yes. That's what I meant to say." The inference of his remark seemed to be lost on Father, his grin unwavering.

Swallowing down a desire to groan, Lillian asked, "How are you feeling, Delyth? Have you been sick at all?"

"Oh yes! The voyage over was a disaster, to be sure. But we managed, didn't we?"

"You were as brave as a man can ask of his wife." Father laid his free hand on top of Delyth's affectionately.

Lillian felt her stomach turn as he spoke the words. *That's just what he used to say to Mother—"you're as brave as a man can ask of his wife." How can he use the very same words to another woman? And to a woman merely having a child, not one suffering through a long and unbearable illness.* Lillian turned frantic eyes up toward Walter. This was not going well.

He seemed to take the hint. "Land sakes, when my sister Lydia was expectin', it was all she could do to keep anything down. Hope you're feelin' better now though."

"Oh yes, much better."

Without allowing for a pause Walter inquired, "And how about your trip by rail? Do you think that'll be difficult in your delicate condition?"

Delyth smiled in a way that seemed a little patronizing to Lillian. "I come fr-rom good stock, I do. And I've done plenty of tr-raveling for all my life. I think I'll be fine. But if not, Elliott's agreed to br-ring me home again by car."

Lillian achieved a strained smile, hoping that discussion of the pregnancy had been dutifully accomplished. She was relieved as the waiter appeared over Father's shoulder with the dessert menus and the conversation focused on far safer issues of which pie to choose and whether to have tea or coffee with dessert.

Mercifully, the topics that followed remained comfortable. Lillian found herself beginning to relax over dessert. Then, just after the check had been placed next to Father, Delyth produced a small package from somewhere under the table. It was the shape of a thin book.

"I made it for you, Lillian—on the ship as we cr-rossed the ocean. I wanted to show you in some little way how much I admire all the work you're doing for the childr-ren."

What on earth? With exaggerated caution, Lillian raised the package, hardly brave enough to hold it in her hands. "Thank you," she managed, then turned her eyes up at Walter.

"That's very nice, Delyth. Can she open it now?"

"Of course. We'd like to watch as you do, Lillian."

Gingerly, she pulled away the folds of paper where they'd been pasted neatly. Instead of a book, Lillian found a small picture frame that displayed a neatly stitched Bible verse with pink and red flowers all around it. She read the verse aloud: "'And whoso shall receive one such little child in my name receiveth me. Matthew 18:5.'"

Lillian smiled, but before she could speak her thanks, Delyth had begun gushing. "I know you work so hard for these childr-ren. What you do is just so important, and so few are gifted in the ways you are. We're just so pr-roud of you."

Lillian managed, "Thank you." Her eyes traveled from Delyth's glowing face to Father's. She'd always wanted so badly for him to feel proud of her. She longed to know that he could understand the deep reasons for it all, the significance of what she and Grace were trying to accomplish. *After all, Father is making sacrifices too. He gave up his own home so that Grace and I would have a stable place to live with the children. Surely he's done so because he knows how important it is, and not just so that Delyth can have a different home than he shared with Mother.* Father's deep-set eyes didn't hold quite the affirmation that Lillian wanted to read there. His smile was light and rather facile. Mother had always been the one who understood the complexities of life—even though he seemed to try his best.

Instead, Lillian turned toward Walter, who was certain to understand, and instantly she noted the pride in his eyes. Walter had shared much of the road that she and Grace had traveled. And yet it occurred to Lillian that it was Walter who was also drawing her away from it all in order to make a new life elsewhere. Her eyes retreated to the table and the gift.

She tucked the frame back inside the folds of paper. "Thank you, Delyth. It's just beautiful. Thank you."

"Maybe you can put it up in the foyer," Father suggested.

Lillian imagined that idea. It felt a little like that would be tooting their own horn. She wondered what Grace and Miss Tilly would think about such a plan—how it would be interpreted by the children.

"It's beautiful. I'm certain it took you hours to stitch. I'll treasure it. Thank you."

Father was bursting with enthusiasm. "We wanted to make something for you that could remind you of our support—how much we value the work that you're doing at our house."

Lillian tipped her head to one side a little, allowing herself to process the comments before attempting a response.

Father continued, "You're different, Lillian. Or I just didn't see it before. But you're an experienced woman now, independent and confident."

Oh, Father, if you only knew. I'm not either of those things at all.

"I'm proud of you, my dear. And I can say without a moment's hesitation that your mother would be just as pleased as she could be to see you now. Caring for orphans, in the home she watched over so well—giving up so much to serve others."

Walter squeezed Lillian's hand beneath the table. She took a deep breath and exhaled slowly. "Thank you, Father," she whispered, fighting to keep her voice under control. "I'll find this needlework a place of honor. Thank you."

"It makes all the difference," Delyth added. "It's much easier to for-rfeit your own desires if it's for someone you love. Just like I gave up my home in Wales—and my family too—to be with your father. Love matter-rs most of all."

On the walk home, Lillian wondered silently what would become of the framed verse. Would it stay with the house if she were to move to Walter's homestead? That seemed the most reasonable assumption. And it seemed clear that most of Mother's possessions would remain there as well. Her soul began to grieve already at the thought.

CHAPTER 21

Relationships

It was Sunday morning now, the first day of August. It had been about a week since Lemuel had returned, since the Voss sisters had moved into the Walsh house—and still no word regarding Freddie. Ben had been told that the Mounted Police had taken over the case—and by now Ben half wished that the boy would outwit them, using the money in the sock to chase down his dreams of a better life. But the girl, that was a more difficult problem. She was alone and unguarded, unless Freddie had managed to catch up to her.

Ben kept his usual distance from the main house, frittering away his time in the barn. The family would soon be off, walking the short distance to the nearby house of worship. Then Ben would head indoors to eat a late breakfast before settling down on a chair in the parlor for a rare chance to read while the house was quiet. Or he might take his book to the old haystack behind the barn to laze with the foxes. There was a wonderful library in Lillian's house. He'd been hungry to take advantage of any time he could find to read. And in the last few weeks those moments had been impossible to find.

The sound of the barn door rattling open interrupted his plans. A loud voice followed. "Ben Waldin, I got a bone ta pick with ya." It was Miss Tilly, standing on the threshold of the barn door, wearing her best dark dress and a little straw hat. Her gray hair was tucked up more tightly than usual.

"Ma'am?" he answered with wide eyes.

"Now, I ain't said nothin' 'bout yer not wantin' ta go ta our church. How ya worship, well, that's yer own business. An' I know ya ain't settled yer faith in yer own heart as yet. I been prayin' 'bout that, an' trustin' God's got a plan fer ya still."

Ben held back an amused smile as the motherly woman scolded out these words, knowing full well how certainly she lived them out in loving ways. However, he dared not allow his mirth to show.

Miss Tilly continued, "But I ain't gonna stand fer ya influencin' none'a them kids away from God. No, sir. I ain't gonna stand by quiet fer that."

This time Ben couldn't hide his reaction. "No, but I . . . I mean . . . What'd I say? What'd I do?"

"That Janie. She's been pesterin' the sisters fer weeks ta be able ta stay here with you. Now, they ain't ne'er said a word to ya 'bout that. An' I held my peace too. But this mornin' she's just got it inta her head ta stay home. An' no, sir, we can't have that, can we? Ya wouldn't want that on yer conscience."

"I'll speak with her."

"Well, ya need ta see to it ya do. We're 'bout ready ta leave." With a huff and a nod of rebuke, Miss Tilly exited the barn.

Ben ran a hand through his unruly waves of hair. *Janie don't wanna go ta church? An' it's cause'a me. No, we can't have that.* Miss Tilly was right. Something must be done. He dusted off his trousers and made a move toward the house in order to speak with Janie. *Naw, that ain't gonna work. She's too tough'a little kid, an' she won't abide me an' her havin' two diff'rent rules.* Immediately he knew what must be done in order to have the proper influence. Still, he dragged his feet.

"Well, God, guess my mam's prayers've been answered at last. I ain't gonna be the cause'a that child turnin' her back on religion. No, sir. You an' me, we're gonna need ta make peace somehow, I guess."

He owned very little that would qualify as church clothes. However, in this region of farming families, he was well aware that many others would be humbly clad as well. So Ben dressed himself in the best garments he had to wear, shaved so quickly he nicked himself twice, and, last of all, dipped a comb into the water left in the basin in order to slick back his hair. Then he hurried to the house, where the others had already gathered in the parlor.

Janie was first to draw everyone's attention to Ben's presence. "What're you doing, Mr. Waldin? How come you're dressed up too?"

He felt the weight of their eyes, though he deliberately avoided Miss Tilly's. "I'm goin' ta church with ya all this mornin'. Thought it'd be nice ta join ya."

Janie drew closer and took his hand. Her face was quizzical for a flash, but that promptly faded to contentment.

Lillian patted his arm as she passed on by, but Grace leaned nearer and raised her face up closer to his ear to whisper, "I'm so glad to have you with us, Ben. I've always hoped you'd join us."

As he sat on the long pew with the others, Ben tried hard not to fidget. But in the moment when he managed to keep his knee from bouncing up and down, his fingers began to tap against his thigh. And when he recognized and resolved that problem, his right boot began to knock against the left. It seemed impossible to keep all parts of his body still at one time. And everything he'd always despised about going to church as a boy came rushing back. He could almost feel his mother's disappointed gaze and hear the harsh rebukes he'd so often received from his father once they'd returned home.

Without warning, Janie rose from her place next to Ben and slid up onto his lap, resting her head against his shoulder. Ben went rigid. This was unacceptable behavior. A child should be seen and not heard—especially in church. She should be seated on the bench, eyes forward, hands folded in her lap. *What on earth will Miss Tilly have ta say 'bout this trespass upon propriety?*

His gaze darted sideways toward her. Miss Tilly merely nodded in return. *What on earth? This type'a behavior—is it tolerated here?* At last Ben's body began to relax, to appreciate the moment of stillness with Janie. But his mind continued to work over this contradiction. In his peripheral vision, he began to notice other families with children around him. Mothers held preschoolers in their laps. Several fathers had stretched their arms out on the back of the bench, allowing their older children to nestle against them.

Ben slowly realized that he'd been so distracted by his own need to control himself that he hadn't observed anyone else around him. It seemed these people had no rule against showing affection to one's own child during a church service. He found himself wondering if perhaps that particular commandment might be one that had not come down from his heavenly Father above. The idea was an unexpected revelation. It made him wonder if perhaps some of his other conclusions about God were based on his own background, and not so much upon truth.

This new notion reminded him of a Bible story he'd read as a child. The little children had been brought to Jesus and, rather than turning them away, He'd welcomed them. Ben felt a smile soften his face just a little, then cleared his throat and managed to stifle his emotions once more, doubting that any church would go so far as to allow smiling during the service. The next time he spoke by telephone with Jane he'd have to see if she'd noticed this difference as well.

· · · ● · · ·

Lemuel pressed the edge of the curry comb deeper into Mirabella's mane, trying to coax out the stubborn burrs that had embedded themselves there. It was good to be allowed to work with the horses again. His dad, though, was always in the vicinity just in case. For a teenage boy, this called into question what the man feared might happen in his absence, but Lemuel had given up resisting. It even felt secretly affirming to have someone watching out for his welfare so persistently after his recent experiences.

He'd begun to grow accustomed to the limits of his vision, testing them from time to time to see if his range might be improving slightly as Dr. Shepherd had hoped. It was impossible to tell. There was still an area to his right that remained in shadow. How much it seemed to improve day by day was open to debate.

"Are you finished with the filly?"

"Almost."

"She looks much better. I don't know where she picked up so many stickers."

Lemuel stepped back to admire Mirabella. This horse was still his favorite, though his mind went back to Star and he hoped again that she was safe—perhaps even back home with her owner.

"Can I talk with you for a moment?" It was a strange question for his new father to ask.

Lemuel set the comb on top of the broad rail and exited the stall. "'Course, do ya need somethin' else done, sir?"

"No, son. I just wanted to chat with you for a couple minutes. Let's take a seat here on these bales."

Lemuel lowered himself cautiously onto the straw, trying not to make eye contact with his dad.

"We haven't really talked about what happened, son. Your mother thought that . . . no, I don't mean to say it that way. Your mother and I discussed how we might be able to help you work through some of the things you're feeling. She's better than I am at that kind of thing, but I wanted a chance to talk about it, man to man."

A covert smile. The words sounded forced and unnatural to Lemuel—as if his dad had switched roles and become the principal instead. *What's he wanna ask me?*

"I'll be direct, if you don't mind." A thick, workworn hand patted Lemuel's leg. "Son, you've had more than your share of misfortune. Most folks struggle with making sense of life with one or two of the kinds of things that have happened to you. We're concerned about how you're coping with this new difficulty— with the loss of some of your sight. But we want—even need—to be sure you know you can talk to us about anything." He chuckled to himself a little.

Turning his head sideways, Lemuel tried to understand what might be amusing at such a serious moment.

"I'll admit that I'm not good at this, Lemuel. I wasn't good at it with your older brothers either. They used to joke about 'having a talk with dad.' But I think it's important to stumble through it . . . if you're willing."

"Sure." The boy nodded, hoping that he could expend as few words as possible in response and still be satisfactory.

"How do you feel about what happened with Freddie? About your decision to go with them and the way they treated you?"

Lemuel pursed his lips. How on earth could all of these emotions be summarized quickly? "It weren't right what he did. I mean, the girl didn't s'prise me, but Freddie an' me were s'posed to be friends."

"That's true. It was a dreadful thing for him to leave you behind. Without God's intervention leading us to you when He did, you would likely have died there."

"Yeah, I know."

His dad shifted positions. "What would you say to Freddie if he were standing right here with us now?"

"Erm, I dunno."

"Will you try, Lemuel? To put into words how you feel about him?"

It was uncomfortable to think about, and even harder to verbalize. He squirmed as he answered, "I guess I'd tell him it was a rotten thing to do—shootin' me. Buryin' me in leaves an' then jus' leavin' me there."

"It was. It was a dreadful thing."

"I don't remember it though. When I got hit by the rock, it jus' went black. Next thing I knew, I was alone an' shiverin'."

"You were knocked unconscious but you awoke in the woods? I didn't know that."

"Yeah, I guess. An' I kep' fallin' back to sleep. I couldn't keep me eyes open, couldn't really see anyhow. An' I couldn't move. I jus' figured I was dyin', is all."

"Oh, Lemuel. I'm so sorry. I didn't know that."

"An' then I woke up when that dog was barkin'. Next I saw you an' I knew you'd get me outta there. Even if it hurt fer ya to move me, I was sure you'd get me home all right. This time I wasn't goin' to be left all alone—this time."

"I'm glad, son. I want to be the kind of dad that you know you can count on."

With just a slow nod in response, Lemuel wondered if his first father had been the kind of person a boy could count on. He really had no memories of that man. In spite of everything, Lemuel had always figured that his first father couldn't reasonably be blamed for dying unexpectedly. However, clearly, the farmer he'd first been placed with had not been that kind of dependable man at all.

"Sir?"

"Yes, son?"

"Can I tell ya somethin'?"

"Of course. Anything."

"Don't be too hard on Freddie, sir. He's hurtin' too—like me. I heard him say that his first dad burned their house down—an' all his brothers an' sisters were killed."

"What?"

"That's what he said. Maybe he was lyin'. I dunno. But, anyway, I tried to remember that with Freddie. He was jus' tryin' to figure stuff out too. It ain't easy after yer first family dies."

No response. Lemuel wondered if Mr. Thompson would prefer not talking about such uncomfortable things. Maybe there was a limit to what he really wanted to hear. Turning just enough to peek at his new dad's face, Lemuel saw that the graying head was bowed. Dad's jaw seemed clenched, and he was pinching at his eyes.

So Lemuel decided to soften his too-candid response. "Maybe it's kinda like this, sir. Kinda like how I can't see so well."

After he cleared his throat, Dad's tightened voice asked, "What do you mean?"

Lemuel sighed, looking toward Mirabella's stall. "I guess I can think like him, like Freddie, more'n you do. An' I had a lotta time to work it out through these last days. I figure that bein' an orphan is kinda like me bein' blind on one side. Ya feel like there's always stuff ya can't see that other folk do, an' it's hard not to imagine sad or scary things're hidin' there. So when somebody says they love ya, ya wonder what ya can't see 'bout that, what it really means. Mostly yer like other people and everybody else might think ya look the same, 'cept everybody else can see that part of the world that you can't—and maybe, somehow, it's yer own fault. So you're always kinda spinnin' in circles, tryin' to look around to find what yer missin'. It gets tirin' sometimes. And sometimes it can make ya mad. I dunno, but I think Freddie's kinda blind like that too."

A shuffling sound came from beside Lemuel. His father reached an arm around Lemuel's shoulders and drew him close. For a few embarrassing moments he sat still while the man seemed to be catching his breath or something.

At last Dad spoke in a husky voice. "Lemuel, I'm so glad you talked to me about this. I've learned a great deal from you today. I hope we can talk often. But mostly, I just want to tell you that . . . well, it's my hope that with every year that passes from now on, you'll grow to trust me more and more. And I'll grow to know you better and better. Because I've never met another person in my life like you. You are an amazing young man, Lemuel. Just amazing."

· · · ● · · ·

Ben had begun a practice of walking deeper into the woods behind the house after the day's work had been completed. It had started naturally enough—just a way to put the complexities of the ever-changing family dynamics and the current difficulties behind him for a while, to clear his head. But gradually he'd become aware that he was being followed. The snap of a branch, a rustling in the grass.

Watching over his shoulder, he'd been pleasantly surprised to see little Sideburns emerge from the underbrush, followed quickly by two of the others. Almost immediately it had become a habit, his favorite time of day, leading the little foxes away to where they might interact with the wild and learn how to forage and hunt. Sometimes he'd been reluctant to return again until darkness had fully engulfed the woods.

But the time was bittersweet too. *Freddie woulda loved bein' here fer this. It shoulda been him doin' it.* Ben tried not to spend too much of the walk lamenting. And yet there was no point in avoiding everything that brought Freddie to mind. It had been impossible to release thoughts of the boy, still lost somewhere in the wilderness between where they'd discovered Lemuel and that far-off town called Sundre. Perhaps waiting was the hardest thing a person was required to do when they loved someone who'd gone astray. Waiting for things to be set right again, hoping that there might still be a way despite all evidence to the contrary. Waiting—hoping—but not knowing.

Veronika was also a concern. Their names were mentioned before every meal as the family continued to pray for their safe return. But there was even less that Ben felt he could do in aid of her. That poor, hurting child had chosen her own path and alienated herself from those who'd committed to caring for her.

On the other hand, each time the girl had been mentioned in prayer, Ben watched her little brother through squinting eyes. *What's the boy thinking? How does he manage?* It defied explanation—his calm, his trust, his seeming disconnectedness. There were no obvious expressions of grief at all. Ben found the boy's reaction confusing. Not to mention the strange interplay between Cass and the home's other residents.

Mamie and her sisters would often attempt to mother him, and Cass resisted every effort. If they offered him help in tying his shoes or serving him dinner, he shrugged them off and physically moved away. He seemed to want nothing to do with another girl who might wish to manage him.

Ben smiled to himself and chuckled as he shook his head. Cass and Janie, by contrast, were two peas in a pod—best mates. They made full use of the outdoors whenever possible, coming in at Miss Tilly's last call for the night when she did final checks.

Grace had suggested that the pair be allowed to walk the short distance into town together in order to pay an arranged visit to friends. She'd insisted that it was the healthiest way to give them normalcy.

On Monday morning, Ben walked with them into town. He'd decided to stop by Mr. Wattley's office, hoping that there would be some news about his plan to legally adopt little Janie.

However, the solicitor had little encouragement to offer. "I'm sorry, Ben. But I've spoken to someone in Judge Brady's office. He was certain that the judge wouldn't grant an adoption to a single man. Apparently, he can be quite persnickety about such things. And I'm all too aware of how difficult it is to change his opinion once he's made up his mind."

"But did ya tell him that I'm the girl's guardian anyhow? Legally. Fer good."

"I did. And the truth is, there's currently no law that specifically governs such matters except that it's left to the discretion of each particular judge to determine what would be considered a 'proper' adoptive placement in each situation."

It was a crushing blow. As Ben wandered back toward the Walsh house, he wondered if there would be any way to convince the judge to change his mind. *If I get folks ta speak up fer me b'fore him? If I get Janie ta ask him herself?* But Ben doubted that a judge would be swayed by emotionalism. The man had probably developed a sufficiently thick skin in such matters.

There was only one other option to consider. Ben could find a wife for himself. That would meet the need for the moment. And certainly, it wasn't as if he hadn't wanted to marry. While he'd been at sea it had seemed too cruel a thing to ask of any woman—to be left behind for the bulk of the year, only to have a husband appear long enough to spend a few days in port before shipping out again.

But things were different for him now. He wouldn't go back to sea, ever. He had Janie to consider now. Was it, therefore, reasonable to allow such a notion to play out? And, was there a woman who might be willing to align herself with him? He doubted that he had much to offer. Mentally, Ben began to search through the possibilities in town. By the time he'd arrived at home once more, he had all but set aside the idea entirely. There seemed to be no local lady who was available and suitable for such an essentially practical alliance. He'd have to find a way to convince the judge instead.

CHAPTER 22

Conversing

Go on with ya. He said no such thing! Oh, Dan, how ya can make me laugh with yer stories." Miss Tilly was chatting on the telephone with one of her sons. She'd recently discovered that the distant man had installed a telephone in his prairie home, and the long miles that had held them apart condensed into telephone wires, reuniting them in an instant. This was the second evening in a row she'd pulled a kitchen chair into the hallway after supper had been cleared away. Then she'd treated herself to a chat with her long-lost son. She'd insisted on paying for the charges herself despite Lillian's strong objections.

Grace passed by her as she entered the kitchen, where Lillian was mending a hole in the knee of Castor's dungarees. "I can't tell you how much I enjoy hearing her speak with one of her kids. Her whole face lights up—and it glows for hours."

"And this one makes her laugh more than anyone else I've seen. Hope we can meet him sometime."

"Aw, wouldn't that be nice." Grace lowered herself onto the chair next to Lillian's. The sigh that escaped her sounded more pensive than worn out.

Lillian set down her work. "What is it? Which worry are you feeling most?"

"Oh, all of it, I guess. Cass keeps talking about his parents—and I always want to encourage him to do so—but it's hard to listen to him. Not to mention that I don't have any more answers for his questions about Veronika than I ever did."

Laughter echoed through the front of the house, causing Lillian to smile in spite of her own more serious conversation. "I understand what you're saying, Grace. He doesn't seem to share his feelings with me to quite the same degree. But I'm glad he feels he can be so honest with you. I think that's very good for his sweet little heart."

"Sure. And I'm glad, of course. But it costs my rather depleted old heart quite a debt to continue to guess and speculate about her whereabouts. I'm tired, sis. I'm just tired out."

Lillian pushed her needle through a fold in the sturdy fabric in order to keep from losing track of it. She wanted to give her full attention to Grace. "I'm sorry, dear. Maybe I should make more of an effort to connect with him. I've spent most of my time with the girls this week, I'm afraid. I've been trying to get the Voss sisters to talk to me—working alongside them on everyday things just to build a relationship. Sometimes I feel like I'm the one pestering them with questions."

"Oh, I didn't mean to sound like I'm complaining. And it's barely been a week since they came. There's bound to be a time of adjustment. Don't give up."

Suddenly Miss Tilly entered the room. Her face was drained of all color.

Grace rose quickly to her feet. "Oh dear, what is it? Did you get bad news from your son?"

"No, no. Dan's fine. But the operator, she broke in. Said she needed the line fer a 'mergency call."

"What? From whom?"

"Was yer Sid Brown in Lethbridge. I asked did he wanna speak with ya—but he tol' me jus' ta tell ya that the girl was picked up near Calg'ry."

"Veronika? She was found?"

"Was Freddie with her?"

Miss Tilly eased herself onto a chair. "Nope, not the boy. But Veronika was caught stealin'. Took her ta the p'lice station."

Lillian turned to see that Grace's face had paled to the same ashen color as Miss Tilly's. "What should we do?"

"I don't know. I . . ." Lillian fumbled for a solution.

"Ya get in yer auto an' drive there. Ya go right now. Somebody's gotta stand up fer that child 'fore she digs herself deeper still. Never was one ta keep her words in check."

Lillian stood slowly. "I'll go knock on Ben's door. I think he's back from his walk into town. I suppose he'd like to go anyway—to ask about Freddie."

"What about you, Lill?" Grace asked. "Do you want to go? Or should I?"

For a moment they regarded each other. "You go," Lillian said meekly. "You're better trained for this."

"Oh, sis, nobody can train for *this*."

After a quick hug, Lillian hurried out to the barn in search of Ben.

· · · ● · · ·

Ben's heart was thumping uncomfortably as he readied the automobile for a trip so late in the day. With another quick trip into town, he'd filled the extra gas can and stored it far in the back of the car, as well as an extra tire and some tools, just to be safe. He had no idea what the roads would be like and was quite concerned that they might have a problem seeing well as they drove by the dim headlamps.

And yet, this was a chance to speak with Veronika. The girl

may be able to give him information regarding Freddie. Ben closed his eyes and whispered aloud, "Please, God, please. He's just a boy. Just a boy." These were the very same words that he'd managed to pray daily on Lemuel's behalf in order to keep his promise. But he figured they still applied in Freddie's case. Perhaps even more so. Teenage boys seemed to Ben to have such a knack for finding their way into trouble. They might be easy to forgive but they were difficult to advise.

At last Grace exited the house. Ben hadn't been told which of the sisters would be joining him on this excursion. But he found himself pleased to see Grace crossing the yard, pulling a light shawl around her shoulders.

"I readied the car. If ya want, ya can sit in the back where ya can sleep a bit."

Grace shook her head. "I don't think I'll be able to sleep. I'm too worried about Veronika and what we'll find when we get there."

"Best we go, then."

They set out into the cool, clear night. Shadows loitered timidly in the ditches along both sides of the road, as if hiding from the large moon and its entourage of stars hanging overhead. By the much paler glow of the headlamps, Ben drove cautiously, reminding himself again and again that at any moment a deer could cross the road from the ditches beside them. It wouldn't do to have an accident while hurrying to the girl's rescue.

Grace sighed to herself several times before actually speaking. "I don't know what we'll tell Cass. He's been doing so well, settling in and thriving. He and Janie are practically siblings now."

"I seen that." Ben smiled toward her, nodding a little.

Her hands were twisting the fringe on her shawl. As she looked out into the night, her words tumbled out easily. "I had a talk with him the other night—just to see how he was doing with it all. It was actually quite illuminating." She sighed. "He's as bright as a new penny, really. I get the sense that Veronika was rather a poor influence on him, stifling his creativity in order to indulge her own." She turned to face Ben as she said, "Do you know that they had secret names for each other? Veronika called him Torrie instead of Cass—but vehemently refused to let anyone else use the nickname. And he called her Polly when they were alone together."

"Why Polly? I mean, I see how Torrie might come outta Castor—but where does Polly come from?"

Grace's head dropped back against the seat. "I guess it comes from Greek mythology. There were twins, Castor and Pollux. Lillian overheard them pretending to wield swords and fight mythological beasts."

Ben nodded. "Sure, I know that story. Castor an' Pollux. I knew men ta set great stock by 'em as patrons'a all sailors."

"Of sailors?" Grace's head lifted. She seemed surprised.

"They was said ta be the source'a the constellation Gemini— watchin' o'er the sea from up above. Twin brothers, they were. Sure, I know them ol' tales. I can point out their stars—show 'em to ya when we stop, if ya like."

"Well, Cass told me that their mother used to read mythology to them. I think Veronika may have taken it a little too much to heart. Cass said that she would even tell the other kids in school that they were descended from Greek gods—which, he seemed to feel, made it more difficult for the two of them to make friends. I wonder just how much that plays into her attitude—that she's better than others." Grace's voice quieted with worry. "That, and the fact that her own mother taught her to despise immigrants— blaming them for the bout of polio that Veronika had as a child." Grace turned her eyes toward Ben in the darkness. "He also said that she told him she was going to save him—to save them both. I think that was actually her motivation for running away. That she'd rescue her brother."

"Ahh, that's what Pollux did in the story. He spoke ta Zeus and got him ta split his own immortality with his dyin' brother. Saved him by makin' 'em inta stars." Ben tried to imagine how the tragedy of their parents' death had twisted the perception of the world inside of Veronika. "I can see she woulda rather been with them uncles. I can see that." He paused. "Why didn't they get sent there anyhow? Nobody e'er told me."

Grace shook her head. "Oh, there was a search made for them. But the men had moved on without leaving any information behind. That was one of the first trails the Mounties explored after their parents died. We just didn't put it together with Cass's version, 'Sunday' for 'Sundre.' It's rumored now that the men live south of Calgary somewhere. So the officers were watching that area closely instead. Maybe that's where she was heading by now too."

"Oh, I see." And then, "Cass seems ta have taken it in stride, doin' well in spite'a all that."

"He is." Grace's voice had cheered with her obvious affection. "He is. He's made some new friends recently—that day last week when he went for a visit to the Caulfields to play with Matty and Milton. They invited two other boys too—little Pat Bukowski and Gordon McRae. You remember, just a few days after Janie went to a tea party with Bryony and Eva Bukowski. I'm glad that Janie and Cass get along so well, but I'm pleased to see them branching out a little too. That's good for them."

"They're a pair, they are."

"Yes. And he does seem to be doing very well. It's just that . . ." Ben waited as Grace sorted her thoughts into words. "It's just that the grief always seems to catch up to them eventually—and will need to be faced rather than repressed. Often it emerges in their early teenage years. I hope to be . . . at least, I wish I could be there for Cass when that happens. It would be such a benefit for him to have people who know him well whenever he's ready to face it all. Yet there's no way to predict where he'll be by then."

For a while the two shared silence instead of conversation. Ben watched the dark skies, picking out the constellations that hung beyond the broad windshield. He wondered if Grace would be interested in hearing any of their names, but hesitated. He wasn't certain how she felt about such things.

At last she spoke again. "Cass and I had a good talk about God too." She chuckled at the recollection. "Isn't it surprising how much a child wants to talk just as you're putting them down for the night?"

Ben nodded, picturing Janie's similar schemes.

"It started out that he asked if he was going to be adopted any time soon. I told him that he didn't need to worry about that for a while. We would wait until we found out about Veronika first. You see, I thought he was worried that he might have to move away from us." The soft voice cracked a little. "But then . . . he asked if *nobody* wanted him."

"Oh no, he don't think such a thing. Surely not."

"One never knows what a child is working through. So little of it shows on their faces." Grace cleared her throat as if she were fending off emotion. "I told him a little of my story, and how God always took very good care of me. And that it wasn't that no one wanted me. They just thought I might still be able to make them sick with the tuberculosis that killed my parents."

It was Ben's turn to clear his throat. "That what ya thought 'bout? When ya was a kid?"

"That was my world, I suppose. I was a child without a family among other children without families. It's difficult not to assume it's your own fault somehow. A child doesn't have anyone else to blame—they often still think that adults are infallible."

"I'm so sorry ta hear it, Grace. Ya deserved better."

"But that's just it, Ben. None of it is about what a child deserves.

Or, at least, every child *deserves* to have a home and people who love him. That's a given—but not always a reality. So instead, we learn as we become adults that there are only two ways to live—to accept and live with those feelings of rejection, or to live with the affirmation of being chosen."

For a moment Ben regarded her, turning his head repeatedly to study her face. "I don't mean ta sound pitiless, but ya said ya weren't ne'er 'dopted. So what is it ya mean, then, miss?"

She returned a smile to him, warm and rich. "Oh, I was chosen. Not by a human family, but by a heavenly Father who has always loved me—the One who knows me best. I'm a part of God's family, and that's the most important family of all."

Her words made Ben suddenly feel shy and withdrawn. She was speaking of things he'd never understood, as if she knew so much more than he did. It became impossible for him to question her further, so he deftly changed the subject instead. "How much farther, ya think?"

Grace leaned her head against the seat once more. "At least another hour."

CHAPTER 23

Conflicted

B ut what do we say to Cass?" Lillian had risen early, her mind wrestling with the difficulties of reacting to the answered prayer that Veronika would be located. Her anxious heart had drawn her to the kitchen, to discuss it all with Miss Tilly before the children woke up. "This little boy has been through so much worry. And now . . . I'm just not sure what to tell him."

"Jus' tell him the truth. His sister's been found. That's good. He'll be happy."

"But we know nothing about what happens next. She was found stealing. It's likely that she'll face consequences. We don't know if she's healthy. We don't know if she's been harmed."

Miss Tilly dropped the wooden spoon into the biscuit dough she'd been stirring and turned her full attention to Lillian. "Now, honey, ya can't carry so much at a time. All them what-ifs and maybes are too much ta bear. This is God's hand movin'. This is what we prayed He'd do. Only He knows all the rest. Ya gotta trust Him."

Lillian filled the small pitcher with honey as she pondered the words. "I just want to be sure I don't say the wrong thing.

It's not God that I'm doubting, *it's me*. It's my role in all of it. It's my inability to understand when it all seems too big."

Miss Tilly walked away, offering a knowing smile as she left. Lillian stood bewildered. This was not what she'd expected. Without explanation, the woman had disappeared into her bedroom next to the kitchen.

But almost immediately she returned, carrying a worn-out Bible. The front cover of the leather-bound book had been refurbished with stitched-on broadcloth. Neatly printed across it in Miss Tilly's handwriting were the words *Holy Bible*. Lillian had seen this treasured book often before.

"Wish I could'a recalled the words jus' right, but I'll read 'em to ya instead. May as well say it proper." She flipped open the book near the center, its exposed pages filled with underlining and notes in the margins. "Gonna read from Job 26. One'a my favorite passages. After describin' all the awesome works God was doin', it says, 'Lo, these are *parts* of his ways: but how *little a portion* is heard of him? But the *thunder of his power* who can understand?'"

Lillian waited, trying to comprehend what the woman was communicating. For a moment Miss Tilly let the words speak for themselves. Then she placed a hand on Lillian's shoulder and stated boldly, "Findin' Veronika is the little portion of Him, Lillian. It's just a hint at all that God's been doin'. But outta our range'a hearin' He's thundering out power—He's movin' the happenin's an' the people He needs ta get His will done. I like ta pi'ture it, the faint rumble of a distant thunder tellin' 'bout all His doin's, with God so big—an' me so small. Makes me not scared'a all them big worries."

Lillian's face withered. "I know what you're saying, but I don't know if I'm able to . . ."

"Dearie, a God who can move kings an' nations can set ya on the right path too. 'Specially when yer heart wants ta bend ta His will. Ya don't have ta trust yerself an' yer own plans—just trust Him."

Lillian nodded, her mind still swirling with unspoken arguments. At last she admitted, "I think I need to take a walk. Do you mind?"

Miss Tilly reached out for a quick embrace. "Sounds like the best thing fer ya right now."

Not bothering with a wrap, Lillian knew her quick steps would be more than enough to warm her in the brisk morning air. When she came to the road, she turned away from town and toward the fields instead. Miss Tilly's words were being laboriously disassembled and reconstructed in her mind as she worked to make sense of it all.

But when she passed by Lemuel's house, she stopped short as she heard someone calling from the lane. "Miss Lillian! Hey, hello."

"Oh, Lemuel! It's so wonderful to see you outdoors."

He waved again as he approached the road. "They hardly let me out, but I can't stay cooped up inside fer good. I was goin' to take a walk."

"Oh, me too. Why don't you come along?" Lillian waved a cheerful hand toward Arthur, who stood in the doorway to the barn. "Okay to borrow him for a little while?"

The man nodded. Side by side, she and Lemuel put the yard behind them. When they reached the road there was no discussion. Lemuel seemed as anxious as Lillian to enjoy the exercise of a brisk pace, speaking very little and in short bursts.

"How are you, dear?"

"Good."

"Are your headaches any better?"

"Sure." He added after a few moments passed, "I heard ya took the bike out."

Lillian laughed. "I'm afraid it wasn't pretty."

"Look. I got me knife back." Lemuel retrieved it from his pocket, holding it up for Lillian to see. The smiles that followed faded slowly. Each fell deep into thought.

Summoning the courage to reveal the latest revelation took some time. At last, "Lemuel, there's something I need to tell you."

"Aw, I don't like them words much."

She tucked a hand around his elbow. "They found Veronika." Silence. "Where?"

"In Calgary. She was picked up for stealing something."

"Freddie wasn't with her?"

"No. I'm sorry. He wasn't."

"Huh. That right?" And then with increased concern, "Was she hurt still?"

Lillian stopped in place. "What do you mean, Lemuel? Had something happened to Veronika?"

His face had taken on the familiar expression of a cornered child who's been asked for an explanation of their guilt. *Is there something for which Lemuel is guilty?* Lillian held her breath.

At last he shrugged and admitted, "I don't like to be a tattle-tale, but Freddie hit her with his slingshot. It was accidently, I think."

"Oh dear! How badly was she hurt?"

Lemuel kicked at a rock. "In her knee. She wouldn't show it to us. Said it might'a knocked her—what was it she said? Her *patella* out of place."

"Her patella?"

"Yeah." His voice lowered to a whisper. "Is that something that girls got down there, on their knees?"

Lillian began walking once more, struggling not to snicker at the boy's genuine concern. She cleared her throat. "Girls and boys both." She managed to sound matter-of-fact. "It just means the kneecap. The bone that protects the knee."

"Well, can ya knock it off? Would that make it hard fer her to walk?"

"I'm quite certain that it would keep her from walking at all. So it seems unlikely that's what really happened."

"Well, she were hobblin' along good enough—just complainin' a lot when she did. Why do ya say it ain't likely?"

"Because, as I understand it, she'd need a surgeon to fix it. It would be very serious. So unless she was completely incapacitated, I think something else might have been at play."

"What's that, miss?"

As gently as she could, Lillian explained her suspicions. "She knew the proper word. So she probably understood too that she hadn't truly been injured. I think she was probably lying to you, Lemuel. I couldn't say why. Maybe she was tired of walking. Maybe it was a play for sympathy, or a way to make things go her own way."

Lemuel muttered, "Aw, she was tryin' to get things her way, all right. She was tryin' to make Freddie move, an' tryin' to keep *me* from leavin'. If it was all a lie, then . . ." It seemed impossible for him to finish his sentence. Lillian supposed it was better if he left it incomplete.

After several moments longer Lillian prodded, "Are you all right, Lemuel? I'm still worried about you."

He shrugged. "Don't worry 'bout me. I'm fine. I'm safe now. I'm back home."

"Are you?" she whispered, her eyes filling with emotion. "Are you back from there? Truly?"

Lemuel's smile drew tight on one side as he shook his head slowly. There was a softening in his eyes that filled Lillian with hope. "Ya gotta give folks a chance to love ya, right? Think you were the one to tell me that, Miss Lillian."

"Oh, we do love you, Lemuel. We all do. I'm so, so grateful to have you home."

· · · ● · · ·

Ben woke to the rumble of an engine passing nearby. He'd stretched out on the back seat of the automobile for what had remained of the night after settling Grace in a city hotel. It was expensive enough for one room. Certainly not worth the trouble of two. But, despite Grace's objections, Ben was adamant that it was necessary considering the current crisis. As Ben pushed up from the bench seat, he tested the stiffness of his joints and back. *I'm gettin' too old fer sleepin' any ol' place.*

Following a hasty breakfast, they drove to the city's Mounted Police station, which was much larger than the small building in Brookfield. Even at this early hour there was movement all around it, people of all descriptions coming and going. Ben held the door for Grace as she squared her shoulders and walked directly toward the reception desk, where an officer with a large mustache was seated.

"Good morning. May I help you, ma'am?"

"Good morning. My name is Miss Grace Bennett. I'm here regarding a child who was taken into custody. Veronika Geary."

"Oh yes, miss. She's not here at the moment. But I'm certain the captain will want to speak with you. Would you take a seat, please? I'll see if he's available."

"Thank you."

The entry room was already crowded. Ben motioned Grace to an open chair in the back corner of the waiting area. He stood next to the doorway, where he could see more of the room and could watch the activity around him. Two officers in scarlet coats passed by him, escorting a downcast young man toward the back rooms. Ben's mind went instantly to Freddie. *Where are ya, boy?*

At last the receptionist motioned him over. "I can take you back now."

Grace promptly appeared at Ben's side. They hurried after the man down a second corridor and into a large office. A quick introduction was offered. "This is Captain James Eichel. Sir, this is Miss Grace Bennett." Then the receptionist closed the door as he exited.

For some reason, Ben had been expecting a burly, broad-shouldered man. Instead, Captain Eichel was thin and small in stature, dwarfed by the dimensions of his desk chair and the size of his office. Thick spectacles sat heavily on his nose. His face flinched frequently as if in an effort to lift his glasses. "Miss Bennett, thank you for coming. And what is your name, sir?"

Ben reached out to shake the offered hand. "Ebenezer Waldin, sir."

"Mr. Waldin, Miss Bennett, please have a seat."

They obeyed.

"I'm pleased you've come immediately. I wanted to discuss Miss Geary's situation before having you escorted to the home where she's being held."

"Held?" Grace's question was little more than a gasp.

"No, no. That's not quite what I mean. Please allow me to be clear. The child is not under arrest. The shopkeeper involved chose not to press charges. However, because she's an unattended minor, we're holding her in custody until her case can be evaluated, so that proper procedures are followed. It's my understanding that you, Miss Bennett, are currently the girl's official guardian, under the supervision of a children's home in Lethbridge." He lifted eyes to Grace, squinting through his lenses as he awaited an answer.

Grace nodded. "Yes, sir. My sister, Lillian Walsh, and I have been appointed as temporary guardians."

"And is it your intention to adopt this child?"

"No, sir. We run a very small children's home and seek to find adoptive families for the children whom we host."

"Good. That's very good." He made a note in the margins of his paperwork, then folded his hands on the desk in front of him. To Ben his mannerisms were more like that of an accountant than a high-ranking police officer despite the familiar red tunic. Captain Eichel's jacket bunched and bulged above his shoulders, as if there were not quite enough of him to fill it out completely. "I'd like to tell you what my many years of service have taught me, Miss Bennett. We've processed more children than I ever wished to through this office. Most are distraught with remorse or angry about something specific. Little Miss Geary is quite another story."

Ben frowned. His eyes flitted around the room, looking for any sign of the man's experience or expertise. There seemed to be several framed certificates of merit on the wall behind him. There was an engraved pen set displayed on the corner of the desk nearest Ben, though the print was too small to read. Still, Ben was already reluctant to receive whatever words of advice might follow.

"I don't believe I've seen a child as easily labeled a delinquent as Miss Geary. She has been obstinate, belligerent, and outright abusive to the staff at the home. I have been very concerned about the reports that I've received. There seems to be no remorse for her actions whatsoever."

Grace cleared her throat. "We are aware that—"

"Please, Miss Bennett, allow me to finish."

Ben leaned forward, bracing his elbows against the arms of his chair. *How does he dare speak ta Grace like this—as if he knows more'n her in just a few short hours' time?*

"It is my belief that, should this girl be relinquished into your custody, she will immediately run away again. This is my belief because it is precisely what the child herself has vowed to do. Therefore, it will be my recommendation that Veronika Geary be surrendered to a detention home for delinquent children."

Ben was surprised by the controlled tone in Grace's reply. Her words came evenly and firmly. "I am unaware of any such homes in this area, Captain."

"True. She would be sent to Ontario."

"And how soon do you intend to do this?"

"I see no reason to hesitate. I'm not aware of any extenuating circumstances to consider."

Grace cleared her throat. "Are you aware that Veronika has a younger brother?"

"Yes."

"And would he not be considered an *extenuating circumstance?*"

"I believe we've taken the needs of the brother into consideration." The officer closed his file. "We feel it actually benefits the boy to be liberated from the influence of his sister."

Ben's eyes widened in disbelief. But the two others were facing off, Grace and the small but grizzled Captain Eichel. The welfare of these children was on the line. Ben sat in silence, watching the battle of wills play out.

"Captain Eichel, I was also orphaned at a young age—and I grew up without my older sister. I can assure you, sir, that her absence will *in no way* be a benefit to Castor. Because retaining an association with family, even one that is far from perfect, is desirable to losing your loved ones entirely. I can speak from my own experience and also from observing many other grieving children."

"Now, Miss Bennett, I—"

"And what of Veronika's uncles? Have they been located?"

The man pushed back from his desk. His face had taken on a smug look. "Yes, miss. They have been located. They are currently awaiting trial for arson. It seems that they burned the field of a neighbor with whom they had a dispute last fall just before harvest."

Grace refused to falter, even at such disturbing news. "Then the *only* living relative available to Castor is his sister. She becomes even more important in his young life. We simply cannot deprive him of that relationship. And, as concerns Veronika, I assure you that Castor means the whole world to her. The boy will be the best possible way to reach her and to restore her equilibrium."

The captain shook his head. "You may know children, Miss Bennett, but I know criminals."

"Veronika Geary is a child, sir. Misguided as she may be, she is still just a child. We have a responsibility to make decisions that improve her lot in life, not ones that condemn her future."

For some time they continued the verbal sparring. Ben held his silence, in awe of Grace's skill at countering the man's attacks. When they stood at last, they were granted the opportunity for a short visit with Veronika in order to convince her toward a more cooperative attitude.

Still in shock, they retreated silently all the way to the parking lot where they'd left the oversized vehicle. Moving in behind the car in order to open the passenger door for Grace, Ben dared to speak at last. "I think ya done right by her. The best any could do."

Grace's face lifted up toward his, but her eyes had flooded with tears. "What if they send her away? What if he never sees her again—and she's lost for good?"

Instinctively, Ben's arms rose up to support her. Grace dropped her face against his shoulder, allowing her sorrow to vent for a moment or two. He patted her back, murmuring the only words he could conceive of that might be useful. "Ya gotta trust the Good Lord, Grace. He'll not let a child'a His fall."

· · · ◉ · · ·

Lillian dropped down onto the sofa, having supervised the feeding, clothing, and morning chores of all five children before sending them out to play for a little while before lunch. But the worry she'd tried to conceal had been far more taxing than managing without Grace for these routine duties. Now she'd arranged herself in the parlor for a rare moment of solitary piano, striking the first chord just as the telephone bell rang in the foyer. She rose reluctantly.

Could it be Grace? Lillian hurried to answer the telephone before its continued ringing brought any of the curious children in from outdoors, ending her respite. "Hello?"

A measured voice queried, "Hello, is that you, Lill?"

"Oh, Walter. I didn't expect your call in the middle of the day."

"I'm sorry if I'm interruptin'. I just got back from town. I was gettin' the mail. But I couldn't wait for evenin' to give you some news, if you have a minute."

Lillian glanced at the raised cover above the piano. She sighed. "Of course. What is it?"

"Are you sittin' down? Because . . . we got it. We got our land!"

At first, she was uncertain what he meant. Then the significance slowly coalesced. Walter's land, the beautiful valley an hour's drive from Brookfield. It had been granted to Walter.

"What did . . . ? Who . . . ? How do you know?"

"I got the letter right here. Says that all I need to do is come in and register for it. It's ours."

Lillian's face contorted. *Oh no, not now.*

"Lill, are you there?"

"Yes. Yes, I'm here."

"Well . . . what do you think?"

Tracing the corner on the wooden telephone box with a fingertip, Lillian tried to sound enthused. "That's wonderful. I'm so happy for you."

"For us. You mean *for us*, right?"

"Yes—for us. Of course."

"Me too. I can hardly wait to begin fellin' some trees to build a barn. I figure I'll do that first and then we can buy lumber to . . ."

Walter's voice was drowned out by the hum of emotion that Lillian was feeling. *We haven't even set a date for our wedding. I haven't told Grace about the land. I haven't told Father how far away it is. Yet in his mind, Walter's already cutting down trees and building things. What if I'm not ready? What if I can't go along with it? Could I really move away? Oh, why did this have to happen right now?*

"Lillian? Are you listening?"

Her mind snapped back to the conversation. "I'm sorry, Walter. What were you saying?"

A long pause. "Is something wrong?"

How could she explain the load that she currently carried? "I'm just a little distracted. I was expecting to hear back from Grace—from the city. I told you about it last night. I thought she was the one calling."

Several drawn-out seconds of silence. "I could call back later." His words were guarded now, his disappointment evident.

"No, I'm sorry. I truly am. It's just so hard to concentrate on other things right now."

"Sure, I can see how it would be. I'll call again later—free up the line for Grace."

"Thank you." Lillian sighed in relief. "It's just so hard for me right now to think about if we'll move to that land and—"

"What did you say?" Walter asked, cutting her off.

"It's hard to think about it. I'm sorry," Lillian answered tentatively.

"No, Lillian. I believe you said *if.*"

Her heart began to race. She'd never heard this tone in Walter's voice before. *What was it I said? I don't remember.*

Walter insisted, "You said, 'if we'll move to that land.'"

"Did I?"

"Yes. You did." Silence once more. "Are you uncertain, Lillian? About marrying me?"

Her throat had begun to tighten. She swallowed hard before

the words began to form again. "Oh no! No. I do want to marry you. I do. I'm sure of it. It's just the land. It's so far away. I—"

He stated bluntly, "You're sure you want to marry me, but you're not so sure that you want to live with me."

"No. I just . . . Don't you see? It's so far away."

"Well, Lillian, where did you imagine that we'd live?"

There were no words left. The line went silent. Then Walter answered himself on Lillian's behalf. "You thought we'd live in your dad's house. You thought I'd just become part of that big, happy family there."

"No. I mean, I wouldn't mind that. But no. I understood that you wanted your own ranch. That's your dream, Walter. I want to support you in that."

"Lillian, do *you* want to live on a ranch?"

She sputtered helplessly. There was no way to phrase any truthful response in the affirmative.

"I don't even know what to say, Lillian. I'm in shock. You're aware, aren't you, that the Bible says that when you marry you leave your own family and cleave to your husband? If you're not ready to do that, then—"

"I am. I *am* ready. I don't have any doubts about you, Walter. I wasn't sure if we needed to go so far away. That's all."

"I see. Well, it's probably best to take a break from this conversation. I'll call you tonight."

"No, Walter. Please listen . . . it's not that I . . . I don't mean to say that . . ."

"Sure, Lillian. We'll talk about it later. I need to do some thinkin' first."

The line went dead. Lillian stumbled into the parlor and closed the door behind her. Dropping the lid over the piano keys, she collapsed onto the sofa to weep in private as quietly as she could manage.

CHAPTER 24

Calgary

The ring of the telephone pealed through the house again midafternoon, startling Lillian so that she almost dropped the primer she'd been using to review reading lessons with Castor, Janie, and Ora at the kitchen table. Three pairs of eyes regarded her with concern.

"Excuse me. I'll just go and answer the telephone."

It was Grace. "We got to see Veronika. She's not doing well. I'm afraid she's going to dig herself into a hole so deep that we can't get her back out."

"Oh no."

"I can only think of one thing to do, sis. I know it's an enormous imposition, and I'm not sure if it's even possible, but . . . well, do you think you could ask Walter if he could drive you here so that you could bring Cass for a visit?"

Lillian pressed a hand against her temple. "I'll ask. When were you thinking?"

"Just as soon as you could come. Things are being decided already. Miss Tilly would have to watch the others. I hope she can do it. I know the canning has been keeping her busy most days."

"I'm sure she won't mind. And if I bring Janie along too, the older girls will likely be more help to her than not."

"That's true. Yes, please go ahead and bring both little ones along."

Lillian's fingertips were making circles against her head as if the pressure would clear her mind. "I guess I'll call Walter. But he's likely outdoors—not near their telephone." And then she added, "How do I get in touch with you again, Grace?"

"I'll have to call you. Say, in an hour?"

"That's fine. I'll expect your call."

Setting the earpiece back on top of the telephone box, Lillian dreaded what was to come. Breathing deeply, she turned the small handle on the side of the telephone box in order to summon the operator. "Mrs. Linden? Would you please connect me to Tommy Gardner's place? I'd like to speak to Walter, please."

"One moment, please."

As expected, it was the Gardner housekeeper who answered the call. "Gardner residence."

"Hello. This is Lillian Walsh. I'd like to speak with Walter, please. If he's nearby."

"Just a minute. I'll get him."

Glancing toward the kitchen, where the children were still seated, Lillian turned her back and ducked her head.

After a few seconds, Walter's voice drawled, "I'm not sure I'm ready to talk to you yet."

"Walter, I'm sorry. I have a favor to ask. And I'll understand if you're not able to help out just now. I truly will understand."

He let out a long sigh. "What is it?"

Her words spilled out. "Grace just called from Calgary. She was able to see Veronika—to speak with her. But it didn't go well. Grace thought that it would be helpful to have a visit with Cass. I know this is asking a lot—and Grace does too—but she wondered if you'd be willing to drive him and me there, if you'd be able to do that today, we'd just appreciate it so much. . . ." Her voice trailed off.

Another sigh. "Of course. I'll come by and pick you up in a little bit."

"You will? That's so kind of you, Walter. I can't even—"

"Sure. I'll be there soon."

Lillian set the earpiece down again. It would be dreadful to see Walter again without having a chance to resolve their differences, and yet she hoped he'd hurry. Even this unexpected journey would be much better than the long afternoon of not being able to see him and to read in his eyes whether or not his feelings toward her had been damaged.

The announcement to the children that a trip in Walter's car had been arranged was met with whoops of enthusiasm. "Go pack some books and toys for the road," Lillian advised. "We'll be driving for a couple hours each way."

Before leaving the room, Cass tugged at Lillian's apron. "I'm gonna see my sister?"

Lillian flushed with remorse that she hadn't even paused to see the situation from the small boy's point of view. Sinking down so that she could speak to him properly, she said, "Yes, dear. You'll have a chance to speak to Veronika. That's why we're going. So that you can see her—so that she can see you. I know there's nothing she wants more right now than to see you, Cass."

His innocent face lit with a smile. "Me too."

· · • ● • · ·

Walter's eyes remained fixed on the road ahead. Lillian sat stiffly on the passenger side of the vehicle, trying not to give in to her temptation to study his face for clues. Janie and Cass clambered around the bench seat behind them, enjoying the outing and settling into the unusual but pleasant place to play. The miles began to slip past slowly. Lillian turned her face toward her own window and lost herself in thought, willing the merciless time to pass.

"What on earth would we do without cars?" She hadn't meant to verbalize the thought aloud. She'd simply been drifting in her mind, contemplating how differently the situation would have played out just a few years before, when there were only slow-moving wagons or trains for such a journey. Now that she'd spoken, it was up to Walter to decide whether or not to respond. She turned tentative eyes in his direction, holding her breath.

"Maybe it was better." His words were presented as usual, deliberate and slow. "There weren't so many crises. Every problem just took time to resolve, so nobody expected any different. They got used to waitin' it out."

Lillian wasn't quite sure what his implications were. Was he answering her ill-timed question, or making a comment about the way she'd requested his help once again?

I'm sorry. I'm just so sorry. She wanted terribly to be able to compose a clever apology, one that the children in the back seat wouldn't understand. But the words refused to form in her mind. "At least you'd have been able to finish a full day of your work for a change. I wouldn't have expected you to charge in and rescue us again."

Walter's eyes remained on the road, but his face softened. "But I kinda like to rescue you."

"You're very good at it. You're very gracious with your time and attention. I hope Tommy hasn't started to resent us all for it yet."

A quick glance her way and his focus returned to the road again. "Guess that's another good reason to be workin' at my own place."

Lillian's eyes closed. *Please, please try to understand that I need to be able to tell you the truth too. I can't pretend to be excited when I'm not.* When Lillian dared another peek toward him, he was looking back. His brown eyes seemed sad, but no longer angry.

Lillian slid closer on the bench seat, whispering, "Maybe we can talk about this when we drop off Cass."

His eyebrows arched and a tip of his head gestured toward the back seat.

Softly, "She'll be with Ben then maybe."

A nod, and silence descended once more. However, now Lillian's nervous butterflies could finally begin to calm. She placed a hand on his knee, leaning comfortably closer.

· · · ● ● · · ·

Ben watched Grace and Cass mount the wide stairs that led to the temporary home where Veronika was being held. Even the small boy seemed to understand the magnitude of the moment. His steps were slow, his hand holding fast to Grace's.

Ben reached for Janie's shoulder, drew her close against his side. The woman and the boy disappeared behind the heavy wood door.

"What do we do now, Mr. Waldin?"

"Guess we wait." Ben looked around. The front lawn of the large home was broad and well-kept. It was framed with bushes and flower gardens, with only a small parking area to interrupt the park-like setting. "I can read ta ya, er I can draw ya a hopscotch game in the dirt over there."

"I brought *The Princess and the Goblin*. Can you read it to me now?"

Ben scratched at his hairline. "What 'bout Cass and the others? They'll miss out if we keep readin' without 'em."

Janie hesitated. "Well, we can read the last chapter over. I'll still like it."

So, taking a seat on a patch of grass in a sunny spot, Ben began reading the old favorite again, one that he'd also enjoyed as a boy. He was glad that Janie seemed just as hungry for printed stories too.

He began, "Chapter seventeen, 'Springtime' . . ."

Janie picked the nearby dandelions as she listened, trying her best to weave them into a crown by their stems. Once the chapter was finished, Ben suggested they go for a walk next. They admired the many flowers, and Janie did five cartwheels in a row across the lawn.

"You do one now, Mr. Waldin."

"No, bunny. I ne'er could move like that."

"It's easy. You just tip over in the middle and the rest of you follows."

Ben smiled. "Easy fer you. Not so simple fer me."

"When you're my papa, I'll teach you."

Freezing in place, Ben tried to think of a way to explain the complications he'd discovered to the child. "Well now, 'bout that. I spoke ta the judge. 'Fraid he ain't gonna let me do that any time soon."

"He's not?"

"No, bunny. He's of a mind that men what ain't married ought not ta be a papa."

"Why not?"

Ben squatted down where he could meet her eyes. Instantly she lifted her hands to fiddle with his collar affectionately. "A child needs a mama too. On that, I agree with him."

"But I don't need a mama. I've got Miss Grace and Miss Lillian and Miss Tilly. That's like *three* mamas. Why isn't that enough for the judge?"

"Because they ain't in our family, Janie. If we get a place'a our own sometime, we wouldn't live with 'em no more."

This thought brought her small hands to the stubble on his chin. "You need a haircut, Mr. Waldin."

"I do."

"Is that why you need a lady? So she can take care of you?"

A slow smile crossed his face. It was a rare bad day that couldn't be improved by a conversation with Janie. He tried again. "The lady, she's not fer me so much as fer you. Ta care fer ya. Ta teach ya ta be a lady too."

"Well." She giggled. "That's one thing I guess you can't do."

"There's others too. Braidin' yer hair an' stitchin' yer clothes . . ."

"I've seen you sew. You fixed the hole in the back of your pants by yourself."

"Yes, but not good 'nough ta wear 'em fer naught but workin'."

"All right. Well, Miss Lillian is going to marry Mr. Norberg. And Miss Tilly is a grandmum. If you need a lady, what about Miss Grace, then? She's not married either."

Ben raised himself to his feet. "That ain't how it works, bunny."

"Why not?"

"Because it's fallin' in love an' promisin' ferever. An' me and Miss Grace ain't—well, we're just friends."

"You sure?"

It was Ben's turn to laugh. "Yes, I'm sure."

"Hmm."

· · ◦ ● · · ·

For some time after turning the children over to the care of Grace and Ben, Walter and Lillian cared for the needs of his automobile. It took two stops to ask for directions in order to find a garage establishment that sold gasoline. Walter worked under the hood for a while, checking the radiator and oil levels. Lillian sat inside with all the windows down, trying to catch as much breeze as was available. At last they were able to veer away from the heavy traffic areas of the city and find a pleasant spot along the Bow River where they could walk for a little while and talk.

Walter took her hand as she exited the vehicle and led her toward a patch of pebbly shoreline. Across the water not far from them, the large limestone buildings of the city center towered, three and four stories tall.

Lillian drew a breath but Walter spoke first, turning so that he could face her fully, scooping up both her hands in his. "I wanted to apologize."

"What?"

"I was wrong to use Scripture to try and win an argument. I'm embarrassed that I did that, and I hope you'll forgive me."

"Oh." This was not how Lillian had anticipated that the conversation would commence.

"I've given it all a great deal of thought." He shrugged. "Well, to be honest, I also talked to my brother-in-law Tommy. And it still took me most of the drive here to figure out that he was right about what he said. I think I blundered in some other ways too."

"But, Walter, it was me. I was out of sorts because—"

"Yes, that's exactly one of the things I did wrong."

Once more, Lillian was shocked into silence.

"You were already worried about Veronika. You were waitin' for a call from Grace. You told me that first thing. But instead of listenin' to you and accommodatin' you, I pushed on with my own agenda. I wasn't attentive to *your* needs."

"Oh." Lillian took a step closer. "Thank you. I— That's very nice to hear, actually."

"And then I started an argument over one single word. One word."

Lillian dropped her eyes. That wasn't really fair. The word hadn't been spoken intentionally, but the weight of it was true nonetheless. "We need to talk about that part, I'm afraid."

"Yes, let's. I'm ready now. We can sit on this log."

They moved to a length of washed-up timber and Walter dusted it off first for Lillian. The action made her laugh aloud.

Again, Walter led the way. "Okay, let's talk about it. How do you really feel about the land? Really."

Lillian took a deep breath. "Well, let me say first that I really do want to marry you. I'm actually amazed whenever I think about it that you're so wonderful to me. You're always kind and generous and thoughtful."

"Not *always*."

"Well, mostly. Almost always. And please understand, it's not that I don't want to live on a ranch with you and make a home for ourselves."

He ducked his head so that he could look directly into her eyes. "Be honest, Lill."

"I'm trying. I mean, you know that I've always been a *town* girl. My mother spent more time making sure I knew French and could play the piano than that I could milk a cow—that I'd read the great works of literature than that I knew how to preserve foods from the garden." Her eyes turned upward plaintively. "But over the last year I've learned an awful lot from Miss Tilly. So, if you'd be patient with me—and maybe, if we could find a little help for me somehow—I think I could manage my own home well enough."

Walter smiled, making his brown eyes glitter with gold.

She continued, "I know you could have found a far more qualified rancher's wife than I—"

"Lillian, stop, please."

She held her breath and waited.

"Don't you know that I've looked up to you ever since you started to tutor me when I was in grade ten? You're so smart and insightful. I love to listen to you discuss complex things. Most of the other girls I know, they couldn't care less about the truly important things in life. But you do. I can almost watch your mind hummin' away as you think things through—it's written all over your face. And you're talented too—and musical. I just wish you could see yourself through *my* eyes. I'm the one who can't believe that you're willin' to marry me. Just a humble start-up rancher with big dreams."

Lillian tucked her head against his shoulder. "Then you won't be disappointed with me if there's a lot I need to learn?"

"I'll be proud of you for bein' willing to share my dream with me. And . . . I didn't get a chance to tell you all of it. There are four new residents nearby who plan to build in adjacent corners of their land. That'll start a new town—and pretty soon, we'll have as many neighbors there as you have here. That land is all bein' settled soon. We won't be alone for long at all."

Those words came as a great relief. But Lillian knew there was more that needed to be discussed. Try as she might, she couldn't make herself articulate the other difficulty. Instead, her hands rose to cover her face.

"What is it?"

"I don't know how to say it," she whispered. "I'm not sure I can put it into words."

"We can face it—together."

Oh dear! This is it. She'd always known in her heart that she needed to be honest with Walter, completely honest. Timidly, she forced herself to speak. "I'm afraid it might be wrong for me to marry you."

"What? Why? How do you mean?"

"I'm afraid I'm supposed to stay with Grace." Once she'd begun, the words tumbled out more and more quickly. "I can't abandon her. I recoil at the very thought of it. I feel like I already abandoned my sister enough for one lifetime."

"You mean when you were little? That had nothin' to do with you."

"But it did, don't you see? I was the one who got a family—a new life. Grace was the one who got stuck without anyone." Lillian blew out a long breath to try to keep the tears from forming. "When you lose your first parents . . . I don't know—it changes you. You don't trust life anymore. In the back of your head there's always kind of a storm stirring around—about why it happened and wondering if it's your own fault somehow—even when logic tells you it couldn't possibly be. So everything that happens kind of gets swirled up into that perpetual storm. Grace is so much stronger than I am in so many ways—but I know she feels it too. It slips out sometimes."

Walter pressed his cheek against Lillian's. "I'm so sorry. I didn't realize you still felt so strongly about that."

"I try not to. I think most adopted kids try not to—especially for the sake of our new parents—our new families. All *they* feel is the joy of having a new child to love—the good families, anyway. But for the child, there's always pain underneath everything—and a strange sense of having to live up to everybody's expectations. My father never understood that. I don't think he means to be insensitive, but I don't think his mind works that way. But Mother's did." Lillian's voice broke. "God gave me a new mother who listened. She wasn't perfect either, but she listened, and that made all the difference for me. . . ." Her throat continued to tighten. Her last words were little more than a whisper. "So I'll never understand why God took her too."

"Oh, Lill." Strong arms wrapped Lillian tightly.

Once she'd managed the most difficult admission, there was much more that Lillian needed to say. "Sometimes, I feel like all I do is try to live up to what I'm supposed to be—like there's a debt I owe to everyone. So I can't complain or be honest about what I really want."

"Oh, Lillian, you can with me. You can always be honest with me. If you don't want to live on a ranch, we'll find some other way. We'll—"

"No, please, Walter. You need to let me finish."

This time it was Walter who wiped away tears. "Okay. Sorry. I'm listenin'."

Another deep breath. "I'm trapped, Walter—between two lives that I love. Loving you and being your wife—and loving my sister, loving the children who don't have anybody else right now. It's an impossible situation. No matter what I choose, I'm going to let someone down."

Reaching to tuck a gentle hand around the back of her neck, Walter leaned his forehead against Lillian's. "I can't promise to give you all the things that matter to you, but I promise to work things out in the best possible way. Your well-being matters to me—more than myself and more than my dreams."

"But don't you see? I can say the same thing. I want *your plans* to matter most. That's the way I want to love you. So, where does that leave us? How do we decide who sacrifices what they want when we each want to make the other happy?"

He laughed, edging closer. "Well, if it's all the same to you, that's the only kind of argument I want us to have anymore. That's an argument where we both win."

Despite her tears, Lillian allowed a smile.

"There's just one more thing." Walter's voice was suddenly serious again.

"What?"

"I think there was one thing that you did wrong when we talked on the telephone—and I want to be sure we clarify it."

"Oh?"

"Lillian, I need you to promise that you won't say yes to me anymore when you're not sure. I need to be confident that you'll tell me the truth even when you're hesitating. Otherwise, I'll never know for certain if you're on board with our decisions or just playin' along."

It would be a difficult promise to keep, covering new relational territory. "I'll try," she answered staidly. "I'll do my very best."

CHAPTER 25

Conclusions

When he spotted Grace and Cass crossing the lawn toward him, Ben rose from his place on the grass and dusted off his trousers. Janie danced forward to greet them, oblivious to the solemnity of the moment.

The look on Grace's face was rather grim. "Kids, why don't you go play under those trees for a few minutes? I'd like to speak with Mr. Waldin, and then we'll all get a snack. Make sure that you stay well away from the road—stay where you can see us."

"Yes, ma'am," they both called.

Ben waited as Grace collected her thoughts, his brows low over his eyes, watching her carefully.

At last she said, "I tried again to speak with Veronika. Even Cass tried to convince her, but she's more determined than ever now to fight against authority. I've never seen a child so angry. No, not angry—but rather, so closed to truth. She just won't let us in—won't hear anything that I have to say."

Ben shook his head. "An' the lad? How'd that go?"

284

"It was the strangest conversation I've ever heard in my life. Oh, Ben, it was frightening." Grace looked toward where the children were playing, as if to be certain they were far enough away before continuing in a hushed tone. "Veronika called him Torrie, which she's never done in front of me before. And he called her Polly—well, not at first. But then she insisted and so he did. There were whole parts of their conversation that I didn't understand, as if the real world and their make-believe one were all twisted up together. I couldn't tell which stories were things that had really happened to them and which parts were things they'd only played."

"I ain't ne'er heard'a such."

"He said to her, 'Polly, what if this time Castor saves Pollux? Somebody else can help. It doesn't always have to be you.' And she answered him right away. She said, 'No, I'm Pollux. I have to be. Mána said.'"

"Jus' that?"

"Just that. Ben, I don't think she's coming back to us at all." Grace's eyes widened. Her hands clenched together in front of her. "And what's more, I don't think we could handle her if she did. She's moved beyond our reach, I'm afraid."

Ben had expected that such a distressing report would have brought Grace close to tears. At this moment she was not, though her words were grave and forthright. However, rather than making him feel a sense of her strength, this lack of emotion seemed a greater weakness. This situation was wearing away at Grace in a way that other difficult times had not. He asked gently, "Where'll they send her, then?"

"To that place in Ontario. It's out of our hands already. The government has taken over as guardian."

"An' the lad?"

Grace turned toward the children again and sighed. "He's left to us. To find him a proper home."

"Without his sister?"

"Yes, without her."

The words sank in, stunning Ben into silence. He was thinking of his sister Jane and the weight he'd carried while wondering if he'd ever see her again.

"I failed her, Ben. I wasn't enough."

"Don't ya say so, Grace."

"Well, the government thinks so."

"Rule'a man comes an' goes. Only God is yer Judge—ain't that what Pastor Bucky said? God's view is all what matters."

Her eyes shut tightly for a moment. "You're right, Ben. Thank you for your kind reminder." When she opened her eyes again, there were tears softening them. "I guess I'll have to pray that there'll be doctors who can help her there. Maybe someone else will understand her mind better than we do, so that they can help her more."

"I guess that could be. I hope so."

· · · ◉ · · ·

Once Lillian and Walter returned to the detention home, the long trip back to Brookfield could begin. Though Lillian would have liked to offer her assistance with the driving, it fell to the men to ferry them home. *Maybe on another day I'll have Walter give me a driving lesson.* She yawned and wrapped her shawl into a ball, stretched out her legs on the bench beside her, and was soon dozing, her head sliding farther and farther down the passenger window as the miles raced by.

They arrived home to find Miss Tilly seated on the front porch, the three sisters having already been tucked into their bed. It was a rare moment when even the seasoned old woman was visibly distraught by the news they delivered. Waving a hand in resignation, Miss Tilly turned and retreated into the house, her head bowed in grief.

Walter drew Lillian into a brief embrace, kissing her gently on the forehead, then hurried away. His car exited the driveway even before the older and more sluggish automobile that Ben was driving pulled into the yard carrying Grace and the children, who had long since fallen asleep in the back.

The next morning, the house seemed oddly quiet, as if an emotional fog had settled over it. Try as she might, Lillian was unable to shake the dark feelings. Castor had lost his sister. Veronika had lost her best opportunity to thrive. Was there anything they might have done differently that could have changed the outcome? It was pointless to ask, and yet impossible to keep the musings from festering in her mind.

By late afternoon, Lillian felt the need to get away for a while. She offered to walk with the Voss sisters into town. They needed new dresses, and Miss Tilly was going to teach Lillian how to lay out the pattern pieces and adjust them for each girl's size. Lillian hoped that being able to choose their own prints might be an enjoyable activity for all. The girls seemed interested in the prospect and fell quickly in step together. Hand in hand, the trio hurried forward as Lillian fell behind. She wasn't concerned. It gave her a chance to tip her face up into the bright sunshine and feel the warmth on her skin. It was good to be outdoors, to walk as a way to work out her muddled thoughts.

Mamie Voss was in the center. To her right, little sister Ora leaned in close as if needing moral support for the excursion into town, her two hands clutching at her oldest sister for courage. Irma, however, was swinging her arm back and forth, dragging Mamie's along by the hand that she held. Lillian smiled in amusement. They'd been able to ferret out so little about these girls—about their story and situation—but their personalities were becoming less and less mysterious.

Mamie was dreadfully quiet but always observant, watching

over her younger sisters doggedly. She managed their daily routines and made certain they cleaned their plates, washed their faces, and did their chores. But Mamie was also very difficult to engage. It was as if a sign were posted over her forehead: *I'm not staying here. This is not my home.* Miss Tilly seemed to have become a stand-in for the grandmother they'd been forced to leave. Mamie was almost always in the kitchen or the garden, wherever the older woman had set up her work for the moment. She was competent and diligent.

Lillian whispered again her constant prayer. *If only their situation at home improves so that they can go home to their family soon. Nothing short of that will bring them peace, it seems. Please, Father, help them go home.*

The youngest, Ora, was a little squirrel always on the lookout for danger from which she should hide. She tucked herself in behind the other two at the slightest hint of risk, only peeping out now and then to sample the pleasures of life if she felt entirely safe, if the situation were completely predictable.

And then there was Irma. Lillian had grown terribly fond of this child. Her head rose in defiance against all that happened around her, the unnamed wrongs that it seemed had been committed to undermine her. This twelve-year-old faced the storms of life with audacity and spunk, refusing to shrink away or be subdued. There was something about Irma that Lillian admired and wished she could emulate.

And it was from Irma that they'd learned why the girls' situation had changed so suddenly. One evening she'd blurted out, "We'd be home yet—'cept our daddy come back ta town drunk all the time."

"Irma!" Mamie had fired back. "Stop it!"

That was all. That had been the extent of the additional information they'd been able to glean from the sisters, even though both Grace and Miss Tilly had, time and again, encouraged the girl to speak her mind, assuring her that this was a safe place for such.

Oh, Father, bless Irma for her courage. Heal her precious heart, but build a hedge around her spirit so that it never ever surrenders.

There were so many ways for families to become broken, for children to be in jeopardy when they needed stability most during their childhood. Walter had said that he'd work with Lillian to find a path forward so the purposes of them both would be considered. Was there any way that he could ranch closer to Brookfield? Was there any property he could purchase here? *If You made a way, Lord, I could keep helping Grace with the children. Isn't that something that You've called me to do? Isn't that worth protecting?*

After Lillian had caught up to the girls and they'd begun their search for fabric, Mamie chose a robin's-egg-blue print with pink flowers scattered across it. Lillian added some lace trim for the collar and cuffs. Ora's material was simple and durable for playing outdoors. Miss Tilly planned to make her a jumper with a drop waist and pleated skirt. She'd also need a new white blouse underneath it. So Lillian found a nice middle-weight fabric for the shirt as well.

But Irma chose a bright yellow print with gray and white triangles scattered across it. She was very specific about how she wanted it sewn too. "Straight down with no waist, and black buttons up the front." As the clerk's scissors worked their way across the breadth of the fabric, Lillian wondered how Miss Tilly would react to such a loud print. *Oh, never mind, it's just a dress. Let Irma have whatever she likes when she finally makes a request.*

· · · ◉ · · ·

That evening, after the children had been tucked into bed, Lillian produced the yard goods, watching Miss Tilly's face as she laid each length on the kitchen table.

"Land sakes." That was all the woman said.

After a little while Grace joined them, beginning to baste the pieces of Mamie's dress together while Lillian and Miss Tilly continued to cut out the other fabrics. The windows had faded into darkness, and they were still just pinning the last piece of the second dress when Ben appeared at the back door for his usual cup of tea before bed. He and Miss Tilly were typically the only ones up at such a late hour. Grace and Lillian often opted to turn in by ten.

"Guess I won't bother ya t'night, then." Ben began to pull his boots back on.

"Nonsense. We're takin' up the whole table, but there's still the dinin' room. Set yerself down there an' have yer dessert. No reason ta let us hinder ya. I put the teakettle on fer ya, see? And there's still some rhubarb pie on the pantry shelf. You can read a bit, if you've a mind."

Irma's dress had been saved for last. Miss Tilly chuckled as she smoothed the yardage out flat with her hands. "I think that shopkeeper must'a been glad ta see this one sold. Bet it's been sittin' on the shelf fer ages waitin' fer just the right one ta come."

Lillian lifted a corner. "It suits her though. Somehow, it seems kind of right for Irma."

Grace laughed. "Well, that it does."

Lillian began laying out the butcher-paper pattern in order to cut Irma's simple pieces. Once the front panels of the dress were free, they laid them out on the table and set the buttons in place.

"I think it's cute," Grace claimed.

"'Twill be one'a its kind."

Lillian yawned over the back of her hand. "That's why it suits her."

Miss Tilly stated matter-of-factly, "Heard that Walt got his land. Ya must be only too pleased ta have a new place fer ya ta start yer future t'gether."

"Oh, you heard."

The scissors stopped, the blades gaping open. "That don't sound like gushin' with joy."

Lillian folded the sleeve pieces and set them on the pile with the others. She glanced from Miss Tilly to Grace. "It's beautiful. The land is just lovely. It's like a piece of heaven."

"Two quarters, eh? Heard it's in a valley with a stream. Yup, I'd say it's a right rare find."

Lillian wrinkled her nose, reluctant to dive into the complicated issue so late at night. "Well, Walter and I talked about it. We're still discussing it."

"What's ta discuss?"

Lillian turned away, straightening the piles of cut fabric. She answered as pragmatically as she could. "It's just that it's so far away. And I'm still helping Grace here—with the kids."

"Oh, sis, you don't think I'd let that stop you from beginning your life with Walter. I'd never hear of such a thing."

"Well, I . . ."

"No, you can't even consider it. Your future is with Walter, wherever he is. We all know that."

Lillian could feel two pairs of eyes evaluating her demeanor. Her shoulders drooped in defeat. There was no point in beating around the bush, so she took a seat at the table, pretending that the pins needed gathering. After a long pause she answered, "Even if I might *want* to stay?"

Grace set her work aside and moved to the chair next to Lillian's. "You can't mean that. This is all that Walter's been talking about for weeks."

Lillian's face began to warm with embarrassment. She tried to explain, "But what if it doesn't have to be so far away? If he could get land around here instead, we could still . . . I don't know. I could be around more—and still help out."

Now it was Miss Tilly who settled onto a neighboring chair. "That ain't how it works, Lillian. I think ya know that in yer heart. Don'tcha?"

Sighing, Lillian tried again. "We talked about it, Walter and I. He said we'd talk about it some more so that we could figure out a way that *both of us* would be satisfied."

"What is it that you're concerned about—really?" Grace was studying Lillian's eyes for clues.

Instinctively, her face dropped into her hands to hide from her sister's steady gaze. "I've tried to picture what it'll be like. Out there, in the middle of nothing. Just me and Walter. He'll be so busy building the barn and the house and everything. What on earth will I do?"

A chuckle from Miss Tilly. "I 'spect you'll have yer share'a the duties."

"But I won't have *this*. I won't have women to share it all with. I won't have someone to ask for help, and people to talk through my day with."

"You'll talk with Walter," Grace insisted.

"It's not the same."

Grace lifted Lillian's hand. "What aren't you saying, sis? I know there's more than this. I know that you and Walter are especially close. What is it that you don't want to admit out loud?"

There it was. Grace had not been so easily deterred. No matter what else seemed to stand in Lillian's way, she was well aware that this was the primary issue.

Lillian managed to mumble, "I don't want to leave you again, Grace. How can I? We just found each other."

"Oh, Lillian." Grace slipped an arm around her sister's shoulders. "You're not going to lose me. And I'm not going to lose you.

Even if we don't live in the same house, we'll never really be away from each other again. We're sisters. But we're also adults. We'll each have access to a car—so we can visit. And, well, you probably won't have a telephone for a few years, but I bet it won't be long. Then we can talk as often as we like. The way Miss Tilly talks to some of her children now."

Lillian turned her eyes up toward Miss Tilly, who had remained oddly silent. Now the woman laid her hand on Lillian's arm, a look of sadness in her eyes. "I ain't gonna lie to ya, dear. It ain't easy ta follow yer man an' be a helpmate. It's a callin'—an' a blessin' too. But it ain't always easy." She pushed the scraps of fabric out of her way, leaning farther across the table. "I can tell ya what I figured out though. There ain't no way ta love 'cept with sacrifice. Ya can't have all that ya want. Ya gotta pick and choose. An' if ya found a good man—like ya did with Walt— then it's worth givin' up a heap'a other things ta make a proper life with him."

"She's right, sis. You need to focus on your marriage first."

"An' soon you'll have kids'a yer own. They'll be yer whole world fer a while. But if ya don't give yerself—all'a yerself—ya can't have the kinda love that ya need ta make it work the way it's s'posed ta. You'll be sellin' yerself short, an' cripplin' yer poor husband. I know ya, Lillian. You love that man too much ta settle fer less than the best fer him."

"I know, I know." Her words were a whimper. "It's just so hard to leave. I want to stay here with you *and* go with Walter too. I can't even imagine actually leaving you all."

"An' someday ya won't. You'll get ta be ferever with the ones ya love. But that ain't earth, dearie. That's heaven. Fer this life, sayin' our good-byes from time ta time is jus' the way it is."

Grace had begun to sniffle too. Miss Tilly's words were blunt but true, at once candid and practical.

"Yer choice, girls, is plain. Ya either take the sacrifice that comes with lovin'—or ya make the sacrifice that comes with not darin' ta try. If ya think ya can protect yerself from it all, ya end up causin' more harm than ya dodge. I ain't seen nothin' betwixt the two. No way to live without givin' up some things too."

"But what will Grace do? I'm worried about you too, Grace. How will you keep up with everything once I'm gone?"

"I'll manage. I have Miss Tilly. And I have this wonderful house that your father so graciously allows us to use. And," she added indecorously loudly, "I have Ben too. At least I hope that I do."

Footsteps crept from the dining room up the hallway, and an uncertain face appeared around the corner by the woodstove. "I'm sorry," he began. "I was tryin' not ta listen in."

Grace answered first. "Oh, Ben, with everything you've been through with us, how can you still doubt that we think of you as family? I wish you'd just surrender to that fact."

Miss Tilly rose from her chair. "'Cause he's still livin' *in the barn*—that's how."

Lillian exchanged glances with Grace. Without hesitation she agreed. "You need to move into the house, Ben."

"No, miss, I—"

"O'course he does," Miss Tilly insisted. "It ain't fittin' fer a grown man ta live in such a state. Now, it's late an' I'm gonna say my piece 'fore I'm off ta bed. Lillian, it'll be nigh unto a year 'fore Walt can get a house built on that land. So, ya got time ta work through yer fears. An' b'fore even that, there'll be a weddin' ta plan. That'll keep ya plenty busy too. But I don't see that it's right fer Ben ta live a day longer where he does. It don't honor him proper fer all that he does here. Therefore, seems ta me it makes the most sense fer me ta take a room upstairs so Ben can have the workroom I been usin' instead. It's first floor an' he can get in and out without wakin' folk. I'll move the pantry shelves into the mudroom or such so's he can have the whole of it. I don't care where ya wanna put me, so long's I keep my mattress. Now, that's my say, fer what it's worth."

The room became silent. Miss Tilly crossed the floor and closed her door behind her.

After several moments, Grace spoke. "Well then. We can figure out how to move things around tomorrow."

CHAPTER 26

Home

Ben stared up at the plastered ceiling. The move into the workroom had been surprisingly easy. Other than her favorite mattress, Miss Tilly had little in the way of possessions. And Ben's duffel bag had been easy enough to carry inside. It turned out that the sisters had decided to share the master bedroom, taking full advantage of the time they had left together. This meant that Miss Tilly could be given Grace's room.

Janie was beside herself with excitement throughout the first day. They were living under the same roof now. She could spend time with him in his room without crossing the yard. There was a small table and a comfortable stuffed chair. When they read stories together in the evening, she could snuggle on his lap or stretch out across the handmade tufted rug. And best of all, at last he'd been provided with a proper mattress filled with feathers.

But Freddie's room was now occupied by Castor. It was as if a period had been placed at the end of a sentence. Ben would need to make peace with the idea that the boy was gone now, just as they'd all been forced to surrender the girl to the unknown.

Unless Freddie committed some crime, even the Mounted Police had little interest in pursuing him.

Ben was glad that he'd refused to take back his money. Hopefully the boy would manage it well rather than squander it. If it could help Freddie establish any kind of suitable life, it was worth the loss, heavy as it was. But Ben had little hope now of striking out on his own any time soon. Janie was content here. His family was settled in Denholm, and they'd been pleased with the idea of a weekly visit.

An' if I had the money back, what would change? He laughed to himself. "S'pose I'd build me a little cabin—er just a lean-to on the back'a the house. So's Miss Tilly had her room back an' there'd be more space upstairs fer kiddos."

What're me plans, then? This it? A hired hand instead'a me own home? Better'n what I had fer most'a me life, but still . . . I can't adopt Janie this way. Can't marry an' bring a wife here. Maybe I just got meself stuck in this place instead'a free.

A rustling sound on the other side of Ben's door made a tingle run down his spine. Was it coming from the kitchen? Or beyond? The house had been quiet for at least an hour.

He rose slowly from his bed, determined to investigate, yet not wanting to embarrass anyone who might have come down for a late-night snack. He had no idea what kinds of activities might go on here in the wee hours of the night. Quietly he turned the handle, opening the door just a crack.

But the dark form standing in the doorway to the mudroom was not one of the women. Instantly Ben bristled. He reached for the nearest weapon, his hand falling on his volume of Shakespeare. Raising it above his head, he threw the door open wide and rushed out.

"Stop!" he shouted viciously.

The form spun to face him. Ben lunged forward, tackling him to the floor.

"Mr. Waldin! It's me."

Now Ben recoiled, pushing off the body that lay beneath him, unable to make sense of what was happening.

The voice whimpered, "It's Freddie, sir."

"What?"

The shock of it all made it impossible for Ben to believe. He leapt to his feet, catching the boy by the shoulder of his shirt and hauling him up from the floor. He pushed him nearer the window, to where a patch of moonlight lit his face. "Freddie? Lad? That you?"

Tears were streaming from the boy's eyes. His lips were contorted by fear and sorrow.

Ben threw his arms around him, clutching deep folds on the back of Freddie's jacket with both hands. "Ya come back. Ya come back."

Holding fast to the weeping boy, Ben was shocked once more by a voice near his elbow.

"Ben, who is it? What's going on?"

He released Freddie from his embrace, still clutching at the jacket with one hand lest the boy somehow get away again. Grace's face glowed white behind the brightness of her lamp. Ben stuttered, "It's . . . it's Freddie. He's . . . he's come home."

The teenager dropped his head to his own chest and heaved another sob.

Grace grasped Freddie's hand, drawing him gently forward into the kitchen. "Oh, Freddie. Oh, son. Come inside, please. Sit down."

Ben followed behind, still holding on with one hand. He drew out a chair with the other and eased the boy onto it, pulling the next seat up in front of him and sitting so close that their foreheads almost touched. Grace lit another lamp, setting it on the table.

Lillian and Miss Tilly appeared on the stairway, tentative at first, then exclaiming at the scene they found. "Freddie! Oh, praise the Lord! You're back."

It was some time before the boy was composed enough to speak. His trembling voice stammered, "I—I brought yer money back, Mr. Waldin. I couldn't keep it. W-weren't right. All yer hard work."

"That don't matter. Ya come home, lad. Ya come home."

· · ◦ ● ◦ · ·

Somehow the children on the second floor slept through the late-night kerfuffle. After about an hour of convincing the boy that he was truly welcome, the women retreated upstairs. But Ben, in his concern that the boy might leave as unexpectedly as he'd come, tucked Freddie into his own bed and sat in the stuffed chair so that he could keep watch, half sleeping throughout the remainder of the night.

In the morning, even before breakfast, Freddie shook Ben's arm. "I gotta go, Mr. Waldin. I gotta go 'pologize ta Lemmy."

"What?"

"It was me what hurt him. All I see when I shut me eyes each night is his bloody face peerin' out from under all them leaves. I tried me best, Mr. Waldin. I covered him over ta try an' keep him warm—even left me own coat on him. But that don't make up fer it all. I gotta go talk to him now, b'fore any more time passes."

Ben forced himself to stand. "I'll come."

"Ya don't gotta."

"I'll come."

Arthur Thompson was duly surprised by their early morning visit. From across the yard he waved as he recognized Ben. Once he'd identified the boy who trudged beside him, he set down his pitchfork and hurried to meet them.

"Morning." It was said with suitable suspicion.

"Morning, Arthur. Freddie come home late last night. First thing he wanted was ta see Lemmy, ta 'pologize."

The man cleared his throat, assessing his guests carefully. "Lemuel's still inside. He's eating breakfast, I believe."

"Mind if we knock?"

"Please, come on in." They followed Arthur up the steps and into the house.

Just as Arthur had supposed, Lemuel was seated at the table with Jesse and Harrison. June was standing at the stove, frying up bacon that sizzled in its pan and filled the room with the aroma of breakfast.

Lemuel stood immediately, pushing his chair back against the wall. His movement brought his older brother Jesse to his feet, a hand on the boy's shoulder. The color had drained from Lemuel's face. Ben was uncertain if the boy intended to flee or fight.

But Mr. Thompson's words interjected calm. "Freddie's come to apologize, Lemuel. He wants to speak with you. Now, is that something that you're willing to do right now? Or would you rather wait until another time? This doesn't need to happen if you're not ready to listen."

Lemuel's wide eyes traveled slowly from Freddie to Ben, from Arthur to June and back again to Freddie. At last he offered, "I'll listen," and sat down, pushing his plate away and crossing his arms in front of him.

Freddie looked up at Ben as if to gain courage. He pulled the cap from his head, twisting it fiercely as he spoke. "I'm sorry, Lemmy. Jus' as sorry as I can be. I shoulda listened when ya tol' me not ta keep usin' me slingshot. An' I shoulda listened when ya told me jus' ta leave the girl be—not ta argue with her. I'm jus' as sorry as I can be that you was the one what got hurt when ya did nothin' wrong." His lip was quivering, though he was clearly trying his best to maintain control. "I'm glad ya didn't die."

This brought a chortle from Lemuel. "Well, ain't that kind of ya."

"I don't mean it that way. I stayed with ya. I watched out fer ya. An' when I heard a dog comin', I got a bunch'a rocks and climbed a tree—so's I could defend ya if it come to it."

"An' that makes it right?"

"No! No. It were wrong. I'll do whate'er I can ta make it up ta ya. I'm so sorry. I am."

"How come?"

"What?"

"How come yer so sorry now?"

Freddie twisted the hat harder. His face turned to stone. "Seein' ya like that, and then bein' alone, it makes a fella think. An' plain as day it come ta me. I don't wanna be like me dad. I don't wanna bring harm ta all around me. Thought I could jus' go away—but then I stole from Mr. Waldin. Everything I did was wrong. I dunno why. An' I don't blame ya if ya can't fergive me. But all I could think 'bout was comin' back and sayin' it, jus' the same."

Lemuel muttered, "I'll think on it."

"Thanks, Lemmy. That's kind'a ya." And then his eyes lifted quickly as he added, "I even walked yer horse back—found where she come from. Went lane by lane till I found someone what knew the owner. Jus' 'cause I knew how much it mattered ta ya."

Lemuel nodded back slowly. "Well, that's somethin'."

"An' I give Ben back his money—well, most'a it. Tol' him I'll work ta pay him back the rest."

Lemuel braced his palms against the table for a moment as if rising from his seat was going to be an effort. Then he stood and walked to Freddie. Without comment, he extended his hand. Freddie grasped it anxiously. "I forgive you," Lemuel said, shaking his head as if in disbelief at what he was choosing to do. "Yer a dumb clod. But I guess I forgive ya."

Ben bid the Thompsons farewell and led the way back to the road. Then his arm went around the boy's shoulders. Freddie seemed surprised but didn't move away.

·· · ● · ··

The following morning, Ben was out on the road early. He'd made a call to the Denholm hotel and had a message delivered to Jane and his parents that he'd be making an unscheduled trip out to see them. There were things that he knew he needed to say, and he felt he might finally understand them enough to try.

For one thing, he hadn't made the trip to Denholm earlier in the week as he'd planned. Instead, he'd been needed to drive Grace to Calgary. Was that just earlier this week? It seemed such a long time ago now.

Coming to a stop in front of the hotel, Ben saw Jane rush out the door. Inside he found Mam resting in her room and spent some time chatting with them about the plans for Jane's upcoming wedding and subsequent move out to Lloyd's farm. Then, at last, he asked where he might find Dada.

Jane said, "He's gone down to the smithy. He was goin' to start out makin' pans and pails for sale in Calg'ry, but he's been told—what with the cost of supplies here—to make tin ceiling panels instead. Better chance'a makin' ends meet. That's been an excitin' thought for Dada, means he could use more of his artistry."

There was no way around it. Ben would walk down the short dirt street to where the blacksmith shop was located, hoping his father would agree to lay down his tools and come outdoors in order for them to speak privately. Ben felt a flutter of fear, much as Freddie must have felt as they approached the Thompsons' house. *What will Dada say?*

So Ben was relieved to be redirected to the back alley behind the shop, where his father was resting, seated on the back of a truck bed and smoking his pipe. It was quickly apparent that he was taking a break from unloading his supplies, half of which were still piled in the truck.

"Can I help ya?" Ben offered first.

"Won't say no."

Dada remained at rest as Ben moved the crates one at a time from the truck to the shop, stacking them with the others.

When there was just one crate left, Ben approached him. "I come ta speak to ya, Dada."

"Oh?"

Removing his cap and stuffing it into his back pocket, Ben raked a trembling hand through his hair. "Don't know if ya heard we'd a boy run away."

Dada nodded. His face revealed nothing.

"It were a hard thing fer me—ta worry an' not ta know what become'a him."

A slow nod, as thin curls of smoke escaped from Dada's lips.

"Made me think what it might'a been like fer you, sir. When I left ya as a lad."

The stony face angled slightly away.

Ben took a deep breath. "Dada, I come ta say how sorry I am. I think I might know now a little'a how it felt when I up an' left ya. When I left Mam an' Jane—an' you. An' I need ya to know, even though it's taken me what feels a lifetime, I'm sorry. I'm very sorry ta have hurt ya like that, sir."

No response. Ben waited a little longer, feeling his hands begin to clench at his sides. And still no response.

"Well, all right, Dada. I'm goin' ta take this last box in an' go say me fare-thee-wells ta Mam and Jane." Try as he did to suppress it, some of his strain showed in his voice. "An' anyhow, that's what I come ta ask ya. So there's nothin' more, I guess."

"Ya didn't ask me nothin'." Still the old face gazed toward the railroad tracks behind them.

303

"What?"

"Ya said yer piece. But ya didn't ask."

Frustration was rising along the muscles in Ben's shoulders. "I don't understand ya. What d'ya mean?"

Turning the pipe over and tapping it against the edge of the truck to knock out the ashes, Dada grumbled, "What did ya wanna ask me, then?"

For a moment Ben stood in confusion, managing at last, "Will ya fergive me, sir?"

Dada pushed up off the bed of the truck slowly. His expression had not changed. His voice had not softened, but he answered gruffly, "Been waitin' a long time ta hear ya ask it. I fergive ya, Ebenezer. Now get that last box, lad. An' we'll go see yer mam."

· · · ● · · ·

Father was keeping another secret. The worrisome thought percolated in the back of Lillian's mind, making it difficult to concentrate on the Sunday sermon. She'd been invited to dine with Delyth and him at the hotel right after church. In fact, Father had invited almost everyone—Walter and Miss Tilly, Grace and Ben. He'd even invited Lemuel, with whom, it seemed, Father recently had struck up a friendship. He'd been dropping by the Thompson farm, renewing his acquaintance with his familiar neighbors, even using his skills with metalwork to help repair their rake.

Father had arranged for Ben to drive their party into town for church. They sat together now in a long row, a strange assembly of people. Delyth and Father had dressed as usual for the other church in town, where they attended regularly. Father, in his houndstooth vest and blue silk tie, and Delyth, sporting a stylish narrow skirt that flared wide at the bottom, were seated side by side with Miss Tilly's every-Sunday dark blue dress and straw hat and Ben's best-of-what-I-own dungarees. Then came

Grace and Lillian, followed by the children all in a row—with Irma's yellow dress glowing brightly at the end. Only Freddie had remained at home.

After church, they'd arranged for Mamie to look after the other children at home and to feed them their lunch. Miss Tilly, of course, had already worked with the fifteen-year-old on the preparations for it. An easy stew was bubbling slowly in the oven. All the arrangements had fallen into place fairly easily, and yet Lillian could not set aside her nerves.

All during dinner in the fancy dining room of the hotel, there was not a hint of the secret revealed. Lillian remained fairly quiet, watching all her friends and family interact together. Father was clearly enjoying his role as the host of their meal. *What on earth is he scheming to do?*

After the meal, they dutifully obeyed Father's further directions. Everyone loaded back into the lumbering automobile, and Ben followed Father's new roadster, passing through town and coming out again on the south side. Then they turned onto a road to the west that Lillian had never traveled previously and bounced along together for at least two miles. At last Father's car turned in at a narrow lane and Ben followed behind.

It took some time to clamber from the vehicles and assemble together in the grass. All the while, Father was beaming. No one seemed brave enough to inquire as to the nature of their excursion. They stood in silence, glancing around themselves uneasily for cues.

Then Father lifted his hands dramatically and asked, "Well, what do you think?"

No one answered.

"What do you think of the land here?"

The fog began to lift in Lillian's cloudy brain. "Oh, are you *buying* it, Father? Are you—do you plan to build on it? Or to rent it out?"

"No, silly." He seemed genuinely surprised that none of them appeared to grasp his intentions. "It's for you—for you and Walter. So he can ranch close by—and you can continue working with Grace at the children's home."

Lillian's mouth hung open. Her eyes lifted to Walter's face. He seemed just as much at a loss for words.

At last Walter managed, "That's kind of you, sir. Very kind. But we couldn't possibly—"

"Nonsense! I'm glad to be able to do it. It's forty lovely acres. Unspoiled land. You could have possession of it in a month and be ready to build as soon after that as you like."

Lillian reached beside her for the support of Walter's hand before answering slowly. "Oh, Father—that's so kind of you—so generous. I can't even express what a lovely gesture this is. But I'm afraid we'd need a much larger piece of land than this in order to ranch the way that Walter is planning. The property he found is a parcel of one hundred sixty acres, and we expect that he'll own two of them."

A calm voice drawled beside her, "Well, Lillian . . ."

What on earth? Is Walter even considering this?

"Maybe we could make somethin' work here. I mean, Tommy thought I might begin to run some of my stock on a part of his land. I could start smaller than I'd hoped. Maybe we could get more land later."

"But it would be in separate pieces, then—it wouldn't all be one parcel." Lillian squeezed Walter's hand harder, turning for support to the others who stood nearby. *Is it me? Should I be excited?*

But Miss Tilly's face was set in a pensive frown. Grace's eyes refused to meet Lillian's now, looking out toward the row of mountains behind them instead. Ben had drawn his cap from his head and was twisting it in his hands the way he did during difficult moments. Even Lemuel, who stood closest to Father, seemed less than enthusiastic, even confused. Still no one else dared to speak.

Walter tried again, turning this time to face Lillian and catching up her second hand too. "It would keep us here, Lill. We could build more slowly over time. But we wouldn't have to move away from Brookfield. It's certainly something to think about." His words were coming more quickly as he labored to assemble a convincing argument. "I could build a house and a barn in the fall. We could marry at Christmas. We'd be all tucked up and cozy before the worst of the weather hit. And I have a car already, so I could drive out to Tommy's and take care of my little herd. That'd work for makin' a start anyway. . . ."

Lillian's chest felt so tight that it might refuse to allow her another breath. She whispered hoarsely, "Walter? That's not what we talked about. This isn't what you dreamed of."

"I know, Lill, but maybe it's a good compromise—a place to start."

The image of the land they'd visited in Walter's valley filled Lillian's mind. The little brook. The rolling hills. The portrait Walter had painted with his words overlaid across it. It would mean that he was giving all of it up in order to keep her close to home and the people she loved.

"No," she whispered. "We can't. I can't. It wouldn't be right."

He shifted in place uncomfortably. His eyes rose to where Father stood awaiting their response. After he exhaled slowly, Walter's focus returned to Lillian again. "It might work."

She said more firmly this time, "No, it would be wrong."

At last Miss Tilly chimed in. "It's a perty piece'a land. Though, she's right that it wouldn't suit fer cattle. Might do fer a few head if it had a proper source'a water. Sure is perty, though, Mr. Walsh. Such a kind thing fer ya ta offer."

Grace moved forward, placing a gentle arm around Lillian. "I know it's a big decision, sis. What an incredible proposition for you! And nobody wants to keep you here more than me. But you need to do what's right for the two of you. You have to choose your own future."

At last Lillian felt able to look back toward Father. He stood in utter disbelief, obviously having never considered the possibility that his generous gift might be rejected. Lillian rushed to embrace him.

"Oh, Father, it's the kindest thing that anyone's ever done. It's just like you to think of a way to try and make everyone happy—to care for the people in your family with astounding generosity." Her hands reached to wipe away her tears so that she could see his face better. "But I can't. I can't ask Walter to give up his dream so that I can have mine instead. You understand, don't you?"

It was Delyth who answered. "Of cour-rse you can't, dear. Even if this land helped to fulfill your father's own pleasant imaginings too. He loves you. Don't you, *cariad*?"

Father sputtered for a moment. "I do. I do love you, Lillian dear. And of course I want the very best for your future. So if that means . . ." Father swallowed hard. "If that means you and Walter must move on to, shall we say, greener pastures—well then, of course I understand that. Just don't leave us out of the picture—too much."

"Never. We'll be around so often you'll soon tire of us."

Lillian reached out tentative arms toward Delyth and accepted a firm embrace in return.

· · • · ·

Lemuel had decided to pay a visit to the Walsh house. After the strange events on Sunday morning, he was curious to get a sense of the women's reactions. Miss Lillian's father had offered a gift of land. Sure, it wasn't as much land as they'd hoped for, but it seemed preposterous to him that they'd turned Mr. Walsh down.

So after all of his regular chores were finished, Lemuel made the familiar walk down the road toward their home, arriving by accident just in time for evening devotions. Without hesitating, Miss Grace herded him to the parlor along with the others so that he could once again participate in the family practice, promising him a cup of tea and a chat afterward. In fact, it seemed that now Mr. Waldin and Freddie had also agreed to attend. Lemuel grinned at Freddie, slightly amused at how the blustery young man had been tamed by his current situation. Lemuel was even more amused to watch Freddie's halfhearted efforts to sing along with the rest of the children.

But Miss Grace asked Cass to stay behind with her while Miss Lillian led all of the other children upstairs for bed. The little boy seemed entirely unconcerned about what it was that she'd disclose. With a nod from Miss Grace, Mr. Waldin and Lemuel remained in their seats. Freddie opted to follow the others out of the room.

Miss Grace began, "Cass, I wanted to let you know that we received a letter today."

"Fer me, miss?"

"It came from the people who are taking care of Veronika."

"Oh. Is she all right?"

"She's fine. She's healthy and well cared for. But they've decided that it's time to send her to Ontario to the other place to live."

"Will she ever come back?" Cass's words were tight and thin. His eyes filled with unspoken concerns.

Miss Grace scooped up his hand in her own. "I don't know, Cass. I wish I did. But you know that she loves you—the best way that she knows how. And you know that you're still the most important person in the whole world to your sister."

"Why'd she hafta go so far away, Miss Grace? Was it 'cause she didn't find our uncles?"

A deep breath. "No. It wasn't that. I'm not sure how to explain it, sweetheart. Her mind is telling her things that aren't true, and she can't seem to understand the difference between what's real and what's . . . what's . . ."

Cass completed her sentence. "Pertend?"

"Yes, I suppose that's accurate. What's real and what's pretend."

Lemuel watched as the little boy climbed up onto Miss Grace's lap, slipping one small arm around the back of her neck. "I wish she didn't hafta go so far away, Miss Grace."

"Me too, Cass."

His eyes squinted up at her for a moment. "But, Miss Grace?"

"Yes?"

"I don't think I wanted her to come back here. Is it bad that I don't want her to live here with us?"

Miss Grace drew him close. "Oh no, son. We all want what's best for Veronika—and for you too. In the East there are doctors who know more about how people's minds work. We think they might be able to help her. And even if she doesn't live with us anymore, it doesn't mean we don't love her. We'll continue to pray for her. We can even write to her. Maybe sometimes we'll be able to talk to her on the telephone—all the way across the country to Ontario. But I don't think she'll come back and live with us again. Do you understand that, Cass?"

The little boy nodded. But when he spoke again, his words were mixed with sniffles. "Am I gonna hafta go away now too? Are ya gonna get me a fam'ly?"

The fear that Cass expressed was one that Lemuel had struggled to hold at bay too. He'd been content in this home. Moving on to any other situation had seemed just another daunting change. *But Mum an' Dad are different than I thought. At first it was hard, but now . . . well, it feels like I'm in the right place finally.*

Miss Grace continued, "Darling, I don't know for sure what

will happen next. But I promise you this: You can stay here until we find somebody who loves you even more than we do—and we love you very, very much. So you know we're going to be very, very careful."

Lemuel cleared his throat, struggling for the right words to express what he had a strong desire to say. "It's true, Cass. I know it, 'cause they let me stay here till they found a better place fer me—a family fer good."

Miss Grace's eyes lit up, her smile softening into tenderness as she managed to reply, "I'm so glad, Lemuel. So very glad that's how you feel."

Cass burrowed deeper into her embrace. Then Miss Tilly arrived with the tray of teacups. Even Miss Lillian returned to the parlor. So Miss Grace led Cass up to bed while the others settled in, sipping their tea solemnly.

At last Miss Lillian broke the silence with a sigh. "It's so good to have you here for a visit, Lemuel. I've been wondering how you're settling back in."

He blushed. "I'm fine, Miss Lillian. I registered fer me last year'a classes at school. Miss Campbell says she thinks I'll be ready to take the entrance exams fer college. I never really thought . . ." He let the sentence hang unfinished.

"Well, we did," Miss Lillian insisted. "We all knew you had it in you. I'm sure you'll be a doctor one day. And I suppose you'll have to go away to the city for that. I guess we're all moving away eventually."

"I suppose so, Miss Lillian." Lemuel grappled for the right way to express what he was feeling. "But some places we don't ever really leave. We jus' carry 'em deep inside." Eyes closed, he added with emotion, "Like here. It's like I got two homes now, instead of jus' one."

Epilogue

Lemuel shifted into a lower gear, easing his black sedan around the last tree-lined corner, where he knew the outskirts of Brookfield would appear. The town had expanded every time he'd visited home since he'd gone away to university. The Walsh house that had once been on the outskirts of town had been surrounded little by little with new housing and businesses. Now Dad's farm stood at the far limit of town, and a developer had purchased the farm across the road from his, intending to build houses there too. That plan, however, had come to nothing when the stock market had crashed a few years back. The field stood empty still, the poor farmhouse deserted.

Lemuel could hardly recall how long it had been since he'd been back. Mum invited him almost every time he chatted with her over the telephone, but following his move to Lethbridge, he'd become suddenly busier. Practicing medicine in the city was very different from the small towns he'd served before. And at thirty-five, he was rather young to be a surgeon at such a notable hospital. But it certainly provided better for his wife

313

and children, now that times were so difficult for everyone. Still, a family wedding—that was always important to come home for. There was no excuse that would be considered acceptable.

He shook his head again at the memories prompted by the familiar landscape. Each farmhouse brought to mind faces from his past. A few of the boys that Lemuel had known had enlisted in the Great War and never returned to Canada. But Freddie had come home a decorated sergeant, soon afterward joining the Mounted Police. He was living far to the north now, where he could still enjoy the frontier lifestyle. George had remained in England at the end of the war, marrying a nurse he'd met while serving overseas.

Lemuel smiled again. Actually, it was because of Freddie and George traveling to England that Janie's sister, Margaret, had been located. By then aged seventeen and just finished at her boarding school, Margaret had been quick to accept an invitation to travel to Canada, where she could reunite with her little sister. Margaret lived near Harstad now and was married to Byron McRae, the eldest of Ernest and Sophie's children.

The difficulties of Lemuel's vision, though it had improved somewhat, had made it impossible for him to enlist. Additionally, his medical degree had not yet been completed in order to allow him to serve as a medic. It had been dreadful for Lemuel to feel unable to do his share in such a profound duty. Even now, he shuddered whenever he thought about what others had been through without him.

His older brother Lou had finally come home from the States in order to enlist. But he was killed early in the war, and Mum still tended the small memorial in his honor over the fireplace mantel. So many years later, and yet the mixture of memory and grief was just as strong—inflamed once more by Lemuel's return to Brookfield.

But good, prosperous years had followed the war, reestablishing hope and revitalizing the country. And even Lemuel had done some conservative investing in the stock market with all of the global enthusiasm. When it had all come crashing down, he'd still had savings to fall back on, unlike so many others he knew. Even some of the other doctors he'd gone to school with had become penniless.

Harrison—always so enticed by the idea of getting ahead easily—had lost everything. So Lemuel's little brother had moved back to Brookfield with his wife and four children to farm with Dad. And Dad had been grateful for more help as he aged, having by then retired as principal. Just a year after returning, Harrison had opened a barbershop "on the side" and had slowly begun to grow a little venture of his own. It was a perfect occupation for this outgoing brother, giving him ample opportunity to socialize, even to this day introducing himself as "'Arrison, but never 'Arry."

Their town and the surrounding ranches had continued to make slow progress forward despite the world's financial woes and the coinciding dust bowl. Sometimes rain still fell on this area so close to the Rockies, whereas out on the open prairies, the terrible drought had hit hard.

As a doctor, Lemuel lived comfortably enough. His wife, Irma, had managed to set up a lovely home for them with very little fuss and expense. Steady, determined Irma—whose character was still so similar to the way she'd been as a child in the Walsh house, where Lemuel had first met her. Despite the dust bowl, they'd managed a comfortable life together. Every night, though, before tucking their two children into bed, Irma would first shake the dust out of their blankets, and every day the wind would drive the dust particles inside through the walls around the windows so that there'd be a fine layer again by the next evening. Irma never complained, however. Surely someday the skies would open regularly once more.

Lemuel glanced across the car at the passenger seat. Irma

had been looking out her window, but his movement seemed to draw her eye. She forced a smile and reached for his hand. Lemuel squeezed back tenderly. They understood each other so well. Memories were complicated things. There was no sense in denying their prominence. They had to be dealt with every time that the feelings arose. And Irma was quite frank regarding her mixed emotions about coming back to Brookfield.

In truth, she was the main reason for their infrequent visits. Irma ended up living for almost three years in the Walsh house with Miss Grace, Miss Tilly, and Mr. Waldin. By then her older sister, Mamie, had married and brought her sisters to live with her and her new husband, a mechanic in town. However, that situation had not been an improvement for Irma. So, at sixteen, Irma had moved to Calgary with two other friends who'd gotten jobs stitching uniforms for the army during the war years. That's where she'd reconnected with Lemuel. He was completing his medical training and, by then, Irma was managing a garment shop. It hadn't taken long for Lemuel to appreciate her determination and straightforward approach to life. Irma had quickly become the central pillar of his world, the first person with whom Lemuel felt he could truly express himself. She was the stronger of the two of them. He was fully aware of how much he depended on his beautiful wife. Together, he was certain, they could face anything. Even the complexities of going home for a wedding.

· · · ● · · · ·

Ben pulled the dark suit jacket over his starched white shirt. He'd never enjoyed wearing a jacket and tie. It was all too constricting, unnatural. But the wedding guests would be arriving at the church soon, and he'd been assigned the task of chauffeuring the bride and her father. He knew firsthand the flutter of activity that was happening in the bedrooms above him. Only four years ago, he'd been father of the bride when Janie had married Frank

Caulfield, the older brother of Matty and Milton. Now Frank and his brothers operated a large ranch south of Brookfield, and Janie could still visit the Walsh house frequently. She'd made him a grandfather too. Janie and Frank had two children, a third on the way. The twins, Matty and Milton, were both married now too, choosing sisters as brides and happily sharing an especially close-knit life, just as they'd always done.

All of them would be waiting at the church soon, ready to celebrate with their large extended family. Whatever Ben's inconveniences on this day—even giving up his own bedroom to dress in the workroom off the kitchen instead—it was nothing in comparison to preparing the bride herself. *No sir, I'll take this o'er bride's father any ol' day.*

Grace appeared in the doorway, laughing at the sight of him. "You haven't really managed your tie, have you?"

"Thought I did it fine."

"Here, let me."

Gentle hands drew the loops apart once more. She started over, chatting as she did. "They're almost ready upstairs. Lillian is keeping relatively calm, but you know she's as edgy as a mama bear on the inside. Have you seen Walter?"

"Not fer a while." The solemnity of the day and the way Grace was looking up at him stirred a memory. "Grace?"

"Yes?"

"Do ya 'member the day I was goin' ta leave ya?"

Her hands smoothed down his lapels, stopping to button his jacket for him. "I do. When you'd decided to move into town— and perhaps take Janie away from us."

Ben brushed a loose strand of Grace's hair back into place. "The day ya asked me ta marry ya."

A soft chuckle. "I remember." She turned her face away.

Pulling her toward him affectionately, it was Ben's turn to laugh. "Ain't many a man can say his wife done the askin'."

317

"Well, you've never let me forget it." Her soft eyes removed all the sting from her words.

His arms went around Grace's waist as he kissed her forehead. He welcomed the memory as it flooded back.

They'd been standing in almost this very spot. He'd been packing his things, intent on exiting the home for good after just a few months of living in the workroom. When Grace had arrived with a handful of cloth napkins that she'd intended to put away in the hutch, he'd announced, "I been thinkin'. It's not right fer me ta live in the house. Folks might get the wrong idea."

Grace had stopped and stared, for the first time noticing that his duffel was packed.

He continued, "Me bein' unmarried, an' you so young an' . . ." He left his description unfinished.

Grace had worked to straighten the last of the napkins, turning her back on him in order to lay them inside the proper drawer neatly. Her voice answered calmly, "I've been thinking about that too. I suppose it might seem—odd—to those who don't know us well. It's not as if we're here all alone—but some folks are pretty quick to jump to false conclusions."

He cleared his throat. It was settled, then. She'd agreed. "'Xactly. A good woman's reputation needs guardin'. Sure don't wanna set tongues waggin'."

Grace had frozen in place, her words coming slower, more carefully. "Where are you going, then?"

"Back ta the barn, fer now. Got me eye on a little house in town what needs fixin'—fer me an' Janie."

Her shoulders stiffened. She drew a deep breath. "I suppose the only way to stop the wagging tongues would be to marry."

"Now, Grace, we talked b'fore 'bout me adoptin' Janie. Said I wouldn't ne'er ask a woman ta marry me jus' ta meet the legal—"

Grace pushed the drawer closed loudly. "Why *would* you ask a woman to marry you?"

"Why . . . what d'ya mean? Fer love. What d'ya mean?"

"I see." She turned to face him, a frown creasing her forehead. "And you don't think you could learn to love me?"

His mouth went instantly dry. "You? What? What d'ya mean—you?"

"It's just that I've been wondering why you've never considered me as an option. It may seem impertinent to ask, but—you must have some compelling reason to discount me as a possibility." Standing before him, she lifted her eyes and, unflinchingly, Grace awaited his answer.

"Oh, Grace, I . . . Ya got ta know I ain't ne'er discounted ya at all. Yer me better in every way. I could ne'er, under any condition, think that ya—"

She took a small step toward him. "Oh, you couldn't? Under any conditions. Well, I could." A deep breath. "And I only have one condition."

"You? A condition?"

"Only one."

"Are ya makin' fun'a me, Grace?"

"No. No, I'm quite serious." Another small step closer.

He cleared his throat. "I got so little, Grace. There ain't ne'er a chance I'd be able ta meet yer condition."

"Well, I believe you could."

Ben fell away a little, studying her closely for a hint of a smile, a flicker of amusement. But there was none. "Yer serious? What . . . ?"

"Cass."

"Cass?"

"He needs a permanent home. I find myself—not—not willing to let him go. He's such a special little boy to me that I . . . Well, I've told myself over and over, 'Don't learn to love them *too much*. They're not yours to keep.' But Cass? And he and Janie . . . Well, you've seen them together. They're already like brother and sister."

It was Ben's turn to frown. "So you would sacrifice yerself by marryin' just ta—"

"No." Her hand slipped into his. "No, Ben. It's not like that." Her eyes pooled with tears now. "Oh, Ben—you just gave me such a scare. When I came through that door and saw you packing, I was so afraid you were leaving for good."

He sighed. "I don't s'pose I could e'er leave ya, Grace. Not truly. But I've nothin' ta give ya. Nothin'!"

"But you have. Everything that I need. Support. Understanding. You love the kids—know how to relate to them far better than I sometimes. You're exactly what I need—who I need. I don't know why we haven't known it all along, but—but God has gradually opened my eyes to His gift. I need you, Ben. Janie and Cass and I—we all need you. Please, please stay with us. Marry me."

He'd already bent down to gather her close. "Ya mean it?"

"I've never been more serious in my life. I think—I think God meant for us to be together—caring for kids who need love. That's why he brought you here—so far from your past. So that, first of all, you could learn how much He loves you, to understand what it is to be His child."

Ben nodded, grateful for the change that the slow process of coming to comprehend salvation had made in his life.

"And also so that I could find someone who understands me like you do. Someone who is always there for me. Someone whose heart . . . beats like mine."

He dropped his cheek against her hair. His eyes closed tightly, as if opening them would make the dream dissolve into mist. "He done that, ta be sure." Then he lifted his head, smiling broadly. "Well, I have a condition too."

Her head tilted so that she could read his face. "And?"

"Soon." The word came out more clipped than he'd intended. But he held her gaze regardless.

"Soon?"

"Soon. I don't wanna live in that ol' barn much longer—an' it'd be best ta have it settled b'fore Miss Lillian weds and leaves here—"

Her raised finger against his lips stopped further explanation. "Soon," she promised.

He pulled her closer as she wrapped her arms around his neck, her fingers playing with the unruly curls around his collar. "Real soon," she whispered, then added dreamily, "You need a haircut," just before he kissed her for the first time.

Now, standing together in the workroom as they prepared for another wedding, Ben tucked his face down against the warm skin of Grace's neck. "I've ne'er regretted it. Have you?"

She laughed. "Regretted asking you to marry me? Not for a moment. And every wedding just reminds me again of what a gift you are to me."

It was Ben's turn to laugh. "You gave me a home, an' a fam'ly, an' a purpose."

"No, God gave you all of that. I just agreed to be yoked alongside you. And that was God's gift to me."

· · • ● • · ·

Lillian lifted the waist-length white veil from where it had been draped over the chair in Mother's bedroom. Mae Anne had chosen a modern wedding dress with sleek and stylish white satin, but she'd also agreed to wear her grandmother's veil—the one Lillian herself had worn when she'd married Walter twenty years before.

Now it was their eighteen-year-old daughter who would carry on the tradition. Draping it over the thick waves of auburn hair,

Lillian pinned it carefully so that it wouldn't come loose and require more pins later.

"You're shaking, Mother."

Lillian withdrew her hands. "Am I?"

"Are you really so anxious?"

How could Lillian respond? It wasn't nervous energy that was causing her heart to flutter. It was all the other emotions. She'd tried all morning not to think about her own mothers, to close the door over feelings that were bursting in her heart. But everything that was happening seemed to draw up the memories regardless. After all, this was still Mother's room. Though it belonged now to Ben and Grace, it would always be Mother and Father's bedroom in Lillian's heart. Everyone else was merely a guest. She felt Mother's lingering presence more in this place than in any other—except, perhaps, at the piano that now stood in the big brick house that Walter had built for them where it could look out over their perfect little valley, the place where they were busy raising six children together—and more cattle than Lillian could count. They'd been truly blessed.

Sadly, there were no visible reminders of Lillian's first mama at all, and yet Lillian was keenly aware of her legacy too—even in her daughter's name, carefully chosen to honor each of these two ephemeral women—Mae Walsh and Suzanne Bennett. And it had always been a source of sorrow that neither of them had been present at Lillian's wedding. Now she was grateful and overwhelmed to be able to achieve what neither of them had, to share this experience with her own daughter as the beautiful bride.

"Where's Daddy?"

"He's gone with James to get your bouquet from the church. Somehow it was taken there when the other flowers were sent over."

"I hope they'll be back soon."

"I'm sure they will. And Uncle Ben is ready to drive you to

the church in Uncle Lemuel's black sedan as soon as we're ready." Lillian laughed. "So he doesn't have to chauffeur you in the big old car he's always had."

"That old thing? It still runs?"

"A little. Barely."

Mae Anne slipped her hands into her short lace gloves. She was the perfect picture of a modern bride. Her lips had been tinged with a modest amount of red, her cheeks blushing under her scattering of freckles. "Did you feel like this, Mother? As if your heart would explode with happiness and sadness—all at once?"

Lillian lowered herself to the edge of the bed, looking at the beautiful young woman before her. "Oh, I certainly did. I think most brides do. But there's no reason to look back and be sad. This is a day to look forward—to your life with Ellis, to all the wonderful experiences you'll have together."

"They won't all be wonderful though. You and Daddy have had plenty of hard times."

"Yes, that's true. But hard times don't have to be the center of your attention. And when you look back at them, you find that they've taught you to be strong in ways you'd never have developed otherwise. I think the secret of maintaining joy is to train yourself to keep the things you cherish in the forefront of your mind. The people you love—the blessings that you've received."

Mae Anne's voice became gentler. "Are you thinking of Grandmother again? Of Grandmama and Grandpapa?"

"Of course."

"They'd be proud of you."

Lillian swallowed down the lump that had risen in her throat and shook her head. "Of me? Oh, I'm not the center of attention today. They'd be proud of *you*, dear. All of them. And Grandfather will be just bursting his buttons to watch you walk down the aisle today—sitting there with Nana Delyth and Auntie

Rebecca. You're a sight to behold. But I'm sorry that you didn't get to have a grandmother around when you were growing up. Grandfather and Nana were gone so much."

"Oh, but I did. I had Grandma Tilly—with Sunday dinners after church at her house for all those years. But . . ." Mae Anne puckered her lips as if contemplating a new thought.

"What is it, dear?"

"I don't know how to say it. But I feel like, like Ellis's family will fill up his half of the church—while our side is mostly, oh, I don't mean to sound unkind, Mother, but they're mostly ghosts."

A quiet intake of breath eased the initial sting of the words. Mae Anne was frequently blunt but never intentionally unkind. "Is that how you feel?"

"A little."

"Well, I can understand that. All your life you've been reminded regularly of people whom you've never known. I can see why they seem like ghosts to you. I hope that in bringing myself comfort by speaking of them often it wasn't too difficult for you. I suppose I still needed them—needed to remember the people I've loved, even though I'd lost them. I so wanted you to know them too. But I hope I haven't made your life seem a . . . a . . . graveyard."

Stooping down in front of Lillian, Mae Anne reached gloved hands to gather up one of her mother's. "Not a graveyard. I didn't mean it that way when I said ghosts. I meant that we've lost so many of the people who would have had special places of honor today. That's what I meant, really."

Lillian added her second hand to their tangle of fingers. Her voice was soft but filled with emotion. These were words she'd spoken aloud regularly to her children over the years in a wide variety of ways. "There will come a day when we'll all be together. That's the thing to remember. That the people we've lost aren't *gone* at all. If they accepted the invitation, they've just *gone ahead* of us into Paradise."

"Oh, Mother. Now you're going to make me cry. And then I'll have to re-powder my face. But . . . I can't help it. That makes me think of Grandma Tilly, the way you said she'd always ask, 'Are all the children in?' when the sun was setting for the day. And how those were the very words they wrote on the ribbon over her casket, just as if she's still looking down from heaven and counting over and over to see that all the little kids she'd loved over the years were accounted for."

Lillian pressed the back of one hand against her eye. She tried to smile away the tears instead. "That was a sight, wasn't it? Our church that day. So many people of all ages who'd been touched by that woman's service through the years. Oh, that was a day to remember." Her voice caught. "Even Veronika came back for that. Cass asked her to come—and she did! Poor, dear Veronika. Miss Tilly never stopped praying for her. Bryony and her family came back from British Columbia, and Hazel brought flowers from her garden in Hope Valley—because Miss Tilly had lived there too. Even Michael and Vaughan drove together all the way back here from their jobs up north on the oil rigs, just to honor her and to support Uncle Ben as he grieved her loss."

Mae Anne dropped a knee to the floor so that she could look more directly into Lillian's eyes. "But you made that much of a difference in children's lives too, Mother. You're a servant too."

"Oh, not like that. I'm not like Miss Tilly."

"Nonsense! What is it that you've always said? God doesn't measure that way. He just asks that we each do our own part—whatever that is—in obedience. And then we leave the rest up to Him. That's what you've always said, Mother." She dipped her eyes coyly. "So, did you mean it or not?"

Lillian shook her head and laughed, despite the tears that were ringing her eyes. "I meant it—but not so much about me."

"Oh, but you did so much for others, Mother. You took care of Grandmother while she was dying. And you searched for Auntie

Grace until you found her. Then you helped her when she was just starting out with her children's home. You . . . you gave up this great big house that Grandfather gave to you. You gave it to Auntie instead so she and Uncle Ben could keep helping kids. And you made a new life with Daddy instead. You've always loved us all—raised us to be servers too. Just imagine how much that'll be multiplied out in the generations to come. I think you're wonderful, Mother. I hope I can be just like you."

Lillian stood and breathed deeply, struggling not to argue. Mae Anne was the proof, if such a thing could be acknowledged. Proof that Lillian dared not—in fact, that she had no desire to—deny that her life had been spent on things that mattered. As timid and doubtful as she'd always felt, the face of her daughter was one of the real proofs that investing in others, especially in children and family, as she'd been called to do, had produced far more than she ever could have imagined.

About the Authors

Bestselling author **Janette Oke** is celebrated for her significant contribution to the Christian book industry. Her novels have sold more than thirty million copies, and she is the recipient of the ECPA President's Award, the CBA Life Impact Award, the Gold Medallion, and the Christy Award. Janette lives in Alberta, Canada.

Laurel Oke Logan, daughter of Edward and Janette Oke, is the author of several books, including *Janette Oke: A Heart for the Prairie*, *Dana's Valley*, and the RETURN TO THE CANADIAN WEST series, cowritten with her mom. Laurel has six children and several grandchildren and lives in Illinois.

More from Janette Oke and Laurel Oke Logan

In this sweeping companion to the Hallmark TV series *When Hope Calls*, Lillian Walsh rushes to a reunion after discovering the sister she believed dead is likely alive. But Grace has big dreams beyond anything Lillian is prepared for. Can Lillian set aside her own plans and join her sister in an adventure that will surely change them both?

Unyielding Hope • WHEN HOPE CALLS #1

With more children on their way from England who need caring homes, Lillian and Grace must use every ounce of gumption to keep their mission alive. But when startling information about the past surfaces and a new arrival comes via suspicious circumstances, they'll have to decide what is worth fighting for and what is better left in God's hands.

Sustaining Faith • WHEN HOPE CALLS #2

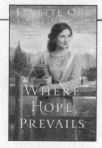

When Beth Thatcher returns to Coal Valley, she has much to be thankful for: her school is expanding, and she hopes to marry the man she loves in the spring. But soon, a new teacher who openly rejects God gives her cause for concern, as do new challenges in her relationship with Jarrick. Inspired by the Original Hallmark Series *When Calls the Heart*.

Where Hope Prevails • RETURN TO THE CANADIAN WEST #3

More from Bethany House

British spy Levi Masters is captured while investigating a discovery that could give America an upper hand in future conflicts. Village healer Audrey Moreau is drawn to the captive's commitment to honesty and is compelled to help him escape. But when he faces a severe injury, they are forced to decide how far they'll go to ensure the other's safety.

A Healer's Promise by Misty M. Beller
BRIDES OF LAURENT #2
mistymbeller.com

Del Nielsen's teaching job in town offers hope, not only to support her three sisters but also to better her students' lives. When their brother visits with his war-wounded friend RJ, Del finds RJ barely polite and wants nothing to do with him. But despite the sisters' best-laid plans, the future—and RJ—might surprise them all.

A Time to Bloom by Lauraine Snelling
LEAH'S GARDEN #2
laurainesnelling.com

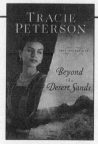

After living an opulent life with her aunt, the last thing Isabella Garcia wants is to celebrate Christmas in a small mining town with her parents. But she's surprised to see how much the town—and an old rival—have changed and how fragile her father's health has become. Faced with many changes, can she sort through her future and who she wants to be?

Beyond the Desert Sands by Tracie Peterson
LOVE ON THE SANTA FE
traciepeterson.com

◊ BETHANYHOUSE